LOOKING GOOD

DIFFICULTY AT THE BEGINNING

BOOK FOUR

Keith Maillard

BRINDLE
& GLASS

Library and Archives Canada Cataloguing in Publication
Maillard, Keith, 1942-
Difficulty at the beginning / Keith Maillard.

Contents: bk. 1. Running — bk. 2. Morgantown —
bk. 3. Lyndon Johnson and the majorettes — bk. 4. Looking good.
ISBN 1-897142-06-4 (bk. 1).—ISBN 1-897142-07-2 (bk. 2).—
ISBN 1-897142-08-0 (bk. 3).—ISBN 1-897142-09-9 (bk. 4)

I. Title.

PS8576.A49D54 2005   C813/.54   C2005-903472-6

Cover image: istockphoto.com
Author photo: Mary Maillard

Acknowledgements: The sentence from Gary Snyder that Pam quotes on page 363 is from his essay "Buddhism in the Coming Revolution" collected in *Earth House Hold* (New Directions: New York, 1969). The song playing in John's acid trip on page 180 and echoed again on page 352 is "Stay" by Maurice Williams. © 1960 Cheerio Corporation, International copyright secured. All rights reserved. Used by permission

Canada Council   Conseil des Arts
for the Arts   du Canada

Brindle & Glass Publishing acknowledges the support of the Canada Council for the Arts and the Alberta Foundation for the Arts for our publishing program.

Brindle & Glass Publishing
www.brindleandglass.com

Brindle & Glass is committed to protecting the environment and to the responsible use of natural resources. This book is printed on 100% post-consumer recycled and ancient-forest-friendly paper. For more information please visit www.oldgrowthfree.com.

1   2   3   4   5   09   08   07   06

PRINTED AND BOUND IN CANADA

ABOVE *The Abysmal, Water*

BELOW *The Arousing, Thunder*

Difficulty at the Beginning
works supreme success.

Looking Good
1969–1970

MY NAME'S Tom Parker, and I was born and raised in Hubbard, North Dakota. I tell people that, and they say, "What's it near?" and I say, "Shit, man, it ain't near nothing," and sometimes they keep on going and say, "What's the nearest big city?" and I say, "Well, if you want to drive for a while, you can hit Bismarck," and that usually stops them. When they were dividing up the states, they should have gone east-west on the Dakotas, not north-south. The eastern half's as flat as a breadboard, but the western half, where I come from, is more like what people think the West ought to look like—like rolling hills, grassy buttes, and a whole shitload of beef cattle. We've even got a cowboy or two, and when I was a kid, I spent half my life attached to the back of a horse, and that's not a bad way for a boy to grow up.

I've got nothing against my home town, but how you got out of the service in those days was like this—when your time was up, BINGO, your time was up. One day you're in Saigon, and the next day you're sitting in an airport back in The World thinking, Jesus, when did the skirts get so short? and the day after that you're restored to the bosom of your family. Now I don't want to make myself sound even crazier than I was. I knew perfectly well I was back home and perfectly safe, but I kept having this FEELING. It's hard to describe. And here's the crazy part. The only thing that would have made that feeling go away was if I was absolutely certain the SPs had secured our perimeter. Sometimes I'd go outside and stare at the sky. When that got too harsh, I'd come inside and stare at the wall.

I've got a lot of relatives. Both my mom and dad come from big families, so I've got aunts and uncles and cousins galore. My old man was married twice, so I've got two half-sisters a lot older than I am, and they're both married. Then I've got two full sisters a few years older than I am, and they're married too. Then I've got a younger brother who was in his senior year of high school when I got out of the service. Anyhow, that's a lot of people. And do you think a single one of them would sit down with me, look me in the eye like they was interested—you know, like they gave a shit—and say, "Well, Tommy, how was it over there?" Nope, not a one of them. I'll tell you what it's like. It's like while you've been gone, you've turned BRIGHT COBALT BLUE, and when you come back, everybody can see immediately that you've turned BRIGHT COBALT BLUE, but nobody ever talks about it.

All except for my old man. He likes wars. He enjoyed the hell out of the one he was in, which wasn't too hard considering he was stationed Stateside the whole time, and he was real interested in the one I'd been in, so there I am trapped in the house with him in the dead of winter, and he keeps telling me that we can still win it over there, and I kept telling him we're never going to win it over there, and Abrams has his head even farther up his ass than Westmoreland did, and none of those dudes have seen daylight recently, let alone the light at the end of the tunnel, and I should know, because, goddamn it, I'D BEEN THERE. Which was true. When Charlie pulled off his world-famous Tet Offensive, I'd been right there to catch his act, and believe me, his act was highly entertaining. So every night I'm fighting the war with my old man over dinner, and it's not lots of fun for my mom and my brother, and when you get right down to it, it's not lots of fun for me either.

I'm kind of slow on the uptake sometimes, but it was beginning to dawn on me that maybe my future in Hubbard, North Dakota, was a little bit on the limited side, and then something happened that made it real clear. I'm laying in my bedroom staring at the ceiling. I hadn't made it downstairs to stare at the kitchen wall yet. And my brother comes in, you know, just goofing off, trying to be friendly. Like he don't know me anymore. And he says something. Now I'd love to tell you what it was, but it's gone out of my mind. I know this much about it—it was supposed to be funny, and I didn't think it was funny at all. It could have been something like, "Hey, Tom, did you kill a lot of slopes over there?" but that isn't what it was—although that was probably kind of like the gist of it. But here's what happens. One minute I'm sitting on the edge of my bed, and then the next minute I've got him rammed up against the wall, and I'm about to pound him out. Got my fist cocked, all set to go, right? And I catch myself at the last possible second. And I step back and let him go, and he's looking at me like his worst fears have come true.

Here he is, folks, appearing right before your eyes, alive and in full color, three dimensional and forty feet tall—THE WAR-CRAZED VIETNAM VET. "Fuck! Tom," he says, like amazed, and he's gone.

I'm standing there, and I swear to God sweat is just pouring off me, and I'm panting like a dog, and I've got that good old accelerated heart rate, and I'm thinking, oh, fuck. That's when I knew I had to get out of there. Well, I went outside and walked around in the cold for a while, and then I came back and walked into my brother's room. He's laying on his bed, reading a book, homework or something, and he looks up. I can see he's really scared of me, and I feel like a piece of shit. But I want to make sure he gets the point. Like the point is the point. "You registered for the draft?" I say.

"Yeah," he says, like what are you asking me such a dumb question for?

"OK," I say, "I'm going to give you some advice. I don't give a shit whether you want to hear it or not, I got to give it to you . . . for the simple reason that I know some things that you don't. Now let me ask you something. When you drive north from here, where do you end up?"

"Fuck," he says, "I don't know what you're talking about."

"OK, let me put it a different way. When you drive north from here, where do you end up?"

He looks at me blank for a long time. Then he says, "Shit, Tom, what are you talking about? You drive north from here, you hit the Reservation."

"Yeah," I say. "Keep going."

"Shit. If you keep on going, there's nothing. You end up at the Canadian border."

"You got it," I say. "Now think about it, asshole."

I'm a great one to talk. I motherfucking enlisted.

So one morning not too long after that, I'm sitting in the kitchen, and I've done my six hours of staring at the wall, and I've drunk my forty-seven cups of coffee just to get myself cranked up to full flame, ready to confront the day and wrestle it into submission, and just for something to do I start cleaning out my wallet. You know all the stuff that gets collected in your wallet so when you reach for a bill, these little bits of paper come pouring out like confetti. Like here's a piece of an envelope that says THURSDAY 1105, and another scrap of paper that says CALL BILL 573-8798, and things like IOU $14.35 signed by a guy who bought it during Tet. And finally this little note with BOB LYONS written on it, and his phone number and address in some place called Watertown, Massachusetts. For a while there, Lyons was the only guy from New England stationed with us, and so you'd hear all these southern accents and western accents and black dudes jive-talking and then there was Lyons, and he sounded like Jack Kennedy. And I remembered one night when we were off-duty and blowing some extremely fine weed, and we're both totally blasted and doing this thing of "what the fuck you going to do when you get out of the service? I don't know, what are you going to do?" And he says, "You ought to come to Boston, Tom," and I say, "What's in Boston?" and he says, "Baked beans," and he laughs. Even then he had a goofy laugh. "No, seriously, man," he says, "it's a real dealer's town. There's a million ways to score."

Ways to score was something he knew about. You talk about people being born to something, you know, like a natural born athlete, well, Lyons was born to deal. Whatever you wanted, he'd get it for you. Mostly what he brought in for us was smoke, but if you wanted a pinch of doogie or even a hit of acid, he could do that too. Why anybody would want to drop acid in Nam is totally beyond me. That scene was already trippy enough without adding to it, but maybe some guys figured that acid would make it look NORMAL, but the point I'm trying to make here is that whatever you wanted, Lyons was your man. He had the perfect dealer's attitude—at the end of the day, you count your bills, and if you got more than you did in the morning, you're looking good. He never burnt anybody, and he never ripped anybody off, and if anybody needed a few bucks to make sure the scene stayed sweet, Lyons was right there laying the bread on them. He used to say he could hire somebody dead. And I'd laugh, right?

We had one master sergeant named Everetts, old crusty fuck from Texas with his hair cut down to an eighth of an inch, looked like a bulldog, and he must have been in the air force so long he'd started out working on aircraft with double wings on them. He liked everything done by the book, and by that stage of the war effort—I'm talking after Tet—most of us had acquired the short-timer's attitude, and you'd hear things like, "That shithead Everetts is worse than Charlie," and Lyons would say, "OK, you don't want him around anymore, let's take up a collection. Wouldn't take more than a few hundred bucks," and most likely I wouldn't have remembered any of that except for what happened. They found Sergeant Everetts in some baby-san's hooch. Somebody had shoved one of those fine government-issue forty-fives in his mouth and pulled the trigger. And I'm thinking, hey, was that a coincidence?

But that's not what I'm thinking in my parents' kitchen in Hubbard, North Dakota. I'm thinking, I GOT TO GET OUT OF HERE. And I knew I had to get out of there before Christmas—because I knew somehow that was going to make everything worse. Weird, huh? You'd think Christmas would be a good time to be home, but I knew I couldn't hack it. So I picked up the phone and dialed Lyons' number. I got his mom and she gave me another number and I called that one, and I got Lyons himself. He was just happier than all hell to hear from me. He was talking a mile a minute and giggling away, and if I'd been listening carefully, I might have detected the fact that he was totally nuts, but right at that time in my life I didn't give a shit. "Tommy," he says, "you dumb fucking cowboy. Get your ass to Boston. I got the sweetest little scene happening, you just won't believe it. I really NEED you, man." So I caught the Greyhound and rode it to Boston.

BACK IN those days when GIs turned into freaks, they tended to do it up right, and Lyons had sure done it up right. He'd been growing his hair ever since he got out of the service, and he had a big Wyatt Earp mustache, and he was into leather, like hand-tooled boots and leather pants and vests, and he even had a black leather hat that came to a point and made him look like he'd escaped from a Mexican movie, you know, one of those cheap-ass ones where the film's blue. And his act was playing in a nice big apartment in Somerville. When you're used to sleeping in a barracks and then all of a sudden you find yourself back in The World where things go QUIET on you at night, you can't sleep for shit, so he's got himself two gigantic fish tanks that bubble and hum, and they're full of weird acid-trip fish you can stare at when you're too whacked out to move. And he's got himself a big pig Lincoln and a stereo that can shatter concrete and a hippie girlfriend that looks like she's about sixteen. And I arrive right on time. Like the same day the shipment comes in. Five keys.

I'd never seen so much weed in my life, and we were wrecked constantly, and I helped him ounce it out, and then we drove around town and sold it like a couple of idiots. We sold it at Harvard and BU and Brandeis and MIT and Wellesley, we sold it to mindless freaks in crash pads, we sold it to a biker gang in East Cambridge, we sold it on the fucking street. We wandered around the Boston Common, and any longhair dude or hippie chickie we saw, we'd go, "Need any weed?" Why we didn't get busted or shot by the Mafia, I don't know, but it wasn't like we were the only folks engaged in that particular line of work. Hell, in those days in Boston everybody was into smoke, and everybody wanted to have a dependable source. So bread was no problem, and, as I may have mentioned, we did not give a shit. Yeah, we were looking good.

If you weren't there at that time, the scene probably sounds crazy, like INSANE, and guess what? It was. I kept running into these political types, and they always had a POSITION. If some dude was being an asshole, he could always run a good rap on you. He'd tell you that being an asshole was required by this, that, or the other shit going down, and it was all laid out by Karl Marx or Fidel Castro or Chairman Mao or some other heavy fuck, so it always came out like if you were the one who wasn't being an asshole, then you were a sell-out, man. But the only POSITION I ever had was this: GRASS IS GOOD. Of course it was illegal, but if you read the Constitution carefully, you'll see that the war I was in was fairly illegal too. And if you believe that GRASS IS GOOD, it follows as the night the day that it's your patriotic duty as an American citizen to supply as much grass as possible to as many people as possible, and the fact that it's illegal makes you kind of like Robin Hood.

Oh, yeah, I did have a line—that famous line you won't cross—and this was it: PSYCHEDELICS, YES; EVERYTHING ELSE,

NO. But Lyons had no line at all, and pretty soon I did detect the fact that a big plastic bag about the size of a brick has arrived from God knows where, full of white powder, and even being a dumb cowboy, I do manage to figure out that it's smack, and Lyons is cutting it with some shit—I'm not sure what he used to cut it with—and he's getting ready to deal it, so I say, "Hey, Bob, I didn't sign on for this," and he says, "Well, Tommy boy, then you should have nothing to do with it, right? I'd be the last person in the world who'd want you to compromise your PRINCIPLES," and he giggles hysterically.

He didn't used to giggle hysterically back in Nam. In fact, he didn't start giggling hysterically until he started shooting himself full of crystal meth. Shit, he gets that fucking crystal in his veins, he's up all night talking a mile a minute, his head bobbing up and down, his eyes staring fire at me like he's straight from the loony bin, and at that time in my life I don't know the first fucking thing about crystal meth. All I know is I've never liked speed—I'm naturally speedy, don't need any help, thank you. So I'm thinking, crystal meth. Jesus, what is this cheap-ass chicken-shit pointless drug? You cook it up in your fucking kitchen out of cold pills and horse medicine and matchbooks and other crap like that, for Christ's sake. Who needs this shit? But Lyons didn't just make it to sell it, he loved it. It was like coming home for him. It was like all the cells in his body were crying out, "Oh, sweet beautiful Crystal, come to me, baby. You're the lover I've been waiting for my whole life." Well, I've had a lot of miles run on me since then, and believe it or not I've even managed to learn a few things since then, and I ain't going to be cute about this. I'm going to tell you flat out what I think. Crystal meth is the worst drug I know of. Crystal meth makes doogie look like cotton candy. CRYSTAL METH IS PURE EVIL.

MY FIRST few weeks in Boston, the only people I knew other than Lyons were these crazy fuckers I'd met at the newspaper office. See, I'd picked up one of these underground rags. It was called the *Biweekly Weasel*, and it hit me just about right. They weren't asking you to sign up with Ho Chi Minh or any weird shit like that, like their POSITION was real simple—the war effort sucked shit and the best thing to do was stop the killing as quick as possible, and I could subscribe to that point of view one hundred percent, so I thought, hey, far out. And they had an ad in there that said, "We need typists, writers, photographers, proof readers, and people to work on distribution," so I walked into their office, and sitting behind a big desk was the hairiest man I've ever seen in my life. When I was a kid, we had a book called *Bible Stories for Children*, and there was pictures of these Old Testament dudes with long curly hair and beards halfway down their chests, and that's exactly what he looked like. He was no spring chicken—like he was getting a little grey around the edges—but he was sure hanging onto every goddamned one of his hairs. Sometimes all you could see of him was the end of his nose, and then he'd kind of wipe the hair out of his face and he'd be staring at you with these hard little blue eyes like ice cubes. That was Ethan. The *Weasel* had two editors, and he was one of them.

Then sitting at a desk off to one side was this little guy, and I almost missed him because he was somebody you could miss real easy and that's exactly the way he liked it. If that Ethan dude was pushing forty, this guy was more my age. He didn't have a beard like Ethan, but he sure had hair. He must have been growing it for years—like it was halfway down his back—and he was sporting these goofy John Lennon glasses. Until he got to know you, he didn't have much to say, and wherever you were, he was always quietly watching you because he figured that anybody could be an agent. The name he was using was "Raymond Lee," and he was heavy into politics, like he wrote all the political shit in the paper, and he was the other editor.

When I walked in there, those dudes didn't seem to be doing much of anything except looking out the window, and the minute I'd got my hands on some bread, I'd bought myself an old crapped-out panel truck, because—well, hell, you can't beat a panel truck—and I said, "Perhaps I can help you out with your distribution." They said, "Sure." I said, "What does it pay?" and they laughed at me.

But I thought, well, shit, if I was driving around town dropping off their rag, I bet it'd give me a few more contacts, and I bet I could move a few more ounces, and I was right, and eventually I got to hanging out at the newspaper office because it was a real trip. All kinds of freaky people floating in there, looking to get out of the cold, and hippie chicks crashed out on the old ratty couch, and runaway kids who didn't know where else to go so Ethan and Ray would have to rap to them until they felt better and then ship them off to one of those radical churches. A bunch of Harvard kids worked on the paper, and they were GODDAMN SERIOUS, but they never did that number on me like, "Oh, you are a Vietnam vet, are you? Well then back off me, you evil baby killer and war criminal." No, it was more like I was John Wayne and I'd just switched over to THEIR SIDE, so they thought I was most definitely where it was at, and I got to admit I worked up a real good song-and-dance routine for those dudes. They required vast quantities of weed just to maintain normal, so they were ideal customers.

And sometimes right out of nowhere, straights would come bursting in TOTALLY OUTRAGED by some article in the *Weasel*, and then, after they'd split, Ethan and Ray would try to guess what kind of agents they'd been. They said you could tell the agents by their shoes and socks. Like the standard-issue agents all wore these absolutely dead-straight shiny black dress shoes, and if they were Cambridge cops, they wore them with WHITE athletic socks, but if they were anybody from the federal government, like the FBI, they wore them with BLACK socks. But the real trippy agents—like your worst nightmare, CIA or Army Intelligence or maybe from some agency so secret it didn't have a name—you'd never know them at all because they'd just look like hairy freaks. Whether any of this shit was true or not, I don't know. I'm just telling you the word that was going down.

The biggest game in town was PARANOIA, and the most paranoid dude going was Raymond Lee. He was so paranoid, that was just the name he was using when he wrote for the *Weasel*. He had another name on the door buzzer of his apartment, and another name for when he did his shit work for money, and he probably had a few more names I never heard about, and I was hanging out with him for weeks calling him Ray before I ever heard his real name.

The way I remember him . . . Well, he was always hanging out on the sidelines, not saying much, checking things out, watching it all go down, probably thinking, hey, is THIS guy an agent, is THAT guy an agent? He was absolutely convinced that the FBI was just one step behind him and if he wasn't as careful as a spy in a movie he was going to end up in the slammer, just like he was absolutely convinced that one of these days the government was going to invoke the McCarran Act and slap us all in concentration camps.

He had himself a little apartment a few blocks from Central Square in the world's ugliest building, and the name on his door buzzer was Mr. Jones—like he'd picked that name from the Dylan song. To get to his place you had to walk down these steep narrow stairs and then all the way back past the furnace, and he had just one room and a kitchen thing off to one side with a little fridge and stove and sink all jammed in together, and off to the other side a little bathroom with a tub about four feet long. I'm a tall guy, and the ceiling was so damn low it weirded me right out. And there was only one window, a slit high up in the wall at street level so you could get this lovely view of the garbage cans, and down below the window was an old wooden table with a typewriter on it, and then there was a narrow little bed with no sheets or anything, just a sleeping bag and a couple pillows, and that's all the furniture there was. Ray had slapped up shelves on cinder blocks that covered every inch of the walls, and every inch of the shelves was stacked with books and papers, and there were quotes from all kinds of hot-shit political types pinned up along with pictures of skinny girls selling pantyhose that he'd clipped out of the *Sunday New York Times*.

Now the thing about Ray—that's what I was still calling him—was that he just loved floating around loose. Like when you get up in the morning and you haven't got plan one and you just follow it out the way the day unfolds until you drift it on through and into the night, and you run into whoever you run into, and you blow a little weed, and you rap about any damn thing that passes through your head, and you blow some more weed, and whatever act's playing, you check out the show—which is pretty much how I spent my entire life in those days. But he couldn't admit he liked doing that. No, that was hippie bullshit, right? He was a heavy political dude with lots of heavy political things he had to get done, right? Trying to end the war, and all that. But I could tempt him real easy, like I'd fall by the newspaper office and whisper in his ear, "Hey, old buddy, I just got in some fine Panamanian Red you just won't believe," and he'd say, "Well, I suppose I could take an hour off," and then we'd be GONE. He was a real easy dude to float around with, and we were both of us amazed at the shit going down, like we'd exchange a look—hey, can you believe this shit?—because it was like the world was always staging another freak show just for our benefit and it beat Bob Hope hollow. So we naturally gravitated into each other's orbits until we were tight running partners.

Whenever I hit a new city, I like to drive around aimlessly until I've got it all in my head, and he was usually along for the ride. The way the politics was going down in Boston, you needed a scorecard to know the game, and he filled me in on all the teams. The Left was splitting apart by then, FRAGMENTING he called it, and there was this alphabet soup of a million different groups, and he wanted to get me checked out on every one of them, but I couldn't keep it in my head longer than about five minutes, so I'd say, "Whatever side you're on, old buddy, that's the side I'm on," and he'd say, "Well, we're sailing under the black flag then," because he was an ANARCHIST. With me, a lot of it just went in one ear and out the other, but I remember one thing he said all the time—"Politics starts with your own life."

———

STONED AS usual, skittering on the crunchy ice, John picked his way along a narrow stretch of cleared sidewalk between the heaped-up masses of snow. This simple two-block walk from Tom's truck to Ethan and Terry's place was starting to feel like eternal damnation. "God, I hate this fucking town," he said. "It's dead. Pinched, mean, bleak. Shabby, squalid, miserable . . ."

"Lay it on me, man." The voice of crazy Tom Parker, a good six-feet-two of him, skinny clown figure in purple bell-bottoms and run-down Beatle boots, mass of hair exploding out in a great puff of a white man's Afro, his arms flailing, careening, leaping across the next stretch of nasty ice, teetering, sliding—zip zap zoop—but never quite falling, laughing like an idiot. "Steady on there, old buddy."

Dope-skewed, John saw the lines of the city bend and loom menacingly over him like something out of a Fabulous Furry Freak Brothers cartoon—past sludge-brown apartment buildings, past witches' houses pricked with yellow cats' eyes, past the flickering cataract blue of TV sets. The hard-driven powder snow bit like quicklime. "Sinister, shadowy, threatening, wretched, obscure," John chanted. "Fearful, suspicious, fanatical. The natural home of the Progressive Labor Party."

"You're a fucking trip, Raymond," Tom yelled back at him. They slammed through the door to Ethan's apartment building, slid to a stop in the welcoming heat. "Made it again, god*damn*," Tom said. "It was the wolves that was getting to me, old buddy. Just a little too fucking close this time."

In Boston, the cheapest apartment was always on the top. They climbed the narrow staircase, floor after floor stinking of rubber, creosote, and years of stewed meat. Ethan had removed the lightbulb from the last landing; to discourage anyone else from putting in a new one, he'd filled the socket with glue. He'd scattered wine bottles and odd pieces of wood in a random pattern on the last flight of stairs. When the apartment door was closed, that final climb would turn into a blacked-out obstacle course as treacherous as a minefield, but now the door was standing open, sociable light spilling down the stairs along with Janis Joplin's moan. "Hey!" Tom yelled.

"Hey, yourself, you crazy fucker," Terry yelled back—and to John, "Ray. How you keeping, man?"

Both Terry and Ethan knew John's real name, but his Boston name had become habitual with everybody by now; half the time he even *felt* like Raymond Lee—the cockroach in the corner. "Surviving," he said.

"With Mercury retrograde, that's good enough." She was a dark girl much younger than Ethan, startling as always—tacky Indian blouse, huge loopy earrings, weirdly rustling Gypsy skirt, small waist and womanly hips, large breasts supported by nothing—Terry, the self-proclaimed witch. Tom shot John a look that embodied his standard line about her—"my favorite sexual fantasy"—and said, "Hey, sweet lady, you're looking good." She returned his smile, pushed a strand of black twisting hair from her damp forehead.

"Where the fuck did you clowns crawl from?" Ethan said, a bass grumble through his beard.

"Oh, we been out there on a tight schedule, running loose," Tom said.

"Running before the wind?" Ethan said.

"Flat out," Tom said.

"Far out." Terry's dry voice turning it into a put-down.

"You know, man," Tom said, his face the very picture of cherubic innocence, "there's only one thing I want to know, and maybe you could tell me. Just what the fuck's happening?"

"I ain't the sheriff," Ethan said. "I couldn't tell you."

"Shit, man, there's just you and me, and if you don't know and I don't know, then who the fuck does? How about you, Raymond?"

"I've been trying to find out," John said, playing along in this old jive-ass routine, "but it stays one step ahead of me."

"Yeah, that's where it's at, man," Tom said, "in that one step. You catch that one step, you there."

"Maybe you don't catch that one step, maybe it catches you," Ethan said.

"Should I be taking all this down for your disciples?" Terry asked straight-faced.

"Well, one thing I will tell you, Parker," Ethan said to Tom, "you deal to any more of my customers, I'm going to kick your ass."

"No need to get personal," Tom said. "There's room for me and you and Jesus too in this fine nation of ours. The demand for grass is infinite. Ain't that the first law of capitalism?"

Ethan threw back his head and laughed. Viking's mustache, patriarch's beard—all that hair, dirty blond streaked with grey—the mouth was lost in there and so were the eyes, small and blue. John had never entirely trusted those eyes. "Might as well feed these assholes," Ethan said.

"Oh, no," Tom said, "far be it from us to intrude upon your sacred dinner hour."

"Sacred dinner hour? Shee-it. Didn't you catch the big mother-fucking sign I got slapped up down on Mass Ave? COME ONE,

COME ALL—FREE EATS AT ETHAN'S. Sit down, sit down."
Ethan slid the jar of chopsticks across the table in their direction;
Terry was already pushing bowls and plates at them—brown rice,
stir-fried greens, a lentil stew scented with garlic, cumin, and
turmeric, whole-grain bread hot from the oven.

John was checking out Terry's latest addition to the ongoing
artwork on the purple and orange walls—another whacked-out
collage—a naked girl with a dog's head and a bomb coming out of
her womb floating above a festive table surrounded by grim-faced
Pentagon generals. In the center of the table a roast turkey was
proclaiming: YOUR PERSPIRATION WORRIES ARE OVER!
"Far out," he said to her.

She winked at him. What secret joke was that? She laid some
paper in front of him. "You ready for the latest load of shit?"

Oh, right, the editorial. This one was getting itself written
the way they always did. Ethan would wander around for a few
days muttering to himself, scribbling onto scrap paper—saving
trees—and then pass the results on to Terry who would trim away
everything that was blatantly off-the-wall, add a few touches of her
own, and type it up. Now it was John's turn. He would work in his
own point of view, cut it down to a reasonable length, polish up the
prose, and give it back to Terry to type into justified columns. The
final version would be published in the *Weasel* under the byline of
"the Editors."

John skimmed through it. "Hey, it's pretty good," he said, "but
what's all this shit about long-chain molecules?"

"Shee-it," Ethan said, "you know, man, like *long* chain . . ."

"Yeah, right. Save the frigging molecules for another time. They
don't belong in here."

Ethan shrugged. "You the man."

"Wow," John said, reading down to the bottom of the first page,
"the SDS kids are going to freak when they see this shit."

Since fall, the *Weasel* had been attracting an ever-increasing
number of politicos from SDS. John had taught them how to justify
copy on the old IBM Executive, how to lay it out, paste it up. They'd
picked up all the tricks of the trade just as quickly as you'd expect

for kids from Harvard and Radcliff. They were very serious. "Fuck them," Ethan said. "This is shit they need to hear, man. Coming in there every day going, 'Revolution, revolution, revolution,' and who the fuck are they anyway? Children of the ruling class, that's who they are. Spoiled fucking brats."

"They may be spoiled brats, but they make me nervous," John said.

"Shit, Raymond, everything makes you nervous."

"Dig it. If it ever came down to the crunch, they could outvote us."

"Oh, yeah? What kind of crunch you think we're coming down to?"

"Wait a minute," Terry said. "What are you saying, Ray?"

"OK," John told her, "there's several tendencies in SDS fighting each other at the moment. The big split's between PL and everybody else. The kids coming into the office now want to use us as a weapon against PL."

"Yeah? So what?" from Ethan. "Those PL assholes are fucking robots, man. Hopeless."

"Sure they are. That's not the point."

"The point? Oh, right, for a minute there I forgot that little number. The motherfucking point. Lay it on me, Raymond."

"Oh, fuck, man, it's just that . . . Well, it could get real heavy. Like Phil Vance, right? He practically lives in the office. Well, he's in a tendency in Harvard SDS. They're kind of like common-sense Marxists . . ."

"Here we go," Ethan said to Tom. "Watch him now. He's going to start drawing those fine distinctions."

"Draw me a few while you're at it, old buddy," Tom said. He was rolling a joint. "Yeah, I could use a distinction or two. Had most of my distinctions shot off in the war effort."

"Fuck you guys," John said. He'd made it his business to know the political tendencies in Boston. He could see the positions as clearly as if they were pieces laid out on a chessboard, and he could predict where each piece was going to move. It would be easy, he thought, to sit there and keep his mouth shut—just eat Terry's good food, smoke Ethan's good dope, laugh at mad Tom Parker, watch it all go down like the next act of a surrealist play—here in this warm steamy kitchen where he felt almost good sometimes, where sometimes he even felt at home. But he couldn't do that. "It doesn't have a fucking thing to do with fine distinctions. All I'm saying is we could find ourselves on the losing side of a turf war . . . whether we want to be there or not. What I'm saying is real simple. We're outnumbered."

"Turf war?" Ethan said. "Outnumbered? What? You think we got territory to defend? Fuck it, man, maybe we ought to take out *insurance*."

"It ain't the numbers anyhow," Tom said, "it's the firepower."

"No, man," Ethan said, "that's the death trip talking. Here's where it's at. You can't get beat if you ain't playing."

"Wait a minute, babe," Terry said to Ethan. "I think Ray's onto something."

"Motherfucking right, I'm onto something. They're all Marxist-Leninist, and they think our editorial policy is just, you know, nuts. They don't dig how open we are. They just see it as *incorrect*. They're going to see *this* as incorrect." He slapped the editorial. "When they decide we're too nuts for them, they're going to impose a correct line . . ."

"What the hell's that mean?"

"Impose a correct line means just exactly what it says," John told her, "*impose* a correct line."

Ethan laughed. "Transcend your paranoia, man."

"How could they do that?" Terry said. "We started the *Weasel*. Everybody knows that."

"Aw, those dudes are too lame," Tom said.

"Yeah," Ethan said, "they're heavy into justifying their columns . . . Dig it, Raymond, you're playing the same game they are. Just going, 'hooray for our side.' It don't mean shit."

"When you can't get something you've written published in your own goddamned paper, it'll mean shit."

"You see that coming down?" Terry asked John.

"Yeah," he said, "like snow in January."

"Oh, man," Ethan said, "we got to transcend the ⟨ politics. We're a new people. I can't say it any plainer ⟨

"Yeah? Sure we are. Like you keep saying. So supposed to do? Give the paper to them? Just walk a⟨ behind like an empty chrysalis after the butterfly's flown away.

"Hey, far out," Terry said, laughing, "I do believe that's what they call a metaphor."

"Whew," Ethan said, "and how about you, man? You the solution or the problem? The butterfly or the chrysalis? You flying anywhere?"

"Hey, steady on there, big fellow," Tom said, "cut him some slack. He's just hanging out like the rest of us."

"Hanging? You better believe it." Ethan reached into the pocket of his flannel shirt, drew out a piece of blotter paper with spots on it. "Big shiny steel hook, that's where he's hanging. He still likes to play with the bright boys at Harvard."

"Fuck you, man," John said. "That's not fair."

"Fuck fair," Ethan said. "Who's talking fair? We're back to the long-chain molecules, you dig? Can't get away from them motherfuckers. They talk about brain damage . . . well, that's just gravy on the side. You get all that and stars too." He pushed the blotter paper across the table at John. "You want to go, man, we'll go with you. What do you say, Tom?"

"Shit, ain't got nothing better to do."

"Not on a bet," John said.

"See, he likes hanging on that steel hook. And that's where he's going to keep on hanging. That one step he's looking for is right there in front of him, ready to step on him, but he ain't ready."

John felt the silence, the eyes. Paranoia was chewing at him like a pack of three-headed dogs.

Tom laughed. "Come on, asshole," he said to Ethan, "you mean to tell me you got somewhere to go?"

Ethan didn't even crack a smile. He continued to stare into John's eyes.

"With Mercury retrograde," Terry said, "fucked-up communications, that's where it's at."

"What do you want from me?" John said.

"Ethan," Terry said, "you're one evil cat sometimes."

Ethan dropped out of role, tilted backward in his chair, and laughed. "Me?" he said, reached across the table, cupped one of his big hands around the back of John's neck, and shook him gently. "Don't want nothing, you sorry son of a bitch. I'm just fucking with your head."

BACK AT his apartment, John lay on his bed listening to the radio. Tom had just left. They'd smoked another joint, and John couldn't quite bring the talk show into focus. He kept getting drawn off into the pauses when the voices had to stop and breathe. The room looked strange, but not unusual—the shadows wouldn't stay in place—and he was still freaked from that nasty head-trip Ethan had run on him. *Acid?* Jesus, that was the last thing in the world he needed. As long as he was stuck in the States playing secret agent, he had to keep his shit together.

He pushed himself upright and stuffed his pipe with weed. If he did a little more smoke, maybe he could sleep. And then what? Get up tomorrow and go through the motions all over again— approximate some semblance of human life here in this unreal city. He'd told everybody in Toronto that he was just going down to check the scene out, that he'd be gone for a few days maybe, a couple weeks at the most, but here he was, still in Boston six months later. Well, shit, nobody had forced him to take this job; he'd volunteered for it—hopeless fool that he was. When he'd first hit town, he'd been floating aimlessly around Harvard Square, wondering what the fuck he thought he was doing, strongly inclined to take the first bus back to Canada, and some hairy street vendor had shoved a copy of an underground rag in his face—the *Biweekly Weasel.* He'd loved the split-fountain covers, the tripped-out cartoons, the Dadaesque centerfold—and the political position. The term "anarchism" never appeared, but the paper felt anarchist to its core. What had finally decided him had been the loony note under the masthead. He'd been sure that he'd finally found some folks who were just as crazy as he was.

> *Weasel.* Any of certain small slender-bodied carnivorous mammals allied to the minks and true polecats. They kill great numbers of rats and other vermin. They are mostly reddish brown with white or yellowish under parts and black-tipped tails, but northern species turn white in winter.

Now he was a motherfucking *editor* of that rag. Well, OK, right, so he should act like one. He took the last few drags on the pipe, set it aside—spread the editorial out on his desk and went to work on it. He knew that he was so stoned he'd get lost in details, but that was actually a good thing for the editorial process. Tomorrow he'd read it straight and check it out again. With a good old number 2 pencil, freshly sharpened, he worked his way down into the thing, adding commas, taking them out, moving sentences, rearranging clauses, until he was hearing Ethan's voice as clearly as if the crazy fucker was whispering in his ear. By now, John had got Ethan's number. With all that hair and hip talk, Ethan might look like an aging freak, but deep inside, he was still an all-American boy who'd grown up on tales of the free press in the days of the Revolution, a true patriot who believed in the right of dissent and every other patriotic chestnut, a rock-ribbed New Englander, who, as much as any old-time Boston firebrand armed with a Bible and a gun, never once doubted that he was *one hundred percent right.* Finished, satisfied, John lay on his bed to read the final version:

```
OK folks, we've managed to keep this motherfucking
rag on the streets for a year and a half now despite
amusing visits from the Cambridge cops who asked us,
"Would you want your daughters to read this shit?",
from irate citizens who threatened to bust up our
office, from a couple of undercover feds who told us
that they were "concerned businessmen" and asked us
if we advocated the overthrow of the United States
government by violent means. We've had letters from
the Minutemen with cute little targets enclosed
indicating that they'd love to blow our brains out.
Our vendors have been hassled on the street. The City
of Cambridge was considering revoking our license. We
```

were ordered not to sell to minors. Well, we're still here, and we're still hitting the streets every two weeks, and if you want to read us, we ain't going to ask how old you are. If you see some vice squad assholes, tell them we printed "motherfucking," and if you should happen across an FBI agent, tell him we used the word "revolution."

You see, in 1776, Boston was the most revolting city on the continent, and we're doing our best to follow in that tradition. "In the course of human events . . ." Well, you know that rap; they taught it to you in school. We began publishing, and we're going to continue publishing, because of a government that lies--lies about who killed King and the Kennedies, lies about the Vietnam war, lies about the pig racist policies of genocide built into the system that runs this sorry country. Clean Gene's gone, and so's fascist Lyndon and his lackey, Hubert Eichmann. Now we've got Richard Milltown, and you know, you can't lick our Dick. He said he had a secret plan to end the war. We're waiting with bated breath.

In case you didn't notice, the pigs just indicted eight more patriots. They say it's about the fun and games in Chicago. (You remember that one, don't you? That's when Fuehrer Daley turned his Storm Troopers loose and the whole country got busted on television.) This time they're out to get everybody: the Panthers, the heavy political Left, the stoned weirdo Left, and even the freaks who think they don't have any politics at all. People ask us all the time if we have an editorial policy. Sure we do. Just look at what's coming down and you'll see our editorial policy. If the pigs can't tell us apart, we figure it's not in our best interests to draw all the fine distinctions that the politicos keep making. We figure sectarian Left politics sucks because if we don't hang together . . . But you've heard that rap too.

We're for anything that fucks the system--draft resistance, draft evasion, going to jail, going to Canada, burning draft records, sanctuaries, mass demonstrations, seizing buildings, freaking out in

the streets, building the new society in the ruins
of the old--anything that works. And we ain't going
to stop till the GIs are home, the Vietnamese are
running their own country, and everybody--black,
white, or flaming pink--is free to walk the streets
of America and run their own lives and . . . how
did they say it? Something about the pursuit of
happiness?

Funny thing. Some people still read those old
pieces of paper, the Constitution and that other
one . . . the declaration of whatever it was. Yeah,
it was a revolution.

2

THE GIRL'S voice: "Hey, hero."

John clung stupidly to the phone, trying to orient himself in the chaotic dark. His glow-in-the-dark clock told him it was 4:10 in the morning. He pumped the words out fast: "Wait a minute. Just wait a minute. Don't say my name, OK?"

"Cool," Cassandra said. "Don't say mine either."

"Can I call you back? Say in ten minutes?" Long enough to walk to a phone booth in Central Square.

The phone line extended to God knows where—tiny unintelligible gremlins back of the hiss. He didn't know for sure the line was tapped, but he always operated on the assumption that it might be.

"Fuck, man," she said, "this is the only time I've got."

"OK, but watch your mouth."

He heard a tense laugh. "Don't I always? Listen . . . If I fly in, will you meet me?"

"Of course I will."

"You got something to write on?"

He always had something to write on. "Yeah. Go ahead."

Speaking just above a whisper, she told him she was coming from Los Angeles, changing planes in New York. He heard the fear in her voice, felt a response like a ghostly tuning fork—that familiar icy vibration. She told him her arrival time and the flight number. "Dig it, if I don't show up, you call my father, OK? Like my *father?*"

"Yeah."

"Tell him some heavy shit's going down."

"Yeah."

"Tell him he better try to find me. Tell him to call the number he's got for me, raise holy hell. And he shouldn't believe anybody unless he talks to me. And if he does talk to me, tell him to motherfucking *listen*. Because if it's not cool, I'll find a way to let him know. And if anything's weird, then he better fly out and look for me. You got that?"

"Yeah, I got that. It's what I do if you *don't* show up. But what if he asks me . . . ?"

"That's all you need to know, man. Hey, and give me a little leeway on that arrival time . . . like an hour. But when that hour's up, you call him. Like before you leave the airport. Got it?"

"Yeah."

He waited, listening to the gremlins. "Try not to look too freaky, OK?" The line went dead.

What was not too freaky? He didn't have a clue where Cassandra was at these days. The last time he'd heard from her had been when she'd sent him that ridiculous picture. He'd got it just a few weeks before he'd graduated from the U of T. The return address on the manila envelope had been Cassandra's home in Raysburg, but it had been postmarked in California. The medium had obviously been the message: she hadn't enclosed a letter with the glossy eight-by-ten of herself in a Bunny costume—nipped waist and four-inch heels, fuzzball tail aimed at the camera, bending forward over a billiard table, staring back over one shoulder with an expression that said, "Can you believe this?" She hadn't signed the photo, but she'd written on it a line from Brecht: "He who laughs has not yet heard the terrible news."

HE GOT to the airport early. The day was iron-blue and cold; the air smelled like snow, but it wasn't snowing yet. He'd thought that with all his goddamn hair, he'd definitely look freaky in his crossing-the-border suit, so he'd chosen one of his other standard disguises, the I-go-to-Harvard look—jeans and the Harris Tweed jacket he'd bought from a used clothing store, a striped necktie worn just the way the Harvard boys did it, as a joke.

The New York flight was on time. He watched the passengers coming out in clusters, walking past him—businessmen with attaché cases, two middle-aged couples, a younger couple with a baby, a trashy little blond in a miniskirt, a cluster of hip kids with knapsacks, more businessmen, but not a sign of Cassandra. He lit a cigarette. His hands were shaking.

All the passengers were out; he could see back the entire length of the hall. He looked for an ashtray. None anywhere. He flicked his ash onto the floor and looked around to see if anybody had noticed—flash fantasy of alarms going off, a hundred Keystone cops springing out of the woodwork—but everything was cool. And the blond in the miniskirt was walking directly toward him. Weird image for the Boston winter. Sunglasses, long skinny legs in shiny stockings, patent leather shoes. Trying for Mod or some damned thing, all gleaming surfaces, but coming off sleaze and plastic. Junk store dolly, waitress on vacation. "Hey, hero," she said, "you're looking good."

He couldn't speak. "Don't stare, for Christ's sake," she said under her breath. "Come on, asshole, walk. You don't know me, OK? You're just trying to score."

He fell into step with her. "Don't fuck around, man, I mean it. I get stopped, you keep right on going. They stop you, *you don't know me.*"

Just as they entered the main building, John saw that two large gentlemen in fedoras and dark overcoats had interrupted the hip kids. The men could have been insurance salesmen, a pair of uncles, high-school football coaches. "Don't even look," Cassandra said under her breath.

He glanced at her. She was as impossibly blond as a rock star's girlfriend. She bit her lower lip, an involuntary gesture. "Shit," she said, "paranoia's got to stop somewhere."

"Does it?" he said. "You got any luggage?"

"Just this." The ordinary looking blue carry-on bag in her hand. "OK, stop talking to me . . . Make like you tried to score and I told you to piss off. Walk on ahead, and I'll follow you to the car."

"What car?"

"Shit . . . OK. Get us a cab . . . Not to your place. Some other part of town. Some place real crowded." He told the driver Government Station.

In the cab she took off her sunglasses, shoved them into a patent-leather purse, grabbed some bills that seemed to be floating loose in there and handed them to him. He counted two tens and six twenties, folded them into his jacket pocket. "Fuck, man," she said under her breath.

No wonder he hadn't recognized her—her face was plastered with makeup, even false eyelashes. But the grey eyes were so much the same he was kaleidoscoped instantly into the unreconstructed and convulsive past. He could see how scared she was. Outside on the bleak streets, the daylight was gone.

John paid the driver. They got out at Faneuil Hall on the cusp between afternoon shopping and dinner time, a million straights wandering the markets—a corny New England winter scene, nostalgic postcard, the snow piled up at the edges of the sidewalks, travelogue of blue ice, cheery yellow lights, hard laughing Boston voices. Right, he thought, the cradle of liberty. "Crowded enough for you?" he said.

"Yeah, perfect . . . What would you do if you were here?"

"Shit." He pointed at the lineup for Durgin-Park. "I'd eat some fish."

"Well, do it. I'll find you."

With her carry-on bag in her right hand, her purse over her shoulder, she went striding off into the crowd. John watched the men react to the miniskirt, check her out, run their eyes up her shiny legs, over the curve of her ass. He could, if he let himself, get just as paranoid about her sleazy sexual charge as he was about the pigs. He added himself to the lineup. Once inside, he nailed down a corner table for two, ordered a pitcher of lager and two clam chowders. Here he was outside the student ghetto once again, surrounded by the good old proletariat; they probably took him for a college boy just the way he'd meant them to. He could feel the abrasive edge of their distaste—it was always the long hair that did it.

After ten minutes Cassandra slipped in quietly next to him, slid her carry-on bag under the table. Blond wig gone, the makeup gone. Now in jeans, a ribbed sweater, and beat up Frye boots, her burnt-sienna hair cut like a Beatle's. "You got a smoke?" she said. He passed her one. "Thanks," she said. She looked straight at him. "I mean thanks for everything."

The strain had pinched the corners of her eyes; her skin looked pale, yellowish, and sick. He took her hands. They were freezing. "Cass, you OK?"

"Shit, yeah. I'm indestructible. I'm fucking Wonder Woman."

"Eat some chowder."

"Yeah, OK . . . I haven't been eating much lately."

"So eat some chowder."

"Yeah . . . Jesus, I'm rank. Getting on the fucking plane, I fucking pissed myself. Can you dig it? It's amazing how your body doesn't want to cooperate . . . you know, like fuck your mind, Jesus, in a fucking miniskirt. It wasn't a gallon or anything, just a few drops, but fuck. All the way across the country, I'm thinking, oh fuck, can people *smell* me? Hey, you're looking good, man. You've lost a lot of weight . . . and Jesus, all that hair. What the hell you doing in Boston? Right up till I called your mom, I thought I'd be flying into Toronto. Woke her up in the middle of the night, and she was nice as pie. Hey, I'm sorry about your dad."

"Thanks."

She was smoking her cigarette in quick short puffs. She stubbed it out. Her hands were shaking. "Did you like my disguise?" she said. "I didn't have time to be cute, just thought, OK, let's just see how motherfucking ridiculous I can get . . . Jesus, I don't want to be a bringdown, but I'm afraid . . . I'm afraid I've kind of run it out."

"It's OK. Eat some chowder."

"I'll be OK."

"Yeah, I know you will. Did you ditch the disguise?"

"Yeah, in a garbage can in one of those markets."

"Good. You want to keep running this secret-agent shit?" he said. "Then we better go back to my place on the subway. A cab leaves a record."

On the MTA, he put his arm around her and she lay against him like a girlfriend. "I could sleep, man."

"Go ahead," he said.

She didn't say anything walking from Central Square. It was turning bitter, and she wasn't dressed for it. He took off his overcoat, draped it around her. She didn't object. At his apartment he led her down the stairs and down the long narrow hall by the furnace, unlocked his door. "Jesus, man," she said, "what did you do? The minute you hit town, say, 'Show me to the nearest rat hole'?"

"That's me . . . the rat in the woodwork. Every building needs a rat in the woodwork. Hey." She was shaking all over.

He put his arms around her and held her. "Fuck," she said, "I'm losing it."

"Go ahead. Lose it all you want."

"Shit. I'm OK. Can I have a bath?"

"Sure." He turned on the water in the tub. He hadn't seen her since he'd left Raysburg for Canada. My God, that had been four years ago. He couldn't stop looking at her. She unzipped her carry-on bag, took out half a dozen flat blocks of a black waxy substance that looked like congealed tar and threw them onto the floor. "Holy fuck," he said, "that's the most hash I've ever seen in my life."

"Yeah," she said. "You want to fire it up?"

He tore off a piece of tinfoil, molded it into his pipe, held it in place with a rubber band. Poked holes in the tinfoil with a pin. Broke off a piece of hash the size of a dried pea, put fire to it, dragged in the thick buttery smoke and held it. Offered Cassandra the pipe and matches. She did a toke, held it, exhaled slowly. "Ah," she said, "there is no pain."

He toked again and so did she. "At this very moment," she said, smiling through the smoke, "some people out in California are extremely upset with me." She reached into the carry-on bag, threw twenties and fifties and even hundred-dollar bills onto the floor. "Have some."

"You already gave me some."

"Take more. Take lots . . . Jesus, Dupre, if I'd miscalculated this one . . ."

"Listen," he said. "I've got another name here. People know me as Raymond Lee. Call me 'Ray,' OK? Get in the habit of it."

"Shit, man," she said, laughing, "couldn't you do better than that? Ray from Raysburg."

"Makes it easy to remember."

She stripped off her clothes. He thought of her as his closest friend, but he'd never seen her entirely naked before. With the hash coming on, he felt the shock of it like two dark notes—one pleasure, one fear. The tuft between her legs was exactly the same burnt-sienna brown as the hair on her head; he didn't know why he should find that so surprising, but he did. "Hey, you like me?" she said, laughing at his eyes. She patted the concavity above her hip bones. "Pretty goddamn thin, huh? It's what you get when you're so weirded out you can't eat. You want the whole show, man, you got to smell me too." She raised an arm, offering an armpit. "My Ban roll-on didn't do it. I'm fucking disgusting. Here, give me another hit."

He held pipe and fire for her. She dragged, then, still holding in the smoke, walked through the door of the bathroom, stepped into the tub, sank into the water. She hadn't bothered to close the door. John dragged. It was strong hash, two-toke stuff. "Oh fuck," she said, "I feel like a snail that's lost its shell."

"That's not a bad thing. Dig your snailness. Whew." It was quality hash, all right. Dynamite.

"What the hell you doing here?" she said. "I mean, what the fuck are you *doing?* Back in the States? Isn't it kind of . . . you know, risky?"

"Oh, you bet your sweet ass," he said. Yeah, back in the belly of the beast, lurking with intent to commit anarchy.

Gradually, as she lay in the bathtub and they talked through the open door, he began to know her again. Her voice, even with all the jive talk, was still the one he remembered. And somewhere, like a whiffling great grey crane, he had diffused with the smoke through the back of the world. He annotated his thoughts, felt them deepen within him—beyond knowledge or memory, he'd come home. Wherever they were together was home, and then she was lying on his bed, wearing one of his t-shirts. He couldn't quite remember how she got there. "How sweet it is," she said, a phrase straight from the old days, and he felt their old telepathic link. "I made it," she said. "Hot fucking damn, I can't fucking believe it. Come on, let's do another hit. Let's get ridiculous."

In silence they smoked another chunk. "What do you think this shit will go for on the street?" she said.

"I don't know. A fortune. I've got a friend who'd know."

She lit a cigarette, held up her right hand for him to see; her first two fingers were stained brown to the second joint. "Been a little nervous lately. You know what we're going to do? Tomorrow we're going to take some of that fucking dumbass money and . . .

I don't know. Anything you want, man. You like to eat fish? Shit, we'll eat fish."

"Beautiful," he heard himself saying hazily from behind the hash.

"God, do I need to sleep . . . If I can ever come down . . . Christ, I'm having a hard time coming down."

Her position on his bed gave her a direct view of the wall where he had taped up his collection of young girls. "Hey, what's this?" she said. Then, laughing, "Why, fuck me blind, it's little sister."

"Yeah, I saw her in *The New York Times.* Couldn't believe it. Blew me away."

"Yeah, shit, she blows me away too. You still read *Seventeen*? For a while there, she was in damn near every issue . . . I mean, Jesus fuck, Zo, come on, you're supposed to suffer. You're supposed to pay your dues. It's supposed to be motherfucking hard. But no, a couple months after she hits town, she's in *Seventeen* just the way she always knew she would be . . . and the moral of that story is . . . the moral of the story is . . . who the fuck knows? Hey, turn on the tube, OK?"

He turned it on. "No," she said, "I don't want to watch anything. I just want the picture happening. You know, for the distraction."

He turned the sound down. "Don't tell her, OK?" he said.

"Don't tell her what?"

"That I . . . You know, that I've got her picture . . ."

"Plastered all over your fucking wall? Why not? She'd love it to pieces."

"No, I'm serious. I'd just as leave you didn't tell her."

"Jesus, Dupre," she said, laughing, "I can't believe it. You're freaked right out. It's just *Zoë*, for Christ's sake . . . OK, OK, I won't tell her . . . but she wouldn't mind. She'd think it was sweet. She'd think it was like, you know, motherfucking *normal.*"

Normal? That was a bad joke. What the hell was normal these days? Or ever? When had *he* ever been normal? Behind the hash, skeins of old memories unraveling, lines leading out in a million directions, images—evocative, repetitive—unwinding past each other out of sequence like pink and green and golden lights reflected in the great sad Ohio. God help me, he thought, because West Virginia was always there at the bottom of everything, because

Toronto seemed now like a dream of joy, but *this* was the perpetual nightmare—Boston—but maybe, after all, nothing but the road again. Yeah, all the roads. In the pressing summer's twilight, Zoë, eerily beautiful—never merely the kid sister, now an icon of something sweet, gone and lost. But wasn't that what the revolution was all about? What it *had* to be about? Yeah, sneak in through the left-hand side of reality, cross the border, and make the impossible possible. But what if they're right, he thought—the most corrosive thought of all—what if we *are* nothing but a bunch of neurotic kids? Maybe he hadn't crossed the border because of any screwy anarchist idealism but because he was hopelessly fucked up. Maybe he didn't know what he was doing at all, was stumbling blindly into the deepening chaos. Shit, that could bum him right out if he let it.

But like Don Juan says, choose a path with heart—and Cassandra was right there. He needed to hear her voice. He stood, walked to the bed, unfolded his sleeping bag and drew it over her. "Thanks, man," she said.

He stood looking down at her grey eyes. "I know you're my best friend in the whole goddamned world," she said, "elsewise I wouldn't be here, would I? But I'm just not into balling tonight, OK?"

"Look, Cassandra . . ."

"Come on, man. Don't start a sentence with, 'Look, Cassandra.' After 'Look, Cassandra,' I know there's not going to be a fucking thing I want to hear."

How could anything be that funny? Laughter was exactly what he needed. And then, as though he'd stepped through a warp, he was suddenly standing by the radiator with a bunch of dirty clothes in his hands. What the hell was he doing there? Oh, right. If he laid out some clothes along the wall, and lay down on them, and used his coat for a blanket, he could sleep. "Hey, man," she said, "don't do that. I can crash anywhere."

"Stay where you are," he said. "I'm fine. I'm whacked."

"What a fabulous friend I am, right? Come dropping in from nowhere, might be bringing serious heat down on you . . . Then I tell you I won't fuck you, and I kick you out of your own goddamned bed."

"Oh, Cass, whatever rat hole I've got . . . it's always your rat hole. You know that."

"Yeah, I do know that. And it goes two ways, man. Yeah, it's amazing what you find when it comes down to the crunch. When I was . . . like it's the motherfucking middle of the night, and I've got like maybe ten minutes, and I'm trying to think of somebody. Anybody. Who really knows me. Who won't ask questions. Somebody I can trust. It's funny, man, because you were the only one there was."

———

NOW I'D like to say that what first turned me on to Cassandra was her mind. But that's a lie. The first thing that turned me on to Cassandra was her ass. The way I met her was like this. I fall by the newspaper office and Ray says, "Hey, Tom, I got something that might interest you," and that didn't sound like "Sell me an ounce," so I was all curious, and we went over to his place, and there was this girl named Cassandra. Sure I was interested. But it turned out he didn't mean the girl, he meant this whole shitload of hash, but I couldn't help checking out the girl, and the last time I'd been laid—well, anyhow, laid so I noticed—had been back in Saigon. And Cass bent over to pick up some of that fine Nepalese hash and my eyes just happened to light on that equally fine ass of hers in those tight jeans, and I thought, OH, YEAH. If she was here to hear me say it, she'd call me a male chauvinist pig, but you know what? I'm straight, and I get turned on by girls' asses. But Cass always figured that you get turned on to the mind first and then the ass will follow. Yeah, and for all the bad-mouthing she laid on the girls she called "fluffs," I did detect the fact that whenever it came time to buy herself another pair of jeans, she'd always pick the tightest pair she could cram herself into, and I couldn't stop thinking about that ass of hers . . . Well, it wasn't just the ass. I don't want to make myself out to be even more of an animal than I am. She fascinated me.

But anyhow, the hash. Even dumb as I was, I'd learned a few things by then, and I knew on this one I could get burnt. I mean, like there was enough of that shit for some two-bit asshole to blow me away for it, or at least do me serious damage, so I took it to Lyons. I'd moved out of his place a long time ago, mainly because I didn't want to get involved with him, but I figured he was the perfect guy for the hash. He thought it was real funny. "Hey, Tommy, when did you start making side trips to Nepal?" He said he could hang onto it and deal it a little bit at a time, but I thought, shit, I could do that. Or he could buy it from me outright. I liked that one, so he gave me a deuce for it. I got screwed, right? Well, it depends on how you look at it. I figured if I hung onto the hash, it could turn into a big problem, and I like to keep my problems little so I might have a fighting chance of dealing with them. Cassandra didn't seem to mind either. I kept a few bucks for my trouble, and Cass shoved a thou in her jeans and gave the rest to Ray. I was still calling him Ray then. "I don't want this," he said.

"Keep it for your getaway," she said, so he shrugged and put it in a book. And she just walked around with that thousand bucks in her jeans until she gradually spent it. God, what a bunch of clowns we were.

That's when I figured out that Ray's real name must be John, because that's all Cass ever called him, and they seemed real tight, but . . . Well, to get right to the point, I couldn't stop thinking about her. There's some guys who will make a move on a buddy's girlfriend, but not where I come from, and there was something about the way John and Cass were together . . . You know when people are fucking each other and enjoying the hell out of it, how it kind of radiates off them? Well, there was nothing like that. They just seemed like buddies. And so what I did, finally, was pull a sneaky little trick. One morning around eleven—early enough so a guy who's out to save the world would probably be up and functioning and anybody else who's mainly a pothead would still be in bed—I drove by the newspaper office and peered in the window, and I'd guessed right. There was John pounding the typewriter. And I kept right on going to his place and banged on his door. Cassandra opens up, and I say, "John home?" and she says, "No, come on in anyway." I probably had an expression on my face like the dog who's just come strolling into the chicken coop, and I couldn't seem to come up with a whole hell of a lot in the way of witty conversation, but Cassandra's a natural-born rapper, and she's laying out enough words for both of us, and finally I say, "Hey, are you and John making it?"

She looks kind of startled. Then she says, "No. He's a friend."

I could see her thinking about it. Like she wanted to make it absolutely clear. "I've known John since I was fourteen," she says. "He's the best friend I've got. We're really close. He's like my brother."

I say, "Oh." And then I think, what the fuck. So I say, "Well, OK then, if he's your brother, and you're not making it with him, maybe you might want to make it with me?"

She laughs her ass off. "That's the straightest come-on I ever heard," she says. "What are you offering, dude?"

"Tell you what, babyshake," I say. "I can offer you exactly what they gave us in the service—three hots and a cot, all the weed you can smoke, and lots of laughs."

"Sounds pretty good to me," she says and stuffs her shit in her little blue suitcase. We went to one of those pancake houses and had us eggs and sausages and a full stack, and then we went back to my hole in East Cambridge and blew some very fine weed and fucked our brains out.

A few days later I got to feeling guilty about poor old Ray . . . John . . . because Cass just called him up and said, "I think I'm going to stay with Tom for a while." And no matter what she'd said, I got to worrying that maybe I'd blown something for him, and so one night I went slipping and sliding over to his place, bringing him some quality Mexican shit that had just come into town. He didn't seem pissed at all. In fact all he said was, "Well, you know, Tom, this place isn't big enough for two people."

THOSE FIRST few months with Cass was the happiest time we had in Boston. We were new to each other, and it seemed impossible we'd ever hassle each other, and we both liked to laugh, and bread was no problem because the dope supply was infinite. We hung out with crazy John, and we'd ride around town like The Three Lunatics, falling by anywhere folks enjoyed a pinch of smoke, picking up hip types off the street and turning them on, and doing a few deals along the way, and just, you know, rocking and rolling and having a good time. John and Cass were a real trip. They were from the same dumb little town in West Virginia, and they'd known each other forever, and she really had his number. So he'd be saying his weird things like, "Remember the sky in the summer back in Raysburg? It's the sky in the summer that gives you the idea that life's worth living. Yeah, the sky in the summer's SUBVERSIVE," or maybe he's laying it on her about the workers' councils and the revolution and how our grandchildren are going to look back and say, "Wow, it's amazing how bad things were in the old days . . . how CRUDE it all was . . . like with states and leaders and hierarchies. It's no wonder that the people back in those days came so close to blowing up the world," and she'd laugh at him and say, "Oh, Dupre, you're so full of shit."

I can't believe some of the bizarre pointless stunts we pulled. There was this one night I was drifting down an alley somewhere, and what do I see but oh, maybe a hundred TV sets, and they're just sitting there, right? And that means that God meant for me to have them for some reason or other. And then it occurs to me that if I sold them to the college kids—you know, the same kids I sold dope to—and I got ten bucks a set, that'd be a nice pocketful of change. So the next thing I know, I'm stuffing them into the truck, and John and Cass are just standing there looking at me like I'm the night's entertainment—and also, you know, because physical labor's most definitely not their thing—but then, eventually, they go what the hell and start helping me, and we filled up the whole fucking truck, even the cab. Left just enough space for them to crawl into the back and crouch there like a couple of moles. We drove around like that for damn near two weeks, I swear to God, and did I sell even one of those goddamned TV sets? Are you kidding?

"DOES HE know where he's going?" John said.

"He's so wrecked he could drive back to North Dakota before he remembered where he was going."

"That's comforting . . . Hey, watch out! That big mother's going to come down on your head."

"No, it's not." Cassandra twisted sideways, shoved her shoulder against the ancient TV set, pushed it firmly back with the others.

She was sitting atop one of the console models, her boots braced against another huge set to keep it in place. In the oversize peacoat she'd bought at the Army and Navy, with her Beatle hair whipping in the wind and her nose running, she looked like a scruffy street kid of indeterminate sex. John was shaking with the cold. Behind them, through the small opening left between the tottering piles of the smaller portables, he could see blowing snow, a virulent whistling across the unwinding pavement. The truck was so jammed that the doors wouldn't shut. "Those fuckers on the tailgate are going to start coming off on the next bump," he said.

"Jesus, man, why do you always sound like Eeyore?"

"Eeyore? Shit, no. I'm Pooh. How cold my ass is growing, tiddely pom . . . Recognize anything? Looks like motherfucking Siberia out there. Are we in Newton?"

The truck had begun to climb a steep hill. John watched the set at the very end shimmy across the tailgate, teeter a moment at the edge, and then flip off in a strangely graceful motion for such a solidly cubical object. It exploded on the pavement. He heard, muffled by the dozens of television sets between them and the cab, the howl of Tom's laughter. "He sounds genuinely nuts."

"Oh, yeah, he's looking good."

"Where the hell is he taking these goddamned things?"

"He hasn't got a clue. But he's determined. Yeah, you bet. Tonight's the night he's going to unload the fuckers. Oh God, he's so hapless." She fished out a baggie of dope and began rolling a joint.

"Cass," John said, "the pigs could pull us over any goddamn moment . . . for any goddamn reason at all, and you're holding . . . and Tom's holding, of course . . ."

"Cool it, man, paranoia's got to . . ."

"Yeah, I know . . . stop somewhere. I think you ought to retire that line."

She fired up the joint, dragged, and offered it to him. "Do a little smoke," she said. "It'll cut the cold."

"It won't cut a goddamn thing. It'll just make it worse."

"Yeah, but we'll be able to dig it more."

"Jesus!" John yelled, bracing himself. Tom must have slammed on the brakes. The truck was skidding, fishtailing. And then, just as suddenly, it was accelerating. John saw another one of the sets suspended a moment in the snowy air.

"Christ, that's loud," Cassandra said. "What makes all that noise? The picture tube?"

"What the fuck is this?" John said, "the revolution as Dada?" He was getting stoned again, as usual, and if they kept spilling TV sets onto the road, they were bound to draw heat eventually—but if he started thinking about that, he was headed straight for a full-fledged bummer, and that he didn't need. He had to get her rapping about something—anything would do. "Do I get to hear about California yet?"

"Come on, man, you've got to be more subtle than that. Be sly about it. Worm it out of me."

"Oh, fuck. Just tell me."

They rode along in silence for so long he was beginning to think she had no intention of telling him anything, but then she said, "You know, Dupre, the possible's always intolerable. Sometimes I think if I could go out and get any kind of a job a boy could do, I'd do it . . . even digging ditches. But that's probably just me bullshitting myself. I'm not built to dig ditches . . . But you know what? The main talent I've got is for living off men. I'm really good at it."

"Like the dudes you used to hang out with in California?"

"Hey, that's good. You slipped that one right in there . . . Yeah, they were a lovely bunch. Real sweethearts. Long-haired sweet-smiling soft-talking pack of cats. You might even think they were hippies if you didn't know better. Heavy into the import business. Brought in many fine products from the lands where the poppies grow. Coin? No problemo. You would have loved my threads, man, whoa, I was just looking so very fine. And it was all so damned easy. Just figure out what the boys want and give it to them, right? Are you getting the picture?"

"Yeah, I'm getting it. Christ, how'd you end up there?"

"I don't know. Maybe it was the next logical step after the Playboy Club. Or maybe I was just drifting."

John stared out the back of the truck at the snow on the moving highway. The dope was coming on unbelievably fast, was opening up a web of interlinking complications in his mind; he found himself caught in them, unable to speak. "Whew," he said. "Keep on talking, Cass. I'm getting stuck in the sound of the tires."

"You talk, man. Your turn. How'd you end up *here?*"

"I told you. It was Chicago."

"Yeah, that's what you said, but Jesus . . . Why didn't you look at all that shit going down on the tube and think, wow, the last thing in the fucking world I'm ever going to do is go back down *there?*"

"That *is* what I thought. Exactly." That one sent them off into gales of whacked-out giggles—and then a tightly impacted silence. Shit, the evil sound of the tires, the evil cold. "Talk, Cassandra," he wanted to say, "talk about *anything*," but he couldn't say it.

He hadn't been with politicos that night; he'd been with the guys in his band—that freaky tribe of musicians who called themselves Hot Dirt. They'd been smoking some dynamite grass in somebody's pad off Dundas. When the cops had begun to wade into the protestors and club them, John had felt it like a shock wave that rolled out of the TV screen and through his guts. The demonstrators hadn't been doing anything. They'd simply been there. The cops kept chasing them. The cops kept clubbing them. A chant rose up; at first, John thought it was, "The whole world is rotten," because that's what the compressed black-and-white image was telling him, but, in a moment, he heard it correctly: "The whole world is *watching*." Yes. There must have been a dozen people in the room with him, watching; they'd fallen silent; with his antennae sensitized by the dope, he could feel them all around him—their horror and their alarm—feel them extending outward, becoming a whole world that was watching. He'd never felt more a part of a whole world— connected to every other human being on the planet—and they were all watching, all witnesses. The shit that America had denied, had kept hidden, was revealed, was displayed, was shoved in their faces, and then the image shattered as though a pig had smashed the TV with a riot baton. John had been screaming, but he hadn't been making a sound. The real reassembled itself, and, on the screen, the cops were still clubbing the demonstrators. His pal Don, their lead guitarist, was staring at him. "Holy fuck, man," Don said, "what's going on down there?" and that's when John realized that he was the only American in the room.

"Whew," John said, "Canada."

"So you dig Canada?" Cassandra said.

"Oh, yeah."

Hey, here we go, he thought—something to rap about. Americans never understood it when he tried to tell them about Canada, so he'd learned to use short pithy statements that would put it all in a nutshell. "Both countries had an election last year," he said. "The good old US of A elected Dick Nixon and Canada elected Pierre Eliott Trudeau. You got it?"

"Yeah," she said, "I think I got it. So tell me again. Why aren't you up there?"

"Shit, I just couldn't . . . I kept having the feeling I had to do something. It was like . . . Oh, fuck. 'There is a tide in the affairs of men, which, taken at the flood . . .'"

"Oh, for Christ's sake."

"All right, all right, but listen. This *is* an extraordinary time. This is . . . Jesus, *everybody knows it.* And I just . . . OK, I don't give a fuck whether it sounds corny or not, but it's like what we're doing now is going to mark us for life. And I just couldn't sit by anymore. I had to *do something.*"

No problem with words now—John heard himself rapping away like a speed freak: "There was something else I saw on the tube. It really changed me." The Buddhist monk who'd burned himself to death in Saigon in 1963 to protest the policies of the Diem regime. "I was in Miami Beach with Cohen, and . . . Jesus, Cass, Miami Beach is like a picture postcard, too beautiful, too peaceful. I'll never forget it. Here's this guy sitting in a perfect lotus position, not moving a muscle, and . . . I mean, he was *burning up.* It just fucking blew me away."

Maybe Canada had been too peaceful, too beautiful. John had lived there long enough to see Toronto as beautiful—that restrained city of quiche and salad—but the killing in Vietnam was still going on, sickening, heartbreaking. The Americans had polarized Vietnam, destroyed the sane middle ground. The whole compassionate Buddhist movement had been swept away; if you were Vietnamese, you had to be either for the Americans or against them. And America herself had been polarized in exactly the same way. That's what Chicago had done. Even the most peaceful protest was not permitted now; the ugly fascist side of corporate liberalism had revealed itself for everyone to see. But there had to be some way to stand up to it—a compassionate way. "And I kept feeling that I had all that evil Karma to work through. Like I might be in Canada, but I was still carrying that American Karma. So I just had to *do something*. Do you get it?"

She didn't answer.

"There's this speech Carl Oglesby gave," he told her. "He was talking about SDS in the old days, what it meant, what it stood for. He said it was 'to make love more possible.' I read that, and I said, wow, yeah, that's it. Or it's like . . . OK, at the end of the Fire Sutra it says, 'the holy life has been lived, what was needed to be done was done.' Well, shit, forget the holy life. Most of us can't even get a sniff of the holy life. But what about doing what needs to be done? What if everybody did that? All these single individuals. What if we just looked around where we were and did what needed to be done? Not perfect, but just the best we could? Wouldn't it all add up? Isn't that what the Movement is? Isn't that what *the revolution* is?"

He looked into her eyes. Intensified by the dope, he felt that old reliable connection between them—a million watts clear channel. She had snot running down all over her upper lip. He fished his handkerchief out of his jeans and handed it to her. "Wipe your nose, for Christ's sake. You look like a pathetic little kid."

She took the handkerchief and blew her nose. "I ain't laughing at you, man," she said. "It's kind of touching . . . like after all these years, you're still a Buddhist boy scout. I think you're nuts, of course. Flaming."

"So what's your answer?"

"Answer? Fuck, Dupre, I don't even know the question. I just try to stay out of the way." He knew that small wicked smile she was giving him now. "How about chicks?"

"What about chicks?"

"You making it with anybody?"

TILT. Here he was, right where he didn't want to go.

"Your silence speaks volumes," she said. "Jesus, Dupre, I can't believe you. What did you lose all that weight for . . . and grow all that hair? You can't make it with Karl Marx, you know. He's dead."

"Piss on Marx. I wouldn't want to make it with him anyway. He threw Bakunin out of the International."

"Hey, I know that trick. It's called 'deflect the conversation through the use of humor.' So where you at? I'm not just fucking with your head. It's *me* you're talking to. And we were getting down to it there for a minute. Seriously, man, what's with you?"

What *was* with him? The dope had just spun him around and landed him right back where he'd started, hopelessly stoned and playing out, yes, what seemed to be a Marxist script—*Groucho* Marxist—riding around in an insane howling black night in the back of a beat-to-shit panel truck stuffed with utterly useless TV sets, accompanied by his best friend who had somehow managed to turn herself into an experienced woman—a former Playboy Bunny, for Christ's sake—whereas he, in the complex and infinitely fascinating area of human sexuality, wasn't much further advanced than when he'd first met her. He'd always loved her, of course, and he almost wished she hadn't fallen out of nowhere into his ratty underground life—but no, he didn't mean that. Love was, as she'd always said, simply love, and he needed her for the same reason he'd always needed her—to save him from God knows what. He hadn't even been able to get pissed off at her for taking off with Tom Parker. He liked Tom Parker—and anyway, why shouldn't Cassandra be with a normal male? She deserved that, didn't she? But fuck normal males; he hated them sometimes. "Jesus," he said. "it's fucking cold. God, it's cold. Where the fuck's he taking us?"

He hadn't meant it as a question she could answer, and she didn't answer. She passed him the baggie of dope and the papers. "Roll one. My hands are frozen."

"All right, Cass. But then you've got to tell me about California."

"Oh, California. You want to hear it, huh?" and off she went, rocketing away on it. "OK, the pigs picked me up, right? That was the beginning of the end. Heavy. I figured they'd fuck me over, but they didn't. They were very polite. Of course forget the Constitution and *habeas corpus* and your one phone call and any of that other good shit, but they were very polite. They stripped me down, buck naked, and locked me in the hole. And there's nothing in there, man. Just a can to piss in and that's it. They let me sit there for twenty-four hours, and then they let me put my clothes back on and sit around for another hour or two waiting to see some heavy dude. And of course you can't smoke all this time, right? And that might sound like a little thing until you've gone from a pack a day to nothing.

"So eventually I get to see the heavy dude, and he says, 'Sit down, Cassandra.' I sit down. He says, 'Would you care for a smoke, Cassandra?' I say, 'Sure.' He gives me a smoke. Then he pushes this sheet of paper across the desk at me. It's a list of names, maybe forty names. And out of those forty names, I know about half of them. He says, 'I just want you to see, Cassandra, that we know who you are. We know every one of you. And we're going to get every one of you.' I don't say a thing.

"He says, 'We'd prefer to get the boys at the top. We don't know a lot about them yet. But if we have to, we'll take the boys at the bottom. Are you with me, Cassandra?' I don't say a thing. He says, 'We could probably indict you right now, Cassandra, and get a conviction, but we'd rather you were doing a little work for us. We don't need you. We don't need your boyfriend.' And he names a few more dudes he doesn't need. I'm sitting there thinking, he's lying to me. He hasn't got enough for a conviction. He could indict me, but he'd never make it stick. But I don't know. And then he starts reading from another piece of paper. It's my whole life. Where I was born. High school. Bennington. Worked here. Worked there. Shit, he even knows I was a Playboy Bunny. Then he says, 'You don't have to answer right now. Just think about it. We'll be in touch with you in a few days,' and I'm out on the street.

"Well, I got back home and Sweet Andrew . . . that's the miserable son of a bitch I'm living with, right? . . . He says, 'Did you do a deal with them?' and I say, 'Are you fucking kidding me, man? You think I'm nuts?' But I can't tell if he believes me or not. OK? So that night we go to bed, and he fucks me cold, man. Like he doesn't slap me around or anything, but it's just cold cold cold. Like I could have been a hunk of flank steak. And when he gets done, he says, 'Hey, Cass, I'm going to give you the straight scoop. If you do a deal with those motherfuckers, here's what's going to happen to you. I know this motorcycle gang, and they're a bunch of evil twisted animals. I'll just give you to them, you dig? And they'll keep you till they get good and sick of you. And when they're done, you'll be nothing but a cunt, and that's all you'll be for the rest of your life. You got that?'

"I say, 'Yeah, man, I got it,' and I'm thinking, Cassandra, it has come time for you to leave sunny California."

"Jesus," John said.

"You know what's horrible? Like the-end-of-the-road horrible? I don't think Sweet Andrew knows any fucking motorcycle gang. The horrible thing is he could even *think* of something like that."

"Jesus," John said.

He'd been left with nothing more to say. The revolution had to deal with that shit. It couldn't just be about stopping the war and civil rights and participatory democracy, or even—God help them all—the seizure of the means of production and the destruction of the State. The revolution had to mean a change in consciousness so shit like that would never happen to girls again. As much as he hated their ideology, he had to give it to the Maoists—they'd tried to make women equal, and they'd swept away their whole sick decadent colonial scene in one fell swoop. But fuck, what was he thinking? Some tendril of meaning just a jump ahead of him, and piss on the Maoists, they weren't worth even a dozen of his brain cells—and he was too stoned, too many weird things just out of reach. Yes, it all *did* have to do with making love more possible. And, yes, McLuhan was right, you had to be *outside* to see something clearly. When he'd been in Canada, he'd been able to see the States clearly, but here he was again, stuck in the belly of the beast, and now what?

Without warning, Tom slid the truck to a stop. His head, grinning, popped up at the end of the tunnel of television sets—the sudden appearance of a demented marionette on a medieval stage. "Let's go, folks," he yelled. "Time to unload these bastards."

John waited for Cassandra to worm her way out; then he crawled after her. The truck was parked in the driveway of an enormous house, an honest-to-God mansion like something out of a Fitzgerald novel. The lawn was covered with a foot of snow, but the driveway had been shoveled clear. "Christ," John said, "who the fuck lives *here?*"

"You think I know?" Tom said and flipped a big console model into the driveway. It exploded like a bomb.

3

JOHN HAD been sitting at his desk in the *Weasel* office for an hour, a sheet of typewriter paper rolled into the old IBM Executive, but he still hadn't written a damned thing. After weeks of chilling rain, the weather had turned around. He'd propped the door open to let in the air and the light, and the day was too sweet—was really fucking with his head. He wanted to be back in Toronto, back in his apartment in the Annex, even, *mirabile dictu*, back in grad school. He missed his Martin, missed his band, missed all those things Canadians took for granted—the sanity, the order, the plain old-fashioned good sense of the place. He wanted to walk down Yonge Street and feel like a full-sized human being again. He wanted to play music again. So why was he still in Boston? It was the same answer as always—because he still had something he had to say. Oh, yeah? Really? Like what?

OK, start with the Resistance. They'd folded, closed down their office, advised their members to join SDS. Not a good move, but he couldn't blame them. They'd been at it a long time now with their draft counseling and sanctuaries; they were tired of helping white middle-class males avoid the draft—and they were just plain tired—but nobody was going to step in and do the work they'd done, and it had been good work. Then there was SDS, and he didn't like anything coming out of the National Office these days. And the assholes in PL never made any sense. Everybody seemed to be getting serious, getting heavy, talking Lenin and cadres, getting down to it—but getting down to *what?* He had to lay out an anarchist alternative, and he was stuck—searching for a clear fresh word—and the day outside was too full of promise, too much like spring.

John liked to be alone when he was writing—especially when he was having this much trouble—but Phil Vance wasn't bugging him at all, was a benign presence actually, musing over his papers spread out on Ethan's desk. "Anything wonderful?" John said, hoping for a little distraction.

"Not in the capitalist press, that's for sure." Phil had gone through the *Boston Globe* and the *New York Times* the way he always did; now he was reading the packets from both versions of *Liberation News*

Service. Like damned near every other New Left group these days, LNS had split into hostile factions—the heavy Marxist one in New York and the freaky hippie one in rural Massachusetts—each sending out its own version of the underground news. "Demonstration in Ann Arbor," Phil said. "Anti-repression teach-in at the University of Michigan. Attack on ROTC building."

"What kind of attack?"

"It doesn't say." Then, glancing over at John with his shy smile, "If they blew it up, they'd probably tell us."

John laughed. He hadn't dug Phil Vance when he'd first turned up—had written him off as just another self-righteous academic asshole from the fantasyland of Harvard—but he'd been wrong. Unlike the rest of the SDSers who came and went, Phil turned up every day and went at the *Weasel* in the same methodical way he'd probably been working on his PhD before he'd abandoned it for the revolution. Phil was always there when John showed up in the morning, was usually still there when John drifted off to get stoned with Tom and Cass. Phil had taken over the HIGH ALERT page. He justified his and everybody else's columns, made the headlines, collected graphics and filed them neatly in manila envelopes, drove around town to pick up the little bits of coin that came in from the ads. On the nights when they were laying out, he turned up with huge pots of home-cooked vegetarian chili and boxes of doughnuts. He even swept the floors—something neither Ethan nor John had ever bothered to do. Doctrinaire Marxist or not, Phil was a joy forever—and John regarded him now with something that bordered on comradely warmth.

Phil made up for being absolutely and irredeemably bald by wearing a full beard and a thick mustache he cut off as straight as a paintbrush. When you added the wire-rimmed granny glasses, he didn't look like a hippie so much as a hard-working small-town New England shopkeeper from 1860—but today he'd blown that effect by wearing a sweatshirt that said (he surely couldn't have been aware of the irony of it): PROPERTY OF HARVARD UNIVERSITY. "Here's something coming out of the People's Park struggle," Phil was saying. "Twelve sheriff's deputies indicted on charges of conspiring to mistreat prisoners. Seems like they beat the crap out of everybody they busted. Like routinely."

"Oh, great. Think they'll get a conviction?"

"Yeah, right. Fat chance . . . And here's something else interesting. Group in Philly is publishing a thing on university complicity. Weapons research. Chemical, biological, anti-personnel, and incendiary weapons. Nice, huh? Lists the guilty universities."

"Can we get that? Reprint some of it?"

"Yeah, we should do that," and Phil wrote a note to himself to do that.

Then, as John studied Phil (hunched over the desk, staring at the LNS copy, thick brows contracted, chewing on his mustache), he realized that he was looking at the future editor of the *Biweekly Weasel*. Right, John thought, I stepped in to take over from Ethan, and one of these days Phil's going to take over from me, and then I'm going to be *gone*. It was a happy thought—and with that, WHAM, he knew what he had to say. "All the things that made the New Left new," he wrote, typing quickly, "the spontaneity, the autonomous local organizations, the . . ."

He wasn't sure what came next, but he had to keep going. He was on a roll. He dropped down several spaces and wrote, "The Man thinks that organizations have to have leaders. To kill an organization, all you have to do is chop off the leaders. But what if there aren't any leaders? What if everybody's a leader, flowing into the . . ." Shit, he could finish that one later too. "With the Man, the movement is always top-down, from the center to the margin. With us the movement is from . . ." Somebody at the door. *Fuck*, he thought. Annoyed. Looked up. Saw that a girl had just walked in.

Not a "woman"—even though John had been training himself to say "woman" for every female over the age of six. He saw a skinny long-legged kid wearing hair ribbons, and the politically unreconstructed part of his mind said "girl." She was already halfway across the office—passing between the layout tables, bounding around the end of Ethan's collapsing bookcase. *Girl?* Yes, barely adolescent—fourteen or fifteen maybe—skin-tight powder-blue jeans, no figure whatsoever, and not just hair ribbons but little-kid shoes with broad straps. She saw Phil, smiled at him, slipped a beat-up leather purse off her shoulder and let it fall onto Ethan's desk: THUNK. "Hey, man," she said.

Like the nineteenth-century gent he resembled, Phil had risen to his feet. Uneasily, not sure why he was doing it, John did the same thing. "Hey, Pamela," Phil said, and, turning to John, "This is Pam. She's been really wanting to meet you, man."

"Pam Zalman," she said, stepped forward and offered her hand. John took it, and she seized him with a grip as emphatic as a boy's. "So you're Raymond Lee, huh?" She had a heavy New York accent.

"That's me," John said, feeling like an asshole.

"I really dig your stuff. I'm an anarchist too."

"Oh, yeah?" Startled and wary.

"Not too many of us around."

"No, not too many. Some of the Resistance people . . ."

"But it's not a numbers game, you dig?" she said. "It's the coherence of the critique," and was already gone, across the room where she grabbed up one of the folding chairs, then was back, slamming her chair down directly next to his. She fell onto it as though it was a kind of prop. "Our ideas are in everybody's minds," she said.

"Not in mine," Phil said, laughing.

"Oh, I know that, you Stalinist schmuck," she said affectionately enough. They were obviously friends. "These assholes never stop with the hyphen," she was saying to John. "*Marxist* . . . and that's OK . . . but then they've got to tack on *Leninist* . . ."

"You're goddamned right I'm a *Leninist*," Phil said, "because it works. I'm an American. I believe in success."

"Hey," she said, still addressing John as though she'd known him for years, "did you hear that? He just told us the truth. Like straight out. They'll always settle for a technical adjustment of the power structure."

By now John was getting the full impact of her—a scary high-wire vibe. He pounded a cigarette out of his pack, offered her one. She shook her head.

"I've been trying to recruit her for the *Weasel*." Phil's amused eyes were adding some further message, but John couldn't read it.

"Terrific," John said, "we always need people."

Hiding behind the ritual—matches, fire, and smoke—John was

examining her. The little-girl look was certainly in at the moment; you saw it everywhere, but not with Movement women, and she wasn't doing that look anyway, at least not in the way it was laid out in the fashion mags. She had long brandy-colored hair neatly divided into two ponytails tied with ribbons the same color as her jeans—and that was Twiggy enough—but a Levi jacket hanging open, and under it, a boy's crisp white dress shirt, and under that (bizarre touch) a boy's white cotton T-shirt. She was so flat-chested she might as well have been a boy. Her Mary Janes looked like she'd walked a hundred miles in them—originally navy but scuffed to beige at the toes—and she was wearing tons of eye makeup—mascara and eyeliner and even a smear of blue on her lids—and Movement women simply didn't do that. John had years of practice at reading the social messages of clothes, but he couldn't read hers. Who the hell was she? "What do you want to do?" he asked her.

"I'm a writer."

"Far out," he said automatically. Nobody would have called her face beautiful. Too narrow, not enough chin and too much nose, but an appealing face—the kind of homely face that could grow on you. Pale skin that had never seen the sun—and eerie eyes. Hazel that mixed brown with flecks of blue and green. Eyes that were looking at him now. Compelling eyes—no doubt about it. If he looked at those eyes long enough, he might even begin to see that odd little face as beautiful. And something zinged between himself and this weird girl—a coded message, an exchange. Untranslatable, but simple as daylight.

Unnerved, he said, "Did you bring anything with you?"

"Of course she's brought something with her," Phil said.

Her compact torso was set upon disproportionately long legs, and she'd settled onto the chair in the screwiest of positions, her left leg drawn up, the heel of one scruffy shoe on the rung, the other leg extended at an oblique angle. Without moving her legs, she swiveled at the waist, and, without being asked, Phil was already handing her the purse she'd left on Ethan's desk. John felt double-teamed. Were they running some kind of number on him?

She handed him a clean typescript, an article that seemed to be—

that certainly was—a political analysis of *The Story of O.* " . . . thus, under the guise of pornography, Pauline Reage has written a profound allegory, as broad in its scope and true to its time as *A Pilgrim's Progress,* of daily life under highly evolved spectacular capitalism."

Jesus fuck, John thought. "Where you from?" he said. "The Cliffe?"

"No. Columbia."

The word fluttered in the office like a suddenly unfurled battle ensign. Those disturbing hazel eyes were looking directly into his, and he finally got it—she was most definitely not a kid. He skimmed the rest of the article, stopped on a paragraph near the end:

```
The powerless are in a constant state of being
fucked up the ass by power. Many of us have long ago
become inured to that state, our assholes having been
methodically stretched by a long, painful education
begun in the family, continued in the schools, and
completed in marriage or on the job. But to maintain
its murderous daily work, power requires far more
than a passively resigned submission that has lost
the will either to suicide or violence. Like O,
the powerless must learn to love being fucked up
the ass, to long for it, to beg fervently for the
return of that huge, adamantine, arrogant, merciless,
commanding cock of power. The effectiveness of
Reage's allegory can be measured by the extent to
which it turns on the reader. Are you wet, woman
reader? Are you hard, man reader? Yes, of course you
are, and therein lies the subversive heart of this
charming allegory: we are all turned on because we
are all O--for the repression of sexuality can only
be maintained by the sexualization of repression.
```

Break. For a while John did nothing but stare at the wedge-shaped patch of sunlight by the door. She had left as quickly as she'd appeared, leaving behind a powder-blue afterimage in his mind. He read her article—twice. It took the second time to really get it. Brilliant? Yes, absolutely. But highly theoretical, damnably difficult, not exactly the kind of thing the *Weasel* usually offered its stoned-out readership. Yes, it was anarchist, but she was working from a tradition he didn't know very well—the Freudian Left—quoting Reich and Laing and the old Viennese trickster himself. He looked up, saw that Phil was looking at him. "OK, man," John said, "lay it on me. Who the fuck is she?"

Phil laughed. "Yeah, she's something else, all right. She's from Columbia SDS . . . one of the women that emerged into a leadership role . . . you know, during the action there."

"SDS?" John said. That was weird. She didn't seem like an SDS heavy, at least not like any of the ones he'd ever met.

"Oh, yeah," Phil said. "She isn't part of any . . . She doesn't reflect the National Office, that's for damned sure. She's highly critical of the National Office. She says she's an anarchist, but she seems more like a council communist to me. Heavy into women's lib. She's in the Collective . . . you know, with Karen."

Shit, John thought, that's all I need. Karen was Phil's— well, in the old days, you would have said simply "wife," but that term had dropped out of the correct vocabulary along with "girlfriend," and Phil usually referred to Karen as "the woman I live with." And "the Collective" was short for the Boston Radical Women's Collective—the dolorous BRWC. John didn't know much about them. No man did. They were a small but influential tendency in the women's movement—theoretical, far left, highly secretive, even paranoid—and anti-men. The best he could tell, they were heavy-duty, full tilt, no-holds-barred anti-men. But they couldn't be out-and-out separatists. Karen was still *living with* Phil.

"The Council's going to start their own journal," Phil was saying. "It's kind of hard because they want it to be woman-produced from beginning to end, all the way to the printing. And Pam wrote that thing, and she doesn't want to wait. She's in a hurry. She wants it out *right now*. I told her to try the *Weasel* . . . Probably not right for us, huh?"

"I don't know. What's she doing in Boston?"

Phil wasn't sure. A few months ago, Pam had just appeared, had crashed with Phil and Karen for a while; then one of the women in the Collective had split town, and Pam had taken over her apartment. "She's looking for some kind of action," Phil said, "like, 'Come on, everybody, I'm here, so let's start the motherfucking revolution.' Oh, yeah, she's crazy."

"Good crazy or bad crazy?"

Phil shrugged. "I've been telling her to come in and just *talk* to you, man. She's crazy like you. I thought you'd dig each other."

John picked up the loose pages of her article, stacked them, restored the paper clip to the upper left-hand corner. "No, it's not right for us," he said, "but that doesn't mean we can't do it."

Later he fought with Ethan over that article. "Shit, man." Ethan tugged on his beard, crinkled his forehead. "I can't make heads or tails of it."

"I don't care whether you understand it or not. We've got to print it."

"Why?"

"Because if we don't, we're damned fools. Because if we don't, she'll go write for somebody else. Because it just may turn out to be the most important article we ever ran."

"Because you got hot pants for her."

"Oh fuck off, man."

"Jesus, Ray . . . or John, or Mr. Fucking Jones, or whatever you're calling yourself today, cool out." Ethan chuckled, slapped John on the top of the head. "Yeah, who gives a good goddamn what it means? The Cambridge Vice Squad hasn't been around for a while, might as well give them a good excuse. Yeah, just what we need . . . an article on assholes."

SHE MET him in Harvard Square in front of Nini's. "Hey, man," she said. A smile lit up her spooky eyes, and he felt the impact of her, the rush—far more stunning than the obsessive tape loop he'd been running in his mind. *Alive.*

He knew she'd want to hear about her article—all writers like to be praised—so that's where he started. "It'll be in the next issue. You've got to come in and lay it out. Yeah, it's great stuff. Amazing. Blew my mind."

"Thanks, man. I put a lot of work into it."

"You want to get something to eat?"

He saw her hesitate. "I've got a hangup about restaurants. You like to walk?"

With long boyish strides, she was leading him into the green and pleasant pastures of Harvard University. She was still wearing the same heavy eye makeup, the same two ponytails, but bound tonight with bits of black yarn. "One of my best friends went to Harvard," he said—and caught himself. No, he shouldn't be talking about old friends—shouldn't be talking about anything that could identify him, give him a traceable past. Here in Boston, there was no past.

"Oh, yeah?" she said. "It's a groove, isn't it? I dig the whole university scene"—expansive gesture—"mystifications and all. Medieval community of scholars. Sanctuary."

She walked, he thought, the way he used to back in Morgantown when ideas had chased him like Maenads, and he realized that she reminded him of a younger version of himself—how weird. She was glancing back for him now, grinning. She paused so he could catch up. "It's ours," she was saying, "anyhow, it should be. Look at how peaceful it is. Never know it was fully complicit with the war machine, would you? Have you checked out Widener? I really dig it. One of the great academic libraries. Shit, man, there's nothing that's not in there."

Maybe *young* was the key to it—a freaky mental twist like déjà vu. A tangle of things coming together in his mind—almost but not quite connecting. "So tell me about Columbia," he said.

"Oh, Columbia?" She shrugged—an eloquent motion of her shoulders. "It was a real trip. We debated everything, like for hours and hours and hours. *Everybody* got to talk. Leaders? When it got down to the action, there weren't any motherfucking leaders. I walked in on Rudd and Papert, the heavy boys having their heavy debate about *strategy*, so fucking serious, and they asked me to leave, can you believe it? Said piss on you guys, vanguards suck shit, fell by Fayerweather, dug it there, stayed there, got busted there . . . Mark Rudd? Oh, he's a good guy but not much of a thinker. A media creation. The TV vultures need leaders. Without leaders, they wouldn't have anything to spectacularize."

He loved watching her walk, watching her move. Like a lean-hipped girl athlete, she was built for speed—quicksilver. Tonight she was wearing the same tight powder-blue jeans, but over black boots just as beat-up as her little-kid shoes had been, and a ribbed turtleneck like the ones Cassandra wore, and a fantastic touch—tight leather gloves, navy, the kind of sleek feminine dress gloves that would have gone with a Bonwitt Teller coat. She seemed to like putting things together that didn't go together—both in her ideas and her clothes.

"Scalp wounds bleed a lot. Oy, I thought I was murdered, but it was just a little cut . . . No, the pigs weren't bad. When they cleared the buildings, anyway. Out on the streets they were motherfucking Cossacks . . . The revolutionary moment . . . Wow, how things got dealt with. Food, sanitation, sleeping arrangements, it all got taken care of. Anarchism in action. *There* was the goddamned revolution. But they tried to siphon the women off into shit work the way they always do. Jesus, I must have made a million sandwiches. While the male heavies fought it out. Yeah, a really big show. The praxis faction versus the action faction. The students were like a hundred miles ahead of the so-called leadership . . . just the way it always is. I learned a lot. Eventually I thought, well, screw that, I can talk too. The next time around, the men can make the sandwiches."

Bedazzled, exhilarated, he trotted behind her. "Where you from?"

"Long Island." Pronounced *Lon-Guyland*. "How about you?"

"West Virginia." Oh, fuck, he thought. That was his second slip. He hadn't been with her twenty minutes, and he was already blowing his cover.

"West Virginia, huh? I don't know a damn thing about it. Yeah, I heard your accent too"—he hadn't said a word about accents, although he'd sure been hearing *hers*—"but I couldn't put my finger on it . . . Coal and Mother Jones?"

"Yeah. But that's downstate. Where I'm from it's steel and the USWA. What's on Long Island?"

She laughed. "Nothing, man. Suburbs."

They'd gone completely around the yard and ended up right back where they'd started—in front of Widener. "Smoke?" he said.

"Sure." But she made no move to take the pack he was offering her.

Disconcerted, something in him stuttering, flapping loose, he pounded out two cigarettes, passed her one, pressed the other between his lips. Lit hers, then his. She'd come to rest . . . Well, no, it didn't look like *rest*—still a coiled energy to her as though she might go bounding off at any moment, but at least she'd put herself on pause, holding her cigarette with a gloved hand. It was not a cold night. Her tight shiny gloves were decorated with bows so small, so discreet, they were almost unnoticeable.

He looked up, found her eyes looking directly into his. His mind was reduced to rubble. Her face was showing— What? Amusement? Something more complex? "I dig boys with long hair," she said.

Even if he could have thought of something to say, he couldn't have said it. "It must be a real trip for you guys to feel how sensual it is," she said.

"Yeah."

He was trying to find a simple strand in this complex tangle. Why had she said *boys* instead of the correct word, *men*? Maybe it had been nothing more than a slip into ordinary language, and she was welcome to call him a boy if she wanted to, but something had just happened; like the Mr. Jones whose name he'd borrowed, John didn't have a clue what it was. Speak, he told himself. "I haven't had a haircut in . . . I don't know. It must be a couple years."

"Groovy." He saw something flicker in her eyes—yes, he could call it "amusement"—as though she'd just heard how empty, even parodic, that single word had sounded. Somewhere else, in a gone life, he might have thought she was flirting with him.

She finally broke their locked gaze, looked out and away (at what? at Harvard? at some Platonic ideal of a university?), her thin lips pressed into a firm line. "They called us reformists," she said, "but it *did* matter what went down at Columbia. I mean it wasn't just to force them to call in the pigs, radicalize the campus. We were creating the new world in the shell of the old, you dig? Like I wanted us to say, 'Fuck the demands, we're keeping the university.' Yeah, man, the universities should be ours. Centers for the development of revolutionary theory."

"Right on."

"But not so right on for the Leninists. Well, piss on them."

She dropped her cigarette and stepped on it. "I don't really smoke. I keep thinking I'm going to dig it, but I never do . . . Hey,

I'm worried I'm keeping you from eating. I could probably sit in that Chinese place for a while."

He'd been hungry when he'd got off the subway, but he was so sick now with the intensity of her he wasn't sure he could eat even a grain of rice. Still, he said the only thing that seemed possible: "Sure. Chinese sounds fine."

"I read all your pieces," she said.

"You did what?"

"Is the first piece you wrote the one on the shift in the Movement after Chicago?"

"Yeah."

"Then I read all your pieces." She laughed reflexively.

He didn't trust himself, not with what he was guessing now—that maybe she was just as old-fashioned kids-in-high-school freaked out as he was. "I was over at Karen's," she said, shrugging. "You know, Karen Vance? We're in the Collective together . . ."

"Yeah, Phil told me."

"And I picked up the *Weasel* . . . saw the last piece you did. Thought wow, a coherent anarchist, far fucking out. Went through every back issue and found all your articles." She shrugged—wry, self-depreciating. "I even made notes. Some things I'd like to rap about . . . if you wouldn't mind . . . Like . . ." She shrugged, didn't finish the sentence.

Up until then, he would have characterized her voice as loud and brash, even abrasive; suddenly it was different. "I can sit in the Chinese restaurant for a while," she said in a low, muted, nearly singing tone. Weird, he thought. "Do you want to do that?" she said.

"BUDDHA'S FEAST," she said, "and please don't put any sauce on it."

"You want plain?"

"Yes," firmly, "I want plain." Most people, John thought, would have left it at that, but she didn't, was staring directly into the face of their waiter—"Nothing on it. *Nothing.*"

"Sweet and sour pork," John said apologetically.

She turned back to John. "You know, the, ah . . . Shit, I hate all the old terminology, but the united-front line. That's what the *Weasel's* taking at the moment, isn't it?"

Yes, it was old terminology—*Old* Left—but he knew exactly what she meant. "Right," he said, "the broadest-based possible opposition."

"And it has worked up till now." Tugging carefully on each finger, she drew off her gloves, pressed them flat, folded them, and laid them aside at the edge of their table. Her hands were just as thin and white as her face. Her nails were short but neatly filed. "But I don't know how much longer it's going to work. I loved the last editorial in the *Weasel* . . . 'If we don't hang together . . . ' Yeah, really dug that invocation of all those old American symbols. The pigs don't *own* those symbols, even though they think they do, so it's great to see a *détournment* on them."

Détournment? he thought. What's she been reading? "But look," she was saying, "maybe some people we can't hang with . . . because they don't want to hang with *us* . . . Like you said in one of your articles, the Leninists have always sold us out every chance they got . . ."

"Right, the First International, Spain, the Ukraine, Kronstadt . . ."

"Yeah, yeah, right, all that shit," she said impatiently, "and they'll sell us out again. So if you're going to have to split with them later, why not now? The question is . . . at what point do you start drawing lines? Like with PL, for instance. PL's not part of the Movement. I don't think it ever was."

"And SDS still is?"

"Yeah, man. SDS is *central* to the Movement . . . Oh, I know what you mean about RYM"—he hadn't said a word about RYM—"its incoherence . . . its failure to engage with the concrete historical situation. But all that crap's in direct reaction to PL. The NO's been forced to take *some* goddamn line, for Christ's sake. With PL at you all the fucking time, you've got to be able to defend yourself. Those sectarian bastards are parasitic on the Movement . . . goddamned miserable vermin. Those motherfuckers suck shit."

Her vehemence made him nervous. He was afraid that there was still living inside himself a hopelessly nice West Virginia boy who wanted even the most heated political debate to be conducted with a certain civility, one that would exclude the reduction of one's opponents to the status of shit-sucking motherfuckers, but she obviously didn't feel any such bourgeois constraint. She was so angry her eyes were sizzling. God, she did have beautiful eyes—huge, luminous. Picking up the color from the walls, they looked green as jade.

Well, OK, he thought, PL might suck shit, but nobody was any better organized. You could always count on them to turn out the bodies, and surely that had to count for something. "It just seems to me," he said, "there's not a lot to choose from in SDS these days. Do you want your repressive top-down mind-fuck Leninist vanguard kissing Ho Chi Minh's ass or Chairman Mao's?"

At the last SDS National Council meeting, the two factions had tried to chant each other down, the RYM faction with "Ho Ho Ho Chi Minh" and the PL faction with "Mao Mao Mao Tse-tung." She laughed. "Yeah. It's pathetic. I was there when they did that, couldn't fucking believe it, man. This is the so-called leadership? This bunch of high school *cheer*leaders? But at least the NO's stumbling vaguely forward in the right direction."

"Is it?"

He was a hell of a lot more interested in *her* than in anything she was saying, but still he was trying to follow her line of thought. He wasn't any great fan of PL, but the people in the National Office seemed like morons to him, and, anyhow, he felt a million miles away from that intensely sectarian, tempest-in-a-teapot shit going down in SDS. All he knew about it was what he read—mostly in *Liberation News Service*. If he was being honest with her, he'd have to say that he didn't think the leadership of SDS mattered all that much; the kids on the campuses were what counted. But she was obviously heavy into the internal SDS debates, so of course all that shit mattered to her—and he'd better watch his mouth.

She was still talking. "You know what I get called? *Old Left*. Well, if "Old Left" means you bother to think about something before you write a manifesto on it, then I'm Old Left. Fuck it, man, I don't know where . . ."

Their dinners arrived, and she stopped in mid-sentence to stare at the steamy bowls. Her eyes had turned off, gone inward; the set of her mouth was tight and disgruntled. He didn't blame her. Without any sauce, her Buddha's feast was nothing but vegetables and tofu; he couldn't imagine how anybody could get off on eating that crap. He offered her some of his sweet and sour pork; she shook her head. "Rice?" he said. Again she shook her head. She began to separate the vegetables, creating small discrete sections on her plate—a row of bean sprouts, another of green peppers, another of carrots . . . "Are you a vegetarian?" he asked her.

"Not exactly." She looked him in the eye. "Ray?"

It took him a heartbeat to remember that Ray was his name. "Yeah?"

"Don't watch me eat, OK?"

"Yeah, sure. OK."

She handled her chopsticks with deft expertise—picked up one bean sprout, put it in her mouth, and chewed on it. How the hell long, he thought, could it possibly take to chew up a bean sprout? She picked up a piece of green pepper. "We really need good theory now," she said. "Can't just go it on guts anymore. Everything's got too fucking heavy and weird . . . Like what do you do with . . . ? OK, there's the united-front line. And it's worked up till now. Like you said, we really *are* all in it together and the pigs can't tell us apart, but . . . Well, what about women and men? If the split comes along that line, what does that do to your broad base?"

The sweet and sour pork turned to a sour mass of sludge in his stomach. He watched her pick up a small square of tofu.

Before he could assemble anything to say, she kept on going: "Dig it, the relationship between women and men is the basic power relationship. Engels had it right. Everything builds from that. *Everything.* All the hierarchies all the way up to the repressive capitalist state. It's fundamental, man. Basic. If you don't deal with the oppression of women, you don't deal with anything."

She gave him an unreadable smile and that eloquent shrug he'd realized by now must be one of her defining gestures. "You want to hear how I'm hung up? The Collective's far fucking out. I love the Collective. But about half the women in there are radical feminists, and they don't want to have anything to do with men . . . shit, not even a cup of coffee. And the other half are Movement women, still attached to SDS . . . and they're all Leninists." She laughed.

"OK, and then there's SDS. And I'm just so fucking sick of the male chauvinism in SDS I could puke. But we're kind of . . . We're trying to deal with it. We did elect Bernardine . . . but then she comes out with all this crap in *New Left Notes*. She thinks the women's groups are bourgeois, says we're flailing at our own middle-class images. Well, piss on her. She's a great one to talk with her miniskirts and Italian leather boots, oh, so sexy . . .

"Well, nobody in the fucking NO's a deep thinker. Their politics is like rudimentary, man, infantile. Most of those people who are running around now calling themselves revolutionary communists wouldn't know Comrade Stalin if he shot them through the head. But it *was* good to see a woman in a leadership position for a change. And Bernardine *is* sexy, damn it. I don't know what to think about that. Part of me wants to dump on her for it, and another part of me says, 'Right on, sister.'"

If he sat there in stunned silence much longer, she'd probably notice, but he still couldn't find anything safe to say. It was no wonder she had trouble with male chauvinism in SDS. Those pea-brained heavy macho dudes would never take her seriously—not with her child's thin white face and her tons of inky black mascara and her twin ponytails and her *hair ribbons*—but *he* was taking her seriously, far more seriously than he would have taken any man. And that, of course, was a kind of male chauvinism too—he couldn't let himself off the hook on that one—but no matter how seriously he took her ideas, he couldn't imagine any way he could stop seeing her as female, responding to her on that level, balancing on the high bright tension of his desire.

"Sometimes I think the radical feminists are right," she was saying. "At this particular historical moment we shouldn't have anything to do with men. Not until we've got our shit together. Men . . . even well-meaning men . . . are just going to fuck us up. And then other times I think, hey, wait a minute, who says I can't do both? Help build an autonomous women's movement and work with men on something else? Something where there's the possibility of theoretical agreement? You see, we get caught in this phony either-or bullshit all the time . . . But if the relationship between men and women is the *basic* power relationship, shouldn't that be the place to start? Isn't that what has to be totally transformed? You dig?"

"Yes," he said, "I do."

ONCE AGAIN he found himself running his old paranoid tape loop: *Could she be an agent?* It wasn't impossible. Everybody in the Resistance had been fond of harmless old Dave with his sad watery eyes and stringy salt-and-pepper beard and gentle smile. He'd told them stories about the Spanish Civil War and led them in chants of Om and turned out to be on the payroll of the Sheriff's Department. Then there had been that live-wire photographer Stan who'd showed up one day eager to work for the *Weasel*. He'd said he was on the staff at *Ramparts*, and he'd been so convincing he'd been hanging around for a month before some odd nagging suspicion had made John call *Ramparts* to discover that they'd never heard of anybody named Stan. When John and Ethan had confronted him—"OK, man, who the fuck are you?"—Stan had stuck to his story, but they'd never seen him again.

But wouldn't an agent blend in more than Pam did? No, not necessarily. Both Dave and Stan had stood out. But would a real agent know as much as she did? Maybe—if she was a highly trained professional, an honest-to-God mole from some creepy agency deep in the shadows. But come on, he told himself—Cassandra's line— paranoia's got to stop somewhere.

They were in Pam's minuscule apartment a short walk from Harvard Square—on the second floor of an old Queen Anne subdivided into student housing. Following her lead, he'd pulled his boots off at the door, had stepped into a space that was white and clean and uncluttered, everything in its place, not a trace of dust on any of the surfaces, not even on the hardwood floor. The light from the huge bay window would be wonderful in the daytime. There was no separate bedroom; a double bed was partially hidden behind a Japanese paper screen. He'd been surprised to see that the white bedspread was decorated with eyelet lace, and with that, he'd begun to pick up something more than merely a love of good order—

something artful and planned, something peaceful, something he felt as intensely *feminine*.

She'd told him a few things about herself—probably because he'd asked her. She wasn't an undergrad; she was working on her PhD in anthropology—which meant that she was a lot older than she looked. For someone who'd participated in the Columbia action, she seemed oddly proud of her school—or at least proud of her department: "Yeah, Boas founded it, Jules Henry went there. We're really radical, man." The only thing she still had left was her thesis: "And I haven't written a word of it, not a single freaking word. I was going to do something on ballet"—*ballet?* he thought—"but then the historical situation pretty much blew me away. I don't know," with a wry smile, "maybe I'll do an ethnographic study of the Movement. But then I think, why would a full-time revolutionary want a PhD?"

No matter where the conversation drifted, she always brought it back to politics. Now she was telling him about the Situationist International—some crazy French group that had been involved in the May Days. A couple of their books already lay at his feet waiting to go home with him. "Best stuff I've seen in a long time. Blew me fucking away, man."

Was there anything she didn't know? "Like Vaneigem says," she was telling him, "the decision to live is a political decision. But then he says, like, why would you want to join a group that expects you to leave your dreams and desires in the cloakroom? So subjectivity is where we start, but if we stop there, then all we'll have is a partial critique, and all partial critiques will fail as they have in the past. Like any illusion of totality will only maintain the totality of the illusion."

She'd rolled a tight perfect joint and passed it to him now with the ritualized courtesy of the true pothead—if you roll it, you give it to someone else to light. As he dragged on it, he tasted the surprise of licorice paper. "So I'll tell you my story, you tell me yours," she said. "You start with, 'I'm fucked up in such and such a way because of what happened to me.' Like Laing says, the politics of *experience*. And we can figure out concrete actions to take *right now*, in this historical moment. That's the beginnings of a council, man."

He passed her the joint. She took a deep drag, held it. "Whew," she said, expelling smoke, "it's new every time."

"Yeah," he said, and it *was* new every time—the rush, the openings in the mind, the weird connections—so why couldn't he just get behind it, go with the flow? Because he had a problem to solve—collecting clues, trying to fit them together until they made a grand pattern, one that would tell him clearly who she was. Under her old scuffed boots she wore not what anybody else would have worn—bulky athletic socks—but instead little white ankle socks; juxtaposed against the flaring cuffs of her jeans, her feet looked improbably dainty. Her voice commanded so much space, ran on so much energy, it gave her an enormous psychic presence, but she really was a small girl, so thin he couldn't imagine her any thinner—and yet there was a bathroom scale by her bed. She couldn't possibly be worried about her weight, could she? But maybe her scanty dinner in the Chinese restaurant had been part of some bizarre diet.

She was passing the joint back to him. He took it and dragged. It was good dope; his brainstem was smoldering like a fuse. Ah, and the whiteness in her apartment was nearly totemic—white walls, white woodwork, white sheers on the window, and all of that white reflected back from a full-length mirror in a white frame. But a pink—yes, pink!—throw rug and, on the largest wall, a huge framed print of two pink flowers. A lavender vase filled with pearly grey pussy willows rested on the top of a white dresser. Floating mysteriously on the wall near her bed was a pale pink ribbon tied into a bow. The desk and the bookshelves were white pine. Over the desk was the picture of a lady from another era; she looked like a stern-faced schoolteacher, somebody's long-dead maiden aunt. "You know her, man," with a hint of a smile. She must have followed his eyes. She must have been just as keenly aware of him as he was of her. "That's Rosa Luxemburg."

"Oh, yeah? Far out. I've never seen a picture of her."

"No, probably not. You can't just walk into a store and buy one. Che and Fidel and Ho and Mao, yes . . . and even Stalin. Shit, can you believe it? You can even buy posters of that pig."

He passed the joint back to her; she took it, held it. Looked away, her eyes focusing on some distant abstract point, her mouth pressed into that firm line he was beginning to recognize—signaling what? "Yeah. So when all those little groups start clumping together," she said, "then we've got the beginnings of the councils, and when they begin to act, then we're moving into the revolutionary moment." She inhaled smoke, held it, blew it out. "And only *then* are we moving into a total critique."

Her doggedness, her persistence, the way she kept coming back to some point she absolutely had to make—it felt compulsive to him, even obsessive, as though she was driven to it, as though she was required to *sell* him something. Wasn't that exactly what an agent would do?

"That's why I can't just go with the radical feminists the whole way," she was saying, "even though I'm sorely tempted. Because I want total power. Half the human race . . . well, slightly less than half . . . are men." She seemed to have forgotten his turn; she dragged on the joint again. "But yeah, I'm tempted. A feminist separatist position is really attractive because it's so goddamn *pure*."

"Like some kinds of anarchism," he said automatically.

"Yeah, exactly."

Forget any hope of her going to bed with him; it was amazing that she was even *talking* to him—and who was he to be thinking about going to bed with anyone anyway? Flavored now like licorice, a waft of his old dark sorrow drifted toward him on the pungent weed, threatened him with the pothead's ultimate nightmare—a fucking bummer. Scrambling for safety, his mind began talking to him, producing words and yet more words. Yeah, he probably *was* doomed to having a series of close women friends who were exactly that—friends—but never lovers. But why should that be? He didn't know for sure, but it was somehow a given, and he'd been doing it for so long by now that it had begun to feel almost normal. In Toronto he'd had plenty of women in his life—friends, not lovers. Usually somebody else's wife or girlfriend so she'd be safe. He liked women, liked being with them, and— Ah, and here was the dark center of the eclipse where he didn't want to go— But anyhow, he'd rather be Pam's Platonic anarchist comrade than not have her in his life at all. Unless, of course, she was an agent.

"But purity just doesn't work," she was saying. "The concrete historical situation is always a mess. Things happen every which way for crazy reasons, and you've got to be able to move with that." And finally she offered him the joint. There wasn't much of it left.

His eyes kept coming back to the painting of the two flowers. One was arranged in front of the other, partially obscuring it. The flower in the back was a cool bluish pink; the one in the front was a warm pink nearly the color of human flesh. Their petals swirled in curves that felt unabashedly sexual; their spiky centers were black and deep maroon. As he stared at the flowers, he began to sense that they were far more than merely decorative; they gave off an energy that radiated throughout the entire apartment—another clue.

The dope, or maybe the intensity of his need to understand her, had clarified his vision until it felt scraped clean, and then he flashed on it—the pattern. The lavender vase was an exact match for the hint of lavender in the background of the painting; the pearly pussy willows picked up a patch of wispy blue-grey in the painting near the left-hand bottom. The throw rug on the floor matched the warm pink; the strange ribbon on the wall matched the cool pink. If what he was discovering was true—wasn't just some freaky solipsistic trick his mind was playing on him—then he'd have to find somewhere that black and deep maroon, and he found it. He and Pam were sitting on two basket chairs; both had been draped with a coarse fabric with interwoven colors of exactly that black and deep maroon. Hey, he thought, far fucking out.

She'd been talking—*of course* she'd been talking; she never stopped—but he'd lost track of anything she'd been saying. He didn't care. "This is really trippy," he said, interrupting her. "It's like you built everything around that painting."

He'd become used to her laugh—the wry cutting edge to it—but the way she laughed now was entirely different. Then, as though the full power of the dope had suddenly jumped her, she began rapping with the cheery abandonment of a whacked-out teenager: "Hey, man, far out, you're the first person who's noticed. Yeah, man, that's exactly what I did. When I moved in here, that's all that . . . Deb had left me the O'Keeffe. She's an O'Keeffe freak, and she didn't . . .

She's out in New Mexico now, in O'Keeffe country, you dig? Like she just looks out the window, and she's got it, and it was supposed to remind me . . . She keeps telling me I've got to get out of the city. Carcinogenic, man, like the city makes nothing but war. So anyhow, the walls were white. I crashed on the floor and woke up in the morning with all that beautiful light streaming in, and I thought, OK, here's where I start my new life in Boston. White and O'Keeffe. Everything will be organized around that. Do you like it?"

"Oh, yeah. I love it."

"Not too bourgeois for you?"

"Oh, hell no. It's peaceful. What the hell's 'bourgeois' mean anyway? Who says it's bourgeois?"

"Oh, I get shit from some of my girlfriends . . . Oops. *Women* friends. But I'm allowed to say that because I am one."

Her eyes were looking directly into his, and he couldn't look away. He felt like . . . a deer in the headlights, a snake in front of the charmer . . . Jesus, what corny images. Her hazel eyes picked up the colors around her; saturated with white, they looked as eerily pale and luminous as the morning star. "You're the first man who's ever been in here," she said.

He wished to God he could fight clear of the dope. Everything was tangling up. His fear was a physical entity, was ice. "Thank you," he heard himself saying.

"You're welcome," she said in a voice that was a mockery of his distant formal tone. He saw again that glitter he'd called "amusement"—although he knew now that's not what it was. "I feel like I should curtsy," she said.

If she was an agent, he thought, she had to be the most unlikely agent in the entire history of American espionage.

"You don't give away much, man," she said.

Now was the time to leave. He could find a way to do it, something to say. They'd been talking non-stop for—God, over five hours. It was getting late. He couldn't take much more. And, in a freaky flash, his mind gave him the same phrase it had when he'd first met Natalie so many years ago—*this girl is special.* But "special" didn't even come close. Yes, that sickening bittersweet intensity, that melodramatic teenage madly-in-love downward spiral he hadn't felt since Morgantown—go ahead, asshole, jump over the edge, who gives a shit if you splatter on the rocks?

There was something else, of course, something obvious: she radiated an eerie boy-girl luminescence—like Cassandra at fourteen, Natalie at seventeen. Then he knew it was himself he didn't trust, his ability to deal with any of this shit, because that part of himself he'd been trying to forget, or at least bracket off, still sometimes wished he'd been born a girl. So what he should do, before things got any weirder, was get up and walk out—but if he did that, what would he win? He'd be protecting himself, that's all. He'd be safe—just another male chauvinist pig who couldn't take her seriously. Right. But how much more seriously could he take her than taking her at her word? What if she'd meant exactly what she'd said: "If the relationship between women and men is the *basic* power relationship . . . isn't that what has to be totally transformed?" He could hear his own heartbeat like a dim thump at the bottom of a lake.

"My name's not Raymond Lee," he said. "My name's John Dupre. I'm a draft resister. I went to Canada in sixty-five. Worked with the Toronto Anti-Draft Program. I came to Boston after Chicago, and I've been here ever since . . . I'm not sure why. Just that I've got to do *something*, although it never feels like enough. I write my pieces in the *Weasel*. Just like you, I try to figure everything out. Before I got . . . How'd you put it? Blown away by history? . . . I was working on an MA at York. I was a *musician*, for Christ's sake. I had a damned good life in Canada, and most of the time I wish I was back there. I'm on the FBI wanted list, and if you're an agent, I've just fucked myself good."

"God, you must really trust me." And then, in a little kid's involuntary gesture, she slapped her fingertips against her lips. Her eyes had never left his.

"Yeah, I must," he said.

"Thank you . . . Now I feel like I really should curtsy," and, blowing his mind yet again, she rose to her feet and did exactly that.

4

THEN JOHN got himself a girlfriend . . . Well, that's probably not what I should be calling her. Like if the word GIRLFRIEND accidentally escaped from my mouth when she was around, my continued existence as a two-balled male might have become doubtful. So let me start over. John found himself a person of the female sex to hang out with—this weird skinny speedy loudmouthed little chick from New York named Pam—and she and John dug each other because they were on the same team. She was the first real heavy-duty women's libber I'd ever run into, and I've got to admit she made me nervous. More than nervous. Listening to her rap sometimes, my blood would run COLD. But Cass thought she was perfect for John. "It's damn well about time," she said. "I just hope he can figure out what the hell to do with her."

"Christ," I said, "I can't imagine wanting to do ANYTHING with her."

"That's because you really are a male chauvinist pig. But she's the kind of girl he's always wanted. I just hope he's not too spaced out to realize it."

She kept worrying about John. I guess that's what you do if you've got a brother, you worry about him. "He's really hung up, man," she said. "I don't know what it is. He wasn't like that when I first met him, but . . . I don't know. He's really fucked up over nothing. I don't think he's ever made it with anybody."

I figured if you'd never made it with anybody, you'd want to start with somebody NICE—you know, kind and understanding and sweet and gentle and feminine and all that other good shit—but then what did I know about being liberated? But anyhow, I never got to the point where I could say I honest-to-God liked Pam, but I got used to her. She and Cassandra were two of the world's most accomplished speed rappers, and when you got them together, it was like contemplating a phenomenon of nature, you know, like a typhoon. John and me would sit there amazed and just look at each other.

And meanwhile Cassandra and me were still living in our little slum dwelling out in East Cambridge, and she'd started bitching about the place the minute she'd moved in with me. "Jesus, Tom, this place is a dump. And there's never any hot water." Growing up with two sisters, I'm pretty well checked out on chicks, and no matter how liberated chicks get, they always want hot water. Well eventually somebody laid it on me that you could rent a whole house in Roxbury for what I was paying in East Cambridge, so we floated over there and looked at the houses, and some of them were really nice, and I rented one of them. Real bright, huh?

It never crossed my mind that there was anything wrong with living in Roxbury just because it's full of black people. I was stationed with a lot of black dudes in the service, and I got along with them fine. I mean I liked black people, I figured they ought to like me. That's how dumb I was. This was like a year after Martin Luther King got killed, you dig? So there was this church around the corner run by white people, and it had a big statue of Christ out front with his arms spread open like you should go up and give him a big hug, and he was all WHITE because he was carved out of marble, and one morning I noted that somebody had come along in the night and painted him BLACK. And the next little event that managed to force its way into my head was when four big black dudes fell by one night and sat around and smoked up our dope and didn't seem to have much to say. I mean, that did seem a little odd. And then one morning I got up and went bouncing out to the truck all set to hop in and make the run for milk and eggs so we could have breakfast, and guess what? There's no truck. That did seem a bit peculiar, right? And I found the truck down at the bottom of the hill. Somebody had pounded the shit out of it and burnt it to a crisp.

Well, I walked back up the hill contemplating that turn of events. Eventually I managed to put two and two together and laid it on Cassandra—"You know, I don't think we're welcome in this neighborhood."

She says, "No shit, horse. Whatever gave you that idea?" So we smoked some more dope, and I began to wonder how I was going to do any dealing when I didn't have transportation and it's an hour on the subway to any place at all. Then a couple nights later somebody chucked a brick through our front window and I went out and found

HONKEY BASTARDS painted on our door, and all of a sudden things seemed clear as a bell to me. "I strongly suspect," I said to Cassandra, "that it is not the world's greatest idea to spend another night here. We better go crash with Ethan until we get our shit together." And she says, "Ethan!" because she hates Ethan's guts. And I say, "OK, let us consider the options. There's always John's place. Of course it might be a little tight with the three of us crammed in there. Particularly in that single bed of his. But oh yeah . . . there's always my old buddy, Bobby Lyons." If she hates Ethan, she hates Lyons ten times worse. "All right," she says, "Ethan's."

It wasn't like we were tapped out. I still had a few bucks, and Cass had whatever was left of her part of the hash deal—and that was probably most of it because I'd been paying for everything. So we packed up our shit and Ethan picked us up, and then we're at his place, sitting on the floor, doing a little smoke, drinking one of Terry's disgusting herb teas, listening to Janis Joplin, and contemplating our next move.

"Go rent us some place," Cassandra says, and pulls some money out of her jeans and gives it to me. For some reason or other that pissed me off, but I kept my mouth shut. So for a couple days I drifted around with Ethan while he was making his dope runs and pretended I was looking for apartments, but when you don't have any wheels, wheels is pretty much all you can think about, and what do I see going by us one evening but a black 1959 Cadillac with a sign on it that says FOR SALE. "Follow that fucking car!" I yell at Ethan like we're in the movies, and off we go. I don't know if you remember the 1959 Cadillac, but it was the biggest pig ever to come out of Detroit—a real monstrosity, I swear to God, damn near thirty feet long. That car had chrome, that car had fins, that car had motherfucking TAIL LIGHTS, that car had it all. So we followed the owner home to Newton, and I bought the son of a bitch. It took all the cash I had with me, and I had to borrow a few bills from Ethan, and when we got back, I couldn't figure out why Cass was pissed off. "Look, honey," I said. "We've got to have transportation. That's number one. Now we can float around and look for apartments. We can take our time and find something nice."

I should have detected the fact that the recent events had weirded Cassandra right out, but I didn't. She launched into me non-stop. "No, Tommy, I do not want to float around looking at apartments. No, Tommy, I do not want to take my fucking time. No, Tommy, I do not want to piss around with this bullshit any longer. Listen, I know safety is a relative term. From the moment we fight our way out of the womb, we are contemplating our own death. That's what they call a GIVEN, an inescapable fact of THE HUMAN CONDITION, and when viewed from that perspective, nothing is safe. We are all, at any moment, a heartbeat away from the end. We could be hit be a car. We could fall down in the shower and crack our skulls. Some bizarre medical condition we don't even know about could snuff us at any moment. A motherfucking meteorite could fall through the roof, for Christ's sake. You, having been in the war effort, must surely understand what I'm talking about—and what I am talking about is the horrible terror of being alive at all—so, yes, when viewed from that perspective, safety is relative. But you must admit, in terms of ordinary life as we live it, some places are safer than others. Boston is, in most respects, a somewhat safer place than Saigon. Harvard Square might be considered safer than East Cambridge. If you are white, places occupied largely by white people are probably safer than places occupied largely by black people. I could go on, but I think you get my point. Now it may be a monumental failure on my part to be concerned about such trivial matters. It may indicate that I am repressed and uptight and unable to go with the flow, but if that is the case, then I frankly do not give a flying fuck. Safety is an important matter to me. So could you please go rent us an apartment? Not on the first floor. Some place in a reasonably nice neighborhood in a reasonably nice building where everybody is motherfucking WHITE? And could you do it within the next twenty-four hours? It's not like we're broke, asshole," and she pulls out a whole bunch of money and throws it on the floor.

Looking back on it, you always know what should have gone down, right? You take, for instance, when the French called up Dwight David Eisenhower, and they said, "Hey, Ike, sorry to bother you, but there's this fascinating piece of the world called Indochina.

Perhaps you might recall that God-forsaken place. Your predecessor, Give-'em-Hell-Harry, took some interest in it. Well, it seems like we're having us a little problem over there, and maybe you could help us out."

Now, looking back on it, we know perfectly well what he should have said. He should have said, "That's what you get for having colonies, you dumb fucks. Go home and eat snails." But that's not what he said.

Looking back on it, I should have said, "Sure, babe, anything you want." But that's not what I said. I said, "Keep your goddamn money."

Cassandra says, "Fuck you, man, I'm going to New York," and she stuffs her things in her little suitcase and calls a cab and she's gone. Like that fast, ZAP. Ethan and Terry are laughing at me, and I'm going, "Shit, what happened?" and I'm thinking, Christ, Tommy, you really are a moron.

The minute she was gone, it finally flashed on me—hey, this is heavy. Like it wasn't just another show I was drifting through. Like as far out as chicks ever got, Cass was always out there a notch farther, and it just seemed stupid for things to end like that. So I knew she had a sister in New York, and I got her number from John and I called it a few times, and eventually I got Cassandra. "Hey, old buddy," I said, "I'm sorry about the way things went down. I'm not too swift sometimes. Is there any possibility you might ever consider coming back to this fair city of beans?"

"Oh, shit, Tommy," she says. "I'm sorry too. I'd just fucking run it out, that's all . . . and sometimes you're just so fucking HOPELESS. Get us a nice place, OK? Little sister's already driving me nuts. I'll be back up there eventually."

I would have just loved to get us a nice place, and I kept INTENDING to get us a nice place, but the problem was that when I'd said "Keep your goddamn money," that's exactly what she'd done—scooped up those bills off the floor and shoved them in her jeans and split—and I was down to zip, and they have this strange ritual there in Boston, which is that the Lord of the Land wants his first month and his last month up front, so I kept making an effort, but I never did manage to put it all together, and it wasn't too bad crashed at Ethan's waiting for Cass to come back. Terry's a hell of a good cook, and of course there was always plenty of weed.

SO ANYHOW, with Cassandra gone, that broke up our little three-some and left John and me alone together to confront reality, and it flashed on us one night that we'd really depended on Cass to keep us from going nuts. Like when she was around, one thing you could always depend on was that she'd never stop talking, so as weirded out as we ever got, we could always count on her voice—you know, like a constant radio transmission we could home in on and get ourselves back from whatever bizarre place we'd been. So without her, we had no reality reference, and we slipped over the edge a few times—like the two days we spent crashed at Lyons' place because the show was just too fucking good in there, you know what I mean? And every time we tried to figure how to stand up, and walk out the door, and drive away, somebody would roll us another joint.

All John could talk about that spring was Pam Zalman. PAMELA, he called her. And a lot of times she couldn't come out and play with him—you know, what with her being heavy into her women's lib shit—and he'd get stoned with me and say, "Do you think she likes me?" like a boy with his first crush, kind of pathetic. Yeah, he was motherfucking LOVESICK.

So one day Ethan and me are laying around at his place drinking our morning coffee at noon when the phone rings and it's John telling us that we've got to get our asses over to Harvard because there's some ACTION going down there. Ethan says he don't give a shit, so I zip by the office and pick up John. I really dug the scene at Harvard, like they say, THE IVORY TOWER. I used to wander around the residence halls at night, knocking on doors and going, "Hey, it's me, Weird Tom the Weed Man," and believe me, mucho dope did I sell. So anyhow, we've got a perfect spring day, the sun like honey, swear to God, and John says, "Yeah, a great day for a building occupation," because the dudes from SDS have seized University Hall and they're flying their red-and-black flag out the second floor window.

Harvard Yard's one big party, hundreds of kids just hanging

out, rapping, getting off on each other, eating ice cream cones, and generally looking good. People just drift in and out of University Hall whenever they feel like it, so we wander around in there for a while. John's taking pictures and asking questions like a real grown-up reporter, and we find this enormous room where there's a meeting going on and check that out, but that's not where it's at, so we've got to keep on going until we locate this little side room, like an office, where there's a few heavies having themselves a real serious rap. I mean REAL SERIOUS. I recognize Phil Vance and some of the other SDS dudes from the *Weasel*, and then I detect the fact that Pam Zalman's there. I go, oh, NOW I see why we had to get our asses over here so fast.

We immediately disrupt their discussion because they have some guys stationed at the door who attempt to dissuade us from entering, and I suggest that they get themselves seriously bent and offer to help them do it, so Pam and Phil Vance start piping up with, "Hey, wait a minute. They're OK. They're from the *Weasel*," and that causes the heavies to launch into a thing about how there was a vote, remember? And it had been decided that there wasn't supposed to be any press in there at all except from Harvard, so Pam says, "Yeah, yeah, right," and leaves the meeting and comes outside into the sunshine with us. She's giving us the straight scoop, and John's hanging on every word. "Motherfucking PL," she says. "They did it again."

Like I said, I never could figure out all the teams they had playing in Boston that season, and everybody disagreed with everybody, but the folks I ran with, one thing they all agreed on was that Progressive Labor sucked shit. John and Pam told me all about it. PL was a heavy top-down organization, they said, and whatever the cats at the top thought, that's what all the members thought, and if the cats at the top changed their minds, then all the members changed their minds, and when PL came into a meeting, they all voted the same way, so going up against them was like ramming your head into a concrete wall. And PL was big on THE WORKERS. Like they dressed real straight—the guys cut their hair and the girls wore skirts—and if they lived together, they had to get married, and nobody was allowed to do drugs, and that was all so they wouldn't piss off THE

WORKERS. OK? Now most of the workers I knew—anyhow, the ones who were our age—were growing lots of hair, fucking every chance they got, and smoking all the weed they could get their hands on, but the dudes from PL never noticed because they were all STUDENTS.

"THREE FUCKING TIMES," Pam keeps saying. You see, they'd had a big meeting to see if they should seize a building, and they'd voted on it three times, and every damn time the meeting had voted it down. But PL had gone ahead and seized University Hall anyway, and all the people who were against PL had to come along with them or get left out in the cold—which is what Pam was doing there with the other heavies. "Eventually we've got to deal with those motherfuckers," she says.

But, in the meantime, there they were occupying a building—PL and the people who hated them all crammed in together—and they were trying to work out something they agreed on, and so far, that wasn't much. The whole thing struck me as ridiculous. "Forgive me for being a dumb shit," I said, "but what is it they want?"

It seemed like a simple question, but they looked at me like I'd just asked them what was the quadratic double factor of minus to the forty-seven. I had another run at it. "The people who seized the hall . . . what is it they want? When you seize a building, aren't you supposed to want something?"

So John explains to me all about the six demands. They had to do with abolishing ROTC and stopping Harvard from expanding into poor people's neighborhoods and like that. "But the issue isn't the issue," he says. "I mean, they're serious demands, but the whole point is to force Harvard into bringing the pigs onto campus and pissing off the moderate students. You know, to radicalize them and to broaden the base of support."

"What? They want a bust?"

"Oh, yeah. You've got to have a bust."

"So you're telling me that the bust's what counts and it don't matter what the demands are?"

"Well, yes and no. You've got to be demanding the right things."

"I know it sounds cynical," Pam says, "but we've got to reveal power for what it is. They try to hide it, but behind power there's always pigs."

The sun's shining, and the kids are milling around with their ice cream cones and bottles of pop, and it looks like one great big be-in, like you can feel this puppy-dog spirit in the air—oh, wow, SPRING!—and I'm thinking, shit, I don't get this. "Hey," I say, "what is it YOU want? Yeah, the two of you."

They look at each other for a minute, and then John says, "OK, in the short run, you want to raise the level of chaos. Like more and more campus disruptions, more building seizures, more draft card burnings, more anything at all . . . to make it harder to conduct the war. Like eventually to make it so hard to conduct the war, that they'll just have to get the hell out of Vietnam. But in the long run . . ."

Pam picks it up for him. "In the long run, you hope that there's going to be a concrete situation where the students outrun the so-called leadership. Where they won't disband when the action's over. Where the action keeps on going and they create parallel structures. Where the revolutionary moment spills out of its container." And on and on she goes, and I haven't got a clue what she's talking about.

Over on the steps of the library some Harvard asshole's mouthing off through a bullhorn. We can't make out much of what he's saying, just things like, " . . . depart therefrom . . . subject to prosecution . . . criminal trespass . . ." I'm thinking, fuck, that poor son of a bitch isn't going to know what hit him.

"If you were Harvard, what would you do?" I ask them.

John just looks at me, but I can see Pam thinking about it. "You know," she says, "that's an interesting question. The administration doesn't want another Columbia. They're scared shitless of that. But if they had any sense, they'd never call in the pigs. They could issue some statements that sounded like they were dealing with the demands, and they could like call for a big meeting of the moderates on campus . . . and pretend they were actually listening to them. And they could create some kind of committee to study the problem, a committee with STUDENTS on it. And as time went by, the people in University Hall would start fighting with each other, and they'd look more and more like assholes, and the broad campus support for the occupation would just dwindle away."

Yeah, she was smart, all right. "Maybe they'll do that," I said.

"No they won't," she said.

———

A GIRL on the phone: "Ray? *Ray?*" He'd been asleep—gone and down a mile—now thinking: shit, why does this keep happening to me? His clock told him it was half past three in the middle of the goddamned night. Yeah, his name was Ray. Of course it was. "Yeah?" he said, keeping his voice neutral.

"It's me." She didn't say her own name, but by now he would have known her voice anywhere. "The bust's coming down," she said.

"What? Now?"

"Yeah now. Soon anyway. There's a million pigs over at the Cambridge Fire Station. How fast can you get here?"

He sat up in bed—fear like heat lightning—and finally got it. She'd called him Ray because his phone might be tapped, and Jesus fucking Christ, she wanted him at Harvard. "Shit," he said, "the MTA's closed."

"Take a cab." It never would have occurred to him in a million years. "You got any money?" she was saying. "Don't worry about money. I've got money. Just get here."

He'd never been any closer to a violent confrontation than watching Chicago on the tube. He threw back his sleeping bag and stood shivering in the dark—afraid that he'd be immobilized—but then, reaching back years, found his old readiness to pull on his boots and be gone. Down what road? Shit, any road would do, and with that, he was launched into a motion that felt inevitable—called a cab, got dressed, loaded his camera with Tri-X, hung it in its case under his coat, and walked out.

He still loved the kick just like in the old days—to be up and out when everybody else was asleep, to be up so early his breath steamed and the sky was blistered with mad stars. The cab pulled up, and he stepped into it, told the driver Harvard Square. Pam was waiting for him exactly where she'd said she'd be, in the spot where she'd met him that first time, in front of Nini's, but Nini's was closed—of course it was, at that cold empty hour. Stepping eagerly toward him, she looked as slender as a boy. Her twin ponytails were gone; she'd bound her hair back and tucked it inside her Levi jacket. "You sure it's a bust?" he said.

"Oh, yeah. Jesus, man, you should see the pigs."

"Shit, that was fast. It didn't even last a day."

"Yeah, well, Nathan Pusey has his head up his ass." She pressed her hand into the small of his back, pushed him the way she wanted him to go; later he would realize it was the first time she'd ever touched him. "We've got to go over the wall," she said. "The gates are locked, and there's pigs at every one of them."

Climbing over the wall into Harvard Yard was simply not possible; he was not agile, not physically brave, but there was no question about it—he was going to get over that fucking wall. She was already on the top reaching down for him. She caught his wrist, and he caught hers—a grip like a trapeze artist's—and hung suspended a moment on nothing but the sinews of her thin arm. Scrabbling, smearing the toes of his shoes against the stones, flailing like a goof, WILLING himself to make it—he was mysteriously up and over. If he'd had a chance to think about it, he couldn't have done it. He landed on all fours, still crouching, heard a man's voice hard with authority: "Hey. What are you doing?"

He sprang up to run, but Pam said "Walk," took his arm, led him into the crowd.

The Yard was full of kids—boys mostly, but some girls too, probably Cliffies. Nothing left of the party mood of the day before; hushed anxious voices, some of them whispering. And dawn was sneaking in—a swell of gunmetal grey on the edge, on the trees still stripped for winter, on the ancient stately buildings of the university, on old John Harvard himself, his statue staring out at his quiet world. "Fuck," John said, "what a horrible time for this. They shoot people at dawn, don't they?"

He was talking too much, but he couldn't help it. "It's classic, right? Dawn's always the time when the KGB shows up."

"Yeah," she said, "the motherfuckers thought they'd pull it off with everybody asleep, right? But we set off the fire alarms in the freshman dorms. There's going to be witnesses. There's going to be lots of witnesses."

A shaft of ugly white light was emerging from behind the church. Headlights. A car. "Jesus, what the fuck's that?" somebody said. John and Pam drifted with the crowd. Some of the Harvard boys still had their pajamas and bathrobes on. Another car and then another car—of course they had to be plain dark cars, John thought; that's what the script called for—and they were driving right into the middle of the Yard, onto the soft spring dirt, onto the tender spring grass. Behind them, some other huge thing lurched in, a dinosaur—wobbling, teetering, righting itself—a motherfucking bus crammed with pigs, their impassive faces framed in the windows. John could feel a wind of sorrow move across the kids—below speech, below voice—a collective silent moan. A girl murmured, "I don't believe this shit."

There were more buses. Pigs in full riot gear poured out of them. Behind the buses was a column of marching men. "You've got to get this," Pam whispered.

Oh, right, John thought, the camera. He unzipped his jacket, swung his Nikon around in front of him. Took off the lens cap, dropped it into his pocket, opened up wide, set the shutter at one-fiftieth. He'd tell the lab to push it to the moon; it was the best he could do. The way his hands were shaking, he was probably not going to get a damned thing but blur anyway.

John looked up and saw that a Harvard boy was staring at him with tears in his eyes. "How could they do this to us?" he asked as though John might know the answer.

"Bummer," John said. Stupid. The only thing he could think of.

"Watch yourself," Pam told him. "They see the camera, they'll beat the crap out of you."

John walked toward University Hall, shooting automatically. There was already a police line going up, and the cops who'd marched into the Yard were headed straight for the building. That's not good drama, John thought. There should be a standoff, a confrontation, the chance to make some speeches—but with no ceremony at all, the cops were getting right to work. Students had packed the steps; the cops clubbed them, grabbed them, flung them down the steps where other cops grabbed them, hauled them off, and shoved them into buses.

With a taste in his mouth like lighter fluid, John broke into a run. Carried along by a wave of kids, he allowed himself to be swept though the police line. He could hear the distinct smack of clubs on bodies. A lot of the kids were screaming now. Even as far away as he was, he could see the blood. A cluster of politicos began to chant "ROTC must go," and, from somewhere else, a counter-chant rose up, "*Pusey* must go," but from the steps, individual voices shrieking—"Pigs. You motherfucking pigs." "Long-haired commies." Just ahead of him, cops were running after students, clubbing them. John sank into a crouch and shot twice, then turned and ran. He'd lost track of Pam.

Winded, he stopped on the far side of the police line, turned back to see what was going on now. The steps had been cleared. Jesus, he thought, that was fast—a matter of minutes. And Pam was magically next to him, her hand on his shoulder. "You OK?"

"Yeah. I'm OK. This is fucking insane."

It was daylight. Sure, he'd watched this shit go down on the tube, but he'd never been right there in the flesh to hear what he was hearing now. Chanting, screaming, pleading, and the most chilling sound of all—kids weeping. Sometimes individual words: *Pigs. Motherfucking pigs. Fascist pigs . . . Please, please don't . . . Fuck you, fuck you, fuck you.* A nasty electronic bullhorn voice, absolutely unintelligible: *Braow da blat blat, blat blat blat.* Something like a pile driver, a regular rhythmic smashing. A new chant started up—picked up more and more voices, built in intensity, until it became a sustained pulse: *Seig heil, seig heil, seig heil.*

Not more than ten yards in front of him, a Cliffie was losing it. Waving her hands in the air, she stumbled toward the police line, wailing, "Pigs, pigs, pigs, pigs, pigs, pigs." John couldn't understand why none of the other students stopped her. A cop broke from the line, ran at her, swung. She twisted away, dodging. The club caught her at the point where her neck met her shoulder. She fell to her knees, screaming and crying. John ran forward, framed her in his lens. As the cop swung straight down, John hit the shutter. The club struck her on the top of her head. Blood spurted out. She screamed.

"Commie cunt," the cop said and kicked her in the side.

John would never understand why he did what he did then—he raised his camera, aimed it directly at the man's face, and took his picture. Instantly Pamela was clawing at his arm. They turned and ran.

She darted like a needle through a surging tapestry of students, dragging him along half a step behind her. Her grip on his hand was brutal. How the hell could she run so fast? He was running flat out, at a speed he knew he couldn't hold for more than a few seconds. He didn't dare look back. He heard screaming behind him. Pam suddenly shoved him to the left, smashed her hip into his to make the point, and they veered off sharply, headed for a building—what building? He only hoped Pam knew. He flicked a glance back, saw the cop—a huge motherfucking man—still lumbering behind them, smashing students out of his way. "Shit, shit, shit," John heard himself chanting, and they were inside, running down a corridor, their bootheels echoing back from the walls. Harvard boys in open doorways stared at them as they sprinted past.

Pam propelled them through a doorway, slammed the door shut behind them, locked it. She bent double, panting. A boy in pajamas stood where he'd frozen, just out of bed, his thin veined feet gripping the floor. His face was white. His lips were trembling. They heard screaming from the hallway. The three of them stared at the locked door. John knew perfectly well the cop could come through it with one massive kick—but had the cop seen which room they'd picked? John stood, poised, trying to soften the sound of his breathing. He counted to a hundred, and then he did it again.

Pamela slowly straightened up. She gave John an odd little smile. "Private property," she said.

"What?"

"All primitive peoples have fetishes. The door to this room's *private property*."

There was a new sound out in the yard—THWUNK. "Tear gas," Pam said. In a moment they could smell the acrid bite of it. She squeezed the Harvard boy's shoulder. "Sorry," she said.

UNIVERSITY HALL had been cleared. The students who'd been inside had been arrested and hauled off to jail. The pigs were leaving, some climbing back aboard their blue buses, some marching off campus, grinning and twirling their clubs. Hundreds of students milled around in the Yard or sat on the steps of the church. Some were still yelling at the cops; others were crying. SDS leaflets, scattered everywhere, were ground into the mud. Keeping well back from the last of the cops, John and Pam were drifting toward Widener. "Were the pigs this bad at Columbia?" he said.

"Oh, yeah. Some of them are just doing their jobs . . . yeah, like Eichmann. But there's others . . . You've read Reich . . . A lot of them are repressed and uptight and horny as hell, and they motherfucking *hate* us, man. Why else would they go after women the way they do? You can't fuck her, but you can bust her head."

John was coming down from the adrenaline rush, sinking into the kind of exhaustion that even sleep wouldn't fix, and it wouldn't take much to keep right on sinking into honest-to-God despair—except that Pam was still holding his hand. It felt like a natural thing, a simple thing, a good thing, to walk with her, holding hands. Unlike herself, she'd fallen silent. Somebody from SDS was yelling through a bullhorn, inviting people to move onto Widener's steps. Ah, yes, another meeting.

"You can't afford to get arrested, can you?" she said suddenly.

"Oh, hell no. Not even for a traffic ticket."

"Jesus, man, you're goddamned fearless."

"Who me? No, I'm not. I'm the original chickenshit." It was important—he didn't know why—that she didn't have any illusions about his bravery. "I'm serious," he said. "Violent confrontations scare the shit out of me."

She squeezed his hand. "Yeah, they scare me too. I get sucked up into the rush of it, and . . ." In a moment she finished the sentence, half swallowing the words. "I don't trust myself."

He didn't know what to say to that. "You saved my ass," he said.

She looked at him without smiling—an inscrutable, level-eyed look. She let go of his hand, drew her hair out of her jacket, unbound it, shook her head. She had wonderful hair, glorious hair—a rich golden brown, not light enough to be called blond but just on the edge of it. He loved everything about her. He was even prepared to love everything that was wrong with her.

She took his hand again. Somebody on the steps on Widener was addressing the crowd. "Who's that?" John said.

"He's PL." She led him away from Widener. "Sometimes I get really sick of this shit," she said. "Sometimes I just want to get out of SDS, work in the Collective, work with people who are . . . like in theoretical agreement . . . like you. Just let SDS go fuck itself. Did you notice how few women there are in the so-called leadership here?"

"There aren't any, are there?"

The kids around the library began chanting, "Strike, strike, strike."

"Yeah," she said, "the strike. Everything's going according to plan."

She was leading him away from that angry electronic voice. The cars and buses had left huge ugly ruts in the soft grass of the yard; she pointed at them. "Great, huh?"

Since their escape from that insane cop, she'd been . . . well, "subdued," he might have called it, but now he could sense that something else was happening. He could feel the energy of it in her hand.

"Ah, the fucking pigs," she said. "I know they're just tools of power, but I hate those bastards. God, and I hate the men who send them out . . . Yeah, the men. The goddamned men. The *men*. Fuck."

He felt chilled. But she was still holding his hand. She stopped walking, turned to look at him. "Those bastards should never believe . . . not for a minute . . . Yeah, they should never believe even for a minute that they've got a monopoly on violence."

JOHN SAT at the typewriter waiting while Pam paced up and down. They were in her apartment, taking turns with the typing. "You know what the fuck I want to say?" she asked him. "The incoherence of their critique guarantees that their every action will be a critique of their incoherence."

"Right on. It's true."

"I know it's true. That doesn't mean we should say it."

John hadn't slept more than two hours at a stretch since the Harvard bust. They'd been working on a special edition of the *Weasel*. Tonight they'd lay it out; tomorrow it would hit the streets. It was, John thought, going to be a damned fine issue. John's pictures of the cop beating the Cliffie would be splashed across the front page with a caption that read simply: OINK! Phil Vance had written the story of the bust from inside University Hall. John and Pam had written the story from the outside—not as two separate points of view but as a unified piece with a double by-line. He'd been surprised at how easy it had been for him to work with her—up until now. Ethan had dumped the lead editorial on them. "I don't know fuck about Harvard, and I don't give a fuck," he'd told them. "You guys write it." They'd been trying for hours.

"Things have got too polarized," Pam said. "PL just never lets up and . . . Shit, you can't make a move that's not . . ."

He waited for her to finish her sentence, but it appeared that she wasn't going to. "Right on," he said, "that's what polarization's all about." By now he'd read all the SI stuff she'd lent him and could quote it back to her: "But like Vaneigem says, isn't there always a third force?"

"Yeah," she said, "but we're right in the middle of an *action* . . ."

"Isn't that *exactly* the right time? And if it isn't the right time, then what are we doing fucking around with theory?"

"Yeah, but . . . Well, you can see where they're coming from. It's like the old action-faction thing. It's the *action* that counts. Let's do something even if it's wrong. And there's something to be said for that. And we certainly don't want to fuck up the action with anything we say . . . or contribute to fucking it up. I know nothing we write's going to have that much . . . And it's so easy to get recuperated . . . Oy, I don't know. If we could just . . ."

They were interrupted by the soft chime of Pam's doorbell. She hesitated a moment, frowning, then said, "Shit," shot out the door and down the stairs.

John heard another girl's voice, knew it, stood up. Footsteps, BANG—her knapsack dumped into a corner—yes, it was Cassandra. "Hey, Dupre, what the fuck's happening?"

"I couldn't tell you." They hugged, and he felt the same old rush he always felt when he first saw her. "Hey, would you mind taking your boots off?" Pam was saying.

"Oh, aren't you the princess?" Cass said, but she pulled her boots off and threw them at her knapsack.

"How was New York?" John said.

"Just groovy as all hell."

"Nice to see you, Cass." Pam's voice was oddly stiff. "Do want anything to eat? Oh, God, I sound like my mother."

"What have you got?"

"Just the weird crap I usually eat. Cheese and crackers? A peanut butter sandwich?" then, laughing at herself, "a grapefruit?"

"Thanks for the offer, but I'll catch Tommy later, and most likely we'll run down a steak. Tell you what, though. You wouldn't happen to have a pinch of smoke? Hey, I dig your space. It's a stone groove."

"Thanks." Pam sent John a look he couldn't read—impatience, annoyance?—retrieved her dope and licorice papers from behind her books, began rolling a joint. "How'd you get my address?" she asked—slightly too casually.

"Oh, easy. I just called my boss in Arlington, Virginia. You know, at the CIA . . . Jesus, I fell by the newspaper office and got it from Phil Vance. Welcome back to the land of the paranoid. Where's Tommy?"

"Still crashed at Ethan's," John said.

"Shit, that's what I was afraid of. God, he's hopeless."

Pam passed the joint to Cassandra who lit and dragged, passed it on to John. "We probably needed a break," Pam said to him.

"You guys into something heavy?" Cassandra said. "I can split."

"No, no, no," Pam said, "it's OK," and to John, "Maybe we could offer comradely criticism . . . ?"

"What? Like Rosa lecturing Lenin?"

"Yeah. Sure. Exactly like that."

"You guys are so full of shit," Cassandra said. "It's kind of endearing."

"OK," John said, "that's how we'll do it. Now we can write that fucker in ten minutes."

"But that's later, right?" Cassandra said. "Now we need a little smoke, right?"

"You the one," John told her.

"Ludicrous," Pam said, shrugging. She dragged on the joint, passed it back to Cassandra, sent John another of her coded looks. This one he could read clearly enough: "Fuck it, what can you do?"

"How's Zoë?" John said.

"Far fucking out of sight, that's how Zoë is. She got into *Vogue*, so she's higher than a kite."

"No, shit?"

"I kid you not, Dupre. She just happened to have an extra copy lying around . . . like maybe four million of them. I've got one in my knapsack for you."

"Groovy," John said uneasily. "How is she? I mean really. She OK?"

"Oh, yeah. Don't know how much coin she's knocking down, but enough to stay in the game. She's . . . Jesus, it's hard to be a Girl Scout in the modeling biz, but little sister's doing her best. In bed by midnight all covered with cream from head to toe. Sleeps with gloves on half the time, can you believe that? She's just so . . . She says, 'Oh, Cass, I was at this reception the other night, and you know what they were doing?' Miss Wide Eyes, right? 'They were doing *Co-caine!*' I'm going, 'No shit, Zo. You've got to be putting me on. Cocaine? I can't believe anybody would do that.' God, she lives in a parallel universe . . . So what are you guys into? Heard there was some heavy shit going down at Harvard."

Grass seemed to have an identical effect on both girls—shot pure energy straight to their speech centers. Pam was doing the whole Harvard thing from beginning to end—the meetings, the factional disputes, the bust. "You guys are fucking nuts," Cassandra was saying. "The minute there's motherfucking pigs, I'm gone."

Getting stoned was probably not a good idea—not if they wanted to get their editorial written by seven—and John felt all the time around him melting down like butter in the sun. Both girls got next to him, and it was all just too fucking much, and if he didn't stop thinking of them as *girls* and start thinking of them as *women*, it was going to pop out of his mouth sometime when his guard was down, and then he'd be in deep shit. How could they talk so fast while he was reduced to his usual bemused catatonia?

Cassandra had moved on to bitching about Tom: "Where the hell's his head at? Oh, I know . . . up his ass. Knew the son of bitch would never move out of there. So here we go again. Yeah, we're going to be looking so good, me and Terry, just us chicks together, man, barefoot in the kitchen, yeah, baking our bread and reading our Tarot cards and rocking and rolling and having a good time."

"You want to stay here?" Pam said.

Cassandra's eyes circled the small apartment, paused on the one and only bed. "You don't want me in your bed, Pamela. I'm a lousy fuck these days."

John would have thought that Pam was unshockable, but he saw that one get to her. She managed to laugh. "I love you, Cass. You'll say *anything*."

"Oh, yeah. Other people have noted that about me. Hey, you want to see little sister?" She opened her knapsack. "Lots of goodies for the Zoë Markapolous fan club," she said to John. "She's intrigued that you're in Boston, man. Very intrigued. She sent all this shit to you *specially*."

John said *Stop!* with his eyes, but if she got the message, she wasn't paying any attention to it. "Here's a whole bunch of tear sheets she had copied just for you, and here's *Vogue*, and here's her latest head shot." Cassandra drew a black-and-white eight-by-ten glossy out of its manila envelope. "Some hot-shit photographer did this for her . . . a true master of the art, Zoë says . . . This anybody you know?"

At first glance it was nobody he knew—but yes, of course it was Zoë, thoroughly disguised. Hair parted in the middle, curling around her face, framing it, setting it off—a thick tumble of curls. Very dramatic lighting, a three-quarter shot. Exposed behind the fall of hair, one ear, stunningly lit, balancing the brilliance of her face. Eyeliner carried all the way to the tear ducts just as her sister had worn it years before, and—although it was hard to tell—probably false lashes. Printed on paper so hard the greys were knocked right out of it—the contrast between white white face and black black turtleneck pushing it damned near into the realm of a charcoal drawing. It wasn't the girl he knew and liked, the little kid he'd watched growing up. It wasn't anybody real. Zoë had no expression whatsoever and didn't need one. "Oh, wow," Pam said, "she's a doll." John was shocked—but he supposed that women were still allowed to say things like that.

"Yeah, literally," Cassandra said.

"Let me see it," Pam said. John passed her the photograph. "Far out," she said. "It's almost Kabuki. I keep having arguments with the women in the Collective about this shit. They say, 'Yuck, that's not beauty,' but I keep telling them you can't deny the power of the image. Like never underestimate your enemy . . ."

"Zoë would love hearing that," Cassandra said.

"No, no, I don't mean *your sister's* the enemy . . ."

"Oh, I know what you mean, Pamela. I'm just jerking you around."

"It's weird," John said. "It's nearly an abstraction."

"Yeah," Pam said, "some cultures use masks exactly like that. It's like the nexus where a whole complex web of cultural values converge. You don't have to *do anything* with it. You just have to *display* it."

"Hey," Cassandra said to John, "she's not just cute, she's been to college too."

"Oh, fuck off, Cass," Pam said, laughing. "But I've thought about this a lot. Like I've been there. I used to be a dancer. I've got pictures of me *en pointe* that are exactly like this."

"A dancer? No shit? Like a for-real dancer . . . up on the stage, the whole bit?"

"Oh, yeah," with her wry smile, "the whole bit."

"Far out," John said. "You never told me that."

"You never asked me."

"How the hell would I even know to ask you?"

"Come on, that isn't what I meant. I didn't think you were interested in . . . like where I'm coming from."

"Of course I am."

"I'll tell you anything you want to know about me," she said. "I'm not a secretive person."

Meaning that *he* was? Paranoia—ping, ping, ping. And grinning Cassandra, who'd watched that small fiery personal exchange go down, said, "Shit, babe, he ain't going to tell you nothing. He's playing secret agent these days. Don't even know his own name half the time," and they were swallowed up immediately by the pothead's collective bummer, immobilized by it—*the weird silence*—each left wrestling with whatever personal demons were emanating from the Void. Could they have planned this? John was wondering. Worked it out ahead of time? Hey, let's really fuck with his head . . .

But he could always count on Cassandra. "Yeah, and here she is in *Vogue*"—her voice like a lifeline. "The freaky thing is, this is what she really looks like."

Cassandra flipped through the pages, found the section with Zoë in it, lay the magazine open on John's lap. Pam knelt by the side of his basket chair—laughed. "What?" he said.

"The caption," Pam said. It was splashed in bold type across the top of the page—THE ACTION FOR SPRING! "God, they're shameless."

The three pages that featured Zoë were variations on a theme, *Vogue's* idea of THE ACTION—a brown jumper with white buttons worn with a white blouse, white knee socks, and white dead-flat patent leather shoes decorated with string bows; a cream jumper with big brass buttons worn with a brown sweater, diamond-patterned knee socks, and brown and white oxfords; a black and white houndstooth jumper worn with a black turtleneck, black knee socks, and black and white spectator Mary Janes. Her head shot might have transformed Zoë into a mask, but in *Vogue* she was a living human being, wearing a brilliant I'm-having-the-time-of-my-life smile, at ease in the childish clothes.

Even though he knew it was dangerous territory, John couldn't restrain his old fascination with this stuff. "You can see why they picked her from *Seventeen*," he said. "It's a *Seventeen* look. But why are they showing it in *Vogue*?"

"That's easy," Pam said, "they want to turn us all back into good little girls."

"God, they keep on doing it no matter what's coming down," Cassandra said. "Does anybody anywhere ever wear this shit?"

"Maybe somebody somewhere," John said.

"Me," Pam said. "Fuck"—to their laughter—"I don't mean *now*, but that's exactly how I used to dress. Do you think I'm kidding? I'm not kidding. My father was in the shmatta trade. I was a very well-dressed little girl, you better believe it. Ten years ago . . . fuck, even *five* years ago . . . I would have looked at this shit and reacted like a trained rat. Like, wow, what cute shoes. I wonder where I can *buy* them?"

"Yeah," Cass said, "we've all been through that one. I used to run right out and buy the *Vogue* patterns so I'd be ahead of everybody else in town." And then, to John's amazement—and delight—Cassandra, the jaded and cynical former Playboy bunny, and Pamela, the full-time revolutionary anarchist, went sailing off into recollections of their fashionable girlhoods: how they'd checked out the clothes, shopped for the clothes, worn the clothes—what it had meant to wear the clothes. "Yeah," Pam was saying, "none of us got out alive. But the thing is, we're *all* wearing uniforms, we're *still* wearing uniforms."

"All except for you, Miss Hair Ribbons," Cassandra said.

"Yeah, it's just a little thing, but . . . I try to find some way to express all the contradictory parts of myself. The revolution's got to mean diversity, not uniformity." She'd lifted the *Vogue* from John's lap, studied it. "You see how they do it. The illusion of life enforces a life of illusion . . ."

"Holy fuck," Cassandra said to John, laughing, "did you get that one?"

"Well, dig it," Pam said, not amused at all, "it's not a difficult concept. Just look. You can see a real person there. That's why she's good for them. She gives the illusion of life."

"Oh, I got it, Pamela," Cassandra said. "I'm just putting you on."

Pam looked up from the magazine directly into Cassandra's eyes. Cassandra returned the look with an intensity that transformed her into the luminescent fourteen-year-old she'd been so many years ago—or maybe, John thought, it was just his own treasonous head kicking him back along the time-track—but he watched the girls' eyes hold each other for so long it was freaking him right out. Goddamn, it was like a staring contest. Then—and he felt it as a physical shock—Cassandra lost the game and looked away. "Whew," she said, "this is some heavy grass."

Pam looked back down at *Vogue*. More time melted and dribbled through the cracks. Nobody was talking, so he'd better do it. "Yeah," he said, "heavy."

"Heavy?" Pam said to him. "Yeah, you bet. Like Debord says, the Spectacle isn't the images. The Spectacle is social relations *mediated* by images," and to Cassandra, "She looks like she's a really nice person."

"Well, that's true," Cassandra said. "Nobody's any nicer."

"How old is she?" Pam said.

"Nineteen."

"Oh, just a baby."

"You bet. But she thinks she's so fucking mature, way more mature than me. I'm just a stoned-out hippie asshole, right?"

"Nineteen," Pam said, the meditative sound of her voice telling John that now she really was somewhere else. "God, it's weird," she said. "What were you doing at nineteen?" she asked Cassandra.

"Shit, I was at Bennington, bummed out of my skull."

"You should have seen her." John was scrambling hard to find a safe space. "White lips and white nails. Heavy into Camus."

"Camus," Pam said. "Yeah. I read him in French. Jesus, I can't believe I did that . . . How about you, man?"

"Me?" he said. "Oh, we're doing nineteen, are we? I was in my first year at WVU. It wasn't a bad year."

Good memories from that year—making out with Cass on a beach towel at Waverly Park the summer she was fifteen. Did she remember? He looked into her eyes, saw a flash of something coming back, couldn't read it, couldn't possibly untangle all the knots—and, shit, that could bum him right out if he let it. It was dangerous to have memories—here in this thickly contracted city where grown men with clubs beat girls on the head until the blood ran down.

Pam began to roll yet another joint. "Nineteen was a pretty good year for me," she said, "although it didn't feel like it at the time. It was the turn-around year, the make-or-break year . . . like the year when I could've really fucked it, but I didn't. I was . . . Oy, I was such a mess. I'd been in and out of the hospital like a yo-yo, but . . . I got out of there for the last time, and my parents had finally split up, thank God, so I was living with my father in Manhattan. I started taking courses at NYU, but I still had some leftover high-school shit to finish up . . . like I hadn't officially graduated from high school. And it was totally . . . like a schlep the whole way . . . where you wake up in the morning and think, hey, I can't do it. But you get up and you do it anyway. And I got through it."

She checked out John and Cassandra as though she'd forgotten them. She shrugged. She didn't pass the joint but lit it and dragged.

"What were you in the hospital for?" Cassandra said.

"Oh . . . like Laing says, I was mad and bad . . . You mean the label they put on me? Anorexia nervosa."

John had heard the term—probably back at WVU when he'd been doing Rat Psych—but he wasn't sure he remembered exactly what it meant. "What's that?"

She smiled. "That's when you stop eating till you die."

5

NOW THAT Cassandra was back, I figured we better get our asses out of Ethan and Terry's, right? I hadn't been dealing much lately, so I was tapped out. I knew Cassandra had some bread left, but I didn't feel right asking her, so I did the only thing I could think of—fell by to see my old pal Bobby Lyons. I hadn't caught his act lately. I'd been trying to stay clear of him. He'd moved, got himself a HUGE apartment on Beacon Hill with an even BIGGER stereo, and even MORE fish tanks, and THOUSANDS of super-freaky day-glo fish swimming like nowhere, and a BRAND-NEW hippie girlfriend, one of the improved models, younger and prettier and even farther out in the galaxy.

Lyons liked to have people around, so I walk in and there's a whole bunch of the new girlfriend's spaced-out little friends, and there's some GIs along with the chicks they've picked up, and there's an entire rock band called Trackless Waste with some groupies attached, and everybody in the whole damn place is whacked right out on whatever substance they dig the most. Lyons is always glad to see me. He's picked up this high-pitched goofy way of talking—like a bat squeaking. "Well, what the fuck's happening, Tommy boy?" Then he does one of those weirdo things he's gotten into, like he gives me a big wet kiss on the ear. Oh, yeah, crystal does wonders for you. "Shit, Robert," I say, "you sure are looking good."

I lay it on him that I want to have some WORDS, so we go in his bedroom. Yeah, he might like having people around, but I do note the fact that he's got a big motherfucking lock on his bedroom door. I tell him I've got to get out of Ethan and Terry's.

"Well, why don't you crash here, Tommy? Hee, hee, hee!" He knows that Cassandra hates his guts.

"Now, Robert, that's not what's happening. Here's where it's at. I've got to make some bread. So I was kind of wondering . . ." I just let it hang. Either he's got something for me or he don't.

"You're in luck, Tommy boy. I really need somebody I can TRUST, you know what I mean?"

Yeah, I did know what he meant.

So I drive over to Dorchester in the middle of the night, and some huge dude meets me in an alley, hops in my car, and we float around here and there and everywhere, and end up in some other alley, and slide into a garage and the door goes down, and there's a bunch of other huge dudes, and not one of them looks like a hippie to me. They put a suitcase in my car, and I'm off to New York. And all the way down there, I'm thinking, why the fuck am I driving a '59 Cadillac?

Guess what? My connection, somewhere the hell and gone in Brooklyn, is another huge dude who hops in my car. And there's more driving around in mysterious ways. And there's another fucking garage with the door shut behind me. This time they let me come into the house. I'm sitting in what looks like an ordinary living room. This huge motherfucker and a few of his pals take the suitcase and go off somewhere. After a while, they come back, and they've got another suitcase. The one I had was big and brown. The one they've got is small and blue. They slap it down on the coffee table and pop it open. It's full of the good old US dinero, and I'm thinking, fuck, what is this, some ridiculous movie off the late show? They're all standing around giving me the hairy eyeball, and it finally flashes on me that I'm supposed to count the shit.

I figure if I'm in a movie, I might as well give them a good show. "Hey, dig it," I say. "I just drive cars. What's in the car, I don't know. You follow me? . . . I don't see nothing. I don't hear nothing. I don't remember nothing. If you guys ain't cool, you'll probably hear from some people, but I won't know a thing about it."

I was a real hit with that one. They thought I was the funniest thing since Syd Caesar. Out comes the whiskey, and we all have a snort, and then I'm driving back to Boston with the blue suitcase in my trunk, thinking, why the fuck am I driving a '59 Cadillac?

I deliver the blue suitcase to Lyons, and we go in his bedroom so he can count the bills. He's giggling away like a bona-fide cretin. "Delicious," he says, "nutritious. Good old US lettuce. You know, Tommy, you should get in the game with me. Like partners, right? Forget that petty-ante grass bullshit, we're talking BREAD, man."

"I'm a small-town boy from the Far West," I tell him. "I dig petty ante. Besides, GRASS IS GOOD. Not that I don't appreciate the offer, Robert."

He says, "Hee, hee, hee," and counts out a thousand bills and hands it to me. "Come back in a couple days. I got some dynamite Magical Michoacan coming in. I'll front you a key of it."

So I should have been off to rent an apartment, right? Well, on my list of things I hate to do, renting an apartment is fairly high. It's the thought of me standing there while some prick in a tie checks me out, and I just know he'll be thinking, oh, sweet Jesus, WHY does this bizarre freaky-looking grotesque asshole want to rent an apartment from ME? And then there was something else happening too. Once I get an idea stuck in my head concerning motor vehicles, it's hard for me to shake it, so I bought a Volkswagen camper. I just couldn't pass it up. I mean it was clean, the engine was in good shape, and they'd even fixed up the back with a stove and an ice chest and some foam mattresses and curtains for the windows, and I thought Cass and I could live in it for a while—you know, roam around the country free as little birds. I got screwed on the trade-in for the Cadillac, but them's the breaks.

Once again, Cassandra was not delighted with me. "It's motherfucking beautiful, Tommy. Sure, we can go floating off any time we want to check out the groovy wonders of nature. But, in the meantime, there are certain things I wish to see appearing before me. My own bathroom, for starters. My own bed . . . in a room with a door that shuts. And you might find this hard to believe, but I wouldn't even mind my own fucking kitchen . . . you know, where it might be possible to fry up the remains of dead birds and animals, something that is definitely not possible at the moment. So you just keep right on in motion, old buddy, and come back and tell me about apartments. Pick up the *Boston Globe*, and I'll give you some pointers. Have you thought about Somerville?"

By now, I was checked out on the workings of Cassandra's mind, so I said, "You bet, sweet stuff," but, with one thing or another, I never got around to it.

———

IT HAD started out with the uncanny juxtapositions—induced by the devastating Mexican weed, "Magical Michoacan" Tom had called it, "some of that one-toke stuff," and for once, he hadn't been exaggerating. As John had drawn in his first toke, that fatal *one toke*, Tom had said to Ethan, "Look at him, the poor fool. Doing it right up. Whew, he'll never know what hit him." The lift had been instantaneous, and John, of course, hadn't stopped with one toke. He'd soared, melted with the shift in the light values. His brains had bubbled and spurted like magma. He'd felt the dope push through his veins like fiery golden wires. Transfigured, he'd thought how the pothead's phrase "behind the grass" was absolutely inadequate—he was certainly *behind* it, but more than that, *inside* it, this singing drug that could terrify him if he let it, but there was too much fascination for terror because he'd fallen out by Zen accident at a perfect location, sitting exactly where he should be (halfway down the kitchen table), looking at exactly what he should be (the Tibetan demon on the wall), and so he was hearing what no one else could hear.

The demon was black, possessed many heads and arms, wore a necklace of skulls, and danced upon skulls. The demon was surrounded by smaller demons, each possessing many heads and arms and wearing necklaces of skulls. If it wasn't for the edge of the poster, the smaller demons might have gone on forever; in fact, John was certain that in the realm where they lived, they did go on forever, becoming smaller and smaller the farther they got from the central demon—finally as small as gnats, a cloud of them in the air, wearing tiny gnat skulls around their innumerable tiny gnat heads. And, at a still higher level, this whole population was just the one demon, the central demon, with his (her?) shimmering manifestations—this deity with whom John was now sharing a comradely and cheerful joke (despite the skulls), because of all the people in the room, he was the only one who'd been given the secret, the key to the puzzle, for if he sat balanced carefully enough, if he looked steadily at his old buddy the Black Demon—

The six people were sitting at the one rectangular table. A line of force that connected John's eyeballs to the demon divided the table—to the right were the men; to the left, the women. The sound of the Jefferson Airplane from behind John's back rode down the line of force, thickened it, and made it impossible for the men and the women to hear each other even though they were only a few feet apart. John, sitting on the dividing line, could hear both sides in stereophonic reality.

And so the right channel brought him:

TOM: Whatever you might think, like it's the first line of defense, or the big retaliatory force the country has . . . well, that's wrong. And they lay it on you right away. The air force's primary mission is to fly and maintain aircraft capable of flying.

ETHAN: (flat) Right, right.

And from the left channel:

TERRY'S SCISSORS ON CASSANDRA'S HAIR: Snip snip.

CASSANDRA: I think it started out . . . you know, back in the stone age or whenever the fuck it was . . . It was just because they're bigger than we are.

PAM: That's absolutely true. Engels talks about that shit.

TERRY: But we're different from them. They're afraid of us, you dig? We're cyclical. We bleed to the moon. We wax and wane. We got tides in our bodies. There's small cycles and big cycles, dark phases and light phases . . .

CASSANDRA: Jesus, Terry, what is this off-the-wall shit? I mean, what's that got to do with anything? If some big hairy asshole wants to fuck you, he's just going to kick your head in, and you can take your cycles and . . .

PAM: No, she does have a point. You see, there's different lines of development. There's the hunter-gatherers and then there's the agricultural . . .

CASSANDRA: Oh, lines of development, huh? Jesus. There's only one thing I know for damned sure. I got fucked over from day one because I was born female. And I've been fucked over ever since.

PAM: (excited) Right. That's exactly right. That's where we've got to start.

TOM: So once your ass is in the Air Force, it turns out that your number-one priority is to keep airplanes flying at all times, and anything additional is like . . . well, you know . . . not where it's at.

ETHAN: Right, right.

TERRY: (in her oracular voice) But there's only one society in which women have been free . . . only one society in which women have had power . . . only one society in which women were on top. And that society goes back thousands of years in an unbroken thread . . . It's the society of witchcraft.

CASSANDRA: (laughing) Jesus, Terry, you're so full of shit.

John, looking only at the face of the Black Demon, could see all of the people at once, hold each distinct and perfect, memory opening like a door to an inner peripheral vision, lucidly, as he couldn't have done if he'd been using his ordinary outward-directed eyes. Cassandra, navy blue from neck to toe, was sitting upright on a kitchen chair, a towel tucked around her neck, as Terry cut her hair. The wickedly bright scissors with their hurtful points were passing in front of Cassandra's closed eyes, safely, guided by Terry's ringed fingers. Sure, deft movements. SNIP SNIP. Cassandra wrinkled her nose as the wet reddish-brown hair fell away.

Pam, the smallest and thinnest, was sitting with her elbows on the table regarding the other two. She was wearing plum-colored hair ribbons and a plain grey shirt bought in the boys' department of Filene's Basement.

PAM: Yeah, it's like that rap Snyder lays out about the age of the Golden Emperor. Whether it's witchcraft, or the Amazons, or the Matriarchy . . . It doesn't matter whether we have any evidence that these cultures really existed because we project them into the future, you dig? They're useful. As myth. The ground of future heresies. So, yeah, what would a progressive society run by women look like?

CASSANDRA: Run by women? Dream on, baby doll.

Ethan, hunched forward, block shoulders in flannel shirt torn out at the elbows, was rolling a joint in hands thick with callus, yellow as horn. He blew through his teeth; his Charlemagne mustaches flared outward. He licked the joint finished, winked, passed it to Tom who took it with short spatulate fingers, grease from the camper engine under his nails.

TOM: (with all the time in the world) So the air force is like a self-sufficient entity, right? It can maintain itself, feed itself, repair itself, keep itself going no matter what's happening. Even if the economy collapses, even if there's rioting in the streets, all them black dudes out there shooting it up, the air force is going to maintain strike capability.

ETHAN: Right, right.

TOM: That's the only thing they've got covered.

PAM: But we've got to try to do something more than just . . . well, imitate men, try to be like men. We've got to look at all the things they've hidden from us all these years, things we've repressed. We've lost our own history.

CASSANDRA: (laughing) Hold it, folks, what's this "we" business?

PAM: (earnestly) We've got to start saying "we" even if it doesn't feel right yet. We've got to start talking to each other. It's going to be all of us or none of us.

CASSANDRA: (still laughing) How about them crazy dudes? The ones with the dongs hanging down?

PAM: (laughing too) Yeah, it's got to be them too . . . eventually. But not now. We've had too many years of not talking to each other.

CASSANDRA: You know, Pamela, everything you're saying is right, and I'll probably join up with you after I start losing my looks. But right now I'm living off men, so it'd be kind of hypocritical of me. (All three women laugh.)

TOM: All them planes up there, man, just maintaining strike capability, man. And no matter what anybody does about it, they're going to be up there.

ETHAN: (finally getting it) Right, right.

John felt the joint pressed into his right hand, took it, inhaled.

TERRY: You want any more off?

CASSANDRA: Cut it all off. I don't give a fuck.

PAM: Don't kid yourself, Cass. You still give a fuck.

CASSANDRA: (annoyed) Oh, you know what I want, do you?

PAM: (looking straight into Cassandra's eyes) Yeah, I do know what
    you want . . . If I could, I'd do it for you.

CASSANDRA: So tell me.

PAM: (to Terry) Give her bangs in the front and take it all off the
    back . . . I mean *all of it*.

TERRY: Shit. What do you say, Cass? It's your hair.

CASSANDRA: (looking away) Yeah, OK, do it.

The music ended. The tone arm hissed a moment in the static
of the blank grooves, then lifted, turned, settled to the side: CLICK,
CLICK. The dividing line fell away, and in the silence Tom's voice
boomed out, full of laughter: "They're up there right at this very
minute with their motherfucking nukes," and, simultaneously,
Pam was saying, "To transform reality, we've got to start with real
transformations."

"It's just a haircut, for fuck's sake," Cassandra said.

"Yeah." Ethan's deep voice rumbled out of his beard. "Yeah, right.
Heavy."

I've got to remember this, John thought. *The Secret Book of the
Black Demon*—meanings so complex he'd never possibly figure them
out; too beautiful, too perfect—like a poem. All he could do was
laugh. "Just look at that crazy fucker," Ethan said to Tom. "He's so
fucking nuts it's a wonder he keeps on walking around in the world."

And, yawning, Terry was saying, "Keep on keeping on. Yeah. We
keep on keeping on with this shit, we're going to crash like a bunch
of junkies." She pushed Cassandra's head down toward the table,
began shearing the nape of her neck.

"Hey, pretty lady," Tom said, "you been to barber college or
what?"

Terry glanced over at Tom and smiled. John felt the energy
coming off that smile—a round ball of heat that shot across the table
right into Tom's eyes. "I come from a big family," she said. "I cut all
the boys' hair."

Ethan, with a lurch of his chair, pushed back from the table and reached for the record. "Hey, man, leave it," Terry said. "You can't hear yourself think."

Then, in the howling silence, John realized that he hadn't outrun his paranoia after all and even the Black Demon couldn't help him. With a buzz like angry bees swarming under the oppressively hard carapace of his skull, he was painfully aware of sound: the idiot child's voice in the rolling boil of the water on the stove, the threatening creak of the chair under all of Ethan's male weight and muscle, the sinister snake's hiss of Terry's gypsy skirt, the silvery deadly snicks of her scissors. He was sweating like Judas.

Everything the least bit out of the ordinary was terrible. His own hair falling around his shoulders was terrible—in fact, what in God's name had he been thinking to let it get so long? And Ethan, of course, was even farther out of bounds; didn't he know how close he came to death at every moment? That the ordinary sane and sensible people who walked the streets of America might rise up and, with hateful thick bricks, hard pointed rocks, stone him out of existence? And Terry? John couldn't even look at Terry—her erectile nipples clearly visible for anybody to see. Didn't they know how dangerous this masquerade was? Didn't they understand how it had to end? One of these days, with no further ado, they'd be exterminated like vermin.

And now John's fried brains were presenting him with an additional convolution of vileness—that the women were spinning off onto their own insane direction, separating themselves, and soon they'd realize just how much they hated men—including him—and then it wouldn't do any good to try to justify himself—no, not any more than it would do any good to argue with the black youths preparing to cut you to ribbons on a street corner, tell them that you hadn't had such a fucking wonderful life yourself, that you'd been screwed around pretty badly too, and, of course, that you'd always been for civil rights. He saw his own doom coming with an awful fatality, the ultimate twist of sadistic humor, that now, just as he was on the point of—well, *maybe* just on the point of, *finally*, goddamn it, after all these years, having some kind of sexual life with a woman, that woman might—for perfectly sound historical reasons—be on the point of repudiating him along with the entire male population of North America and their annoyingly demanding penises.

"Tea time," Terry said, throwing down the scissors. "Anybody got the munchies?"

"Oh wow, look at Cass," Tom said, "shorn like a little lamb. How you doing, little buddy? What's happening?"

"Shit, I couldn't tell you."

"Fuck, I thought you could."

Pamela stood up, walked around the table, and slid into the chair next to John's. She touched him on the back of the hand. "Hey, where have you got yourself to, man?"

Relief sang through him, immense and corny as a thousand violins. "Whew," he said. His jaws had been clamped tight; they ached with release. "I don't know. I was just off . . . sort of running around in my head." Act normal, he told himself.

"If you don't know, and I don't know," Tom was saying to Cassandra, "then who the fuck does?" Terry set a teapot and a huge hot loaf on the table. Ethan immediately seized the loaf, sawed off a huge piece of it, and shoved it into his mouth. Glancing up, John was caught by Tom's amused eyes. Gesturing with his head toward Ethan, Tom mugged amazement—"Can you believe that animal?" John laughed.

Then Terry, with no warning at all that she was about to do anything the least bit unusual, in a single dramatic gesture, smeared a deck of cards from one end of the table to the other. John felt his body jerk back as if he'd been stung. "Pick yourself," Terry said.

"Shee-it," Ethan said, laughing, "now we're getting down to it."

No one spoke. No one moved. "Pick yourself," Terry said again. They were Tarot cards.

"Seven come eleven, baby needs a new pair of shoes," Ethan said, chuckling.

"Is this . . . ? Are we supposed to . . . ?" Pam said.

"Pick yourself," Terry said, looking up and away, not meeting anyone's eyes.

"Hey, dig it," Ethan said, addressing the table, "seriously, she's far out with this shit. She's got the gift big time."

"Pick yourself," Terry said.

John had seen Tarot cards before, but he'd never really looked at them—their sinister faces as evocative as masks. And so what the hell was he supposed to do? He'd seen himself in the cards the first time Terry had said it; now he couldn't stop seeing himself. Any minute now someone would say, "Hey, man, that's your card." But maybe not. The point of the game seemed to be that you had to do your own choosing—anyhow, that was the way Terry had phrased it. Well, shit, no one else was making a move—in fact, the people seated around the table were starting to look like a waxworks display, so maybe he should be the one to break the spell.

He drew the card out of the deck and handed it to Terry. She would surely see how perfect it was: an old man, a wanderer with his cloak and staff and lamp, staring down, lost in thought. John hadn't been able to read the name of the card, but he saw now that it too was perfect: The Hermit. "Far out," she said and gestured with her head: "Come on."

"Wait a minute . . . What?"

"We're going to find out what's going down in your life, man," Terry said.

"You the one," Tom said, laughing, "check it out."

"I don't know," John said. Everybody was looking at him.

"That one step you been looking for?" Ethan said. "Well, it's stepping on you, man . . . Seriously, Raymond, when you been offered a righteous gift, you take it."

THERE WAS nothing for John to do but stand up and follow Terry into the bedroom she shared with Ethan—a space he'd never seen. Saying nothing, she began lighting candles—lit them with ritualized concentration as though timing her actions to intoned words he couldn't hear.

Spooked, smoldering with apprehension, a fuck of a lot more stoned than he'd even thought, he hovered already halfway trapped inside this hippie melodrama—yeah, it could be as ridiculous as *Alfred Hitchcock Presents* or the prodigious unfolding of an inscrutable mystery—and, in the wavering candle-light, images were emerging from the walls (yikes!), almost like tapestries, something like a unicorn, and then a man with glaring eyes sprawled on one side staring upward at a woman wrapped in a diaphanous blue gown; she was turning her head, painfully, inhumanly, to stare back at him, holding something upraised that looked like an open book, as the doubtful forest lowered around them. Before John could meander away into that kitschy landscape, Terry gestured him to an old carved table; he sat down at it. She lit incense—four tapers—and the small chamber (no, not simply a "room") began to seethe with the most dismal of Oriental fumes. It was all a load of crap, of course, but he was freaked right out of his goddamn skull.

Terry placed his card, the Hermit, in the center of the table, handed him the rest of the deck. "Shuffle the cards till they know you," she said.

His hands were greasy with sweat. He had to wipe them on his pants. He shuffled the cards a good dozen times. "OK," she said, "now cut them into three piles. Use your left hand . . . Yeah, man, we're invoking the left hand of darkness."

Trying to get a flicker of humor back into the murk, he said, "Do we want to do that?"

"Oh, yeah. It's the heart line, the female line, the unbroken line that goes all the way back to Egypt."

He cut the deck; she swept it up instantly and began to snap the cards down, making a pattern. "This covers you," she chanted, "this crosses you, this is behind you, this is beneath you . . ." and he imagined himself standing up without a word and simply walking out. Yes, he could do that—walk easily enough through Ethan's living room and not say a word, walk past everyone still sitting stoned at the kitchen table (although that would be harder), and walk right out of this cryptic nightmare to arrive safely at home once again in the Holy Land of Canada. "Oh, fuck, man," Terry said, "that's heavy."

"What's heavy?"

"The whole fucking thing's heavy. I've never seen the cards so clear, man. Whew. Your power's in the Page of Cups. That's the fish rising up from the Deep Mind, and that's how you know things . . .

like out of nowhere. Things you've got no right to know. That happens to you, doesn't it?"

She was right. He was horrified. "Yeah," he said.

"Well, trust that shit, man. Don't push it away from you. OK, and you're crossed by the Hierophant. That means you've got to work through all the old crap. All the old authorities, you dig? The heavy straight dudes telling you, 'Do this, do that.' You've got to get clear of that shit, make your own rules, but that's already what you've been doing, right? So just keep on keeping on."

Whatever was pulsating in what was left of his mind was keeping him stuck, stowed in an indeterminate anteroom, not believing a damned word of this shit, believing every word of it, compelled by Terry's glittering eyes, by the urgency of her voice: "The Ten of Wands is behind you, so you're just leaving a time of danger and disguise . . . like hiding out, creeping around in the shadows, staying one jump ahead of the Man. Well, that freaky time's almost over, but not just yet. But see there? The High Priestess is before you, so your future's going to be full of mystery. You can't try to *think* your way out of it. If you walk out of here and you remember only one thing, that's it. *Don't try to think about it.* You with me, man? Just let yourself dissolve in the weirdness."

What if she knew something? (Sweat scalding his armpits.) What if this was something more than cheap-ass stoned-out hippie melodrama?

"And look at the outcome card, man. The Hanged Man. That's going to be you, Ray . . . John. You see, I don't even know what to call you. But it's all going to get clear. *You're* going to get clear. You're going to prophesy. You're going to glow with a weird light. You're going to speak the truth. And this is how you've got to get there, man. The Six of Cups is beneath you. It's back there in the past somewhere. There's something in your childhood that's really heavy, right?"

"Yes."

The flare inside his dried-up skull—awareness. He couldn't avoid it—not when it had just flashed on him as heavy as that. In Morgantown, he'd stared at that image of himself until it had burned itself into his psyche—or until what was already in his psyche had risen up burning to meet it.

"It's not like . . ." Her hands made swirling motions in the air, describing convolutions of smoke. "It's solid, right? Real. You know exactly what I'm talking about, don't you?"

"Yes."

"How old were you?" she asked him.

"Seven."

"Yeah. I was seeing you about seven. Well, you remember that place where the world cracked open? Right under your feet? Well, that's like that Don Juan thing . . . 'the crack between the worlds.' You've got to slide back through that crack."

Oh, my God, it was true. She really was a witch. He stared at her, trying to reorient himself in this newly flung dark. She'd always been just as disguised as he was, but he saw her clearly now—how she could, in a flash, pounce on the tiny mouse of his mind and claw it to the marrow. "We think time's going in a straight line," she told him, "but that's not where it's at. We just see it that way because our perceptions have been clouded. There's no past and no future. All times exists all the time."

"Jesus, Terry, how the hell . . . OK, our perceptions may be clouded, but how the fuck do I go back there and slide through the crack?"

"Shit, man, I can lay it down for you, but you got to pick it up. You can look at it this way," aiming the back of her stiffened hand at his chest, "or this way," turning her hand over, offering him her cupped palm. "Every nowhere's a somewhere, you dig? . . . But just let it be right now, OK? Look at what's in your home. It's the Page of Swords. That's Pamela, right?"

"I don't know."

"Sure, you do. Don't bullshit me."

"Yeah, it's Pamela. Of course it's Pamela."

"Well, dig it, she's *already* there in your home . . . Yeah, I know you want to know what's going to happen with her, but the cards don't want to tell you that . . . But is there anything else you want to ask me?"

"Terry . . . What the hell am I supposed *to do?*"

She laughed. "That's like . . . Well, say you got a huge power line with all this current running through it. That's like one little electron asking, 'What am I supposed to do?'"

He could almost see it—enormous forces converging, conflicting, making a pattern, himself at the center, perpetually right on time, skittering along like a ping-pong ball down a raging rapid—and, looking, he saw the watery womanliness of crazy Gypsy Terry with all her talk about cycles and phases, how she *was* timed to the moon, and something else—arcane, oscillating, veiled, esoteric, sinuous, sphinxlike, labyrinthine, and every other silly-ass portentous word he could dream up. And powerful as all hell. Yes. He wanted her for an ally. Maybe she had enough power to save him.

"There's just one thing more, man," she said. "You're crowned by Zero the Fool."

"What's that mean?"

"Nobody knows. It's called 'Zero' because it's outside the deck."

———

SOMETHING WAS up with the chicks. I mean the whole women's liberation thing was just boiling away in Boston, and like I said, Pam was heavy into it. She belonged to this women's group that everybody said was the meanest outfit in town, and she was always trying to convert Terry and Cass, and even if she never got them to heed the altar call, she sure left them with plenty of shit to think about. And besides, they didn't need Pam Zalman to ORGANIZE them. It was just in the air. And us men—and we're all porkers at heart no matter what we might say up front—were getting worried, just the way we were supposed to, each in our own way. For Ethan what it meant was that women weren't going to screw anymore, and therefore he was against it because he figured everybody ought to screw as much as possible or they were ANTI-LIFE, and besides, he didn't want Terry to stop screwing HIM. But I knew it wasn't that simple. Like the chicks did have a lot to complain about—any idiot could see that—but the rap that some of them were laying down was just SO DAMNED WEIRD that all you wanted to do was back off them quick.

I'd always had it in my head that if I ever got to the point where

I gave a shit about anything again, I'd probably get married and have a family. It wasn't like I was in a great rush to get there, it was just something I was pretty sure would catch up with me sometime, like dying. But the way the women's libbers were talking, getting married and having a family was definitely not where it was at. It's crazy, because when Cass and me first got together, if she'd said to me, "Hey, Tom, why don't we get married and have a kid?" I would have said, "Christ, are you fucking nuts?" But now she was saying she was NEVER going to do that, and I kept thinking, hey, why not? And I can remember thinking, well, fuck this bullshit. One of these days I'm going to kiss good-bye to Boston, Massachusetts and all these insane bizarre freaky weirded-out people and go back to North Dakota and marry a girl who thinks being liberated means wearing a miniskirt.

So anyhow, Cass and me crashed on that big foam-rubber pad covered with burlap that Ethan had put down on the living-room floor for him and Terry to lay on when they were stoned and listening to records and watching the picture roll on the tube. So when they flaked out, we flaked out, and when they got up, we got up, and seeing as it wasn't us who was paying the rent, we did our best to fit into their space. And all the time we were there, Cass was laying it on me how Ethan was a male chauvinist pig, and she was right, that's what he was. Shit, he was ten times worse than me. When Cass had been off in New York, Ethan and me had got into the habit of doing our dope runs together, and we kept on doing that after she came back, and he made it real clear that this was MEN'S BUSINESS and he was not big on Cassandra coming along. For a while I'd pretend I didn't notice, so I'd say to her like, "Come on, old buddy, let's put it on the road," but he made her so uptight she just gave up—"Well, I guess I'd better stay here with Terry tonight," with this bitter little smile. And that left the chicks exactly where Ethan wanted them to be. Yeah, it was all going down just the way the women's libbers said it always did.

So pretty soon it's running like a clock with Ethan and me stumbling out of bed at noon every day, and Terry the witch makes our breakfast appear magically on the table without us having to do anything about it, and then she makes the dishes magically disappear, and guess what? Those dishes end up washed and dried and put away without us having to think about it. And Cass, who is just about the most undomestic chick you can possibly imagine, is out in the kitchen helping Terry do it. And Ethan and me retire to the living room to have our morning smokes and cups of coffee like a couple of four-star generals and plan our major strategy for the day—mostly rapping about our latest ventures in the import and retail business. And I heard all about the LIBERATED ZONE he had up there in New Hampshire, and how he figured one of these days he'd move his ass back up there permanently, cool out, finish building his house, get out of the freaking evil city, man—like the tribes were coming together, and we're a new people, and all that shit. And somebody else could run the *Weasel*. Like John maybe. And of course that would mean John and Pam running the *Weasel*, and then, lined up right behind them on the flight line, that uptight SDS guy, Phil Vance—but I don't think that ever crossed his mind.

OK, and I should tell you this other little thing that went down one night. Now when Cass and me first got together, one of the things I'd noticed instantly was that, when it came to sex, she could pretty much take it or leave it. Not that she was down on it. When we did get to bed, she seemed to enjoy herself, but it was obvious that it wasn't something real high at the top of her list. And the way that Cass and me generally decided to screw was me saying something like this—"Hey, old buddy, don't you think it's about time to get a fuck in?" or kidding her about it, like, "I don't really want to fuck you, sweet stuff, I just want to put it in to SOAK," and I'd get her laughing, and we'd go to bed laughing, and laugh our way through it, and get up laughing. But Ethan and Terry played it different.

Terry was one of these girls that . . . OK, I know I'm going to sound like a total male chauvinist pig, but shit, it's THE TRUTH, you know what I mean? There really are girls who get just as horny as guys, and they like to get fucked, and if they don't get fucked, they get bitchy and weird. And Terry was like that. And so when she was feeling a bit on the deprived side, she'd start sending Ethan THE MESSAGE. Like she'd come drifting by and stick her tongue in his ear. Or run her hand up the crack of his ass. Or the clothes she wore. Terry always looked like she was going to a Halloween party anyway, but when she was sending him THE MESSAGE, there was usually some other little thing, like maybe a skirt and no panties, right? Or one of those flimsy little blouses imported from India and no bra. And she had, believe me, a real healthy set on her.

So one night Terry's doing her number and so far Ethan hasn't detected a thing. He's just plunked down like a mud fence, sucking away on the water pipe and telling me AGAIN about being in the Merchant Marines. And meanwhile Terry is getting more and more upfront until I'm getting really itchy and embarrassed, and I think even Cassandra's embarrassed—although she's pretty hard to embarrass—but she's looking at me and laughing, like, can you believe this shit? And finally it hits Ethan right in the middle of his dope-fried brain: WHAMMO. Oh yeah . . . TERRY. WOMAN. NEED SEX. NEED SEX WITH WOMAN. GOT WOMAN HERE. FUCK WOMAN NOW. You know, like that. And so quick and hard that he just goes nuts, and they can't even make it into the bedroom. Yeah, before you know it, there's Ethan and Terry fucking on the foam-rubber pad right next to us. I look at Cass, and she looks at me, and we're going, what the hell? So we rip our clothes off and then we're all screwing away on the floor, the two women on their backs and the two men on top like billy goats pumping away and maybe a foot between us.

Pretty soon we're all yelling and screaming and having orgasms and looking good, right? And then we're all crashed out on the floor, intermingled and panting and blown away, right? Like my head is resting on one of Ethan's big hairy arms, and Terry is sprawled out mostly on top of Ethan, but partly on top of me, and Cass is sort of layered in on top of Terry. We're all a bit surprised. Nobody says anything for the longest damn time, and then Ethan says, "Well, that was friendly, wasn't it?" and we get up like nothing much has happened and Terry makes some tea.

OK? Now I realize there's some information about this that I haven't laid out yet, so let me go back and do a rerun. When Terry would do her numbers on Ethan, it might take him a while to get

THE MESSAGE, but I usually got it pronto. And there was this one thing that got stuck in my head like a hunk of film I couldn't shut off. Terry's long smooth legs, and her feet pushing on the floor, and she's still got her skirt on but it's hiked up around her waist, and Ethan's between her legs, and she's shoving her hips up into him, and she's grabbed ahold of his ass and she's pulling him into her, and she's panting, and when Terry comes, she yowls like a goddamned cat. It gets next to me, buddy, I'll tell you.

BUT ANYHOW, here's what's happening. Ethan never hits the sack before three or four in the morning, but Terry crashes about midnight, and that gives Ethan an excuse to turn up the stereo as loud as he's been wanting to all along, which is FULL TILT, so Cass and me are stuck there with our eardrums getting beat to shit until he decides he wants to cash it in. And this don't really bother me because after four years of living with a bunch of animals in a barracks I can sleep through anything, so when the next morning rolls around, I sleep till noon the same as Ethan. But Cassandra is a real light sleeper, and Terry's up in the kitchen banging away at the crack of dawn—making bread and all that other good shit witches do—and Cass is wide awake. So she's getting cut off at both ends and only grabbing like four or five hours sleep at the most, besides which she's doing a pack of smokes a day and all the dope she can get her hands on, and I guess that's how she got sick with bronchitis.

One morning I touched her and she was like something that had been left out in the sun too long. She seemed really young, like ten years old, and said in this little-girl voice, "Hey, Tommy, I don't feel very good." I brought her some orange juice, but she couldn't drink much of it because her throat hurt too much. She went back to sleep. I wandered out into the kitchen, bouncing off the walls, and Terry said, "What's the matter?" so I told her. Ethan had crawled out of the sack by then, and Terry said, "Cool it, man. Cassandra's sick."

"Oh yeah?" he says and goes in to look at her. "She don't look too good." He's got that one right. She's goddamned WHITE. And Terry's bending over to wake her up and get her temperature.

I'm getting that old gnawing-on-a-dry-bone kind of fear. It's like when you have one of those premonitions that something awful is going to happen and you'll take any excuse to think THIS IS IT. "Far out," Terry says, "it's damned near a hundred and four."

"Is that bad?" I say.

"Not exactly the picture of health. I'd better break her fever."

I say, "Break her fever? What is that?"

"Cool out, Tom. Sit down. Relax. Smoke up or something."

But I can't relax. You don't know how much somebody matters to you until they ain't around anymore, and that's an experience I've had a little too much of. It's not like I thought Cass was going to die or anything, but weird shit goes down all the time, and you can't really predict it. "What are you going to break her fever with?" I say.

"Catnip."

"Catnip?"

In the living room Cass says: "Catnip?"

"Look, Tom," Terry's saying, "you want to do something, you get the vitamin C and you count out twelve grams and you put them in the blender with some ice and honey and orange juice and you blend them up." And she's grabbing a couple jars. One's labeled catnip and the other one wormwood. I say, "Wormwood?"

In the living room Cass says: "Wormwood?"

"She knows what she's doing," Ethan says.

Well, Terry did break Cassandra's fever, knocked it down to a hundred, made her sip that vitamin C drink, and finally just let her sleep. Then she told Ethan and me to haul ass. "Huh?" Ethan says.

"Out," Terry says.

So Cass was sick for a few weeks. First it was in her throat. Then it moved down into her lungs and turned into bronchitis, and she had this horrible cough that would just damn near tear her apart. And forget about us getting out of there. Cass wasn't going anywhere. And all that time, Terry took care of her. The first thing she did was move her into the bedroom, which Ethan didn't much care for because it was HIS bed. And he kept trying to crank up the stereo, and Terry would turn it down and say, "Come on, man. Grow up."

That first night Terry read the Tarot to see why Cass had got sick. It was real complicated, and I can't remember most of what she said, but there was a knight riding along on a horse at full tilt with a big stick in his hand, and Terry said that was me riding into Cassandra's life and putting her through some heavy changes that put a strain on her spirit. And there was another card that was a picture of a woman blindfolded and tied up with a bunch of swords stuck in the ground around her. Cass tried to laugh at that one. "She looks like something out of a porn book," she said in this raspy little voice.

"Yeah," Terry says. "That's exactly right. She's in bondage. And that's where you're stuck at the moment . . . but dig it, that won't last forever."

She said that Cassandra would only be real sick for two weeks and then she'd start getting better, and that turned out to be true. And she said that Cassandra was about to go through a whole bunch more heavy changes—like no R and R on the horizon for mucho moons. And I remember the last card. It was the Star. Terry said that if Cassandra didn't lose her courage, she'd eventually get through all this shit and end up clean and clear and simple like bright water. I don't know if that turned out to be true or not, but I sure hope it did.

6.

"ALL THE men can go off to the suicide center and get themselves quietly gassed to death?" John said. He was pacing back and forth in Pam's apartment while she stood motionless and watched him. Her hint of a smile could drive him nuts if he let it.

"There's a certain element of satire," she said.

"Oh, you think so, do you? I think she meant every fucking word of it."

"I don't know. I've never met her. A lot of it could be a put-on . . . or maybe not."

"Put-on, hell. She shot Andy Warhol, didn't she?"

"Come on, man. Nobody's offering it seriously as a program. It's an interesting document. You've got a wound that's been festering for a few thousand years . . . and you lance it . . . you're going to get pus, OK?"

"Why the hell are you defending her?"

"I'm not defending her. Like . . . Fuck, why is this such a . . . Why are you so uptight? Don't you see the humor in it?"

"Humor? Jesus. Men are really women and women are really men . . . The male is an incomplete female . . . a walking abortion. That's supposed to be funny?"

She shook her heard and laughed. "Fuck, man. Yeah, it's horrible, but . . . It *is* funny. Like the ultimate *détournement* on sex roles. Flip everything around one hundred and eighty degrees and see what it looks like. Like Swift's modest proposal . . ."

"So this modest proposal is to kill all the men . . ."

"Hey, cool out, OK? You're talking like I presented you with a critique and asked you to sign it. But that's not why . . . If you take another look . . . I mean, isn't it a fascinating document? A really interesting document? If you simply think that women have been denied the right to be like men, then isn't it the logical . . ."

"Fascinating document? Interesting document? What makes you think that people won't think it's meant straight?"

"Maybe they will. And maybe it is. Jesus. Where the hell's your anarchism? Trust the masses . . ."

She'd stopped smiling, had settled into a stance that looked poised and stubborn, her legs widely spaced, her feet in their dainty white socks pressed solidly into the hardwood floor. A part of his mind was saying, can this really be happening? Are we really having the first honest-to-God fight since we met each other—and are we having it because the Collective published selections from *The SCUM Manifesto*? It was nuts. He knew it was nuts, but he couldn't stop: "You voted to publish it."

"Yeah, I did."

John had long ago drunk his tea, but he was still clutching the cup in his right hand. The part of himself that remained detached— that was sadly watching this shit go down—told him that if he squeezed the delicate white cup any harder, he was going to break it, but he didn't care. It felt good to squeeze it. "If you published it, you dig it," he said.

"Oh, fuck, man. You're intentionally not understanding me." She started to say something else but stopped; then she smiled again—the faintest hint of a smile. "She really got to you, didn't she?"

His fury was so intense it couldn't make words. He clamped it down, controlled it. His mind was racing. He needed to find something that would really devastate her. "The other women in the Collective . . . Your comrades in the Collective . . . How many of those women really hate men?"

"What the fuck does that have to do with anything?"

"Then why the hell did you publish Valerie Solanis? Oh, we don't *really* hate men. Oh, no, not us. That's a goddamn filthy rumor. We'll just find the biggest fucking man-hating dyke we can find and publish her . . . Jesus, Pam, you've told me about those women. OK, so how many of them hate men?"

He saw her face go cold, turn into a mask. "Fuck you, man."

"How many? A few? Most of them? It's a political question, damn it."

"It's none of your goddamned fucking business." He'd got what he'd wanted. She wasn't talking in that quiet voice anymore. She was just as furious as he was. "Fuck you, John. I never want to hear 'dyke' again, you got that? *Never.* Jesus fucking Christ."

"Sorry. But I'm mad, goddamn it . . . I'm just asking you. It's *political*, goddamn it . . . the dominant tendency . . ."

"The dominant fucking tendency . . . Oh, fuck the dominant tendency . . . Jesus . . . What the hell do you want? . . . OK, the dominant tendency is separatist."

"Ah, now we're getting somewhere. So what about you?"

"Why the fuck would I be . . . ? What would I be doing . . . ? Shit. Having this goddamned stupid pointless fight with you? Jesus, man, don't you know me at all? Can't you read my theory from my practice?"

He saw her eyes look down at his hand; then she looked into his face. He was still squeezing the cup with his thumb and three of his fingers, but his index finger was pointed at her. Her eyes were saying something like, "Look at what you're doing." He didn't want to look at what he was doing.

"You may not be there yet," he said, "but you're tempted, aren't you?"

"What? To a separatist position? You're goddamn right, I'm tempted."

He'd heard a flicker of something in her voice—an opening, a way out. If he laughed, so would she, and it would be over. He couldn't do it. "Fuck," he said. "Go ahead. Why stop with half measures?" Clutching the cup, he jabbed his extended index finger directly into her face. "Go ahead. Quit fucking around with men. They're defective . . . just walking abortions. Go on, you can do it. You can hate men with the best of them."

BANG

He was left standing, stunned and stupid, his fingers vibrating with pain. The cup was gone. He'd heard it smash into the wall, shatter into a million fragments. Whatever had happened was already over. He remembered his hand, his index finger stiffened, pointing at Pam's head. Then an explosion. Shock. Waves of pain still running from his fingers up the length of his arm. Pam's eyes had no expression at all. They were looking into his eyes. In memory—a crackle of powder blue brief as a strobe flash. She'd kicked the cup right out of his hand.

He laughed. He sank to his knees laughing, then rolled onto the floor, convulsed, destroyed. She was laughing too—giggling like a little kid.

"Oh, fuck." He sat up, found that she was kneeling next to him. He shook his fingers.

"Did I hurt you?" she said.

"Yes."

"I'm sorry."

"No, you're not."

"You're right, I'm not."

"Jesus, Pam, where'd you learn to kick like that?"

"Karate," she said, shrugging.

"My God, I didn't know you were doing that. Why didn't you tell me you were doing that?"

"You never asked me."

"Christ, you keep saying that. It's nuts. What else am I going to find out about you that's a total shock?"

That one sent her off into another giggling fit. "Shit, man, you should have seen your face."

"Oh, yeah, I can imagine."

"Hey, look," he said, "I'm sorry. I'm really sorry."

"Me too. I didn't think you'd take it that way."

Then, as though taking an invisible cue, they both fell silent. She was looking at him. She offered him her hand. He took it. She stood, pulled him to his feet. He tried to find something to say but came up with nothing. He tried to clear his throat, but his mouth had gone dry. He produced an idiot's small discreet sound, something like a cough.

She was close enough that he could have reached out and placed his hand on the base of her throat—and he discovered with some alarm that he wanted to do exactly that. Touch her smooth live skin, trace her clearly defined collarbone to the deep hollow just above her sternum. He wanted to read her entire body, locate the mass of each muscle, the shape of each bone. He wanted to touch every vertebra, joint, tendon, and rib, every concavity or swelling or long fine line, every hardness or softness, every sinew of her. Then, in slow motion, she ran her fingers though his hair, held him, resting a hand on either side of his neck, looking. "I don't think of you as a man," she said and kissed him open-mouthed.

Tension coiling toward immensity, slush of fear in his chest, muscles tightening, he allowed her grave deliberate motion to push across a dangerous barrier. A girl hadn't kissed him like that—as skillfully and aggressively—since Natalie. (How many years ago had that been?) It was wonderful to get turned on again—to know it in every singing nerve in his body. He wanted her so much that maybe it would be all right this time—if only he could get his treasonous brain to turn off. He was an animal touching another animal, moments away from being blasted away to nowhere like the white porcelain cup.

But he'd been here before, and no, nothing was going to be all right—not now and not ever. That old whipped-dog misery. He pushed her away, a movement as instinctive as if she'd caught fire. Christ, now he'd done it. He'd have to explain—come up with more words, more lies. "What's the matter?" she said.

"Nothing," he said.

"Do I turn you on?"

"God, yes." He hated himself. His entire body was shaking. Surely she could see it.

"What's the matter?" she asked him again. "What just happened to you?"

"Pam, I don't know what happens."

"OK, let's try to figure it out."

"It shouldn't have to be something you figure out, should it? I mean . . . is it amenable to political analysis?"

"Shit, man, if it's not amenable to political analysis, then there's something wrong with our politics."

Not getting it, not wanting to get it, he stared at her, tried to read her—find a way to translate her into something familiar. Then, finally, he did get it. When she said "total critique," that's exactly what she meant.

He stepped toward the door. Moving quickly, she blocked his way. "Don't go," she said.

He had to get out of there. He had to say something that would allow him to escape. After all these years, he still believed in the transcendent power of the old magical formula; as terrified as he was, he knew he had to say it. He thought it might somehow get him off the hook. "Pamela. I love you."

"Oh, baby," she said in that oddly muted, nearly singing voice he'd heard only a few times before, "you don't know what you're letting yourself in for."

"I've got to cool out."

She was firmly positioned in front of the door. He didn't want to try to move her. "Come on, Pam," he said.

"*You* come on," she said, offering a hand. He couldn't take it.

"I've got a real hang-up with saying the words," she said, "like saying the words you just said. But I've got feelings too. Really strong feelings. So don't think for a minute you can say that to me and then just walk out of here." She took his hand. She must have felt how cold and wet it was. "Oy, you're a mess. Come on, it's OK."

He allowed her to lead him away from the door. But she was leading him toward the bed. "Pam?" he said.

"We're not going to do anything."

"Look, for Christ's sake . . ."

"Come on, man. We're not going to *do* anything."

She was gripping his hand as tightly as on that awful morning when she'd saved him at the Harvard bust. "I don't think this is a good idea," he said.

She led him behind the screen. It was a big bed, bigger than a double. Someone who wanted to sleep alone would never have picked a bed like that. "Pamela?"

"We're not going to do anything."

She drew him onto the bed, lay down next to him. "OK, you can breathe again," she said.

He lay flat on his back, stared at the ceiling, listened to the moist thudding of his heart. She took both of his hands into hers, rubbed them. "Come on, baby, trust me. We're not going to do anything. It's just a nice place to have a conversation, OK?"

TALKING WAS something he could do. She'd led him across a fundamental divide—he knew that—and now they were on the dangerous side of the Japanese screen. The light from the big bay window set the rice paper aglow, and they were lying together inside that flat diffused light, saturated by the clarity of the whiteness—lying on their backs, not touching each other. Like the bedspread, her pillows were decorated with eyelet lace, and he felt again the vast calm of the space she'd created, felt almost protected by it. He could almost trust her. "I don't really know you," he said.

"Come on, man, you see me practically every day."

"Yeah, but how many more things are there . . . you know, like karate? You say you're not a secretive person, but . . ."

"I'll tell you anything. What do you want to know?"

"OK. Let's start with karate. How'd you get into that?"

"A lot of us are heavy into karate these days. As a direct reaction to male terror. Dig it, rape is a political act, an act of terror aimed at *all* women. Learning to defend yourself is like basic. The women in the Collective all study Korean style, so I do that with them, but I studied Goju in New York. I've got a brown belt in Goju. After ballet, karate's the perfect thing for me. I need . . . I have to do something *physical*, man, or I just go crazy."

"All right. And ballet? Tell me about ballet."

"Fuck. You want to be here for a week? I don't even know where to . . . OK, look,"—the pale pink ribbon floating on the wall above their heads—"I wore that in my hair when I was Clara in the *Nutcracker*. The only real solo role I ever had. I was the best goddamn Clara you ever saw. I saved that ribbon for years, but it made me sick . . . even to look at it. It was a big deal for me to put it up there."

He waited for her to go on, but she didn't. "Tell me about the hospital," he said.

"I knew you were going to ask me that. OK, I started fainting in class. I wasn't living with . . . I was still living with my parents. I don't know how my father got involved, but he came over to the school and took one look at me and said, 'What are you doing to my daughter?' and he slapped me in the hospital like instantly. Boy, was I mad at him. I wanted to kill him. But he saved my life. I was really fucked, man. My head was fucked. I thought it was normal to faint every day. I was working my ass off . . . *of course* I was going to faint. The only thing that was wrong with me was like four or five extra pounds. That's what I thought. And if I lost that weight, I'd be perfect, and then maybe Mr. B would choreograph a ballet for me. Jesus, man, when I hit the hospital, I weighed eighty-four pounds."

Again he waited for her to go on; when she didn't, he turned to look at her. Her eyes searched his face. He couldn't read her expression.

She sprang up, brought back the dope and papers, sat on the edge of the bed and began rolling a joint. "What are you going to call a Jewish girl?" she said. "Esther, Ruth, Miriam, Deborah? Shit, no, that's too easy. I swear to God, my mother must have thought about it for days to come up with the right name . . . Fuck me, man . . . Pamela Lynne Zalman."

SHE WAS an only child—"and that's one more kid than my mother should've had." Her father owned his own business, made good money. For as long as she could remember, her parents hated each other; when she was little, her father wasn't around much. He'd wanted a son, so Pam was a disappointment straight from the womb. He was second-generation, had once had a big family in Europe, but most of them had died in the camps. The only relative Pam knew on her father's side was Baba Zalman who lived all alone at the end of a subway line, read a Yiddish newspaper, and taught little Pam to spit when she passed a church so she wouldn't get struck by the evil eye. But Pam's mother supplied a vast collection of living relatives—the aunts and uncles and cousins Pam remembered from her childhood. Pam's mother was known as a great beauty, "a real pritzteh." The spoiled youngest of six children, Mrs. Zalman wanted her daughter to be the next Shirley Temple. "Well, shit, man, you can't say I didn't try."

It wasn't that Pam didn't know what she was supposed to do or how to do it—"that little-girl cuteness"—but she could only do it for a while, always screwed it up eventually, reverted to her real self, "mad and bad," a tiny bundle of raw nerves and craziness. She was a picky eater, painfully underweight. ("Yeah?" John said, "so was I.") She was highly verbal, learned to read by four, could never keep her mouth shut, and couldn't sit still. Dance classes were OK because they were physical, but school was hell. "If you sat me down and tried to *tell me* anything, you might as well have been speaking Russian." If she didn't like what was going on, she just got up and walked out. She wasn't just a brat; she was a thug. She broke dishes, cut up her clothes, cut off her hair, murdered her dolls. She bit and kicked and punched other kids. Sometimes she kicked her teachers. She was the only girl in her entire school ever to get paddled by the principal. She was always peeing her pants. She slept in diapers until she was nine. She told John all of these things in a deadpan voice, her eyes fixed on the O'Keeffe painting. He knew why she had to tell her story that way.

Ballet saved her. She wasn't one of those little girls with sugarplum fantasies, didn't care if she ever got to wear a pink tutu. She loved the work at the barre. "I didn't know it, but I desperately needed some sense of control. I used to have this sensation like I was going to fly apart into a million pieces. It's terrible, man. It makes you crazy. And ballet gave me like a way to squeeze myself together." She loved the Cecchetti syllabus, the way each step leads to the next, the way it all fits, the logic of it. When she was twelve, a talent scout from the School of American Ballet was auditioning kids on Long Island. "I was like this little mechanical ballerina doll. You wind it up, and it dances. I had no expression at all . . . never smiled . . . but oh boy, did I have technique. She asked me to do a fouetté. I couldn't believe she meant just one. I got this screwy idea in my head that she wanted me to do the thirty-two fouettés from the third act of *Swan Lake*, so that's what I did. Afterward there was this dead silence. Of course she took me."

Her mother rented a dark little apartment on the Upper West Side so they could be near the school, but cramming Pam and her mother together into the same small space was a lousy idea—"two freaked-out hysterics in a sardine can"—so when Pam was fourteen, she started boarding with the family of another dancer. "It was like the Garden of Eden. Melanie and I were very close. Compared to my meshuggina family, I thought hers was motherfucking *normal*. We were going to this special high school for actors and dancers, and they didn't give a fuck what we did, and we spent most of our time in ballet classes. I was in heaven." When she was sixteen, André Eglevsky borrowed her for his production of the *Nutcracker*. Everybody loved her. She thought her career was taking off. Everybody loved her but Mr. B.

"I never did figure out why that son of a bitch didn't like me. Maybe it was because I'd done most of my training somewhere else. Maybe it was because I didn't look like Suzanne Farrell. Maybe it was because I talked too much, asked too many questions . . . Maybe it was because I was so crazy . . . like you could just *feel it* radiating off me. But everybody knew he liked his girls thin as pins, so I thought, hell, I can do that. All I have to do is stop eating."

The doctor in the hospital said she had anorexia nervosa, atypical. "Well, of course it was *atypical*. Nothing about me's ever been typical." For the next three years Pam was in and out of the hospital. She tried to keep dancing, but it was impossible. Without dance, she had nothing to keep her from flying apart—she *was* nothing. She bounced from doctor to doctor, shrink to shrink. "Most of them were quacks . . . or real idiots. I was smarter than they were."

She'd do anything to avoid going back to the hospital. She'd learned all the tricks of the trade by then. "Sinkers are great, man. They're cheap, they're small, you can buy them in any sporting goods store. If you're wearing a blazer, you can put them in every pocket. You can sew them under your skirt. If you get a heavy-duty panty girdle, it's amazing how many sinkers you can stuff into it. Those assholes would weigh me and say, 'Oh, Pamela, you're doing so well.'"

When it was obvious that she was losing weight again, they sent her back to the hospital. Once she was in, she wasn't allowed to exercise—not even allowed to walk. If she wasn't gaining weight, they'd shove a feeding tube down her. "Like it was all designed to punish you, make you even crazier." One of the few things they let her do was read. She read obsessively. "It wasn't for escape. I was like a feral child. I didn't know a fucking thing, man . . . gornisht. I had to construct the entire world from scratch. And it was like really personal . . . *how the fuck did I get here?*" The right book hit her at the right time: Jules Henry's *Culture Against Man*. "It blew my mind. I thought, whatever he's doing, that's what I want to do."

Slowly, her life turned around. Her parents split up, and she moved in with her father. "He'd give me this look . . . like appalled and disgusted and just dripping with pity. 'Oy, oy, oy, what *is* this miserable little thing? It won't eat, it won't talk, it won't dance, it won't do anything. It just lies there and cries.' But he never gave up on me."

She finally found the right doctor. He weighed her stripped naked. "Don't give me any of that crap about modesty, Pamela. I know that all of you girls lie automatically." He gave her blood tests to make sure she hadn't drunk gallons of water. "You fall an ounce below a hundred pounds," he told her, "you go straight back in the hospital. I won't even let you go home first." And she found the right therapist. "After all those charlatans, I didn't believe in anybody . . . and then there she is, this funny middle-aged fat lady with glasses. Martha. So fucking far out, man. It took me a while to . . . But yeah, she trained with Paul Goodman. Gestalt therapy's like . . . Do you know anything about it? It's *anarchist* therapy. That's how I got onto the whole anarchist trip."

By the time Pam was nineteen, her doctor said she was "stabilized." She was working with Martha twice a week. She finished her last courses for high school the same year she started at NYU. She had a goal again: she was going to be an anthropologist, better than Ruth Benedict, better than Margaret Mead. She was as nutty and compulsive at NYU as she'd been with ballet; if she ever got anything less than an A+ on anything, she cried for days. Of course for a doctorate in anthropology she'd have to go to Columbia—there really wasn't any other choice. They didn't just admit her, they gave her a scholarship. She got involved in SDS. History came along and blew her away. "And that's the story of my mishigas, man. Now what's yours?"

SHE PASSED John the freshly rolled joint and the matches. He took them but said, "No, not yet. In a minute. OK?" Right now he didn't need the doper's weird web, certainly not the doper's paranoia. He sat up and swung his legs over the side of the bed so he could sit next to her, so he could feel the floor under his feet.

He felt poised, balanced. It was like that deliberate moment he always sought just before he performed—that sense of *gravitas* as he stepped from secular to sacred space. The first night in the Bohemian Embassy—where Ian and Sylvia had played, by God—about to offer up his shit-kicker West Virginia voice, his repertoire of strange old mountain tunes to a huge bare room full of somewhat cool, somewhat reserved Canadian kids. To sit down in front of the mike, adjust it, pick up his Martin, check the tuning, look out at those polite faces. He was waiting for them just as much as they were waiting for him, and he felt—yes, of course, fear. Wiping his sweaty hands on his jeans. But also the kick, the juice, the clarity. Whatever I've got, you're going to get it, like it or not. And they had liked it. That had been, not Raymond Lee, the cockroach in the corner, but John Dupre, the full-sized human being. As he would be again.

What she'd told him had changed everything. It was more than merely trust. He couldn't have felt any more linked to Pamela if they'd shared the same womb. It was high summer in Boston, and she was wearing what she always wore in the heat—her powder-blue jeans and a boy's white shirt with nothing under it. She was sitting sideways on the edge of the bed, one leg drawn up. The light through the paper screen was so flat and white it seemed to cast no shadows. Looking at him, waiting, she was a living Vermeer. Soon he would have to say something, but not just yet. The windows in her apartment were open, and he could hear the traffic outside, distant voices, someone's stereo—not the drugged-out rock he might have expected in that hip building but a snatch of something crystalline and precise, Vivaldi or even Bach—and with that, the entire universe ignited with relatedness. Even the smell of her, not strong enough to call it a perfume, just the faintest hint of sweetness—allusive, evocative. "Fasting," he said. "Yeah."

He saw a wary movement far back in her eyes—knew that she was ready to defend herself. Karate must have been the perfect metaphor for something she'd known her whole life.

"There's a point," he said, "after . . . well, maybe after three days . . . when your hunger starts to feel pleasurable. Something sharp to push yourself against, like an inner knife blade. And then there's the euphoria, like wow, impossible to describe. And the whole world gets hard-edged and clear. So clear. So fucking clear. Like an etching."

He saw her surprise, puzzlement. "What are you . . . ? Are you asking me what it's like? Shit, man, you're right on."

"No, I'm not asking you. I'm telling you. I've done it. Not like you. I only did it twice, but . . . OK, it's like you're right on the edge, and if you keep going . . . everything will get pure and clean and brilliantly focused . . . like sunlight on a mirror."

"I can't believe this. Are you putting me on?"

"No, I'm not putting you on. Listen. Everything's charged with meaning. Your mind makes unbelievably brilliant leaps . . . It's like the speed, the clarity. It's like . . . Food would just slow you down. Food would just get in the way."

"Yeah, that's right. Exactly right."

"What you're trying to . . . This is hard to say . . . What you're trying to break free from . . . It's the 'witness of the body.'"

Even her mental karate hadn't prepared her for that. Her eyes filled, spilled over. She looked away from him, wiped the tears away with the back of her hand. "I'm sorry, man" she said. "This is heavy for me."

He'd never imagined her crying. It hurt him to see it. "It's heavy for me too," he said. "Listen. It feels like something really . . . just unbelievably significant. Like a huge mental breakthrough's going to happen at any moment. It's right around the corner. A clarity you can't simply choose. It's going to enter you from the outside . . . in a blaze of brilliance. Soon everything's going to be *blindingly* clear."

"Yes."

"But then you keep on going, and it gets farther and farther away. You get sick and crazy. Really crazy. You keep running the same weird tape loops in your mind."

"Yes."

"The only thing you can think of is to keep on going. You can't let go of it. If you ate anything, you'd lose it. And you just get crazier and crazier."

"Oh, yes. Fuck, yes. Did you stop yourself or did somebody stop you?"

"I stopped myself."

"How did you do it?"

"I honest to God don't know. What I associate it with . . . This is going to sound weird. It had something to do with playing the guitar."

"Yeah, I can understand that," controlled distant voice, "how that might work. But I couldn't stop myself. If my father hadn't stopped me, I would have died. You hit a point where . . . It's like dying's absolutely beside the point. Like *your body* is absolutely beside the point. That's how you got there in the first place. So dying doesn't even enter into the picture, you dig?"

"Oh, yeah. I didn't go that far, but . . . oh, yeah."

He saw a second wave of tears wash through her. She didn't try to hide them. "Oh, man," she said, whispering it, "I was so fucking crazy."

His own eyes were stinging in sympathy. Because he didn't know what else to do, he wiped the fat drops off her face. He kissed her forehead.

She wrapped her arms around him, and he held her for a moment, her head pressed into his chest. How could he ever have been afraid of her?

"I wasted so much of my life," she said.

She kissed him lightly on the cheek, stood up, withdrew to the other side of the room. He could feel her urgency like a physical force—her need for space around herself, for distance between them. She stood in the white flat light, looking at him. He could have sworn that he'd never seen anyone as clearly.

"John" she said, "we're a council. We've been a council for a while now. It doesn't matter that there's only two of us. Maybe we'll have more members, and maybe we won't . . . and maybe . . . Maybe we'll go to bed, and maybe we won't. Do you understand what I'm saying?"

"Yes."

"Just don't . . . Like saying 'don't worry' is bullshit, because if you're going to worry, you're going to worry. But I really wish you wouldn't. I mean . . . I don't know how to say this. Don't worry for my sake, OK? The important thing is that we're a council. The apparent contradiction between the individual and the collective vanishes in practice, you dig? That's what we're doing right now."

———

FOR ABOUT a week all Cassandra did was sleep. Like it wasn't just the bronchitis, I think she was worn down to the nub. But then she started feeling better, and she kept trying to get up while Terry kept running her back to bed, like, "Wait until that cough starts breaking up," because Cass would start coughing sometimes and you'd think she was going to bring up half her guts. And every day Ethan was saying, "Hey, she's looking pretty good. Don't you think so, Terry? Look how she's getting her color back." Meaning, looking almost good enough to MOVE HER ASS RIGHT ALONG OUT OF HERE. But Terry just ignored him and kept shoving Cassandra back into bed and feeding her herbs, and I thought that was really good of Terry. Before that, I didn't think she liked Cass all that much.

And a lot of times Terry would go in and sit on the edge of the bed and rap with her, and I thought, hey, that's really NICE. But then later on I started getting this uneasy feeling, and I'd be wondering what the hell they were talking about in there. Sometimes I'd hear snatches of Terry telling Cass about the Ancient Mother. Like all these little statues they found all over the East which were of women, "just cunt and tits," Terry said, and to her that proved that women's magic went back millions of years and would always be around no matter what kind of silly-ass God any man might invent, so I figured that they were mainly talking about Terry's witch trip, but I wasn't sure, and I couldn't help wondering if they were ever talking about ME.

And there was one other thing. Even now I can't bring myself to wish it never happened. As long as Cass was sick, we were goddamn well STUCK there, and it was starting to freak me right out. It was motherfucking CLAUSTROPHOBIC, you know what I mean? There was nobody forcing me to hang out in that insane place. Like I could have got in the camper and gone anywhere I damn well pleased, but I kept thinking I shouldn't desert Cassandra in her hour of need—although I don't know what I thought I could accomplish just by being there and bouncing off the walls. But I didn't feel much like dealing at the moment, and I didn't want to go float around with John because floating around with John meant floating around with Pam, and, to tell you the truth, Pam Zalman pricked my ass, and I sure as hell wasn't going to go hang out at Lyons' place. And then there was Ethan, and he'd turned into my good old buddy, and that made things even worse—because I was developing a pretty bad case for Terry. And you know the most bizarre thing? Like all the time Cass was in New York, the three of us got along just fine. Ethan and Terry just opened up their place for me like there'd never been any question of me going anywhere else, and they'd never said a word about me kicking in for the rent—or even for the food, for fuck's sake—and that's amazing considering Ethan's one of the cheapest sons of bitches ever to walk God's green earth. And all the time Cass was in New York, I had no problem with Terry. Like she was just a fantasy, right? Like I admired her from a distance, right? But she was my good buddy's old lady, and that took care of that. But now somehow everything had got twisted, and it was so harsh I couldn't even stand to talk to her, and she must have noticed because I remember her looking at me with a strange expression on her face, like . . . I don't know. Like she'd just noticed me for the first time.

Well, one afternoon Ethan's off somewhere and Cassandra's asleep, or at least she's supposed to be asleep. The bedroom door's shut, and Terry's cleaning the bathtub. I don't know what to do with myself, feeling itchy and restless and low. I've been trying to read something, I can't remember what, but I just can't get into it. So anyhow I get up and drift into the bathroom thinking maybe I can get into a rap with Terry, and she's cleaning the bathtub with some of that good old foaming cleanser. There's blue foam all over the inside of the tub and she's scrubbing away at it with a sponge. I don't have my boots on, so she don't hear me coming, right? I'm standing just inside the bathroom door, and she don't know I'm there, and she just goes on scrubbing away at the bathtub.

It's all burnt into my brain like I was branded with it. Terry's barefoot, and one of her long brown legs is straight back, and she's up on her toes, and I can see the creases in the bottom of her foot and the little pattern of dirt from walking around barefoot, and the other leg's bent, taking most of her weight, and I can see the shift in her muscles as her body moves, and her black hair's hanging down so I can't see her face, and she's wearing a very short white skirt and I can see almost all of her ass, and her ass is round and hard and I can see the muscles shifting in it as she moves, and she's got on shiny peach-colored panties and they fit her just tight as a drum, like there's the crack of her ass and the little hollows at the sides. She shaves her legs all the way up, they're smooth and brown and I can see the long smooth muscles under the skin, and she's bent there over the tub. I can smell her sweat, and the bathroom smell of the cleanser. And her panties are so fucking shiny and tight.

She finally straightens up and catches me staring at her. I can't say a word. She just stands there with the sponge in her hand looking at me, don't smile or anything. There's little drops of sweat all across her forehead and her upper lip, and I'll never forget her eyes. Big and round and black and shiny. And I've been CAUGHT, of course, because what I want is just written all over my face, but I can't stop. Looking at her, and wanting her, and the wanting just hanging out front. And maybe I could have stopped it if I'd done it right then, but she has on one of those real thin blouses, and no bra, and her nipples come erect. I mean it's not gradual, they just pop right up. And I'm GONE.

To this day I don't know whether she stepped toward me or I stepped toward her or we just met in the middle. All I know is that her shiny panties are on the floor and my pants are down around my ankles, and when I put my fingers in, she's already wet like the ocean, and then I've got my hands on her ass, easing her on down to the floor, and I've come into her with the most incredible wonderful feeling of coming home. Some part of me that's still halfway in the real world hears Cassandra in the next room, just on the other side of the door, COUGH, COUGH. And so I'm trying to be absolutely quiet. Terry's still got the sponge in her hand. She throws it away. And she gives the bathroom door a little kick. It swings shut, not quite all the way, leaving about an inch of space. She don't say a word. I don't say a word. We're just going at each other like a couple of silent wildcats.

Right then I couldn't think of a thing. But later, after I got my brains working again, I contemplated the fact that there are some women in the world that your body just fits with, you know what I mean? It helps if you like each other, but that's not a requirement. And Terry was one of those women. So it didn't matter a damn what our minds were doing, our bodies belonged together. It's amazing how different women are from each other inside, but she really had that . . . I don't know how to say it. It's like she wanted me in her as much as I wanted to be in there. I felt that when I came into her. All that wonderful smooth wetness.

We're panting. We're biting each other. And I can't PLAN what I'm going to do next. I can't even THINK. But somehow I can manage to keep myself quiet. So there's this weird silence, just us breathing, and I'm pushing her into the floor, just dying to get into her deeper and deeper. She bites down on my shoulder so she won't yell out loud, grinding her teeth and tongue into me, the air kind of whistling through her nose, and I can feel the rise and fall of her ribs, like the way you feel a horse after you've been galloping. And goddamn, I can feel this fluttering inside her. Her whole body's jerking and twisting, she's drawing blood on my shoulder, and there's a little stifled moan deep down inside her throat. And that just does it for me, and I'm there.

And then we're just staring at each other. Neither one of us has said a word yet. And I hear in the next room, COUGH, COUGH. I slide out of her and stand up. I offer her my hand, and she takes it and stands up. I look into the bathroom mirror to see how my shoulder is, and there's this perfect ring of bloody teeth marks, and I'm thinking, shit, how the hell am I going to explain THAT to Cassandra? I look at Terry. She's still looking at me. She steps over to the toilet and tears off some toilet paper and wipes between her legs and then pulls her panties back on. I'd somehow got my jeans off, don't quite remember doing it, so I get them back on and pull them up and fasten my zipper and my belt. Then we both take a deep breath, and she opens the door, and we walk out into the kitchen and fall down at the table. And I'm hearing, COUGH, COUGH.

I give Terry one of my smokes and she fires it up, and I fire one up, and we sit looking at each other across the table, smoking, with these perfectly serious blown-away faces, and still neither one of us saying a word. Finally she gets up and goes to the fridge and brings us some apple juice. And we drink that. Still looking at each other and not saying a goddamn thing. My brains are starting to work again, and I'm feeling this great incredible calm and at the same time this great incredible sadness. We just sit there, oh, for about forty minutes. Then she says, "You know, Tom, Cass is a hell of a lot better. You could probably leave any day now."

I FIGURED we better haul ass out of Ethan and Terry's pretty damned fast—like it was one of those famous do-not-pass-Go moments—so I laid it on Cassandra, "Hey, babyshake, you're looking good again, and the weather's got real nice, and we got us this fine set of wheels, let's go see the sea." She gave me no argument, so we stuffed our shit into the camper and bid sayonara to Ethan and Terry and drove away into the sunset and made it as far as the vacant lot by the *Weasel* office.

What hung us up was THE REVOLUTION. When you look back on it, that trip seems like loony tunes, but it didn't at the time. Everybody was heavy into THE REVOLUTION—it was in the air, it was in the water, it was in the goddamn sun coming up in the morning. Like you'd be wandering around the Boston Common, and you'd run into the most hopeless mind-fucked blotto-paper kid you could possibly imagine, and the most subversive thing he's ever done in his life is dropping out of high school, but if you rap with him five minutes, he's talking THE REVOLUTION. Of course everybody had their own way of thinking on the subject. Now me, I figured that as time went on, there'd be more and more people on our side and less and less on theirs—because we were RIGHT, and not only that, we were YOUNGER THAN THEY WERE—and eventually we'd just take over the world. I mean, we had dope, so how could we lose? And yeah, I know it's a joke, but part of me believed it.

Well, SDS had themselves a big convention in Chicago, and Pamela the Great went to it, and when she came back, she told us all about it, I mean every fucking detail. Yeah, she brought us right up to date on THE REVOLUTION—from the perspective of the anarchist team, you dig? Cassandra thought politics was horseshit, but she got a laugh out of it too, like she used to say all the time—"What fools these mortals be!"—so she kept egging Pam to tell us more, more, more. You know, just to see how ridiculous she could get.

You think I ever got it straight? Fuck. All I ever figured out was that before the convention there was one SDS, but after the convention there was two of them—each one saying it was the real one and the other one was a bunch of assholes. One of them was the PL team and the other one wasn't. The one that wasn't was calling itself WEATHERMAN.

I say, "OK, now who the fuck is Weatherman?"

Pam starts drawing those famous FINE DISTINCTIONS, but John knows me, so he boils it down to the idiot's level. "They're mainly people in the NO and around the NO . . . That's the National Office, you know, the so-called leadership. They think the armed struggle has already started, like by the Vietnamese and other third-world peoples, and all we've got to do is jump on the bandwagon."

So what's the SDS convention got to do with why Cass and me can't take off to go see the sea? Just hang on, I'm getting to that. Well, when Pam came back to Boston, she wrote up a long rap about what went down at the convention—TELLING IT LIKE IT WAS. And that heavy SDS guy Phil Vance was practically running the *Weasel* by then, and he read it and made his pronouncement—"Yeah, can't argue with that. Yep, that's really what happened." So far so good. But then John and Pam laid out another rap about WHAT IT ALL MEANT, and Phil read that one and said it was COUNTER-REVOLUTIONARY BULLSHIT and the *Weasel* sure as hell wasn't going to print it. So John says, "Fuck you, man, there's only two editors on the *Weasel*, and Ethan's one of them and I'm the other, and we're going to print it," and Phil says, "Fuck YOU, man. This rag's run on participatory democracy, so we got to go to THE MASSES on this one. Yeah, we got to have us a motherfucking MEETING."

I was pretty sure some vital thing was still eluding me—in the big picture, you dig? I ask Pam if she's in Weatherman, and she says no fucking way is she IN Weatherman, their politics sucks shit, but at the convention she was AROUND Weatherman because she was heavy into throwing out those PL motherfuckers and Weatherman was all for that too. I say, "OK, how about Phil Vance? Is he in Weatherman?"

No, no, no, John and Pam are telling me. He's not IN Weatherman, he was AROUND Weatherman at the Convention the same as Pam was, but now that he's back in Boston, he's AROUND that New Left group at Harvard, the same as he always was, but that group is . . . OK, here's where the DISTINCTIONS start getting way too fine for me. First of all, Phil really isn't IN that group either, he's AROUND it. And then that group—you know, the one he really isn't IN? Well, they think Weatherman's bullshit, but since we're back here in Boston where the home team is PL, then they're sort of like . . . oh maybe . . . just a little bit AROUND Weatherman because they hate PL. You following any of this?

I pondered this IN and AROUND business for a long time. Yeah, I used up many a brain cell on it. And then it finally flashed on me. Suppose you got a big pile of shit by the side of the road. Well, a lot of dogs will be AROUND it, but there's only a few going to be stupid enough to get IN it.

So anyhow, Cass and me can't take off to see the sea because they're going to have their heavy-ass meeting any day now, and we've just got to be there. It's like the Wild West, right?—you got to hang around Dodge City just a little bit longer, old buddy, because WE NEED YOUR GUN. Now me, I didn't give a rat's ass, but I wanted to help out John if I could because he was a friend of mine, but of course helping out John meant helping out Pam because he figured whatever she was laying down was the Gospel. I'm pretty sure he wasn't IN her yet, but he sure as hell was AROUND her. He was just about as AROUND her as a man could get.

––––––––

PAM HAD been moving, making one of her quicksilver runs, darting neatly around the sullen lumpish objects of the world, but now, with no warning at all, she snapped to a stop. John, following, bumped into her—was blown away once again by her smallness, hard edges, her unmistakable *bones*; she reached behind her in an instinctive gesture, her hand on his wrist, both steadying him and distancing him, protecting her space. She'd been stopped by Karen Vance: "What the fuck is this shit?" She was waving a copy of Pam and John's critique of Weatherman.

John drew back another step to give the women room; he didn't hear Pam's answer, but the hard tone of her voice cut through clearly enough. The July night was unbearably hot and muggy—as oppressive as anything he remembered from West Virginia. The inside of the *Weasel* office was filling up with SDS kids; they made things worse, brought their own body heat with them. "You followed Bernardine out of the hall the same as I did," Karen said. He had no problem hearing *her*.

"Sure I followed Bernardine out of the hall." Pam's New York accent was sharp enough to score glass. "We were finally, finally, *finally* going to get those motherfuckers off our ass. *Of course* I followed Bernardine out of the hall."

Since Pam had come back from Chicago, the convention had been all she could talk about. Bernardine had split SDS, and Pam, of course, had been all for the split. John could have guessed that Pam would have backed any move to expel the mindless robots of Progressive Labor, but he'd been surprised that she'd followed crazy Bernardine—but, on second thought, maybe not too surprised. Pam might have hated Bernardine's incoherent Leninism, but (and he would never say this to her) she clearly loved Bernardine as an icon: her showgirl's figure and her miniskirts, her high sleek boots and her chutzpah. Yeah, Bernardine was damned near mythic—a woman not the least bit afraid of transforming the high dangerous charge of her sex into the usable power of leadership. Yeah, that's what turned Pam on. He couldn't imagine Pam following any *man* out of the convention hall.

"Where were your fucking objections *at the time*?" Karen was yelling, stabbing the air in front of Pam's eyes. She was a head taller than Pam; she had to lean down. "We debated this shit. What? Have you got amnesia? I remember what you said. You said Bernardine was right on . . ."

"Well, fuck. She *was* right on about PL. We were debating PL. That was damn near the most brilliant fucking speech I ever heard in my life. But *Weatherman?* Have you tried to read that crap?"

The meeting hadn't even started yet, and already the two women seemed to have opened the debate right there in front of the layout tables, so intent on confronting each other that the whole rest of the world could go fuck itself. They were supposed to be allies—both members of the BRWC—but John couldn't see the faintest sign of sisterly warmth passing between them. Even the way they looked proclaimed their radically divergent tendencies. Pam was wearing what she always wore; perhaps to match the gravity of the occasion, she'd tied her pigtails with *black* satin ribbons. Karen Vance (no, not Phil's *wife* but *the woman he lived with*) was in baggy green corduroy pants, frayed at the cuffs and worn at the knees, a furiously wrinkled plaid shirt several sizes too big for her, and—despite the heat—steel-toed construction worker's boots. Karen had a grey tired angry face that would have fit easily into a photograph of Dust Bowl survivors from the thirties; her hair was chopped off as raggedly as if she'd done the job herself with a pair of garden shears. "Yeah, it's crap," she was saying, "but so what? It was just something to get us together. From here on out, it's the action that counts."

"Jesus!" Pam exploded, turned to John as though calling on him to bear witness. "Did you hear that shit? Jesus fucking Christ, she actually said it," and turning back to Karen, "No. No no *no*. You can't have coherent practice without coherent theory. And the critique's got to be total. All partial critiques will fail as they've done in the past. The proletariat must become aware of itself as . . ."

Karen had finally registered John's presence. She shot a dark look his way—annoyed, offended—what's this *man* doing here, watching this shit go down? "Pamela, Jesus! Where the fuck do you think you are, Paris?"

"Well, where the fuck you think *you* are? Moscow? It's Narodnaya Volya, for Christ's sake. And you know how fucking successful they were. There's no excuse for ignorance. Ignorance is a motherfucking luxury we can't afford."

The small space was filling up. It felt like a steambath in there. He could have sworn that most of the kids walking in now had never set foot in the office before—but, of course, nobody was going to ask for their credentials. The members of the original *Weasel* staff weren't just outnumbered, they were lost in the crowd. The SDS forces were packing the meeting just as John had known they would. Great, he thought, we're fucked before we even start.

Taking a step toward Karen, dropping her voice, Pam said, "Why are we doing this? It's bullshit. *We can't go on sucking off other people's oppression.* How many times have I heard you say that?"

He saw Karen react to the peace overture—a softening. "Shit, Pamela, I'm not saying there's not a lot to criticize. I'm not even saying they're right. I'm just saying we shouldn't be dumping on them right now . . . that it's like counter-revolutionary. What the fuck have *we* been doing? And they're dealing with male chauvinism . . . internally."

"Oy," Pam said, rolling her eyes toward the ceiling.

Then, to John's surprise, the two women wrapped their arms around each other and hugged. Karen whispered something into Pam's ear.

Pam stepped back, disengaging, took John's hand and led him away. "What did she say to you?" he asked before he could stop himself. But they were a council, weren't they? Didn't he have the right to know?

"Fuck," Pam said, and then, bending close, echoed the gesture of Karen's whisper. "She said, 'It's not personal.' Shit, man, she ought to know better. What the fuck have we been talking about for months now? It's *always* personal."

———

THAT MEETING was something else. I'd never caught one before—like your genuine, world-famous REVOLUTIONARY MEETING—and believe me, it was highly entertaining. And it went on for HOURS. Phil Vance was the referee, and he started off by laying it on us what we were supposed to deal with. Like the *Weasel* had always been into that good old freewheeling debate, but, dig it, some of the brothers and sisters were having themselves some serious doubts about Pam and Ray's rap—whether it was CORRECT to publish it what with all the shit going down in THIS MOTHERFUCKING REPRESSIVE IMPERIALIST COUNTRY.

Now if anybody had asked my opinion, I would have pointed out that we've got free speech guaranteed by the Constitution of the United States—a document much neglected in recent years—but any fool could plainly see that rapping about the Constitution would get you nowhere that night. Well, you know who had the right idea? Ethan. He didn't even bother to show up. He said the same thing he always said—"If somebody's going to shoot me, I just ain't going to come around." Terry had been hammering at him, like, "For Christ's sake, babe, that rag's ours. We just can't let those dudes take it away from us," and he'd say, "You can't lose if you ain't playing," and, "There's nothing to defend," and other acid-head shit like that. I think he'd got to the point where putting out a newspaper was just too much old-fashioned WORK for him. Yeah, in his head he was already living up in THE LIBERATED ZONE, heavy into the ganja and watching the weeds grow. But Terry had put a lot of herself into the *Weasel*, so that gave her yet one more item to add to her list of all the reasons why Ethan was an asshole.

So, anyhow, the meeting. You never saw so many people in the *Weasel* office—everywhere, sitting on the floor, crammed along the walls, hanging from the rafters. There was a lot of talk about OUR GALLANT ALLIES, THE VIETNAMESE, which pissed me right off, and then we got down to the debate. The first up for our side was John—"Ray" they was calling him—and he laid it on them about SDS in the old days and how everybody doing their own thing was where it was at. And he argued against what he called THE LENINIST MODEL. What the fuck's that? I don't know. But I guess if you're operating with THE LENINIST MODEL you get to put the limits on the old free speech, and he didn't want any limits. He said if somebody disagreed with what he and Pam laid down, then they could write their own motherfucking article, and the two sides could slug it out in print—like THE MASSES could read all about it and decide. And then John passed the ball off to Pam, and she was TOTALLY INCOMPREHENSIBLE, which impressed everybody no end.

The chicks were especially impressed. I should say something about the chicks. The ones that were heavy into woman's lib were all clumped together and dressed up like they'd been hired on as somebody's demolition crew, and when any of the dudes was talking, they watched him like a hawk, and the minute he said ONE WORD they didn't like, they kicked into this chant—FIGHT MALE CHAUVINISM, FIGHT MALE CHAUVINISM. They even did it to poor old Phil. At one point he got so frustrated he said, "Would any of the WOMEN like to chair the meeting?" and they all went, oh, no, man, no problem, you're doing great, but that didn't stop them from hitting him with the old chant the next time he slipped. And so what it came down to was that if you had the misfortune to have balls hanging between your legs, it was real hard to lay out much of a rap.

Yeah, we had us a lot of cheerleading that night. It took me right back to high school. We didn't just have us FIGHT MALE CHAUVINISM, we had HO HO HO CHI MINH, and we had POWER TO THE PEOPLE, and I don't know what all. And there's this moment when Pam's rapping, and she's bad-mouthing Weatherman and she says, "We've got to mean what we say and say what we mean," and that's just too much for Cassandra, so she starts up this chant—I MEANT WHAT I SAID AND I SAID WHAT I MEANT, AN ELEPHANT'S FAITHFUL ONE HUNDRED PERCENT. It was pretty goddamn hilarious, although you probably had to be there. So that little handful of us—the old-time long-hair whacked-out weirdo freaks—and we're all sitting together, and we're stamping our feet and clapping our hands and chanting away, I MEANT WHAT I SAID AND I SAID WHAT I MEANT. Even Pam thought it was funny. Yeah, it cracked her right up. And the heavy SDS dudes were all exchanging these disgusted looks—like see what we got to put up with? Jesus, these goddamned irresponsible hippie assholes.

Well, after—oh, maybe after the first nineteen or twenty hours, it was starting to get real clear that what was going to decide things was which side had the heaviest chicks. Now, the heavy chick for the other team was Karen Vance, and . . . Well, you remember, she was living with Phil—no, no, no, not really IN marriage but just sort of AROUND it—but the way they were acting there in that meeting, if you didn't know them, you'd think they hardly knew each other. So that gave me the very strong suspicion that the fix was in. And our heavy chick was Pamela the Great, and she was pretty good. Like she could run that mouth of hers a hundred miles a minute, and she was checked out on THE REVOLUTION from one end to the other, and she could cite you chapter and verse.

———

PAMELA KEPT moving as she talked—pacing off the length of the room, deliberately, as though measuring her steps. John knew that she was trying to stay ahead of her nerves, and she seemed to be doing OK so far. "Lenin made Stalin possible," she was saying, "but the honest mistakes of a genuine proletarian movement are a million times better than all the cleverness of any motherfucking vanguard."

He was so freaked on her behalf he was sick with it. He had to remind himself that she was the same girl who'd once been able to do thirty-two fouettés, so it shouldn't be a problem for her to maintain control of her *appearance*. She was looking directly into people's eyes, taking a few seconds with each of them, forcing them to connect with her personally. "Weatherman says follow third-world leadership. Weatherman says the revolution's already started, but *you've* got nothing to contribute. Fuck, no, you're just a white middle-class asshole. Maybe you're even a woman, and then you're *really* nothing. Yeah, chicks, get on the bandwagon. Support the real revolutionaries. The blacks, the Vietnamese. Yeah, it's always somebody else. Well, that's bullshit."

Now she stepped back, putting distance between herself and the crowd. If that small area in front of Ethan's desk was her stage, she'd just taken command of it; now she could address the collective, the whole. "We've got to start from where *we* live . . . yeah, with subjectivity . . . the *wildest dreams* of subjectivity. But we can't stop there. We've got to create situations where the revolutionary moment spills out of its container. And dig it, a Leninist cadre is a container, a motherfucking jail. Fuck Lenin. He was a pig. Fuck the vanguard. We've got to do it ourselves. Our brothers and sisters in France came *close* to doing it, and the next time they are going to do it. And *we're* going to do it. That's why we criticized Weatherman. They've got an incoherent critique, a partial critique. They don't want enough, but we want the whole fucking world. We want the world and we want it now. All power to the councils."

John could hear murmuring here and there. He could see that Pam had got to some of those crazy SDS kids—especially the women. Ah, some of them looked so goddamned *young*, and he could feel their puzzlement—and then he flashed on what was going down. She'd got to them for the wrong reason. They were asking themselves the fatal question: "Is she more revolutionary than Weatherman, *more revolutionary than I am?*" Because, in the current climate, the only possible position to take was the one that looked the most revolutionary. Oh, fuck, John thought, it's all hopeless.

KAREN VANCE walked to the front of Ethan's desk, occupied it— taking center stage. Her appearance—grim and serious and tired— opened her statement. "The Vietnamese are winning," she said.

The chant came smashing instantly back: *Ho Ho Ho Chi Minh, the NLF is going to win!* Smiling, she waited until it stopped. "You know why the Vietnamese are winning?" she said. "The pigs may have the technology. The pigs may have the planes and the bombs and the bullets and the napalm. But the Vietnamese have got the politics."

It was that quick, John thought—she had them all in the pocket of her old worn baggy pants. Her height, her manner, her absolute self-assurance—she made Pam seem, in contrast, small and strident. It shouldn't come down to the goddamned image, but of course it did—maybe it always did—and yeah, on that particular night, with that particular crowd, eye makeup and hair ribbons were not going to do it. No, Pam couldn't do a trip like Bernardine's. It took Bernardine to do Bernardine.

"We've heard plenty from our anarchist comrades," Karen was saying. "You know, it's funny how if you look at it closely, anarchism can sound like liberalism. Just kind of disguised. Or like hippie bullshit. Yeah, it can sound like a big incoherent slithery blob of nothing. Like, 'Fuck leaders, man, you can't organize *me*. Yeah, I'll come to the peace demonstration maybe . . . like carry a candle maybe . . . if I'm not too stoned.'"

Oh, she's good, John thought, horrified. Everybody was laughing. Of course they were. Everybody needed a good laugh.

"Fuck this shit!" A voice. Too loud. A *male* voice. Who the hell was that? Spinning around, John saw that it was Tom Parker.

Tom was already up and moving. "You fucking assholes."

Nobody seemed able to react. Stunned, frozen. And now Tom was up there in front of everybody. Yelling. "You know what? You're fucking assholes, that's what. Our fucking goddamn allies. Jesus fuck."

Phil: "Hey, Tom. Hey, Tom, now, just a minute, man . . ."

"Want me to tell you about our goddamn fucking allies? Jesus, fuck."

"Hey, there's a speaker's list," Phil said, stepped forward. Then, in an explosion of movement too fast too see, Phil was careening backward, arms flailing, losing his footing. What the hell? Had Tom hit him? Shoved him?

Phil went smack into the crowd; he was caught, steadied, held upright—his eyes popping, his mouth hanging open. Already a big Harvard dude was coming to his defense, rushing Tom, and this time, John saw the motion. Tom sidestepped. Made a small, neat, deft flick with the side of his hand. Delivered to the front of the throat. That huge guy was nailed, stopped, shocked to nothingness, soundlessly, his eyes spilling with tears. Jesus. Heavy. John's heart was beating him silly.

"Stop it!" Karen Vance was yelling. "Stop it, stop it. Let him talk. He's got a right to talk."

Talk? Tom was already laying it down. "Our goddamned fucking gallant allies! Jesus. Let's say there's some dude been playing ball with the Yanks. And Charlie comes by to have a little chat with him, you dig? Well, you get yourself some bamboo, and you sharpen it up real good, and you roll the point around in shit. And you know where you shove that goddamned thing? If it's his wife and daughters, it goes up their cunts. If it's his sons, it goes up their assholes. You want to shove it up far enough to do the job, but you don't want to shove it up too far because you want them to take their time on the way out, you dig? And he's got to watch that evil shit going down, you dig? And then they gouge out his eyes and cut off his balls and leave him there *to think about it*. You getting the picture? That's Charlie I'm talking about. Our gallant Vietnamese ally."

What had happened to mellow? To the joker, the trickster, the whacked-out slack-limbed clown? Gone. Not a trace of him left. Transformed, pacing, smashing one fist into the big open palm of his other hand. "Jesus! Listen up, assholes, because I'm giving you the straight scoop now. Don't matter who's doing it—evil shit is evil shit. *They're* doing evil shit, *we're* doing evil shit, and we got to stop this evil shit. People want to go to demonstrations, that's just great. They want to carry candles, that's just great. *Because we got to stop this evil shit.*

"It's their fucking country over there . . . you got that right. If they want to fuck it up, that's their right. Yeah, and we've got to get our asses out of there. Got to deal with *our own* motherfucking country, because . . . Jesus, you assholes, listen up. Our liberties are going down the tube. Yeah, we're flushing them away at a great rate. 'Congress shall make *no law* abridging the freedom of speech.' It don't say, 'not many laws.' It don't say, 'Congress has got to be careful what laws.' You want to hear it again? *'Congress shall make no law abridging the freedom of speech.'* And that takes care of that, you dig? We should have got that one over in like five minutes.

"And while we're on the topic, you assholes want to hear another one? *The Congress shall have the power to declare War.* You seen any declaration of War? Fuck me. Damned if I've seen one either. Jesus, you assholes, what are you doing rapping about Stalin and Lenin and Russia and France and motherfucking Nam? Why don't you try rapping about America? Open your eyes. Everywhere you look, evil shit going down."

Tom launched into another word run and then stopped. In mid-sentence. Gulping air. His eyes darted across the surface of the crowd. For the first time, he seemed to be able to see the immobilized faces in front of him. He made a pushing gesture—as though trying to free himself from yards of stinking fabric. "Oh, fuck this shit," he said, and walked.

————

TO THIS day I don't know what came over me. Well, you know what was getting next to me? It was all this shit about OUR GALLANT ALLIES, THE VIETNAMESE. That's Charlie they're talking about. Hell, I had a good healthy respect for Charlie, but he wasn't MY gallant ally, and I guess I just flat-out lost it. Like the next thing you know, WHAM, there I am up in front of everybody shooting off my big mouth, and then I start hearing this little voice in my head, and it goes, "Hey, Parker, what the fuck do you think you're doing?" All of a sudden I catch up to myself, and there I am right smack in the middle of this dead silence with everybody staring at me. Yep, here he is, folks, the FUCKED-UP VIETNAM VET FOAMING OUT RIGHT BEFORE YOUR EYES.

So I just walked out of there. Like I'm a couple blocks away, and Cass is running after me. "Tommy! Come on, man. Slow down." I grind to a halt, and she says, "Shit, that was beautiful."

Well, I don't know how beautiful it was. I was pretty sure I hadn't scored any points for our team, not to mention the fact that I'd probably pissed off a number of my regular customers. And I was thinking, OK, Parker, you're coming up against it. You really can't trust yourself, can you?

———

"MOST OF us here tonight are revolutionary communists," Karen said, "and there's a world revolution going on at this very minute, an armed struggle against American pig imperialism."

After Tom had given up the stage, she'd done what no one else had been prepared to do—addressed the howling vacuum he'd left behind and addressed it with absolute authority. She'd told them that American servicemen were victims of the war as much as the Vietnamese. She'd told them that Mao had been right—a revolution was not a tea party.

"And that brother was right too . . . about one thing. All that crap about freedom we learned in school . . . well, that's been exposed for what it is. Liberal pig bullshit. We only have as much freedom as the pigs can afford to let us have. And that's not much. The repression's coming down, brothers and sisters. It's here."

Karen sliced the air with her stiffened fingers. "Our phones are tapped. People are going to jail. People are dying. The Attorney General of the United States is talking about putting us in concentration camps. And there's agents everywhere now. There's agents *in here tonight*, and don't you forget it. Some of us here tonight are going to do jail time because of the agents in here tonight, so we can't afford any more of this jive-ass shit."

If I was a scared kid, John thought, I'd want to be hearing a voice exactly like that. A voice that knows exactly what it's talking about—a voice that knows *the truth.* "We've got to have good politics," she was saying, "and that's what we're doing here tonight. We're here to decide whether or not the *Weasel* should publish an article. Either by itself or along with some response to it . . . what good liberals would call 'the other side.' And those are political questions. Let's not lose track of that.

"That article is a criticism of Weatherman. Just like our anarchist comrades, I read Weatherman. Just like them, I think there's a lot of crap in it. But there's one central point that's true. The Vietnamese are winning. And the question is, do we want to help them or not? Are we going to be part of the solution or part of the problem? OK, so what are *we* doing? The bombs keep falling. The Vietnamese keep dying. More American servicemen are getting killed . . . or fucked up like the brother we just heard from. And are we just going to sit back and criticize somebody who's trying to do something about it? Is that a revolutionary act or only an excuse for our own middle-class wimpiness?

"Of course SDS is going to make some mistakes, but if you want to make an omelet, you've got to crack a few eggs. And dig it, here's the main thing I want to say. The pigs can take care of themselves. There's lots of people working for the pig capitalist press who can criticize Weatherman. And they will. Am I saying we should agree with everything in Weatherman? Oh, hell no. Now's the time when we've got to get our shit together, and that means debate. Ongoing struggle. But I think it's bullshit to criticize a revolutionary organization *in a public statement.* Crap like that just helps the pigs. And I, for one, will have nothing to do with it."

ALL THE windows in Pam's apartment were open, but there wasn't even a puff of a breeze. Perched on the edge of one of her basket chairs, doing nothing more strenuous than watching her, John had to keep wiping the sweat off his face, but she'd hidden herself away inside a thick blue sweatshirt that said *Columbia University Athletics.* She sat, huddled, her knees drawn up to her chest, drinking her second cup of hot tea, awkwardly smoking one of John's cigarettes. He wished she'd switch to dope but didn't say so. "Motherfuckers," she said.

They'd been purged. The meeting had voted, by a large margin, not to publish their critique, but it hadn't stopped there. Ethan and John had been voted out of their positions as editors; they'd been replaced by Phil and Karen Vance. An entirely new editorial board had been elected. Not a single member of the original *Weasel* collective was on it. What he didn't say to her—what he had no intention of saying to her—was that he was almost glad. It made everything *clear*.

She was talking in short telegraphic bursts, but he could supply the missing links: "Fragmenting. A plague. Locusts. The first-born. Fuck . . . We keep saying, 'Come on, it's just more male-dominated bullshit,' but they keep going, 'The Vietnamese, the Vietnamese.' Well, shit, you heard her . . . She's going to drop out of the Collective, I just know it. Maybe Judy and Miriam too. Leaving us crazy man-hating bitches behind. No, that's not funny, is it . . . ? Why did she . . . ? Weatherman? Spectacular show of opposition. Easily recuperated . . . With every split, you lose the chance to . . . Like *the dialectic*, you dig? But it's easier just to say fuck you and walk away."

She stubbed out her cigarette, leaving most of it unsmoked. "She's sleeping with Ben Pavalick, did I tell you that?"

"Ben Pavalick?" he said. "Who the fuck's Ben Pavalick?"

"Weatherman, that's who."

"Now wait a minute. Karen Vance is sleeping with some Weatherman dude?"

"Right on. And like Weatherman's into smashing monogamy, so guess who gets fucked . . . as in *fucked over?* The women, right? As usual . . . Yeah, fuck theory, she's going to follow her pussy. Oh, Jesus, what a vile thing to say. If a man said that, I'd motherfucking kill him. But it's true. Oh, *fuck*."

She was crying. All out, full tilt, her face pressed into her knees. He took the teacup from her hand, set it down. He wanted to touch her but didn't know if he should. Sometimes when he tried to touch her, she shot away like a struck billiard ball. But he couldn't stand it—had to do something even if it was wrong. He allowed his hand to rest lightly on her shoulder. She seized his fingers and held them. Her skin was cold and wet. "Oy," she said, "I bet you didn't know you were getting such a weepy girl."

He hadn't known that he'd got a girl at all. Yes, they might be a council—she kept saying that they were—but it hadn't changed much of anything between them, or hadn't changed anything *enough*, and he was beginning to resent the politics that seemed to separate them even as it united them. "Pamela," he said, "do you want to eat something?" For days, he hadn't seen her eat anything that a rabbit wouldn't eat.

She looked up at him, her face streaked with black mascara tears, and he felt the full impact of the scary blast she was aiming at him. He expected her to say, "Fuck off, man," but, after a weighted pause, she said: "Your analysis is absolutely *correct*, comrade. I've got to come down." She smiled slightly. "This is motherfucking insane. Make me some oatmeal, OK?"

He found the steel-cut oats easily enough. She'd labeled everything. "Tom broke through the dreadful passivity," she said, "but we couldn't respond. We were frozen, man. *I* was frozen. That was the revolutionary moment . . . if we could have met his subjectivity with our subjectivity."

"What?" he said stupidly. He was stopped in her kitchen, the jar of oatmeal stuck in his hands, staring at her across the full length of her apartment. She was still huddled up like a child in the basket chair. What the hell was she talking about? Did she honest to God believe that they could have started the revolution right there on the spot if they'd done the right thing?

"It was our passivity that allowed Karen to impose a correct line," she said. "We've been trained for that. Dig it, the ego has to become masochistic in order to survive . . . That's how power maintains itself."

"What should we have done?"

He kept waiting for the answer. "Pam?" he said.

Her eyes met his. She was smiling slightly. *"Pam?"* he said.

"Let's seize the paper."

"What?"

"Just one issue. *Our* issue. It'd be the perfect *détournement* on those assholes."

He understood her immediately. He didn't want to do it.

"Yeah, so they voted you out, but fuck that shit. You've still got a key to the office, don't you?"

———

AFTER THAT, I'd pretty well had it with THE REVOLUTION. Like John was the only one that made any sense, and I figured all the rest of those assholes were running for Sheriff. Yeah, and it was long past time for me and Cass to grab us a little R and R out in some picturesque locale far far away on the edge of the deep blue sea. Unfortunately, before we could make our break, there was this perennial problem with the coin, and so, yet once again, I did what I always did when in dire straits—fell by to see my old pal, Bobby Lyons.

Cass won't even set foot in his place. She's got a book, she says, she'll just wait for me, so he buzzes me in, and the whole banana-split scene's still playing, like I don't know if anybody ever slept in that damn place—crystal city, right?—and we go in his bedroom and shut the door, and he lays a capsule on the table. It's just a capsule, right? I mean it's day-glo orange, could be strychnine for all I know, but he wants to fuck with my head over it, so just the way I'm supposed to, I ask him what it is. He hisses at me like a snake—"Aaaaasssssid."

"Is it any good?"

"Taste and ye shall know."

"Not at the moment. Just TELL me."

"Your brain's going to look like a GI omelet."

I ask him the price and the price is low. The price is EXTREMELY low. "You must be making this shit yourself," I say.

He giggles hysterically for a while. Then he says, "Yeah, fuck, lucked out, got me a real good cook. Ain't no recipe he don't know, and he uses all the finest ingredients. Yeah, you could say he's a motherfucking CHEF."

I'm doing my arithmetic, thinking that I can mark it up a couple hundred percent to dealers, mark it up even more on the street—like I don't even know what this motherfucking day-glo shit is yet, but in my head I'm already dealing it. It's an incredible price. And like he knows exactly what I'm thinking. "That's just the price to YOU, Tommy."

I say, "Can you do me a thousand caps up front? You'll see the bread in a week or two." It's a joke, right?

But he says, "No problem, darling. It's because I love you. But just don't mention our little transactions to anybody, if you follow me." I look at that goofy smile of his and all of a sudden I KNOW just how big he's got.

I walked out of there with a thousand caps of so-called acid. I wasn't about to play guinea pig with any weird drug I'd got from Bobby Lyons, so I went straight over to Ethan's, laid a cap on him, and he ate it right up. Well, he tripped out heavy for a day—like the whole goddamn twenty-four hours—and when he got coherent again, he pronounced it SOME RIGHTEOUS SHIT, although he said it was a little on the speedy side. I sold him half my stash— which did my heart good because he thought I was nothing but a jerk-off, not a real man of business, you know, like him. "Fuck," he says, "where'd you get these goddamned things?"

I just winked at him. "Friendly neighborhood source." Pissed him right off. And then I unloaded the rest with some street dealers I knew, saved like forty or fifty caps to sell as the spirit moved me, went back and paid off Lyons, and lo and behold, I was heavy into the bread. So Cass and I should have been hitting it on down the road, right? Wrong. So why's that? Turns out that there's another major development in THE REVOLUTION. Now we've got to seize the goddamned newspaper.

———

JOHN WOKE and saw a girl. She was an inexplicable silhouette, small head and slender torso set inside a black rectangular frame, lit from behind by harsh flaring yellow light. He knew that he'd been dreaming, knew that he was awake, but time had come untied, was flapping loose, and he didn't have a clue where he was. The rank, muddy smell of the Ohio River was a dream, surely, created from the mold and dust and cobwebs and old unpainted wood of the loft in the *Weasel* office. Yes, this had to be real—the stacks of unsold back issues piled up next to him; he was using one of the stacks for a pillow—and the girl looking in at him had to be Cassandra standing on the ladder. "What's happening?" he said.

"Hey, hero," she said, "I couldn't tell you."

What the fuck was he doing? He had no business being asleep. They were in the middle of *an action*, for Christ's sake. When he'd climbed up into the loft, all he'd wanted to do was cool out for a while. "Jesus, was I ever down," he said. "Dreaming. I can still feel the . . . like the filaments. But it's all vague now. I was dreaming I was back home."

"Home? Where's that?"

Good question. "Shit," he said. "What time is it?"

"Beats me. I've given up on time." She climbed into the loft with him. "It's getting light out, so it must be another fucking day. Move over," and stretched out next to him. "You know, Dupre, that old paranoia? Well, sometimes it turns out . . ."

"What's Pam doing?"

"Oh, Pam. Right. The center of the universe. Working on her page, I don't know. What did you think she'd be doing . . . handstands? You fall for the weirdest girls, you know that? You got a smoke?"

"Yeah, sure." He pounded two out of his pack, lit them both, and handed her one. When he'd climbed up here, his own page had been laid out, and about half the front page. When had that been? After three, nearly four—the hour of the wolf. If it was daylight, they must be damned near ready to go to the printer. "What weird girls?"

"You fell for me, didn't you?"

THUNG: reverberations, echoes. "Yeah," he said, "I sure did." And maybe Cassandra had been in the dream—or maybe Pamela. There'd been a hard-edged dangerous feeling to her like Pamela, but she'd also been the girl who'd been in his dreams forever, the one who was never quite there, not quite in the car when he reached for her, and not quite in his bed, and not quite at the end of the street when he got there, running. "Well, it was mutual," she said.

Now it was summer again, the stink of his own sweat in a loft in an old crappy building in Cambridge, Massachusetts, and down in the office at the bottom of the ladder was *the real* in all of its nasty hard-edged immediacy—an action, the revolution, a whole bunch of shit that needed to be done. Pamela was down there. But here he was being drawn back into the seductive past. He teetered a moment, not sure which way to go, but he felt a nebulous emotional blur pulling at him. He couldn't let it go. Fuck the real.

"Everything feels connected," he said. "Jesus. I can't quite remember the dream, but the *feeling* of it . . . Summer. Like that Rilke poem: 'Lord, the summer was so full.' That thick heavy feeling of summer . . . flowers, the mosquitoes, the smell of the river . . . Like something's right on the edge of happening . . . God, Cass, do you remember the smell of the river? . . . Hey," and finally catching up to her, "what do you mean *it was mutual?*"

"Mutual means mutual, asshole. Of course I remember the smell of the river."

They were lying on their backs side by side. He turned to look at her. Those clear grey eyes—he'd always thought of them as familiar, but they didn't look familiar now. "God, you're nuts," she said.

Time.

"OK," she said, "let's go back and wallow in it. That's always good for a laugh. Make ourselves feel really good, right? Ah, our lost youth . . . how motherfucking sweet it was, right? Listen, there's something . . ."

"It *was* sweet."

"Sure. Sure, it was sweet. You think I'm saying it wasn't?"

"Jesus, the summer you were fifteen, I dreamed of you night after night . . ."

"Oh, fuck. Oh, yeah. The summer I was fifteen. Heavy-duty summer. Motherfucking ridiculous is what it was . . . Hey, listen to me for a minute, OK? I called this chick . . ."

He waited for her to continue, but she didn't. She sighed. "Shit. Of course it was sweet."

She dragged on her cigarette, was seized by a spasm of coughing. For a minute, he didn't think she was going to stop. "You OK?" he said.

"Oh, yeah, I'm the picture of health . . . Jesus, Dupre, you piss me off sometimes. Like the old days when you and William would . . . In some ways you haven't changed a bit. You're so full of shit. You think you're the only one with feelings. Like it's all one big fucking Rilke poem, and you're the hero, and the chicks in your life are just . . . fuck, I don't know. Bit players. Window dressing. The summer I was fifteen, I was horny as a river rat, and I didn't even know it. I just walked around constantly in this state of exquisite agony. You could have fucked me any time you wanted, you know."

The sloping ceiling over his head was too low for him to sit upright, but he pushed himself up onto his elbow and looked down at her. "What?"

"What do you mean, *what?* I thought you knew. Didn't you know it? . . . Do we really have to go back and wallow in this shit? . . . It was a weird scene, man. It felt inevitable from the first time I kissed you. You kept falling by and making out with me, and Jesus, man, I'd never even had a goddamned *date*. What were my parents thinking? They must have been insane. Like certifiable. Yeah, the legendary summer I was fifteen. And we'd go out to the park all the time and lay there on a blanket for *hours*. And if I was lucky, once in a blue moon, I'd get to come. But most nights I just went home and jerked off."

"Jesus Christ, Cass, why are you telling me this *now?*"

"I don't know. Why shouldn't I? It's like . . . Well, OK, the summer I was fifteen is not your private property. I was there too."

John fell back, lay there, smoking, staring at the cobwebs and dirty beams a few feet above his eyes. He could feel his heart slamming his ribs. "I was scared of sex," he said.

"Yeah, me too."

"I didn't have a clue how to do it."

"You think I did? We could have figured it out."

"Don't tell me these things. Jesus."

"Why the hell shouldn't I? It's so fucking long ago, man. So, OK, asshole, have you made it with her yet?"

He couldn't answer.

"You give me a royal pain in the ass," she said. "It's almost like you enjoy being miserable. She really digs you, man. Look, chicks can read each other a lot better than guys can read them, and she's . . ."

He was left hanging in the middle of Cassandra's stopped sentence. Pamela was what? Yes, *the real* had caught up with him all right. His antennae were fully extended. He needed every clue he could get.

"It's all there," Cassandra said, "like obvious. It's in the way she looks at you, the way she touches you. You and your goddamned fantasies. Well, there she is, man, flesh and blood, hair ribbons and all. She's perfect for you. Christ, Dupre, she must think you're the biggest tease in the world. So are you going to make it with her? Or are you just going to spend the rest of your life jerking off to pictures of my little sister?"

"But, Jesus, nobody ever tells you how to *do it*. How the hell do you *do it*?"

"Look, put a pillow under her ass so she's tilted up a bit, and then you just shove it in between her legs, right? It's not particularly complicated. And she'll help you. Just make sure she's good and wet first. And if you lose your hard-on, don't take it like the end of the world. Just do some more weed and try it again."

But since Pam had come back from Chicago, she'd been on the dark side of the moon, and he felt again the absolute *certainty* of Cassandra. "You wouldn't want to *show me*, would you?"

"Oh, hell. Sure I could. Of course I could. It's be easy. But . . . Oh, Jesus. Listen, John, we're completely out of phase now. I'm sick of men. I'm sick of sex. Sometimes I have more fun blowing my nose."

"What are you doing with Tom then?"

"He makes me laugh . . . But you know what sex does, don't you? It messes up perfectly good friendships."

"Does it?"

"Yeah. Every time. Without fail. And right now I'd rather have a friend than somebody else to screw me. Friends are rare. I can always get laid."

"Well, I can't."

"You are an asshole."

He was beginning to believe her. Maybe it was possible. "Cassandra," he said, "where's the clitoris?"

"Don't you know? Oh shit." She laughed until she started to

cough. She hugged herself, squeezed her chest and coughed, her body contracting.

"You better do something," he said. "Could you maybe not smoke for a while? That sounds awful."

"Yeah, fuck."

"Maybe you need to take antibiotics or something."

"Yeah, probably. But then I'd have to see a doctor, wouldn't I? And I'm so fucking paranoid . . . Well, shit, I could make up some off-the-wall name for myself the way you do. *Candy Necropolis.* How do you like that one?"

He laughed. "Listen," she said, "there's a warrant out for my ass in California."

"No shit?"

"Yeah, no shit. You better believe no shit. This ain't just the old paranoia. This one's for real. I called this chick I know back there, about the only one I can trust. Or maybe can trust. Who the fuck knows? I told her I was working at the Bunny Club in Vegas. It was the most motherfucking ridiculous thing I could think of. Don't even know if there *is* a Bunny Club in Vegas, but there's bound to be one, right?

"I just couldn't go on *not knowing.* Yeah, the bust came down on the whole fucking lot of them. They're all out on bail. Groovy, huh? That's what you can buy when you're heavy into the coin . . . out on bail and mucho lawyers. And boy oh boy, are they not happy with me. Sweet Andrew especially. Yeah, he couldn't take the joke. He'd like to do me some serious damage, that's what she told me. There's a warrant out for me too, but he thinks it might be phony . . . that, like, maybe I did do a number with the pigs. And he can't get behind the fact that I ripped off his cute little ass, and . . . Well, you know, *serious* damage. Oh, he'd never do it himself. He's kind of squeamish. But he'd hire it done. He wouldn't think twice about it."

"Did you tell Tom any of this?"

"Are you kidding?"

"Why not?"

"Why should I? The less people that know about it, the better."

"You just told *me.*"

"Shit, Dupre, talking to you's like talking to myself."

"Jesus, I don't know what to say."

"Well, there's nothing *to* say, right? But I've got no reason to be in Boston. Like it's not a place anybody would guess. You could stick a pin anywhere in a map of the States and that'd make just about as much sense. Anyhow, I keep telling myself that. Fuck, I don't know. It's all a freak show, right? Ringling Brothers . . . Come on, let's get out of here." But she made no move to do it.

"OK, the clitoris," she said. She unzipped her jeans, pushed them down. She wasn't wearing anything underneath. "Go ahead. Feel around for it."

He was too shocked to do anything but what she'd told him. "Where?"

"Right in there."

"All I can feel is hair."

"Up higher. You've got to open it up a bit. That's right. Inside there. Spread it open."

"That little thing? There?"

"What did you expect, a doorknob? Yeah, that's it."

"Amazing."

"Hey. Be gentle. It's really sensitive. Just run your finger around and around very lightly. Yeah. That's exactly right. Very nice. And if you keep doing that, she'll start to get wet. Then you reach into her and get your fingers wet, and ah . . . Yeah, just keep doing that. Yeah, that's it, you're doing just fine. Don't be in a hurry. Girls don't get turned on as fast as boys, so don't try to come into her till she's sopping wet. And she'll be right there with you, you know. You can *talk* to her."

"Jesus, Cass, you give me hope."

She arched, lifted her pelvis clear of the floor, worked her jeans back on, and zipped them up. "Well, shit, man," she said, "isn't that my main function in life . . . to give you hope?"

TOM AND Terry had been standing close together at one end of the layout tables. John saw them step quickly back from each other. Tom's eyes found Cassandra. "Hey, old buddy, what's happening?"

"I couldn't tell you."

"Well, shit, babe, if you can't tell me, nobody can."

Ethan was sitting on the floor, his back propped against the wall, his legs splayed out into the room like dead wood. His head had fallen to one side; he was snoring. John stepped over the legs. But where the hell was Pamela?

Terry yawned elaborately—exaggerating it? Her curly black hair was hanging in her face. John looked at the frieze she'd been constructing around Ethan's article, a Kurt Schwitters insanity like the collages on her kitchen walls—naked women, bombs, dogs and cats, dead Vietnamese, bits of copy from the *Boston Globe*, fashion models, bursts of napalm, chicken legs and hot dogs. "Will it print?" she said.

"Oh, yeah," John said, "no problem."

At the end of the table where Pam had been working there was no one at all. Her absence vibrated far back of words—trippy, ominous. It was like—what? Looking at the favorite chair of someone who's died? Just *remembering* that they'd died—and a wispy filament of dream still left, some connection. Dreaming of a dead person? "I think she went for a walk, man," Terry said. He looked up and saw her dark eyes. OK, witch, he told her silently, stop reading my mind.

He looked at Pam's completed work. It was something she'd written quickly just to fill up the back page, but it must have been shit she'd been thinking about—although he'd never heard her talk about any of it. The only illustration was a single photograph, a mushroom cloud. His eyes ran down the copy. Additives in bread, nuclear waste, second-generation breeder reactors, DDT in plant life, fragile pelican eggs. The last sentence read: "The denial of the feminine is the destruction of the planet."

He stepped through the open door of the office and out onto the sidewalk. The advance notice of dawn was visible as the most minimal release of darkness toward blue. A small slender figure was walking toward the office—Pamela. She saw him and waved. What he was feeling was so mixed, so elusive, so goddamned *poignant* that he didn't know whether to call it joy or despair. She waved again, and he saw now that the gesture was not a greeting but a demand. He began to walk quickly toward her, then broke into a jog to match hers. She caught his hands. "Phil's onto us," she said.

"What? How do you know?"

"I saw him drive by."

"Shit. What the fuck's he doing up in the middle of the night?" The office, of course, was lit up like a Christmas tree.

They heard the sound of tires, and there, right on cue, was Phil's old maroon Volvo turning at the far end of the block. It pulled up on the other side of the street. The headlights went out. John and Pam ran back to the office, plunged through the door. "We've got a visitor." John said.

Terry kicked Ethan's feet. He made an explosive sound like "ungh," his mustaches flaring, and jerked upright.

Phil was standing next to his car, staring at them from across the street. Now, more than ever, he looked like a nineteenth-century shopkeeper—puzzled and arcane. He crossed the street. John stepped back out of the doorway.

"What the fuck *is* this?" Phil said. His eyes were darting around. Nobody said anything. He walked along the layout table, checked out the paste-up. "You anarchist clowns," he said sadly.

Ethan pushed himself to his feet, stretched. "Anybody know this shithead?" he said.

"I think it goes to Harvard," Terry said.

"You better get your ass out of here," John said to Phil in a low conspiratorial tone, trying to pack in a whole extra layer of meaning: *Come on, pick up the vibe here, man. This could get heavy.*

Phil continued along the layout table until he came to John and Pam's critique of Weatherman. "Fuck," he said. He stood, reading it. "Fuck, fuck, fuck. What the fuck you . . . We voted you *down*, man."

He stared at the copy a moment longer, then reached out and grabbed the laid-out page. Pam was on him instantly, one of her small hands clamping his wrist. "Phil. Don't." Their eyes locked.

"Would you folks like this dude removed?" Tom inquired from the far side of the room.

"Put it down," Pam said.

"Fuck you," Phil said. "We debated this. We had a vote."

Tom stepped closer, said directly to Pam: "How about you, sweet stuff? Would you like this dude removed?"

Pam looked into Tom's eyes. John couldn't read her expression. "Yeah," she said flatly, "remove him."

Tom took a few leisurely steps around the layout table. "Come on, old buddy," he said to Phil, "you and me's going to take a little walk."

Phil let the page drop. Pam stepped out of the way. "Check out the dawn, you dig?" Tom said, smiling. "Contemplate the deep imponderable mysteries of life."

"Fuck you," Phil said. He took off his glasses, folded them up, and slipped them into his pocket.

"Shit, you don't need to do that," Tom said. "Mellow, you dig? Love, peace, and brotherhood . . . all that good shit." In the friendliest possible way, Tom let his hand fall onto Phil's shoulder.

"Fuck you," Phil said, batted the hand away and took a swing at Tom's smile.

With hardly any effort at all, Tom stepped aside just enough to let Phil's fist smash the empty air. With the assurance of a master carpenter driving a tack, Tom snapped his own fist directly onto the point of Phil's chin. Phil's head jerked back; his teeth made a distinct CLICK. His knees began to buckle. Tom caught him around the waist and hustled him toward the door.

John whipped the door open. Tom assisted Phil through it and encouraged him on his way—thrust him into a slack-kneed stumbling run.

Phil almost fell. Caught himself. Panting, crouched forward, hands on knees. He straightened up, turned, came right back at Tom, throwing punches. Tom deftly avoided every one of them. He tapped Phil lightly in the solar plexus. Phil grunted and doubled up. "Oh, for fuck's sake," Tom said. "Don't be ridiculous."

Again Phil flung himself at Tom—punching, clawing, grabbing at Tom's shirt—and then Tom hit Phil so many times, so fast, that John—sick and fascinated—couldn't count the blows. Tom hit Phil with his fists, his elbows, and his knees. He seemed able to hit him anywhere, any time he damn well pleased. He slammed him up against the wall, grabbed his face with one hand, and hammered his head into the bricks. "Stop it," Cassandra yelled. "Jesus, man." Pam was yelling something too, but John couldn't make out the words.

Tom threw another round of punches and stepped back. Phil collapsed onto the sidewalk. Tom kicked Phil in the chest. Cassandra grabbed Tom by the arm. He spun around, sent her flying. She fell backward, slid on her bottom, jumped up, ran at him: *"Stop it!"*

"Hey, man, cool," Ethan yelled and grabbed at Tom's arm.

Tom stopped, froze—like he'd just dropped back into the real from another time-space continuum. He saw Cassandra still sitting on the sidewalk where he'd dumped her. He saw John watching him, saw the others watching him. He saw Phil lying by the wall, saw the blood. Now John could identify the look on Tom's face. He'd seen it before when Tom had walked out of the *Weasel* office in the middle of his speech, but then John had been so surprised by it that he hadn't been able to call it by its correct name. Terror.

"THERE'S PROBABLY some . . ." Some *what?* John thought. He kept waiting. "I can't," Pam said. "Will you call Karen? Jesus fuck, I can't . . ."

"Sure. Do you know her number?"

"I just can't do it. Do you understand? I. Just. Can't. Do. It. Her fucking number?"

It had all happened too fast—time warp, film run through the projector at double speed—and John's head had been left behind in the blur of crazy black-and-white action, maybe on the street outside the *Weasel* office, maybe on the taxi ride to Emergency. He hadn't been inside a hospital in years, and without telling him about it, they must have stopped painting the goddamned places white. This one was a nondescript snot-pale green, and Pam was a jagged whir of motion—walking, turning, stopping, walking. Shaking all over. And there were people in the waiting room. Bleeding people, passed-out people. Old people, young people, a woman with a crying baby. Somewhere in the bowels of the building a bell was ringing—or something like a bell. The doctor had looked improbably young;

he'd had huge sideburns and a thick black mustache.

"Shit," Pam was saying, "he got exactly what he fucking . . . What the fuck was he thinking? Why did he . . . ? Jesus, fuck, man, what's he *think*? The revolution's going to be a fist fight? Oh, fuck!" She caught John's hands and drew him through the big doors, outside onto the street, outside into the city.

"Little boys in fucking kindergarten." She was rapping compulsively. She certainly wasn't enjoying anything she was saying. "Jesus. 'It's *my* fucking candy. I'll kick your fucking ass, man.' Jesus, I could live happily . . . the rest of my goddamn life happily, oh, *I'd love it.* Never have to see another man again. Never *see* one, never *talk to one,* never have to *deal with another motherfucking man again in my whole goddamned life.* Jesus, fuck, keep them in kennels for breeding purposes. Yeah, throw them some food over the fucking walls, hose them down every once in a while. Collect their sperm in motherfucking test tubes. Let them punch each other around, kick the shit out of each other, fuck each other up the ass . . . like goddamned motherfucking *chimpanzees.* Jesus, they fuck up everything they touch. *Men?* God*damn* them. 'OK, boys, we're going to drop our fucking pricks on those motherfuckers. That'll show them. Yeah, we're going to *come* all over Vietnam.'"

The light was flattening out the city like rice paper—which was a damned good thing because there was some kind of hermetic horror going down and his mouth tasted like zero. He pounded a cigarette out of his pack, offered one to Pam. She grabbed it, and he lit both smokes. The words, hard as blown metal, were still ratcheting out of her. "Yeah, you've got to call Karen. I can't call her, I just can't. Fuck her. See what she says about this one. Yeah, tell her old Phillip got his revolutionary ass kicked, the dumb shit.

"Oh, fuck Karen. *Male-fucking-identified* is what she is. Goddamn, the bitch, she'd grow balls if she could. Dealing with male chauvinism? Oh, yeah, you bet. Motherfucking *hypocrite.* 'In practice, the woman question vanishes as an issue.' Yeah, right. I want to see it vanishing from *her* practice. That goddamned fucking *cow.*

"Shit, I hope he's all right. Stupid, stupid, stupid. Motherfucking shmegegge. But he didn't deserve that . . . Oy, fuck, man, I've got blood all over me." It was true; her white shirt was splashed with it. She'd held Phil's head in her lap on the ride over.

So he was supposed to call Karen. And then what? There was something else. But he'd gone numb or some damned thing. He couldn't *think*, and it was that hour when every bird in the city sings its head off. She even had blood on her hands. Maybe he was supposed to go into the hospital and sign something. And Pam was still hammering him with words. But he had to call Karen. That's right. That's where he had to start.

A cab pulled up. Someone was getting out of it. With no warning at all, Pam turned and ran to the cab. "Wait, wait," she yelled, but the driver didn't look like he was going anywhere.

She bent down, said something to the driver, turned and ran back to John. She was crying openly now. "I didn't mean you. I didn't mean you, I didn't mean you. I'm so fucking freaked, man. Oy, I'm so fucked up. I've got to . . . Jesus. I'm below a hundred. Oy, I can't stop. I need fucking help, man. I'm *fucking ninety-four pounds!* But . . . Jesus, listen. I didn't mean you. Do you understand me? You've got to understand me. Like politically, I think of you as a woman, *do you understand me?* Oh, fuck, John, I've got to go *home*." She hugged him so hard it hurt. "Be *careful*. Oh, fuck. I'll call you."

8

WELL, YEAH, I might have been a little bit rough on Phil Vance, but I guess I must have lost it there for a while. In those days I was definitely not in the headspace where I could have a friendly little duke-out with some clown and RESTRAIN MYSELF, if you know what I mean. I brooded about it for a while, and then, like with everything else, I went, oh, what the hell—he was only in the hospital that one night, and they checked him out and there was no serious damage done to him, and I was glad to hear that because I had nothing against the guy. He just had no business fucking with me, that's all. But I couldn't run that one too long before some little voice in my head goes, "Come on, Parker, who are you kidding? You're a MENACE TO THE CIVILIAN POPULACE." It never would have occurred to me to go to the VA with any of this shit. What the fuck did I have to complain about? I'd been in field maintenance, for Christ's sake.

Anyhow, I took the special issue in to the printer, and when it was ready, I picked it up and drove around town, delivering it to all the usual places, and so there it was, out on the street, and I figured that was pretty much the end of the line with me and the *Weasel*, so now there was absolutely nothing preventing Cass and me from going to see the sea. Well, what we discovered real quick is that they've got a conspiracy there in Boston, Massachusetts—like nobody wants you to see the sea, like every time you try, you run into a gate or a fence—so the first chance we got was in Marblehead, which they say is named for one of the early governors of Massachusetts. They've got sailboats in Marblehead, and they're real pretty, and we stood there and watched them for a while, and then I got this profound idea. "Hey, old buddy," I said, "why don't we try some of that day-glo orange shit to see if it's any good?" So we each popped a cap. That was the first mistake. We waited a while and all we could feel was speed coming on, so we figured it was nothing but icing sugar and candy color and a big healthy hit of crystal. That was the second mistake. Then we decided because the sea was so groovy in Marblehead, we should keep right on going up the coast to see how much more of the sea we could see. That was the third and final mistake.

There's one good thing about me—no matter how ruined I've got myself, I can always drive. So the next thing I know we're in North Dakota, except that somehow or other we're in New Hampshire at the same time. I remember thinking, shit, it's amazing I never realized before how easy it is to be in two places at once. And my Uncle Doc, the veterinarian, turned up along with some hitchhikers we picked up, and one of them was driving the camper for a while, and he was kind of an unusual dude because he had a Santa Claus suit on, and when I looked out the right window it was pine trees and New England, and when I looked out the left window it was dusty drab North Dakota with those low rolling hills. We did a lot of laughing through this shit.

It was kind of exhausting there for a while, but we did finally manage to pull over—you know, just off the main base flight line in Ton Son Nhut—and tried to cop some Zs, but then my father turned up. And you know what he does, the evil son of a bitch? He climbs right in the goddamned camper bed with us—like he pushes his way in between me and Cass—and I've got to argue with the old bastard all night long. Well, eventually we achieved unconsciousness. And when we woke up, we were in Maine of all bizarre places, and I drove into the nearest town and we had us a nice stack of hots. I bought the local paper and discovered that three days had vanished. Cassandra was coughing like she was going to die, so I turned around and headed back for Boston. Naturally we just had to drop another cap to get us back to town.

OK, so a few more days get lost somewhere out there in the far galactic regions of awesome cosmic black space, and then we're coming down. Oh shit, I mean COMING DOWN. We're parked in downtown Boston, and it's very early in the morning, this cold grey spaced-out morning, and we're sitting on the fucking roof of the camper, right? We're sitting there cross-legged eating doughnuts. Cassandra looks at me and says, "Tommy, I think we better try to get straight." She looks just GHASTLY. Her hair's all stiff with dirt, and she's wearing the same clothes she's been sleeping in for a week— work shirt and jeans and her old beat-to-shit boots—and from the looks of her we might have spent a few nights in a hog wallow, and I've got a pretty good idea I'm not looking so fucking wonderful myself. I guess if the *Wretched American* came by right then and took our picture, we would've been perfect for one of their stories about the HIPPIE MENACE.

I say to Cassandra, "You're right. We better get straight." So we start talking about who's the most soothing person we know and we decide on John. She says, "Yeah, we can depend on him. He'll be the same goofy fucker he always is. That's what we need. REALITY REFERENCE." And all the time we've been rapping, the streets have been grey and blank and totally deserted. But suddenly, just like somebody threw a switch, there's people hustling everywhere. There's hundreds of them, and they're all in a hurry.

Me and Cass look at each other and we both start to laugh. It's the straights going to work. And they look so absolutely ridiculous we're busting our guts. I mean it's better than a Charlie Chaplin movie. So here comes this poor secretary up the street, and as soon as she gets a glimpse of us, her nose goes straight up in the air, and she starts really stepping it off, going faster and faster. Cassandra gives her this big wolf whistle.

Well, that poor secretary is just immaculate, man, she's motherfucking CLEAN. If she'd had some flaw, Cassandra might not have gone nuts, right? But the poor secretary is just exactly the way she ought to be from top to toe. She shoots one glance over at us when she hears the wolf whistle, and I see her go like totally paranoid, and her nose is really up in the air, and now she's really moving. Cass jumps off the camper and lands right behind her.

"Jesus Christ, Tommy," Cass yells at me, "she's beautiful. Not even a run in her stockings. Hey lady, you sure are looking good." And the secretary is trying to pretend she isn't hearing any of this shit. "Get a load of the shoes. Bonwit Teller's, I bet. Right, lady?" The secretary sort of halfheartedly starts to run, her plastic heels banging down, PING, PING, PING. And Cass is running right along behind her.

I can't believe it's for real. Cass flicks up the poor girl's skirt in the back. "Get a load of the slip." And the secretary breaks into the closest she'll ever get to a dead sprint. Cassandra can't keep up because she's started to cough. The secretary is at the end of the block by now, and she peers back over her shoulder to see if she's safe yet, and Cassandra yells after her, "PLASTIC CUNT."

I'm just blown away. Cass had started the whole thing laughing, but it's not funny anymore. It's absolutely vicious, like sheer hatred. And she walks back to the camper out of breath and coughing and I say, "Hey, wow. You were really hard on her."

She says, "Yeah, I don't know what got into me. Shit. There's nobody in the world more fucked over than secretaries."

SO, FOR our next trick, we go sailing over to John's. He's still in the sack, but he don't give a shit. He's been freaked for days, and he's just DELIGHTED to see us. He even makes us a big mother omelet for breakfast. He's got himself tied in a real knot—like he's in one of those famous YOU CAN'T POSSIBLY WIN spaces. Seems like Pamela the Great has pissed off to New York, leaving him holding the bag over their COUNTER-REVOLUTIONARY article, and all the heavies in town are out for his ass. And he sure ain't working for the *Weasel* no more—like he can't even go in the office or maybe they'll lynch him. And this would be the ideal time to go skittering back to Canada—like all the signs are right—except he can't do that because he's waiting for Pamela to come back.

I say, "OK, old buddy, here's the straight scoop. One thing you should never do with chicks is WAIT FOR THEM, you dig? Because once they figure out that you'll WAIT FOR THEM, they'll take all the time you've got."

Cass says, "Jesus, that's about the piggiest thing I ever heard in my life."

I say, "Yeah, but ain't it the truth?"

She says, "Well, I got to admit there's a grain of truth buried in there somewhere."

John says, "Fuck, Ethan and Terry invited me to go up to New Hampshire with them. Maybe I should do that."

I say, "NEW HAMPSHIRE? Jesus fuck, man, we just came back from New Hampshire. You got to avoid that place like the plague.

It's real freaky up there," so I get to tell him all our war stories about that ridiculous day-glo acid. I figured he could use a laugh or two, right? Like he couldn't believe the guy in the Santa Claus suit. I say, "Shit, that dude was as real as anything else."

Cass says, "That was no dude in a Santa Claus suit. That was motherfucking SANTA CLAUS."

So we're doing a little smoke, and we're yucking it up and looking halfway decent, and even John kind of cheers up, like, "Well, maybe I will go to New Hampshire. Shit, I'm not doing anything here bouncing off the walls. You guys want to crash here while I'm gone?" Sure, we say. He calls up Ethan, worried, you know, that maybe they'd already left, but of course they hadn't left. It wasn't even noon yet.

"Terry said they were thinking of dropping some of that day-glo shit once they got up there," John says. "It's really some heavy shit, huh?"

"Like a stone," I say.

"Like the anchor on a motherfucking ocean liner," Cass says.

"Shit," he says, "doesn't sound like a game for beginners. Well, I guess I'll play babysitter. I'm not going to go NEAR that shit . . . not on a bet. As long as I'm in the States, I've got to stay STRAIGHT." That's pretty funny, right? He smoked weed the way most people breathe air.

He throws some shit in his knapsack, and Ethan and Terry swing by and pick him up, and that leaves me and Cassandra. Home. I mean, it's a fucking rat hole, but right at the moment it's our rat hole. "OK, Tommy," she says, "let's do DOMESTICITY."

So we made a run to Central Square and loaded up on the grub and came back and locked ourselves in and cranked up the shower full tilt, and we washed every part of each other there was to wash, and we kept wandering in and out of the bathroom—to cool off we'd go peek out the window—and then we'd jump back under the water, and you better believe we came out CLEAN CLEAN CLEAN. So eventually, Cass says, "Hey, we better knock this shit off. Zoë's getting soggy." Like all the pictures John had up on his walls were getting kind of steamed, and we were running out of hot water anyway, and then we got a fuck in, and that was nice, and I fried up a bunch of potatoes, and Cass made a big salad with some of that Greek cheese that smells like dirty socks, and we broiled up a couple of steaks—both of us heavy into the carnivore trip, blood running down our chins—and I dug out some hash, perfect for when you're coming down, and we watched some dumb show on John's old tube, and we were looking good, right? And then at some point, like on one of those flip-arounds you get on hash where you go, POP, oh, gee, I just thought of something weird, and it turns out to be REALITY, so anyhow, Cass does one of those pops, and she looks at me and says, "Hey, you know what's going to happen, don't you? Those assholes are going to get John up there in the woods and dump him full of that motherfucking freaky acid."

———

JOHN DROVE north. They'd left the long hot summer behind; up here, climbing these narrow roads higher into the mountains, it was almost like fall. The sun couldn't force its full energy through to the ground, could do little more than play a brilliant game of peeka-boo through the top branches of the monotonous stands of pine. When they'd run out of freeway north of Boston, Ethan had said, "You drive," a variation on his earlier pronouncement, "You know, man, the only way not to be hiding is *not to be hiding*," so John had taken the wheel and driven the forking roads that led through neat, orderly New England towns. He'd watched the church spires drift by, the village greens designed for small-scale democracy, and he'd understood why this was country that had gone for Clean Gene the year before, why this was country that was sick of the war. And pushing on up into the wilderness of austere peaks, light as caustic as etching acid, drab Christmas-tree green that went on forever, he was returning Ethan's pickup truck to the White Mountains where it had been registered, outfitted with license plates that carried the bitter message: NEW HAMPSHIRE—LIVE FREE OR DIE.

They'd been fifty miles north of Boston before John had remembered the simple fact that New Hampshire bordered on Quebec. If he'd brought not just some of his stuff with him, but everything he needed, this could be his getaway. He kept a knapsack at the back of his closet expressly for that purpose, so why hadn't it even crossed his mind? There was no doubt about it—he'd run Boston out, used it up, used *himself* up, and for what? He'd written a few good articles that he couldn't have written in Toronto, and for what? Well, if he was going to be back at York in September, he'd better let them know, but *was* he going to be there in September? He didn't know anything. He wasn't used to driving. He felt disembodied, almost depersonalized. His mind had been cut loose, left free to circle around in huge spacey loops, and all of those loops led back to Pamela Lynne Zalman. "Shit," he said, "I need to cool out."

"Fuck, man," Ethan said, "don't let it get next to you. We went out with a bang."

"Yeah, it might have been a bang," Terry said, "but it had a certain whimper quality too. A real bummer after all the energy we put into that cocksucker."

"Art ain't eternal, babe."

"Don't give me that Ken Kesey crap."

The *Weasel*, they were talking about. With some surprise, John realized that he didn't give a fuck. "You always told me there was no territory we had to defend," he said.

"You got that one right," Ethan said, "and ain't it a weight off your mind? Just dig it for a minute. Don't you feel lighter? Shee-it, moving into the *liberated zone*. That'll rearrange your head for you, man. Check back in with the earth, right? Like, man, we *grow food* up here, can't get any more revolutionary than that. And some far-out chicks thrown in for good measure," with a chuckle, "and maybe we can even do us a hit of that old death and rebirth."

"Not on a bet," John said. But why not? One of those day-glo orange capsules might give him a fresh insight—and that was something he could certainly use at the moment. He'd been wanting to try acid for years, but he'd always known that dropping it in Boston would be suicidal. Off in the woods with Ethan and Terry, however—perfectly safe. Yeah, he couldn't imagine a better place for his first trip. "How much farther?" he said. "You want to drive?"

"Shit, no. You can bring it on home, man."

More head games. And it was silly and dangerous bravado, but John kept on driving, knowing he couldn't afford to be stopped, not with a driver's license that said he was Joseph Alfred Minotti. He'd bought the damned thing in the underground, had never tested it on a cop, but he had serious doubts that he could convince anybody he was a nice Italian boy from East Cambridge. The road forked again. "Left," Terry said.

"I've had it," John said.

More road, more trees. Every pine looked like every other goddamned pine. "This is it," Terry said. "Up that driveway."

John drove out of the trees, up a hill onto cleared land where a dome sat like a landed spaceship in the suddenly too-bright afternoon sun. He turned off the engine; it went on knocking for a moment, then fell silent. He let go of the steering wheel, sank back, let his eyes fall shut. He could still feel the road unwinding under him.

Ethan reached across Terry, grabbed John by the back of the neck, and shook him gently. "Guess what, motherfucker?" he said. "You're here."

ETHAN WAS snoring on the bunk. "Real head stuff, right?" Terry said. "Puts him right to sleep."

John laughed, heard the sound of his scraped nerves—an annoying sound like the switch got stuck—and if he didn't stop it, Terry would know he was scared shitless. He was waiting to feel some effect, any effect at all, from the capsule of day-glo orange powder he'd swallowed.

Terry pulled off Ethan's boots and covered him with the sleeping bag. "Never know how he's going to do behind any particular drug," she said. "He's ripped out so many of his brain cells by now, his head probably looks like an anthill."

"You feel anything?" John asked her.

"No, just kind of edgy."

"Yeah, me too. Like? Nervous?"

"Yeah. Feels like mescaline coming on," she said, "but I can't tell yet. Could be milk sugar and candy coloring and our heads doing the rest. You want to sit outside, man?"

John followed Terry outside. The day was cooling down; the red-gold light of the setting sun was long and slanting, and John felt it ignite something far back in his mind—the slow fuse of memory. Terry led him to the very top of the hill. "This is nice," she said. "We can watch the sunset."

Ethan had built two structures on his land. The first—a rough, hastily slapped-together cabin called "the shack"—was hidden by the trees at the foot of the hollow; it had been mere shelter, a base camp where Ethan had lived while he worked on "the house," that spacious, breathtaking Buckminster Fuller dome. John was going to be staying in the shack, Ethan and Terry in the house. It hadn't occurred to John that they would want their privacy, but of course they did—it made perfect sense—but he couldn't imagine anything worse than tripping out all alone in that crappy little box in the dark woods at the bottom of the hill. They wouldn't expect him to do that, would they?

Terry sat down on the ground facing west; he sat down next to her. "Jesus," she said, "it doesn't feel like ordinary acid. They must have cut it with speed or some damn thing, crystal maybe. I'm afraid we're going to speed all night . . . you know, at some point just turn around and face the other way and watch the sun come *up*."

"Yeah, I feel janglier than all hell."

"Just *sit here*, man, and look out over the valley. Like there's nothing you've got to do. Just wait for the twilight. Like Don Juan says, 'The crack between the worlds.'"

John felt a chill of excitement deep inside his body—like a spray of ice water delivered by enema. "This is my first trip," he said.

"Yeah, I know. Just trust your head, man."

The rim of the sun was still visible behind the trees. John stared in that direction until his eyes began to ache, then looked away. The blue-green shadows had appeared, for a moment, curiously in motion. "No," Terry said, "it's not just speed. It's a hell of a lot more than speed."

"I'm scared," he said. Shit, he hadn't meant to say that.

"Just get behind it. That's just the way it comes on."

He felt as though each of his internal organs was being whisked, carefully, with an ice-cold camel-hair brush. He clenched his teeth and tried to get behind it—whatever the hell that meant. "I'm getting this horrible shaky feeling. Does it ever stop . . . the shaky feeling?"

"Yeah," Terry said, "I'm getting it too. It's just a part of getting off . . . like how you get off the launch pad, right? It should stop once we're into the trip." She smiled. "Either that or we won't be able to notice anymore."

It was nothing like grass. He'd hoped that's all it would be—the same quality as a high on Magical Michoacan, only more intense, more profound—but everything was sharp, winding tight. He drew out his cigarettes, looked at the back of his hand. For a moment each of the tiny hairs was stiff with electricity. He looked up quickly. Amazing how long the sun could continue to hang behind the edging of trees, amazing that the wind was not the least abstract, was rather a clearly defined presence as it passed over the length of the valley with a sensuous stroking motion, turning back the hissing leaves. Unpleasant. Blinking, a bright flicker behind his eyelids, he'd seen for a fraction of a second a hand stroking a long sleek leg in a nylon stocking. He shuddered.

Immediately his mind was talking, generating a continuous stream of safe protective words—about how the city was evil after all, just as Ethan said it was, abstract and artificial. You learned concrete, subways, street patterns; you didn't learn the names of the trees. You became a city boy, at home in any urban center in the world, foreign and uneasy the minute you drove a hundred miles out of town. And it was no wonder that Ethan didn't give a shit about the *Weasel* anymore; looking down from the top of the hill, John could see Ethan's mind at work. There was Ethan's house like something out of the *Whole Earth Catalogue*, all glass and freshly nailed wood smelling like a clean new beginning. And there was Ethan's garden, the neat rectangles of it—corn and beans, tomatoes and lettuce, radishes and onions and carrots. "A little slice of paradise"—that kitschy phrase—the Peaceable Kingdom, the New Jerusalem. The tribes were coming together, Ethan said, a loose anarchist structure. They were even getting the locals involved—and back in Toronto, people had been talking about doing the same thing in Northern Ontario. Yeah, that's where it was at—not in the motherfucking city with its mad politics. Pamela's mad politics.

But wait a minute—it had nothing to do with the city. What was he doing out here with some alien chemical, some unnamed day-glo powder, filtering out of his digestive juices and into his bloodstream and headed for his brain cells to fuck them up irredeemably? He wanted everything to fall into place—the whole huge demonic pattern. No, more than that, he wanted to come up with something even bigger than Pamela's total critique—to *transcend* the pattern—but now he knew that his mind wasn't going to follow any assignments. His mind was going to do what it fucking well pleased.

He found a cigarette in his hand. Lit it. Said again to Terry, "I'm scared." Looked into her black gypsy eyes.

"It's OK to be scared. Just don't go away inside your head."

"Do you really *know* anything?"

She didn't hesitate. "Yeah, I do. I'm in contact with some heavy entities. I can call on them if I need to. But listen. This is important, man. *Don't go away.* Just keep in contact with me no matter what happens, OK?"

Her words frightened him profoundly. He couldn't speak. Dragged on the cigarette. Felt the smoke all the way to the base of his lungs. Remembered Pam's line—the personal is the political. Or was it—the political is the personal? Either way would do. That double-faced motto vibrated with power, hidden meaning. If he could pry it open . . . "I'm having . . ." he said slowly. "Well, I guess you could say . . . I'm having a profound case of misgivings."

"A little late for that. We're not exactly right around the corner from Mass General and their handy-dandy stomach pump." She reached out and squeezed his hand. "Don't worry, man. Just get behind it, whatever happens. Trust me. And Ethan brought something along in case you bummed out. I wasn't supposed to tell you, right? He was hoping you'd do it on your head the whole way, but he's got some thorazine. If it gets too dreadful, we'll dump you full of it."

"That's comforting. How the fuck did Ethan know I was going to drop acid?"

"I don't know, but he did."

Jesus. That was heavy. Ethan and Terry had *planned it.* They'd worked out all the details ahead of time. It was some kind of horrible test—but no, that was crazy, just more of the old Boston paranoia. "Trust me," she'd said, but could he do it? And the damned recalcitrant sun was still hanging behind the trees as though it had no intention of ever setting. Terry was sitting cross-legged, her back upright, her hands resting on her thighs, centered and one-pointed, in a perfect half-lotus like a buddha—if a buddha would have worn dainty hand-made leather sandals and a lavender miniskirt. He tried to connect back to the night she'd read the Tarot for him, the feeling he'd had for her then—that she was wise, sphinxlike, ancient, in tune with womanly forces far beyond his paltry masculine comprehension—but now she just looked like a pretty chick. Great figure, beautiful eyes, younger than he was. He hardly knew her. How the hell could he expect her to lead him through anything?

He watched as she linked her fingers, stretched her arms over her head until her elbows made tiny snapping noises, arched her back. She uncrossed her legs, slipped off each sandal—quick sliding sound of leather against bare skin. Maddening. Lay back on the ground and stretched. He thought he saw blue light, crackle of Reichian electricity down one of her long legs—tension crotch to knee, down the inner thigh. Once he would have known the name of the muscle. I sing the body electric, followed immediately by: we're here to do a deed without a name. Shut up, shut up, shut up, he told his chattering mind.

Caught in a tangle of drawn and knotted sensations, disconnected mental fragments arriving without any warning. He'd trusted Pamela. He was in love with Pamela. Why the hell hadn't she called him? What the hell was she *doing?* And a nasty flash of insight—that he was bouncing from girl to girl just like in his WVU days. A repeated pattern? Yeah, and Terry was supposed to be safe because she was somebody else's girlfriend? But the only girl he could really trust was Cassandra, and now she was somebody else's girlfriend too, and he was tripping out (oh, my God, he could feel it), alone with Terry—whoever the hell she was—on a hilltop in alien New Hampshire. Fear of getting lost (I've always wanted to ask you).

Was he still smoking a cigarette? Yes, he was still smoking a cigarette. And he was saying it out loud: " . . . to ask you what your *real* hair looks like?"

She laughed. She sat up and, for a moment, the entire world tilted with her like a gyroscope righting itself. "Christ, you've got eyes like a hawk. Yeah, old watchful Ray. My real hair's mouse-brown and straight as a poker. Hey, can I do one of your smokes? Mine are in the house."

She was talking, but he couldn't quite follow her. " . . . when I turned into Terry. Been stoned for days, man. You could still get pure Sandoz acid, like straight from Switzerland. Oh, incredible. Looked in the mirror, saw my eyes looking back. My dark eyes. Thought, that's *real*, man. Not Maggie but Terry. Saint Terry. Saint Teresa. No, Saint Teresa's shadow. Demon Terry. Terry the witch. Looked and said, you're a gypsy child, they left you in that fucking awful nest like a cuckoo child."

Listening, he tilted toward her. It was possible she hadn't said a word.

Twilight was pressing in around them. Just a single line of light left of the sun. Trees going silhouette black. Clarity returning, making him remember the uneasy confusion where he'd just been. She was saying, quite distinctly, in an absolutely normal voice, " . . . drinking beer with Jill, and there was Ethan staring at me. Like I'd never seen a man with so much motherfucking hair in my life . . . and giving me *the look*. You know the way he can stare at you like a goddamn madman? And Jill says, 'You aren't actually going to *talk* to him, are you?' And I say, 'Sure.' And an hour later Ethan and I are floating around town in his truck, laughing like a couple of fucking idiots . . . just whacked out of our gourds on pure Sandoz acid."

There was nothing the least bit strange going on here. John was merely asking her, "But how does Ethan handle it? I mean it's a contradiction, isn't it? With his naturalness thing?"

"Oh sure. He handles it by pretending it isn't happening. Like I was born with black hair, right? I just go off and get it done in the daytime when he's not home. He never says a word. It's almost like he's forgotten Maggie with her straight brown hair."

And John was asking in a perfectly ordinary way, "Why do you dress like that?" Pointing with his glowing cigarette tip, in the increasing dark, to her flimsy Indian blouse, her tiny skirt, her bare thighs.

She grinned at him. He could barely see her. "I like fucking men up," she said. And then her face took on a peculiar, comic expression as though she'd deeply surprised herself with what she'd just said. John began to laugh. Terry began to laugh. The laughter turned into solid blocks, a row of them like dominoes, and marched down the hill. Then they marched back up the hill again. Like a row of soldiers: HA, HA, HA, HA, HA. Don't pay attention to that or you will go crazy. The inside of Terry's mouth was pink. How could he see it in the dark? "It's magic," she said, and they both laughed again.

"Yeah, it was right after I dropped out of BU," she was saying, "and I was working for this motherfucking insurance company. Boring? Jesus Christ, you can't believe it . . . but the men in there . . . Oh, it was beautiful. I'd wear these miniskirts, like *short*, man . . . Show them my ass, and Jesus. I bend over the filing cabinet, see those dicks jump up in their pants all over the room. Oh, just fucking beautiful."

John had never heard anything so funny in his life. He was rolling on the ground laughing. He was pounding his fists into the dirt. "I didn't think you knew," he gasped.

"Are you kidding? One poor asshole in there, man, I'd go bend over his desk, stick my tits in his face. No bra, right? And I'd just watch him go to pieces. And then I'd reach up to adjust the blind so my skirt rides up. He's fucking foaming, man."

The laughter was marching around in circles on the top of the hill, a regiment of Prussians—HA, HA, HA, HA, HA, HA. John knew he had to stop it. "And then in the bar I said to him, 'Why are you so fucking *lame?*'" John was laughing so hard that the tears were streaming down. "'You fucking limp-dicked dude,' I said. Oh, man, you should have seen his face." Terry was rolling on the ground laughing. Suddenly John knew that he had invented all of it, that she hadn't said anything like that.

John and Terry were sitting cross-legged looking into the twilight. Neither of them was laughing. "What were you saying?" John said.

She turned her face toward him. Her eyes looked unusually large and bright, like great sheened pools of dark oil. Slowly and deliberately, with a ritualized mime's gesture, she extended her hand, one lacquered scarlet nail, and touched him in the center of his lips. "Evil," she whispered.

"What did you say?" John yelled, staring at her. "Terry? What have you been saying?"

"See the little boy, right? The little boy growing up in some pissy little mill town, right? See the dude who was in the Merchant Marines. It's all still there, back of all that hair."

She was talking quickly. John was rolling on the ground laughing. "He likes coming in the back way. Like dogs. Wiggle my ass. Say, 'No, man, not in the mood right now.' Get him so hard he's dripping in his underwear. Can't stand it anymore, rips my panties off, pushes me down, comes in the back way. I feel him coming in, man. So much of a hurry, man. And it's a little boy coming into me so fast he can't hold it back. Comes into me hard and squirts right away."

Hey, this was private shit. John knew that he shouldn't be hearing any of this private shit. "Terry," he yelled into the dark.

"Maybe a week or so I don't want to, right? Until he's going fucking bananas. Say, 'Oh, I've got cramps. Can't make it.' He's getting nasty. I can see him start to itch, start to burn. Wake up in the morning with big fucking boners poking up. Say, 'No, man, don't feel very good yet.' Oh, I love it, the way he starts looking at me. Then maybe we're off at somebody's house, lots of people around. He's trying to *do business,* right? It's a deal, takes time. We can't leave. And I show him, just for a minute, just to him, that I haven't got any panties on. 'Terry, you fucking bitch,' he says when nobody can hear him. I say, 'Oh, daddy, I want it.' When he sees me talking to another man, he goes nuts. His hands are shaking. He's blown it. He can't do a thing. One time can't even wait to get me home. Right there in somebody's yard in the dirt like a fucking goat."

John knew he had to stop her from telling him any more of this private shit. But he was alone in the dark.

"Terry," he yelled. "Terry, where the fuck are you?"

"I'm right here."

No moon and the night was black from end to end. But he could just barely make her out. He ran toward her. She was standing under a tree, looking up into the branches, rubbing the bark with her hands. "This is sure some heavy shit," she said. "This is stronger than any acid I ever took."

"Terry," he said, "I'm getting lost."

John and Terry were crouched on all fours facing each other like two animals. He couldn't understand why he'd thought it was dark; he could see her perfectly. He seemed to remember that he'd been barking. Had she been hissing like a cat? Her eyes were very big. "I can see into you," she said, smiling. Their noses were almost touching. She hissed like a cat. She arched forward and licked him quickly on the lips. "You're clear like glass to me," she said. *You fucking love it.*

"Terry," he said, "I can't see."

But he could see perfectly. She raised one hand, fingers arched. A cat's paw. Sharply pointed scarlet nails. She batted at him with those shiny scarlet nails.

She turned away, still on all fours, and arched her back. She made a low resonant sound like a purr. He slipped his hand between her legs. She was sopping wet. "I'm going to make you squirm, man," she said, "I'm going to make you suffer. Yeah, you're going into hell, man. You're going to cry and beg, but you won't be able to *do anything.* Never, never, never. You do know exactly what I mean, don't you?"

"Terry?" he said.

They were sitting cross-legged on top of the hill. They were nowhere near each other. John was staring straight ahead.

He closed his eyes a moment to try to orient himself. What if Terry had never said any of those things? What if he'd made it all up, been hopelessly lost inside his own head? He opened his eyes. The sun was still high on the edge of the horizon. Terry was sitting in a perfect half-lotus like a buddha, looking down over the valley. She wasn't wearing red nail polish. Of course she wasn't. In all the time he'd known her, he'd never seen her wearing nail polish.

"Terry," he said carefully, "are you getting off on this stuff?"

She turned to look at him, her head strangely tilted. Where her eyes should have been were empty black pools.

John was crashing through the woods in the dark. He bumped into a tree, stopped, panting. "Terry!" he yelled. The night was moonless, and he couldn't see anything but shapes.

"It's all right, man, I'm right here." He felt her hand on his shoulder. She was out of breath. "Here, let me lean on you," she said, laughing. He felt her weight on his shoulder. She slipped her sandals on. "We'd better go back to the house," she said, "or we're going to get lost out here, and that'd be a real bummer, as whacked out as we are." She took his hand. "It's this way. Can you see?"

"Not a whole fuck of a lot."

"It's right there. That big black shape is the house. We should go in and make a fire. It's kind of freaky out here."

"You're telling me."

"How are you doing?"

"I don't know. It's hard for me to figure out what's happening."

"Just get behind it and keep in touch with me. Keep talking. I won't let you get lost." They were out of the woods now, holding hands, crossing the clearing toward the house.

"It's an incredible relief just to be able to talk to you again," he said. "You know, talk in a normal way."

"I know what you mean. You can really go off into a weird space behind this shit. Look, the clouds seem to be clearing over there. Maybe there'll be some stars."

"That'd be good."

"Are you hungry? We brought a ton of food."

"Maybe a little. This drug is so crazy and jangly though . . ." He laughed. "Christ, Terry, I was having the most incredible hallucinations. I guess that's what they were."

"I thought you were. What were they about?"

"I thought we were pretending to be a dog and a cat."

Deep in the back of her throat, she laughed. Then she mewed and, with a quick, deft motion, flicked her tongue across his lips.

He stopped, frozen to the spot. Everything remained precisely the way it had been a moment before. Still the same overcast, dark night, still the same black shape of the house a few yards in front of them. She was still holding his hand. "Terry," he said, "what's going on?"

"Meow," she said, let go of his hand and jumped away laughing. The hair stiffened on the back of his neck.

Huge, windy slam in the dark. A crash and a howl like a hyena. Ethan's voice. "Wow, man! Far fucking out!" Ethan seemed to be bouncing up and down. He seemed to be rolling in the dirt. He seemed to be crouched on all fours howling like a wolf.

Terry was meowing like a cat, and Ethan was howling like a wolf.

"Where the fuck's Ray?"

"I don't know. He was here a minute ago. . . . Ray . . . Hey, *John*." Burrowing into the dirt. Hiding among the leaves.

"Hey, John. Come on, man. You're going to freak us right out."

He rose to his feet and walked toward the house. He knew he could manage to maintain, knew that he had to. "It's all right," he yelled, forced himself to laugh.

"Shit, what the hell you doing, man?" Looming just ahead, Ethan, the sharp *male* smell of him. Heavy *male* voice. John drew himself up inside, hard and careful. "You go running off into the woods, you're going to bum yourself right out, man," Ethan said.

John forced his voice to sound light and casual. "Having a great time. This stuff's really incredible. I was just going through a lot of shit in my mind . . . you know, like sorting it all out."

"Come up to the house. We'll have something to eat."

"Think I want to be alone. All my stuff's down in the shack. Think I'll just sit down there and meditate for a while."

"Are you sure?" Ethan tilted forward out of the dark. John felt the large hand on his shoulder.

"Yeah, I'm sure."

"OK, but if you start to weird out, you either come back to the house if you can, or you yell if you can't. Just yell in a loud voice, man, and we'll be down that fucking hill quick as a wink."

JOHN LAY on the floor of the shack in his sleeping bag. It was worse now, and he knew he could never get back up the hill. He also knew he was so terrified of Ethan and Terry that he could never, no matter how bad it got, yell for them to come down. He tried to light a cigarette, but stopped, afraid of the fire. But maybe he'd already lit a cigarette and forgotten it. He searched for it, felt nothing but the dirt under him, the rough wood of the walls.

Forgotten? What about the light? Now he was keenly aware of it. The low golden blaze of the late-afternoon sun was transforming everything, making even the dirt and wood astonishingly beautiful, and then, like the screwing down of an aperture, he was slowly squeezed back into the thick antique dark. He pulled the sleeping bag up around his ears. That chilled trembly feeling hadn't gone away, and he heard the harsh sound of his own breath.

"Hi, do you want to dance?" Shimmering white solarized images of the park with the trees in full leaf, the hot summer sun of West Virginia, and her eyes impossibly brilliant, her hair streaming out behind her longer than in life. She's never quite there, not quite in the sleeping bag with him, not quite in the car when he reaches for her, not quite at the side of the house where she'd been only a moment before. She leaves behind an afterimage, like that perfume called F Sharp; she's just around the corner of the hallway, rock 'n roll playing, the high whining voice through a distant tinny radio speaker: "STAY . . . just a little bit longer. Well, your mommy don't mind. And your daddy don't mind."

"Cass," he said. "Cassandra. Please help me."

She was immediately kneeling next to him in the dirt by his sleeping bag. She took his icy hands into hers. "Dig it," she said, "the possible's *always* intolerable."

He saw that she was a beautiful boy. How could he have known her all these years and never figured that out before? "Cassandra," he said, "how do I get off?"

"You don't get off. You just hang on."

"Help me. I'm lost."

"No, you're not. It's the world that's lost." With birth, with aging, with death, with sorrows, with lamentations, with pains, with griefs, with despairs.

John came back to find his lips moving. He'd been muttering to himself. In a briefly lucid flash, he felt the dirt under his fingers. He couldn't trust what his hands might do the next time he was gone. They might gouge his eyes out or tear his balls off. His fingers were bleeding.

He unzipped the sleeping bag and ripped it away from him. Had to get some light in there—had to do it quickly while he could still think. He lit a match, saw the straight wooden lines of the shack swaying around him in the flame. He put the match to a candle on the shelf. For a moment he thought that he wasn't tripping at all, that everything was perfectly normal. He pulled his boots on.

Then he saw the candle bend and rotate, a pulse of fire that could blot him out. He blew against it, and the dark closed him in like a hand. He jerked the door open and ran out into the night. The moon seemed to be chasing him up the hill, but he knew that it was only the clouds moving. He could stay on the trail, claw and scramble forward. He could get there on sheer will. He knew he had to be with people. His fear of Ethan and Terry was just another face to the demon in his own mind. "Ethan!" he shouted.

"Steady on there, big fellow," Ethan seemed to be saying. But no, it wasn't Ethan's voice, and what was he doing wandering around on top of the hill again? Where had Terry gone? Why the hell wouldn't that damned sun set?

He couldn't understand how he could have been so confused. He wasn't on top of the hill at all. The house wasn't hard to find. He could see light pouring out from under around the edge of the door. Inside was safety—talk, food, thorazine—but he stopped, stood still, and strained to hear a sound, any sound, any ordinary human activity. He couldn't hear a thing. What if they were fucking in there?

The door swung open. A girl was standing in the doorway. She was the dark center of an eclipse, a silhouette of the iconic. Jukebox laughter blurred and was gone, and of her dress, from the curve of it, he knew she was in disguise. Pamela? Rain, sweeping water, torrents down, but no, that was the sharp points of her nails—but, wait a minute, that wasn't right. Nothing in his head was right. *Jesus,* he thought, *I can't deal with this shit.*

The acid was rolling over him like a tidal wave—something like a road, bouncing over the railroad tracks, and if a road can— Heels and my prom dress? Cassandra, even further on the bus, ride jumbles it up, but wearing with— With nothing seriously left of him, death coming at any rate and slid off his lap, smoothed down her skirt, an itsy-bitsy voice: ice-cold, fallen, seen things, well, you're stuck with it forever. *Focus, asshole.* Yes, he could—a nipped waist and a full skirt: "Come on, Alice, sit by me," with a sensation like Zoë was the girl.

Flame of a match lit Revington's dark face, flowed, and that's what models did, disguised—incredible. The air was music. Yes, it was making him see things: she wore a classic ball gown with a should-have-known-years-ago. The divide in space, it can also divide in time, carried along on the deep fast channel; his life had divided at a crucial moment, and a (why don't you ever *listen* to me?) whole between us and you; there's a great gulf fixed, other life had been waiting for a shudder of brilliance, him, her, the entire—that is, from where it had lurked and had time. All he had to do was step back to that crucial moment, that crack between the worlds, and not chicken out, getting back there flying, just as easy as Alice stepping through: he'd been looking down at his feet so that laughter drifted across the water, and they which would pass from hence into muddy sleep. In black patent, he hadn't known which or the girls, of as a man, and outside it was raining. She looked up now and saw. Took his hand. *Come on. Alice. With me.*

The train comes by every hour it seems like, where they'd played dolls and dressup, and with that, the whole track inside, and what must be the voices of children, open doorway, looking out. The relief was, of course, but let's say there is a hell. She could see John Dupre at the end of the Purkinje Shift, shape of a girl, standing in, seen men shot, seen men burnt alive. She could feel how freaked, and that glittering mask, that she was dark sorrow, lips burning. *Wir sindt nicht einig,* she that was Nancy Clark thought, darkly as roses.

She knew she had to thrust her mind against the edge of real objects, trace her clearly defined, out in the sad muddy Ohio, try to maintain contact—they disguised themselves. The people are music, still stuck there in the dark that'd make you puke, with closed eyes, so tight she could feel pink and green and golden lights, she wore a classic ball gown, he knew he should recognize her, she wore a classic ball gown with a but-he-couldn't-quite-remember, baby gets upstairs for a cold shower? No, he knew he had to get back, Cassandra said it was, she thought, biting into the palms of her hands, she'd gone the wrong way, but this acid thing we mistakenly call "life," continue the way she'd been going—this time was easy, just as easy as looking glass. Confused, embarrassed—Way to go!—with the boys, Zoë dressed as a princess, she you can go so great he began to cry, crouch, staring in, of the past rewound, and she was terrified he was—the poor fucked-up, chilled by a draft of his old, to contact her own body, something outside his own mind. She clenched his fists, clenched—

John let his hands fall open, took a deep breath, and opened his eyes. He was crouched in the dirt just a few feet from the house. That goddamn freaky acid came in waves; he'd figured out that much. It had just rolled over him, but now it had left him free and clear—for the moment. He had to get to people before the next wave hit him. The door was partially open; he could hear Ethan and Terry laughing inside. He could feel the tears running down his face. He ran toward the light yelling, "Ethan? Terry?"—felt his body go rigid in the sleeping bag, the dirt under his fingers digging in, the pain and sticky warmth of his own blood. *Oh my God,* he thought, *I haven't gone anywhere. I've got to start all over again.*

9

THORAZINE. JOHN didn't know where Ethan had got it, and he didn't care. When he'd been able to convince himself that it really was dawn and not just another fake version, John had crawled on his hands and knees out the door of the shack and into the cold low-lying mist of a morning that had seemed almost real enough. He'd been able to see the ground, the trees, the sky again in something close to an ordinary way, and he'd been so thankful that he'd kissed the dirt in front of him. He'd scrambled up to the house. Ethan and Terry had still been asleep. "Hey, sorry. I'm kind of bummed out. Thorazine?"

The trip had left him with unpredictable chilly events he would later call "images," although they weren't entirely like things he *saw*; he knew them as internal, mental, like skips on the record of his memory or misfires in the engine that generated his thoughts; if he took enough Thorazine, it seemed to erase those errors, but he could feel it erasing something else too—maybe something essential—and it didn't even touch the jangle. John walked for miles around Ethan's property, up and down the hills, trying to damp down the fire of an animal life that was threatening to consume him. He didn't know how many days had passed. The jangle kept getting worse. He had trouble with words. His mind was still full of them, but he couldn't control them and they resisted being transformed into spoken language. He paced up and down, woke time after time to discover that once again he'd been hopelessly lost, muttering to himself, that once again he'd been staring at something—a bit of bark, a tree at the edge of the skyline—his eyes so fixed that they burned like hot augers turned in against him.

He thought about the rope so much he forgot that there had ever been a time when he hadn't been thinking about it. The rope was in the back of Ethan's truck—good thick sturdy rope—and the roof of the shack was crossed by a single fat beam. There was even an old wooden kitchen chair, so he had everything he needed. He didn't know how to make a hangman's knot, but he was pretty sure that if he tied a loop at the end of the rope and secured it with a series of half-hitches, ten or twelve of them, and then threaded the rope through the loop, that would do the trick. He'd read somewhere that it helped to rub the rope with lard so it would slide more easily, and Terry, of course, didn't have any lard—it was an animal product—but he decided that butter would probably do the same thing. He would spring up from the chair, kick it out of the way. He would do it in the very center of the ceiling so, as he was dangling, he wouldn't be able to reach any of the walls. He would wait until Ethan and Terry drove into town—they kept talking about it—so if he screamed, they wouldn't hear him. If he screamed, it would be a simple animal reaction. And then the mistake would be erased.

He listened to Ethan and Terry talk. Sometimes their voices made sense and sometimes they didn't—drifted in and out of comprehension like an untrustworthy transmission crossing a star-smear of static. "That was some evil shit," Terry said—or something like it. "The trippy part was really heavy, but way too much speed."

"Yeah, whoa, way too much speed . . ."

"Kind of like mescaline."

"You got it, babe. Not quite, but almost. Warped. Kali emanations, you dig? Shee-it. Heavy."

Terry made tea out of catnip, hops, chamomile, linden flower, and motherwort. She and Ethan drank it; she made John drink it. "We got to get you off that motherfucking Thorazine. You keep on taking that shit, it'll turn on you."

For the first time since he'd come back, John felt something that was almost like a real emotion, something that generated a single consistent line of thought. They didn't understand. They couldn't take his Thorazine away. When it got really bad, Thorazine eased it, smoothed out its edges. They had no idea how horrible it could get without Thorazine. And consciousness was an animal byproduct anyway, certainly not something one should be attached to—particularly seeing as the "one" that was thinking about being attached to it didn't exist in any meaningful way—but, at any rate, one could certainly not be aware of *not* having consciousness—and all of that crap was just words going around anyway. Words came and went. They did funny things. They turned into each other, wouldn't sit still, melted away into static and somebody yelling. He took the rope from the back of Ethan's truck and hid it under his sleeping bag. He had to get the mistake erased while he still remembered how bad it was.

"How much of that shit's he been taking?" Ethan said.

"I don't know, man. He's been popping it like candy."

One morning when he woke up, there wasn't any more Thorazine. "You got to get back, man," Terry said. "You got to deal with it, that's all."

He knew she was lying. She'd hidden the Thorazine somewhere. Ethan caught him going through their knapsacks. "She chucked it in the woods, man."

"Where?"

"Shit, buddy, gone. Into nowhere. Vanished without a trace. No more motherfucking Thorazine, you got that?"

John jumped up and down and screamed: "I can't stand it, I can't stand it, I can't stand it, I can't stand it, can't stand it, can't stand it, can't stand it can't stand it can't stand it . . ."

"Hey, steady on there, big fellow."

John batted Ethan's hand away, ran outside. Waving his arms in the air, he jumped up and down and screamed, jumped up and down and screamed, jumped up and down and screamed. He fell over onto the ground. He'd screamed himself hoarse. He was crying. Ethan offered him a hand. John took it, allowed himself to be hauled to his feet. "Come on, motherfucker," Ethan said, "you're going to learn to drive nails."

NOW JOHN couldn't tell how much of the weird shit in his head was left over from the day-glo acid and how much was from coming down, cold turkey, off the Thorazine. Driving nails was good. So was sawing wood—and carrying wood, and holding it in place while Ethan drove the nails. So was hoeing weeds in the garden, picking vegetables, hauling water up to the house from the well. So was walking endlessly around and around, and up and down the hill behind the house. He remembered quite clearly that these were things he ordinarily would not do, things he ordinarily would not have enjoyed doing, but he did them anyway and began to find comfort in them. His mind was beginning to organize itself again—he felt it fighting to recreate itself in a way that resembled what it used to be—and he knew that working with wood could be called "a Zen exercise," but there was a problem with names. The names that were ordinarily attached to things weren't the real names. Shit, he knew that much. He remembered Bill Cohen. Words were no damned good.

John had already left behind the mechanical infantile mannequin that had jumped up and down and screamed, jumped up and down and screamed—couldn't quite remember, in any convincing way, what it had been like to be that thing. He wasn't as jangly as when he'd been on the Thorazine, but he knew he had to keep moving. He felt bursts of electrical energy—a million tiny burns, in motion, terrifying—like ants skittering, biting, down his neck, up his back, along his arms, between his legs. Things that shouldn't move sometimes moved; the motion of the wind through the trees spilled over into the house, and the entire wood and glass construction rippled with it. Shadows were bad; they slithered. Colors weren't stable; if he stared at them too long, they went cobalt blue or canary yellow on him. But the worst were "mind-feeling-things" (he couldn't think of any other name for them): sometimes like a draft of dark sorrow—like the sudden recollection of a dear one's death—at times so sweet and poignant they were unendurable. The mind-feeling-things were not attached to images or memories; they simply appeared, related to nothing, and carried with them a hint of a greater meaning—infinitely complex yet simple as water—that he could grasp if he could only move forward half an inch through some dense mental fluid.

He could talk again. "Non-existence . . . kind of generates existence. And the other way around too, like . . . OK, so how could something cease to exist that used to exist? And how could something come into existence out of nothing? Do you know what the fuck I'm talking about? . . . And it's like kind of pointless to pick one or the other."

"Oh, yeah," Terry said. "You're there, man. Like this," and she aimed her hand at his stomach palm down. "Go ahead and kill all

187

those motherfuckers, they're dead already. And that's *true.*"

She turned her hand over, making her palm into a cup. "But OK, this is the other side. And it's true too. If you check out, man, you're just going to blow your incarnation. Do you want to come back as a maggot and have to work your way all the way back up again?"

John wondered if she knew about the rope. If the world was still operating the way it was supposed to, she couldn't possibly know about the rope, but shit, he wouldn't put it past her. He hid the rope in the woods. He knew in his heart that it was not possible to live without Thorazine. It was too much work. In the shack, he stood on the chair, reached up and over the crossbeam. He lifted his feet from the chair, allowed his entire weight to hang from the crossbeam. He wanted to know for sure that it was strong enough to erase the mistake.

JOHN MET the neighbors. He didn't talk to them and didn't bother to remember their names. He helped Ethan finish an entire section of the house. He helped Terry cook, learned to bake bread in the wood-burning stove. Kneading the dough was good. So was batting it down when it rose. Every day Terry made him drink a mixture of brewer's yeast, raw wheat germ, and blackstrap molasses. It tasted like shit. She made him eat raw vegetables. He ate carrots and tomatoes and onions and lettuce and parsley—all still warm from the sun. At night, the three of them sat down together like a family and ate brown rice and lentils. Terry taught him how to season the lentils with mustard seeds heated in oil until they popped, with whole cinnamon and cloves, with cumin and turmeric and coriander and chilies, with sea salt and a pinch of raw sugar. The sun was making him darker, lightening his hair; he was getting thinner. He had to poke a new hole in his belt. One night as he lay in his sleeping bag in the shack, the terror came back. It arrived on the voice of the mosquitoes buzzing around his ears, then swelled into a howl. It rolled over him, wave after wave, as he shook and wept. He brought the rope back from the woods, untied the loop in the end, and returned it to Ethan's truck. He walked up to the house. "Hey, do you guys mind if I sleep in here?"

"Hell, no, man. There's plenty of space."

If he wanted to live, he had to put up with the jangle. It was an animal thing. He knew that wanting to live was stupid, pointless, and hopelessly mired in ordinary human consciousness, but he was terrified of that rope now, that crossbeam; the thought of what he'd almost done iced his guts until, for minutes at a time, he couldn't breathe. If he wanted to live, he'd have to learn again to do what he'd done his whole life—hide the mistake so no one could see it. He stripped to the waist, tied his hair into a ponytail the way Ethan did, and sweated in the sun. They made a new fence. Glad to find out how bone-grindingly hard it was, John dug post holes. To keep the sweat out of his eyes, he tied a bandana around his forehead the way Ethan did.

He began to look forward to the evenings. He would have worked himself into exhaustion by then. His mind would have cooled by then. He didn't dare to smoke dope, but he liked it when Ethan and Terry did—how silly it made them. He drank the truly vile tea she brewed for him—skullcap and valerian root—and felt almost peaceful, almost at home. He liked Terry's freshly made bread without any butter on it. He liked the light of the kerosene lanterns. Ethan had an old cracked Stella guitar; it was a piece of shit, but John tuned it and played it. He didn't sing, just picked out old tunes that felt right for the place—the mountains of West Virginia folded into the White Mountains of New Hampshire. The Dupres must have lived much like this in the old days. He played "Reuben" and "Spike Driver's Blues" and "Bonaparte's Retreat."

"Hey," Ethan said, "you ain't half bad, you know that?"

John began to enjoy falling asleep—the way he often used to, as he realized now, back in Canada, and even further back, in West Virginia. No location was ever simple; just as he could turn New Hampshire over and find West Virginia embedded in it, he could turn West Virginia over and find Canada. The last time he'd felt fully and completely all right had been in Canada, where he would return—as his mind, drifting away, always told him. The images that slipped in and around him now were no longer menacing because the central mind-feeling-acid-thing had come out of hiding—from where it had lurked and had time. Yes, time was not a simple one-way flow any more than location was a simple point on a map. It was true that his life had divided in time as well as in space. If he went far enough back along the track, there was no mistake. Getting back there was just as easy as flying in dreams. You run gently forward. You leap up. And then you're airborne. You sweep your arms like a swimmer.

One morning Terry said, "I'm going to drive back down to Boston. You want to go back to Boston?"

"Sure," John said, although he didn't know what the fuck he was going to do in Boston. He'd been in New Hampshire for nearly six weeks.

———

AUGUST IN Boston is a bitch. It's like that summer-in-the-city song—I kept hearing it in my head, clanging away. And the weird thing about John's apartment was that what made it unfit for human habitation—like being underground with no light—made it NICE in August. It never got too hot down there, and you never had to notice that the sun outside was baking the piss out of everything, so we spent a lot of time not going anywhere, and Cass got heavy into DOMESTIC, so pretty soon we're sleeping on a brand-new foamie with SHEETS on it, and we've replaced his old beat-to shit TV with an up-to-date model, and we've even bought us a little stereo and a few records. The old weird hashish seemed to go perfectly with the space we were in, so we got ourselves an honest-to-God hookah to do it in, and I filled the bastard up with Napoleon brandy. You better believe it was mellow.

For a while there we were looking good. It's not like we never went anywhere. When the evil sun fell behind the tallest buildings, we'd emerge like a couple of skunks into the cool of the evening and drift around town because I had to stay in the game, you know what I mean? Like checking in with Lyons and moving a few ounces. But anything else . . . Well, there was this music festival happening, the one they called Woodstock, and we almost went to it, but when we got right down to the full horror of maybe packing up the camper and driving all the way there, we just couldn't quite get it together, so

I won't be able to tell my grandchildren I caught the big show. And you know what Cass likes to do? Cass likes to lay around and READ BOOKS. Well, shit, I've read a book or two in my time, but as to spending day after day LAYING AROUND READING BOOKS, that's a whole other matter. We had to keep going over to Harvard Square so she could buy more of them.

I didn't know when the hell John was coming back. For all I knew he'd pissed off to Canada and was never coming back. The Lord of the Land—slimy little fucker—showed up, and he was kind of surprised to see that Mr. Jones's act wasn't playing, so I laid the bread on him for August AND September, hoping he'd go away, which he did just happy as a clam, so there was no reason why we couldn't stay there right on into the fall, LAYING AROUND READING BOOKS. When John finally showed up, I'd never been so glad to see anybody in my life.

I noted right off the top that Terry was with him and Ethan wasn't, and I filed that one away in the back of my brain for later contemplation. John had turned into one of these spacey Macrobiotic back-to-the-land freaks, brown as a nut and skinny as a stick and wearing some bleached-out old Mexican shirt that was probably Ethan's, hanging open so you could count his ribs if you felt inclined to do that. I noted that he was real quiet, even more quiet than usual, and he'd got that ten-mile stare like the guys who've been out humping the boonies too long. And when you asked him anything, there'd be like this . . . I don't know, this take-up time before it all clicked into place and he'd say something back to you. "I'm all right," he kept saying, but I didn't think so. I knew he'd dropped that fucking day-glo acid before he even told me.

Well, Cass was all concerned with the state of John's head, and she had to hear all about it, and Terry looked kind of jumpy, like twitchy and irritable, and she says, "Well, I got to split, folks, catch you later," but not before she gives me THE LOOK, and all of a sudden I'm left standing there holding up the wall, thinking, hey, wait a minute, why did I just get THE LOOK? I say, "Hey, old buddy," to Cass, you know, like, "you and John catch up on the state of the cosmos and maybe fire up that old hookah and like . . . and maybe you could start getting our shit together, because I'm going to go see if I can find us a place." She just laughs at me, but my show's already on the road.

Ethan and Terry's door was standing wide open so I walked right in. Terry didn't seem the least bit surprised to see me. She closed the door and locked it. She says, "You hungry?"

So we do some smoke and she slices up some of that fine bread she bakes. She tells me that the folks on the next farm over laid some far-out blackberry jam on her. She shoves the jar at me and says, "Yeah, man, take a little hit. A ray of sunshine in every bite. Homemade by honest-to-God hippy-trippy-dippy assholes just like out of the newspapers."

I don't know where she's at. I'm just sitting there trying to catch it as it goes by. She says, "You know, if any of us had any morals left, we wouldn't be selling that heavy mind-fuck day-glo shit on the street . . . like to any dumbass fourteen-year-old with the bread to pay for it."

"Oh, yeah?"

"But we transcended morals, right? That's death-trip talk, right? We're a new people, right?"

"You the one, babyshake."

"Oh, Jesus, Tom, I can only do Earth Mother for so long and then I've got to feel pavement under my feet. I used to wear stockings to work, can you believe that? Weird, huh? Every fucking day. And you know what's even weirder? It wasn't that bad," with this hard little laugh. She says, "Tom?"

"Yeah?"

"Fuck me."

Well, I did just that, and it was pretty damn spectacular. Then we had us some more smoke and some more bread and jam and tea. She says, "Ethan may be a crazy old fucker, but he's MY crazy old fucker."

I say, "Yeah, right. And he's a friend of mine."

"Oh, yeah," she says. "If you asked him, he'd say that too. You know, Tom, this state of affairs does not exactly fill me with joy."

"Well, me neither, sweetheart."

"You know what? It's so easy, it's disgusting. There's no reason in the world you shouldn't fall by here any time you feel like it. Either you got Cassandra with you or you don't. And either Ethan's here or he isn't. You see how motherfucking easy it is?"

Yeah, I did see how easy it was.

I hightailed it out of there. I figured if I was gone too long, it'd look kind of weird, and I should have been headed straight back to John's but I didn't do that. I just drove around. I don't even remember where, but I just drove around. And I came THIS CLOSE to aiming it all west. Like there was nothing at John's place really I needed, and I had coin in my jeans—plenty for gas and hamburgers and even checking into a motel along the way, if that should turn out to be my inclination. And if you like to drive, it don't take that long to drive from Boston to North Dakota. I like to drive. I can drive for days, man, and not think twice about it.

But here's what's happening. There had to be some reason for all this shit, you know what I mean? Some PURPOSE. Like why was I at Ton Son Nhut when Tet came down? Like why did I go to Nam at all? Like why didn't I stay in Hubbard when I got out of the service, and why the fuck did I go to Boston, and why had I been hanging out with some crazy anarchist draft-dodger from West Virginia, and why was I living with Cassandra and screwing Terry? You see what I mean? It was all just too nuts not to MEAN SOMETHING.

———

IT WAS weird to be back inside a small box at the bottom of a large box located near Central Square in Cambridge, Massachusetts, in the United States of America, in the belly of the beast, but it wasn't any weirder than being anywhere else. Whenever John looked at the pictures of the girls he'd taped to his walls, he felt his old familiar dark sorrow—but now it was so intense that he almost ripped those images down. Instead, he forced himself to look at them until he caught up with the thing that had lurked and had time—or until it caught up with him. It wasn't just girls in general, it was Zoë—like she was the entrance to a seriously heavy mind-time-place-thing. He took down all of the pictures but hers.

Back along the time track—it was not far at all; it was gone and lost—he swung gently on the front porch glider with Zoë and remembered Rilke's German. She sat next to him with her back straight and her knees together, in a posture that was almost prim. She was so different from Cassandra. He remembered remembering the rain at the end of that summer—and taking rollers out of Zoë's hair, the way each section sprang back into a perfect cylinder once it had been released. He'd never taken rollers out of a girl's hair before, but it had felt like a perfectly natural thing to do. So had separating her eyelashes with a pin—individual hairs, each growing out of sensitive living tissue—but the summer had thinned out, given up its stifling heat. *The summer was so full*, John thought, Rilke's words coming to him now in English.

It wasn't just poetry, or memory, resonating in a mind-feeling-place; Boston itself was drifting into melancholy autumn. Tom had paid John's rent for September, so there was no reason for him to go anywhere—just as there was no reason to stay where he was. Ethan had given him the old Stella guitar. "Yeah, man, that poor fucker would get lonely if it didn't go home with you." He restrung it with light-gauge strings, sanded down the bridge. It was still a piece of shit, but he'd transformed it into a somewhat more useful piece of shit. He played for hours. He never would have guessed that he remembered so many tunes. Some of them didn't even have names. He never sang. He thought at first that it was because he couldn't trust his voice, but then he amended that formulation: it was because he didn't want to *hear* his voice.

He ate the vegetables Terry had given him. He drank Terry's herb teas. Using a bit of the money Cassandra had given him from the hash deal (he'd stashed it in *Memoir of a Revolutionist* and had almost forgotten it), he bought more vegetables. He bought lentils and beans, split peas and tofu, brown rice and miso. Maybe he'd been reborn as a vegetarian. He ate as much as he wanted, but he kept getting thinner. None of his clothes fit. He bought a new pair of Levis. His waist had shrunk from thirty-four to thirty—a *loose* thirty. He bought a pair of lightweight hiking boots and walked for hours along the Charles River. Thinking of Bill Cohen, he walked around and around Harvard Yard. He hadn't been that thin since high school.

He felt like he was fourteen again—but not like it at all. He felt like he was back in Morgantown again—but not like that at all. Each time he remembered remembering, it thickened the depth of the central mind-meaning-thing. He wanted to talk to Pamela. He asked himself if he was still in love with her. He wasn't sure now what "in love" meant—a metaphor for something he could almost grasp if he could find some way to move toward it.

JOHN RAN into Phil and Karen Vance in Harvard Square. He was about to cross the street to avoid them when they called out to him, "Hey, Raymond. What's happening, man?"

There was no reason not to talk to them any more than there was a reason why he should. He waited for them to walk up to him. "My God, man, have you lost weight," Phil said. "Are you OK?"

"Yeah, I'm fine."

They were dressed like twins—same checked shirts, same baggy pants, same construction worker's boots, same chopped-off hair. Phil was shorter and thicker, was bald and had a beard—those were the only differences between them. "Great to see you, man," Phil was saying. "Where the hell you been?"

It would have been impossible to answer a question like that in any kind of concise way—certainly not using ordinary words—but John had learned by now that when people asked things like that, they didn't really want to know. "Up in New Hampshire with Ethan and Terry," he said.

Did he want to have lunch? they asked him, smiling and smiling. It took him a moment to realize they meant right now. He couldn't find any reason not to, so they went into the nearest box where food was sold to people. He didn't want anything made of ground meat, but that's what they sold in that particular box, so he ordered a cheeseburger. He couldn't understand why Phil and Karen were being so friendly. Had they forgotten the newspaper seizure? Being with them was forcing him to play a difficult old tune with his mind, and it had been so long since he'd played it, he kept missing the strings.

"You should call Pam," Karen told him. "She's worried about you."

So they still liked Pam too, did they? Maybe politics didn't matter as much as it used to. Or maybe it was when he and Pam had taken Phil to emergency—maybe that had made them all friends again. And of course Karen and Pam were in the Collective together. "Is she back?" he said.

"No, she's still in New York."

Karen wrote Pam's father's phone number onto the back of a leaflet she'd been carrying in her knapsack. The front of the leaflet said: WARGASM.

"I dropped acid in New Hampshire," John heard himself saying, but why shouldn't he say it? "Like heavy. Like one of the most unpleasant experiences of my life. I'm just coming down from it now."

He thought they weren't going to say anything to that, but then Phil said: "You ought to come to Chicago. Roast some pig. That'll put your head back together."

"Chicago?"

"Yeah, man, you know, the October action. The Four Days of Rage. It's going to be so fucking far out, man. Thousands and thousands of kids. We're going to kick out the motherfucking jams. Going to trash that fucking pig city."

Now they were both talking to him. They took turns. When one stopped, the other one started. Lots of jailbreaks happening now—going into high schools and giving the kids the straight scoop on the revolution. Slapping around a few pig teachers if they got in the way. And so-and-so had trashed some pig center at Harvard, far fucking out, man. Yeah, getting into some serious anti-imperialist ass kicking now, bringing the war home to the mother country. They were living in a collective in Dorchester, relating to working-class youth, trashing the pig inside themselves, getting rid of the last of that wimpy Movement shit, doing karate every morning, getting toughened up.

Tough enough to take on Tommy Parker? John wondered. He didn't think they had a chance. And John took one bite of his cheeseburger—the sadly congealed animal cells created by murder, the sleekly globular fat, the hot orange slime, the rasp of salt, all of it pressed between a puffed-out white paper bletch. He couldn't eat it. He'd be lucky if he could retain what was already in his mouth and swallow it. And trying to chew that dead mass of protein flipped him elsewhere—to a noble section of gleaming track at some considerable distance—and he saw that what he'd mistaken for two people sitting with him were really chilly images. The rubbery horizontal slots in the lumpy pinkish balls were continually moving, continually emitting streams of ordered sound that appeared to be designed to imitate human speech. Each entity had two shiny wet globes set above the slots; the globes kept rolling around. One entity picked up the hot stinking thing in front of it and thrust it into its slot—and then, just as quickly, the images shivered and he saw them again as people. Oh, my God, he thought, they're Weatherman.

"I've got to go," John said, "got to meet somebody. I almost forgot. Running on a tight schedule."

"Fall by the office," Phil said. "Get into the paper again. We're doing some far-out shit. We'd be glad to have you, man. You could really make a difference."

John knew that he had to walk to burn off the jangle. He aimed himself toward Central Square in the heat of the afternoon. All those words coming out of Phil and Karen—the thick dense code of the Revolution—but he'd cracked that code a long time ago, and now he was remembering. Yeah, he was remembering *everything*. What was he feeling? Was it anger? By the time he got back to his place, he knew that he could still make words happen. He wrote in a fury:

```
SNCC, the Resistance, the Old Mobe, the New Mobe,
Women's Lib, BRWC, SDS, PLP, WSA, RYM I, RYM
II, Weatherman. As the technique of production
progresses, the worker on the assembly line makes an
increasingly smaller segment of the finished product.
Mirror image of automated technology, our opposition
becomes increasingly fragmented as we create smaller
and smaller interest groups competing with each other
for the goods of the world AS IT IS. Each fragment-
-in danger of splitting into yet smaller fragments-
-tries to struggle harder for REAL power, entering
```

competition with such worthy opponents as the Oil
Lobby, Crest, Carl Oglesby, General Motors, the
Anti-Defamation League, Mao Tse-Tung, Coca-Cola,
and Colonel Sanders' Southern Fried Chicken. Black
power, red power, gay power, Jewish power, student
power, women power, power to the people, a powerful
new washday whitener, a new car with the power of
a thousand horses under the hood, your perspiration
worries are over with a NEW REVOLUTIONARY PRODUCT
MORE POWERFUL THAN A SPEEDING BULLET—but THE power
is unitary, maintained by the powerlessness created
by such fragmentation. Soon riot police will become
obsolete, for, even now, magicians a thousand times
more clever than Henry Kissinger wait in the wings
for their chance to adjust the social order. They
will have degrees from Harvard, they will be masters
of technique, and they will cast no shadow at all.

The next day he needed to confirm what he already knew, so
he walked over to the *Weasel* office. It was the same familiar box
where he'd spent so many hours, with the same tables and desks and
chairs, but now Ho and Fidel and Che looked down from the walls.
Somebody had put up a hand-painted banner that read: LONG
LIVE THE VICTORY OF PEOPLE'S WAR. Phil was sitting at
what used to be Ethan's desk. "Hey, man, great to see you. You want
to help us lay out?" The place was packed with SDS kids. "No,"
John said, "not this time. I'm out of practice. I'd just fuck it up."

He sat down at what used to be his desk and read the LNS packets
he'd missed while he'd been gone. He read what used to be *New
Left Notes* but was now called *Fire*. He read the issue of the *Weasel*
that was spread out on the layout tables. WARGASM . . . BRING
THE WAR HOME . . . SDS IS CALLING THE SHOTS THIS
YEAR . . . WE ARE WINNING . . . PART OF A WORLDWIDE
STRUGGLE . . . SMASH MONOGAMY, SMASH RACISM,
SMASH IMPERIALISM, SMASH PIG AMERIKKKA . . . MAKE
YOURSELF INTO A TOOL OF THE REVOLUTION . . .
SMASH THE PIG IN YOURSELF. It was all aimed at the October
action: FOUR DAYS OF RAGE. As he was leaving, he saw an

image he'd missed. From around a corner, on the side wall next to the lay-out tables, Comrade Stalin was staring down at him.

Back in his small box, he read what he'd written the day before. It wasn't direct enough, clear enough. He tried again:

```
Heroes, machismo mongers, revolutionaries who've
never been in a fist fight! BRING YOUR BALLS
TO CHICAGO! SDS is calling the shots this year.
We're going to fuck the city up for a few days,
get ourselves beaten up, jailed, tear-gassed, and
probably this time around some of us killed. Oh,
wow, real death! We haven't got anything to offer
YOUR head. You don't count, being white middle-class
assholes, but you'll have a great chance to work out
your wet-dream fantasies of violence right there on
the motherfucking street. And of course we'll get a
lot of press coverage.
```

That was as much as he could do. He was afraid that now he could only write in short bursts, that he couldn't finish anything. And who would publish it? Nobody.

He thought of calling Pamela at her father's, but what could he possibly say to her—using words that were no damned good? Some words were even worse than no damned good; they were lies. But then, later, as the evening cooled, he heard Rilke again, sounding, and spoke the words aloud, quietly—words written in another dense code, but words that were the opposite of the crap they were pumping out in the *Weasel* office. Rilke's words didn't lie, didn't hide, didn't snap viciously shut to kill off any chance of possibility.

It was amazing that he could still remember so much German after all that time, and surely he must be remembering it because each word was perfect. *Du im Voraus.* How could Rilke have found each word, so exquisitely right that no other word could possibly replace it? *Verlorne Geliebte.* You couldn't translate Rilke. Maybe you could get the raw meaning, but you couldn't get the music—the way each word fell into place with absolute inevitability. *Nimmergekommene, nicht weiss ich, welche Töne dir lieb sind.* And with that, the door opened to the dark sorrow—unbearable, unbearable—and Rilke's

German resonated, opened door after door after door.

He'd told Phil and Karen that he was coming down from the acid, but was that true? Yes, so far as he could tell, it was true. Soon he'd be normal again—as crazy as everybody else. That day-glo orange powder had given him an experience so intense he couldn't hold it—like sitting next to his father's bed while his father died—but it hadn't added anything new. It had rearranged things, intensified things, but everything that was happening now had always been happening. Each night, just at the edge of sleep, he heard voices far behind the blur of words. "The whole track inside" wasn't its real name, nor was it what we mistakenly call "life." Back of all that—before the track had divided, before the great gulf had been fixed, before the mistake had been made—the train would always come by for him in the extinguished lamplight just at the edge of sleep. It was as easy as flying.

SOUND. BY now he was sure that he could tell the difference between what was real and what was not, and this was a real sound—hard leather heels walking quickly down the narrow hallway past the furnace, approaching his door. Not a cop's walk—too light and rapid for that—but someone who didn't care about making noise, and he caught up to the full inevitability of it: *of course* he would know her sound; he'd been waiting for her so intensely he'd almost forgotten he'd been waiting. He opened the door before she knocked. "Hey, man," she said, and the jangle poured over him like napalm.

He contracted back into himself, withdrawing from the doorway. He didn't know what to say. Maybe he should try her name. He said it. "Pamela."

She took two steps inside. She turned toward him, then stopped, her feet in shiny black boots planted firmly on the floor a foot apart—a karate stance? She took a deep breath. He saw that she was shaking all over—just slightly, just enough to give her away. "I'm sorry," she said. "I'm so sorry."

"Sorry for what?"

"I'm sorry I ran away. I freaked, man. You probably felt deserted . . . Shit, you *were* deserted. And *I* did it," and then, like an aside to an audience, "That's me trying to own my actions, right?"

He could feel his heart tripping out. Adrenaline. The living animal. He should say something.

"I *did* desert you," she said. "I couldn't . . . I didn't have any choice, but I felt like shit about it. I still feel like shit about it. You don't run out on . . . I can't even say the word with a straight face, but we haven't got another one. You don't run out on your *comrades*."

Maybe it was *comrades*, or the long swingy navy coat, belted at the waist, or the knee-high boots worn over her jeans, or the way she'd just burst in and delivered her speech with no preliminaries: she seemed too flamboyant to be real, like a character out of *Dr. Zhivago*—but then the hard-edged immediacy of her, the astonishing unpredictable *presence* of her, made her perfectly real. She wasn't wearing ribbons in her hair, had brushed it straight back, Alice-style, and secured it with a plain black band. Simplicity. But it was the most eye makeup he'd ever seen on her—dancer's eyes, meant to carry all the way to the back of a darkened theater—and inside that fabulous artifice, the corneas of the speckled hazel he remembered remembering. *Alive.*

He watched her breathe. Deliberately. Telling herself to breathe? She stepped forward, reached out, and ran a gloved finger over his cheek just under the cheekbone. "Oh, baby," she said, her voice changed, now singing and sorrowful, "what are you living on? Air?"

He stepped back because he didn't have any choice. Air? He couldn't get enough of it. He was gobbling it up, trying to drink it down like a milkshake. He withdrew until the wall stopped him. Through a twist of the kaleidoscope, he saw her another way—she wasn't merely giving him a highly mannered performance, she was like a *little girl* giving a performance and nearly perishing of stage fright, a far younger Pamela embedded in the current version.

He couldn't very well say, "I forgive you." People didn't say things like that anymore. He said what he could. "It's OK." That sounded all right so he tried it again. "It's OK."

"I called you and called you and called you," she said.

"I was in New Hampshire."

"Yeah, Karen told me that." She shrugged—another apology. "I just got in last night. I called her . . . I didn't want to *call* you. Like it's been too long. Like it couldn't just be *a phone call*. She told me you'd dropped acid and it was . . . A bummer? Is that right? Jesus, man, how are you?"

"It was, yeah, a garbage trip. It was like . . ." Stick to formula words. "It was one of the most unpleasant experiences of my life. But I'm all right."

She was studying him. God knows what she was finding or how she was translating it. She undid the belt on her coat, unbuttoned it, shed it, and threw it onto the one and only chair. He could see that she'd been eating. She looked healthy. She was wearing a pink sweater. Pink! She didn't take her gloves off.

He knew that she'd dressed for him. He saw her knowing that he knew it. "Yeah, check me out, man, brand new from top to bottom. My father said, 'Pamela, what are you doing schlumping around like that? You look like a DP. Go buy yourself some decent clothes,' and he hands me the charge card. Like a year ago I would have told him to shove his charge card, but . . . I don't know, man, I've changed my ways . . .

"Oh, baby, you look . . ." She shrugged, exasperated with herself. "You look kind of scary . . . I don't mean . . . You look *cute* that thin, but . . . Shit, I shouldn't encourage you . . ."

"Have you been eating *anything?*" she said.

"Oh, hell," she said, "I'm saying all the wrong things. I know that nobody can make us eat if we don't want to, but . . ."

She had to be as frightened as he was. Even her legs were shaking. "I'm talking about your *head*, man. What the fuck are you *doing?*"

"I don't know," he said. "I *have* been eating. I'm not . . . Yeah, I have been. For real. And trying to write an article. It's not . . ." That was as much as he could say right now.

"What's it on?"

"Oh, shit. Just another critique. I guess it's supposed to be a critique of Weatherman. It feels kind of futile."

"Yeah? Well, our critiques will always be futile until futility writes the critique."

"Do you think that way naturally, or does it take an effort?"

He saw the surprise on her face. Then she laughed—a sharp, brief, staccato sound. "Glad you still got your sense of humor, man."

"I don't know if it's humor." He hadn't been trying to be funny. He'd really wanted to know.

She walked to his desk. "Mind if I look?"

"Oh, hell no."

She read through it quickly. Of course there wasn't much to read—his pathetic two paragraphs. "Right on," she said in a bugle-bright voice. Then, turning to find his eyes with her eyes: "It's good. It's necessary. I can see what you were trying to do . . . where you were going. It doesn't have to be long. Another two or three pages. Do you want me to finish it?" Meaning: Are we still a council?

"Yes," he said, "you finish it."

She nodded. What needed to be done, would be done. Like Lenin. No, not Lenin, God forbid. Like Rosa. She took off her gloves. Another pair so tight she had to tug at each finger. She flattened them, folded them, laid them on her coat. Now he knew why she wore gloves like that—although he couldn't have found the words to explain it to anyone who didn't already know. He saw her start to say something but give it up before she could find the words.

Instead, she paced. Looked at his guitar. Looked at his notes on the walls. Could she be doing it simply by walking, taking a quick tour of the inside of the box—finding a way to deal with the jangle, taking it all as it came? (He could never do anything that simply.) She circled away, passed the partially open window. It was raining—he'd been aware of the steady autumnal sound of it since morning—and he caught himself in the act of inhabiting his own small space. Some of his notes were on the walls; others he'd rejected, crumpled up, thrown into the corner. He was one of his own notes—infringed, taped, and baffled. He was a Charlie Chaplin hobo, scrabbling over scree and escarpment to vanish into an airy nothing.

"Wer jetzt allein ist . . ." a voice in his head reminded him. But he was *not* alone, at least not at the moment, and Pamela was talking about New York. The Movement fragmenting even worse than in Boston. A lot of Leninist bullshit, everybody talking about cells, cadres, revolutionary violence, Weatherman. She'd seen some SI people, but they were paranoid and jumpy and didn't want to talk

to her. Women were leaving the male-dominated groups—a good thing—and there was a lot of terrific women's lib organizing, the only hope on the horizon. And she'd taken some ballet classes, the first time she'd set foot in a dance studio in eight years. "So fucking weird, man. I thought I would freak, but I didn't. Well, not too much. Just wanted to see where I was at with it, if I could do it . . . a lot of my psychic energy still tied up in that shit. Even took pointe classes, if you can believe it. I thought I was in good shape, but oy, was I sore. I couldn't walk the next day."

Now she was looking at Zoë. Watching her look, he could feel the energy crackling off the wall where Zoë, undeviating, was multiplied— What was it Debord said? Where Zoë was mediated by images. "Are you close to her?" Pam said. He'd known that she was going to ask him about Zoë.

"It's not . . ." He wanted to draw a curtain over the images—but then, no, he didn't. "Yeah, I guess we're close . . . Well, not really *close*, but . . . It's hard to . . . She isn't just Cassandra's little sister. She's *my* little sister."

Pamela looking at Zoë—it was a mind-feeling-thing.

"John?"

"Yes."

"Are you all right?"

"Yeah, sure, I'm fine."

"How much weight have you lost?"

"I don't know."

"Haven't you weighed yourself?"

"No. I haven't got a scale. It doesn't matter a damn anyway. Look, Pam, I haven't been fasting. I swear to God I haven't."

Her level stare said: I don't believe you.

"I was in the hospital a motherfucking week, man," she said. "As soon as my doctor weighed me, ZAP, there I am, back in again. The son of a bitch. I said, 'Oh, for fuck's sake, give me a break. I'm only a couple of pounds under.' He said, 'That's good, Pamela. That means you'll only have a short visit . . . ' And I've been really careful. I mean *really* careful. I'm healthy as a horse. Yeah, pink-cheeked and rosy, a hundred and twelve pounds."

As she talked, she was moving closer. "And my head too," she said. "Like I saw Martha twice a week. Whew, did some really good work, man, and like . . . It was a quantum leap. I can't wait to tell you. I've changed my ways, man. I'm at a whole new level."

She was waiting for him. Impacted, he couldn't do anything but watch her. She shrugged. "I stayed with my father and his new . . . It was the best time I've had with him for years. Shit, if you didn't know better, you'd think we were two normal human beings. Yeah, and his new wife. She's only ten years older than I am, and she was scared shitless of me, you know, that I'd fuck up her scene . . . like, 'What are you doing with *my father*, you goddamned *little girl?*' And of course she's heard all about the hysterical crazy daughter . . . mad and bad. So I got her alone and said, 'Look, Elaine, I'm not going to give you any grief, mazel tov and all that . . . like we're going to get along just fine,' and we did get along just fine. You would have thought we were a nice normal family. He even lent me one of their cars."

She stopped. He could see her frustration. He knew he had to give something back to her. "Good," he said. "That's good."

"Hell, I even had tea with *my mother*. That's how fucking noble I am. I ought to get some kind of award. I couldn't eat for twenty-four hours afterward, but other than that, I was perfectly fine. Hey, don't just stare at me with those big sad eyes."

"I should have put the whole poem up," he said suddenly, the words blowing out of him with no warning. "I don't know why I didn't. Jesus, it's kind of obvious . . . Rilke. Did you ever read Rilke? I just put up the end part . . . the part that says, 'Whoever's alone now is going to stay alone for a long time.' But the damn poem starts with, '*Herr: es ist Zeit. Der Sommer war sehr gross.*' Yes. That's so heavy. 'Lord, it is time. The summer was so full.' Yes. That's like really important. That's like, you know, really *heavy . . .*" He shrugged. He couldn't begin to tell her how heavy it was.

She was giving him a different look now. He saw the tension in small muscles around her eyes: *Yes? OK, you can tell me everything.* He couldn't do that. It wasn't that he didn't want to, it was that words were no damned good.

"No, I've never read Rilke," she said. "I never read *any* poetry.

I never have time. Like where we're at now, the only possible art is political art . . . But I don't know. It's too easy to get arrogant on that shit. Maybe I should . . . Should I?"

"Should you what? Read poetry? Yeah, sure . . . How can you live without poetry? Rilke? I don't know. Maybe you'd like him, maybe you wouldn't. Maybe it's just my thing. For me, he's like the poet of the past. There's . . . About the only good thing I got out of that acid trip . . . It's hard to explain. There are these mind-feeling-things . . . like really intense. And Rilke's one of the ways back into them."

She seemed to be waiting for something more. He'd thought for a moment that he'd clarified everything; now he saw that he'd clarified nothing. All he could find were shifting fragments, glass shards shaken in a glass bowl. Well, no, there was one other thing—what he'd guessed. *Sisters?* Cassandra's little sister? What he'd been afraid might happen, had happened—he saw Pamela now as *his* sister; that is, he saw her plain little face as entirely beautiful. "Jesus, it's hot in here," he said. He was sweating out of every pore.

He stepped toward the gas stove to turn it off. Saw a flash of it—clear and brilliant—the flame sodium yellow and copper blue. Then he was stopped, staring at the radiator. There was no gas stove. There was no Rilke poem taped to his wall, and there never had been. This was not Morgantown. This was Cambridge. "Pam," he said, frightened, "I'm still kind of out of it."

"Yeah, I know."

Again he fled to the far side of the room. To feel space between them. Nowhere near enough space. Unbearable bursts of electrical energy—a million tiny burns—down his neck, up his back, along his arms, between his legs. This is dangerous, he thought. I've been here before, and this is dangerous.

"How out of it?" she said. "Where are you? Come on, man, talk to me."

He felt the same luminous— Whatever it was, it felt much the same as when she'd walked into the *Weasel* office for the first time, but now, while he hadn't been paying attention, she must have slipped by him on one of the strands, because he met her like someone who's been for miles, who didn't have time. Transcribed by his own notes, he felt himself tipped, body over time—

"Say anything," she told him. "I don't give a shit what it is. Whatever's in your head. Anything at all."

He could have sworn he was seeing *her* and not his own mind stuff. "I'm glad you don't wear lipstick," he said. He saw that surprise her. It had surprised him too.

"Well, nobody does right now, but that's just . . . OK, it's too big a symbol for me. Way too heavy for me. Lipstick is *my mother*, you dig? I could wear a dress before I could wear lipstick. Come on, what else?"

"There's something really fluid about you . . . alive about you. The way you move . . . even just the way you sit . . . You're always graceful."

"Thanks. That's nice. That's a nice thing to tell an ex-dancer."

She stepped toward him; he saw her blur into a mind-feeling-space he might have been able to call "anguish" if he hadn't known that words were no damned good. It was impossible to separate his feelings from hers; he saw a stutter of incompleted motion rippling out from her, a strobe-light image he was afraid was more mental than real, and he knew that there was only a limited amount of time he could go on doing this. "Do you still love me?" she said.

He answered without hesitation, "Yes. I love you."

Then he could hardly believe it—although he wanted to believe it. He could see her relief. It made him want to cry. And, with a painful thud like a dislocated joint finding its way home, he was back. He was nowhere else but here. He was right here.

"That's good," she said. "I'm glad. I was afraid you'd stop."

"No, I didn't stop. Were you really afraid?"

"Yes, I really was afraid. Fuck you, man, I have feelings. I throw up words around myself like . . . you know, to protect myself. But I have feelings. Like *strong* feelings. Pack up your shit, man, we're getting out of here. This place is weird."

10.

HER APARTMENT, just as he'd remembered it, was white and calming, and everything that wasn't white was one of the colors of coolness. Outside it was still raining, and she'd become matter-of-fact; if he wanted to, he could read her as coiled back into a quiet anger, but he knew that's not where she'd gone.

"We're a council," she said, "so there's no private property, you dig? But having said that . . . Shit, I sound like a goddamned professor . . . *But having said that*, I also want to say I'm a neatness freak. If you look around, you'll see that everything has a place. If you don't know the place, ask. If you think it's a dumb place, we'll talk about it, but . . . No, I don't think it's a petit-bourgeois hang-up. We're not going to waste our time doing the politics of housework, are we?"

"No."

"OK, and . . . No, don't unpack yet. We'll do that later. We'll work everything out. We'll figure out something we can both eat. We'll go to the laundromat . . . Do you want to take a shower?"

Late afternoon, and the rain driven hard against the windows—that was all he could translate. Something seasonal. Something Northrop Frye would write about, an autumn ritual—dried peas shaken in a dried gourd. She seemed to be waiting for him to reply.

"You always trusted me, didn't you?" she said.

"Yes."

"Even that first night when we went to the Chinese restaurant and you hardly . . . So there must have always been . . ."

"Pam," he said, "you're as scared as I am, aren't you?"

"Oh, yeah." Her signature shrug. "Yeah, I am." She crossed the empty three feet of space between them and took his hands. Hers were cold and wet. "Oy, I'm so fucking nervous." She looked young to him. He squeezed her hands.

"You didn't know me at all," she said. "Why did you trust me?"

He felt her single-pointedness, her tenacity. It made him smile. He was about to say, "I don't know," but he did know. "I believed what you said. That you *meant* what you said. That you'd *do* what you said. And there was . . . A vibe . . . Oh, for Christ's sake. There's no words for it."

"Me too. When we first saw each other in the *Weasel* office . . . like really intense . . . and when we walked around the Yard and talked for hours and hours. But I'm not . . . I work hard to look solid, but I'm not. I freak sometimes. Sometimes things blow through me like smoke. You've got to know that about me. You can trust me, but . . . sometimes I freak, that's all."

"It's OK."

"No, it's not OK . . ." and then, as though addressing herself in another voice, "Shit, Pamela, go ahead and push the wall."

"It *is* OK."

"Yeah, right now. It's OK right now. Do you still trust me?"

"Yes."

"Even though I'm scared . . . ? I figured out a lot of . . . It's not a *bad* scared. Oh, fuck. Look, if we were in an action together? Something dangerous? Would you trust me?"

"Yes."

"Would you trust me with your life?"

With that one, he was back in *Dr. Zhivago* or some other melodrama much like it, but he answered her honestly. "Yes."

"OK, then trust me now." She kissed him lightly on the mouth. "Come on, baby, take a shower."

He followed her into the bathroom. "I don't care if we use each other's towels," she said, "but here's a clean one." It was neatly folded. "There's some conditioner in there." The shelf above the bathtub. "God, you guys are ridiculous," she said. "You grow all that hair, and then you don't know how to take care of it."

He hadn't known how chilled he was until he felt the heat of the water. He kept making it hotter. He used her soap and her shampoo. He'd never used conditioner before, but he followed the instructions on the label. What was happening was inevitable. It didn't matter what he thought about it; it didn't even matter how he felt about it; he was being carried along on a deep fast channel. He dried himself with her towel, then wrapped it around his waist. He took a single step through the doorway, hesitated, the slick of the hardwood pulling at his moist bare feet. His body was steaming, scented with her flowers.

She had been standing at the window, looking out at the rain. She turned to look at him "Oh, aren't you lovely? I shouldn't encourage you, I really shouldn't, but oh . . ."

She was offering him something. A cup. The twin of the one she'd kicked from his hand. "It's cocoa," she said. "I drink cocoa when I'm headed for fail-safe . . . but I can't force myself to drink whole milk. It's skimmed milk. Motherfucking ridiculous, huh? It's got honey in it. If you haven't been eating much, you'll really taste the sugar . . . Can I look at you?"

He took the cup from her—a girl, fully dressed—and she took the towel. Whatever had been protecting him in the shower—had made him resigned, detached, nearly *depersonalized*—was blown all to hell. Maybe it had been illusion after all—or, that is, maybe it was *all* illusion, because life was jangle, a raging animal fire that only stopped at death. "Oh, God," she said, "you're so scared. I'm sorry . . . I didn't mean to . . ."

Her hands were automatically folding the towel. She walked away from him and put it down on the kitchen table. "Hey," she said, turning back, "I'm just kind of shy, OK? Like a hundred and twelve feels heavy to me. Just about as solid as I want to get. But my goddamned doctor would like me at a hundred *and twenty*. In the hospital they even got me there once. That was a few years ago. But I was only there for like . . . I feel zaftig at a hundred and twenty. I hate it. Like weighted down, bottom-heavy . . . like my goddamned mother, for Christ's sake. And even a hundred and twelve still feels . . . I will let you see me, but this is . . . Oy, why can't I ever just shut up? You can see why I was always in trouble at school. But I wish you could see me at . . . I don't know, maybe a hundred and five . . . Fuck, Pamela, maybe zero? Negative weight? Pure spirit? Oy, this is ridiculous. We can't see ourselves. That's part of the . . . I know in my head that a hundred and twelve is perfectly all right, that I'm not the least bit fat, but . . . We've got to be mirrors for each other. You look just lovely, by the way, but you're not allowed to lose an ounce. I mean it, not another fucking ounce. Are you OK? Are you shy? Like I don't want you to feel demeaned. Now I feel terrible. Oh, come here. Come on."

She caught him in a clumsy embrace. She sat down on a kitchen chair, pulled him along with her. Startled, he set the cup down on the table. She kissed his cheeks and eyelids. She drew him onto her lap. It was beyond strange. Naked as a jaybird, he was sitting on a girl's lap. He could feel the rough denim of her jeans under his thighs, the powder-puff texture of her sweater against his bare skin. "Why pink?" he said.

"Why not pink? . . . I'm sorry, that's a smartass answer. That's what I'd say to Deb. You know Deb? This was her apartment. We were close, but we argued like all the time. She's as bad as I am, and we . . . like two dogs with a bone. For hours, man. Pink? I thought you'd like it, OK? The ambiguity. I thought you'd like it."

"Yeah, I like it. I'm having trouble talking."

"Yeah, I noticed."

"This feels so goddamned weird," he said. "I must be too heavy for you."

"No, you're not. Are you kidding? Oh, wow, you have long lashes, but they're pale like mine."

He felt her shift position on the chair—opening her legs wider to take some of his weight directly onto the tight crotch of her jeans. To answer her, he kissed her; he'd meant it to be tentative, exploratory, but she responded immediately, her tongue in his mouth. His sullen penis finally woke up. She ran her fingertips over his chest, his stomach. She stroked him fully erect. "It's so . . . velvety," she said. "I've never . . . You've got to give me a chance to get used to you. I'm not . . . I usually sleep with women. You knew that about me, didn't you?"

He felt the shock of it, a spooky gust of rain blown against his naked back. "No . . . Well, maybe on some level . . . I knew *something* about you."

"I have slept with boys before, but . . . It was like I just sort of . . . OK, man, here I am, do your thing. But . . . like only . . ." To stop the words, he kissed her again, felt the change in her breath.

She drew back to look at him. He'd never seen her eyes that close before. "But this is . . . Like one of the arguments we used to . . . like Deb and I . . . She'd say, 'We can't play roles anymore. We can't play games. Games are always the Man's games,' and I'd say, 'OK, then show me what *authentic* looks like.' It's like everything we do is a game. They haven't left us anything that's authentic. It's like . . ." She stopped in mid-sentence, shook her head and smiled. "Oh, for Christ's sake," she said. She licked his nipples into two small points of fire.

He stroked the back of her neck, felt the lines of muscle under the soft pink fur of her sweater. Sitting naked on her lap had opened the door to a mind-feeling-thing—girls had sat on his lap, and he knew now why they'd done what they'd done when they'd been sitting on his lap. "Like Rousseau," Pamela was saying, "all that crap about natural man. But like Lévi-Strauss went all the way to . . . Ah!"

He'd thrust his tongue deep into the tiny pocket of her ear. The next breath she drew was as ragged as a torn sheet. He wanted to hear her gasp again, so he bit her earlobe—felt the large long muscles of her thighs contract, her feet pressing hard into the floor. She wrapped her fingers into his hair, pulled his face to hers, and kissed him—not gently. Whispering, she said, "I was afraid you'd be strange, but you're not strange at all."

Reaching behind him, she thrust the palm of her hand between the cheeks of his ass, her fingers pressed over his sphincter, and squeezed. Now it was his turn to gasp. With her other hand—her short neat nails—she tapped on the underside of his penis. He arched back, the world going flash yellow. "Oh, God," he heard himself saying. She held him suspended at the end of an impossible ribbon, kissed him deliberately, methodically, while he hung and burned, unable to think. "I am so turned on," she said in a matter-of-fact voice, "I think I am going to die."

She released him and stood him up. She offered him her hand and he took it. She led him behind the white screen to the white bed with its eyelet lace. The fear had left him alone for a while, but now it was back, eroding him. He could try to ignore the mistake all he wanted to, but it was still there, and it was still a mistake. His miserable penis was losing its blood; pink and clean, it flopped and swung as he walked. "It's OK to be scared," she said.

She motioned for him to lie on the bed. Blanked, he fell onto it, stared at the white ceiling. "Will you play with me?" she said.

He could tell that she really wanted an answer. "Yeah, sure . . . if I can."

"Of course you can. There's nothing to lose because there's nothing to win. We've got all the time in the world, and we're just *playing*, OK?"

"OK."

"Listen. Here's the game. Just like with kids, there's rules. And here's the rules. You're not allowed to move. Not at all. Nothing. Not a muscle. Do you understand?"

"Yes."

"Is that OK with you?"

"Yes."

She arranged him the way she wanted him to lie—on his back, pillows behind his head, his arms lying at his sides, his legs apart. She walked to the dresser, returned with a pale grey scarf, folded it over itself to make a long narrow stripe, and laid it gently over his eyes. "Is that all right? I don't want to scare you."

"Yeah, it's all right. If I'm scared, I'll tell you."

First things—not darkness but a watery blur of lights, pink and green and golden—and then his hearing opened out to enormity. The zipper in her jeans, the sleek sound of them being pushed down and off. Other sounds not quite identifiable, cottony and evocative. He felt the clean weight of her on the bed. She kissed him. "You're such a pretty thing," she whispered, her mouth close to his ear. He felt her fingers on his hip bone. He flinched, his entire body contracting.

"Oh, jumpy," she said. "Lie still. I told you, you're not allowed to move. You're not allowed to move *at all*."

He heard the lid being unscrewed from something—metal on glass—then a sweet familiar scent. Something edible. Apricots. "Ah!" His sound. Involuntary. Her hands on his stomach. "What's that?"

"Shhh," she said and pressed more firmly, the fingers of both hands in the concavity under his ribcage, tracing his stomach

213

muscles. "Baby," she murmured to him. "Sweetheart. My angel."

Not able to see her, he couldn't prepare for the sensations, defend against them. With the tip of her tongue, she outlined his lips. She touched him lightly at first, then more firmly—circled the backs of his knees, then drew her fingers along the insides of his thighs, always returned to his hip bones, to his stomach. Nerves sandpapered raw, violently aware of her touch—delicious, maddening, dangerous— and the only way he could bear the delicacy and the fire was to brace himself against it, to recreate himself as a steel rod wedged against concrete. She was in no hurry. Reading her fingers on his skin and muscles, he knew she would eventually touch his penis—all of her motions were aimed there as clearly as if she was drawing a hundred tiny arrows pointing that way. And the damned thing was or wasn't hard—he couldn't be sure—although he felt a clotted ache. Standing out. Or not. Giving him away, whatever it was doing.

Her fingers were suddenly in the sensitive creases at the very tops of his legs, at the edge of his groin; his entire body contracted. "Lie still," she said.

She touched him there again. He flinched away, gasping. "I said *lie still*." She smacked him on the hip. Hard. Stinging. He heard her giggle. "Oh, boy," she whispered, "do I ever have your number."

She kissed him, slowly, deliberately. She licked the whorls of his ear. "Come on, baby," she murmured, "let go."

The strange land they were exploring was hers, and he began to see the logic of it. There were two ways not to move—he could become as rigid as a spike or as soft as water. He'd been there before; that is, like a covenant, it had been waiting for him from where it had lurked and had time, and he chose soft. It was not merely compliance, or even taking a dark pleasure in compliance. It was what Pamela had always wanted—a total critique. Of course he would have to let go, but he wanted more than that. He wanted to throw himself open to her, to give himself to her in a way that meant acceptance and welcome. He wanted to be velvet for her.

He let the fear go, gave up trying to be clenched or hard. He melted into the bed, opened his mouth to her tongue, felt her hands on him—wherever they were on his body, whatever they were doing with it—felt her as a blessing, an unwinding, an opening warmth. Dissolving downward, he slipped beyond time. She drew the scarf from his eyes. Blazing with light, he saw her. Like waking from a dream and not finding the unbearable poignancy of vanishing love, drifting away, lost forever—but instead finding love exactly where it should be. She was sitting astride him, complete and shining.

Her naked body was even whiter than her face—the lovely tracery of blue veins, her chest that swelled slightly outward into two gentle circles tipped with pink disks, the deep hollows under her collar bones, the hard sinews of her shoulders, the precisely curving instrument of her ribs. He could see her breathing. Then, jagged-edged, he was conscious of himself, of his traitorous body. But, looking down, found a miracle—nothing of himself left standing out. His penis was gone. It had vanished without a trace. He was as smoothly drawn as a girl. Then, catching up to her, he saw how easy it had been. She had slipped herself delicately over him. Now he was inside her, and she was protecting him. They had become marvelously and beautifully fused at the hips. He could never have imagined such grace or such a gift. His eyes burned, then blurred. "Oh, baby," she said, "don't *cry*."

She bent forward to kiss him. "Move, sweetheart. You can move now."

He did what he'd wanted to do since he'd met her—held her, explored her, felt her vertebrae and the hard musculature of her back, felt the power of the muscles in her thighs and buttocks. They were moving together, fused at the hips. There was nothing left to solve, nothing left to do. He was being carried along on a deep fast channel. The motion wasn't hard to find; it was as easy as flying. It flowed through him and into her as he went white and brilliant.

Returned, he could hear the hard autumn rain and the crystalline music of the neighbor's distant stereo. He and Pamela were still melted together—although they'd turned onto their sides. They lay together side by side. She stroked his face, licked away his tears. "Oh, what a watery boy. It's OK. It's OK. You can cry all you want. It's good to cry."

She gently drew her hips away, and his penis came flopping

out—wet, happy, and deflated. She laughed. He found, to his surprise, that he could laugh too. Looking into her eyes—the magical flecks of blues and browns in the hazel. "Make me come," she said.

"Here," she said, guiding his hand. "It's easy," and pressed her mouth against his.

"That's right," she said. "That's exactly right . . . You don't have to be quite *that* gentle."

It happened sooner than he would have expected. She arched—her angel's pale hard body contracting in his arms—"Ahh, ahh!"

Amazed, he looked at her, watched her breathe. "OK, that's better," she said. And then: "We were driving each other crazy before. Like that's not a metaphor. Like literally crazy."

Softened, she settled into the curve of his arm. "Something you should know about me," she said. "After I come, I go straight back into my head. Like instantly. My mind just takes off a million miles a minute . . . Are you OK? Was it OK for you?"

"OK?" he said. *"I love you."*

"Of course you do. And it's mutual. Like the feelings you have, well, I . . ."

"Oh, shut up, Pamela," she told herself, "you shmegegge."

Staring at the ceiling, she said, "It's the words. I keep hearing my mother saying, 'I love you, Pammy,' and all the time she was trying to kill me. Well, fuck. I've got to get over my mother, don't I?"

She looked into his eyes again. "OK. All right. Baby, sweetheart, I love you too . . . Oy, you're crying again. My sweet angel. Shhh. It's OK, it's OK. I do love you. I do."

She jumped out of bed, brought back the dope and her licorice papers. It was something he'd already known about her—that she could stand to be close only for a while. He hadn't smoked dope since his acid trip, but he thought that he could smoke dope now.

"I was afraid it might not work," she said. "Well, I was pretty sure it would work. That's a game Melanie and I used to play. She was my first girlfriend. If it goes on long enough, you go like completely fucking nuts . . . *hysterical* you want it so much. I thought if it worked on a girl, it would work on you. It's one of the things . . . You know, I didn't understand for the longest damned time. I just didn't know what to *do* with you. And then when I was back home . . . It wasn't even in a therapy session. It was after I'd *walked out* of one. And it flashed on me. Oh, that's it. He's not a man. He's an androgyne just like me."

———

SO AFTER John came back, Cass and me crashed in the camper because we didn't have anywhere else to go, right? Like all of a sudden we were kicked back out into the cold cruel world like a couple of blind dumb puppies—that's pretty much the way she saw it. And you know, when she puts her mind to it, Cass can be a real fucking pain in the ass. And if you keep wearing away at me, I'm not exactly the world's most laid-back dude either. So, from time to time, when both of us got to the point where we'd be looking over our shoulders and hoping to God we wouldn't see the other one looking back, I'd dump her at John's or in a goddamned bookstore, and then I'd shoot over to have a nice quiet cup of tea with my good buddy's old lady—anyhow, just so long as my good buddy happened to be in New Hampshire. It was one of those situations I think they call UNSTABLE. Yeah, and more than likely it would have blown to shit eventually, but one night I'm at Lyons' picking up a key, and we're making the air vibrate, and I say, "Jesus, fuck, Robert, this back-of-the-camper horseshit grows old on you real fast. We sure could use us a place to crash."

He says, "Funny you should mention that, Tommy boy. There's this dude I met, name of Garvin. And he's got this house over in Somerville, living there with his old lady. And he's having a little trouble making the scratch for the first of the month. So if you was to fall by there with something in your pocket more than your pecker, he'd welcome you with open arms."

That sounded promising, so I drove straight over there and Garvin wasn't home but his old lady was. Her name was Lorraine. I told her I was a friend of Bob Lyons, and she goes blank. I mean MUD-WALL BLANK. She says, "Bob's got a lot of friends, doesn't he?" If you think you've heard NOTHING in somebody's voice, you should have heard hers.

I allowed as how Bob did have a lot of friends and she made

coffee. She had very pale blue eyes and they weren't giving away a whole hell of a lot either, but they sure were checking me out. I'm thinking, shit, what does she take me for? A nark? A rip-off artist? Bob's HEAVY, for Christ's sake?

She was a strawberry blond, a real one, all the way down to the roots. When she'd been in her twenties, she must have been the kind of chick that guys would cream themselves just watching her sit down, but she'd had lots of miles run on her since then and it had made her careful and tired. She wasn't dressed in what you'd call the best of taste. Well, let's say you're sitting in a bar minding your own business and all of a sudden you hear a voice in your left ear—"Hey, sport, buy me a drink?"—and you look over and there's a LADY on the next bar stool. That's what she looked like. But she had a real slow easy way of talking. I said, "Where you from?"

She says, "Texas."

I say, "Far out. Yeah, FAR OUT WEST. I'm from North Dakota," and she smiles for the first time. So I break out the smoke and we do that, and I say, "Look, sweet stuff, I don't know what you took me for when I walked in here, but Lyons and me were assholes in the service together, and that's about it as far as it goes with him and me. I'm looking for a place for me and my old lady to crash, and that's all . . . the end of the song, there is no more."

She says, "Shit, man, you never know who's going to walk in the door, right?"

I agreed with her that, yes, it was true, you never did know.

So she showed me around, and it was just an ordinary big old house, but compared to John's place, it was the Taj Mahal. And the rent was low because it was in Somerville, and it had three bedrooms, and there was a nice big one with good light, vacant as could be, and by then, Garvin was back. There must be some kind of tradition with junkies that some of them don't have first names because I've met other junkies like that, but whatever Garvin's first name was, nobody ever mentioned it. Even Lorraine called him Garvin. He was skinny as a rat's tail, and not too long ago his head had been shaved—like, you know, SHAVED. He was maybe ten years younger than Lorraine but already he was looking chewed and tired and careful. And they were both giving me the MUD-WALL STARE.

Lorraine says, "He's all right," meaning me, and Garvin gives me that funny handshake with the thumb up in the air which I never know what to do with. "What are you into, man?"

"Oh, I do a little dealing."

I see this long look go back and forth between them—like, oh fucking shit, our worst nightmare come true. He says, "Smack?"

"Oh, hell no. I just move a little grass around town."

They both say, "Grass!" and then they crack up like it's the funniest thing they've ever heard.

Garvin never looks at you when he's talking to you, and he talks out of the side of his mouth like he's letting you in on who fixed the next race. So he's peering away at the corner of the room and slipping me the straight scoop sideways. "I was supposed to get this warehousing gig, you dig? They said they'd let me know next week, you know how it is, man, 'Don't call us, we'll call you.' Shit. Bet you been down that road plenty times yourself, huh? I applied all over town. Nothing. Not even the mayonnaise plant. Used to be you could always get something at the mayonnaise plant. But nothing. I should have motherfucking re-upped, you know what I mean? So what with one thing or another, we're kind of tapped out, man."

"I think I can do the rent this month," I say.

He nods a couple times and goes, "Beautiful," and that's that.

THE BIG thing about Garvin and Lorraine was that they were REHABILITATED. Garvin had got himself a fairly substantial habit in Nam—like he was the only guy I ever met who used to wish he was back there. "Jesus, man, you wouldn't believe how pure the smack is in Saigon. Ain't cut with nothing!" Well, the US Army turned him loose, and he came back to The World, and the first thing he discovered was that if he wanted to maintain his habit, he was going to have to be knocking down the bread like Howard Hughes, and the second thing was that the good folks at home weren't exactly killing themselves to hire fucked-up ex-GIs. So he checked out the inventory of skills he'd picked up in the War Effort and decided he'd try out the good old time-honored Break-and-Enter Trade. And he did that, and it worked out just fine, and he figured he was well on his way to being reintegrated into civilian life. Then one night he shoved a color TV through a window and set it down, and then he shoved his ass through the window and turned around to get a good grip on the TV, and lo and behold there's a Boston cop waiting for him. So he went up before the judge and got to do his song and dance about how pure the smack was over in Saigon, and the judge, being an upright citizen, was APPALLED, right? And he said, "This poor boy does not need to be PUNISHED, he needs to be REHABILITATED." So instead of going into the slammer, Garvin went to a hospital for junkies, and that's where he met Lorraine.

"It wasn't so bad in the hospital," Lorraine says, "was it, Garvin? We was smuggling reefer in by the key, and they didn't give two shits about that . . . so long as it wasn't doogie. And they didn't care who's in whose bedroom, right? We got to have these encounter group things just like Synanon and sit around and yell at each other, and that was always good for a few laughs."

"Yeah," he says, "and three squares a day and snacks in between. Shit, it wasn't bad in the hospital."

How Lorraine got there was like this. She'd been minding her own business just walking out of Bonwit Teller's, but she couldn't find a good word to say to the rent-a-cop about why she was wearing five dresses under her coat, so she got to do HER number for the judge. "Well, what do you expect, your honor, man, with me up to a bag a day?" And he says, "Lorraine, don't give me that crap. You have a record as long as my right leg." And she says, "Well, judge, that's because I've never been REHABILITATED."

"What do they do in there?" I say. "Do they taper you off or something?" I told you I've always been the perfect straight-man.

"Shit, no," Lorraine says, "they just withdraw you."

"Withdraw means withdraw," Garvin says. "It ain't as bad as all that. It's not like the movies. It's just like having the worst case of flu you ever had in your life, that's all."

So here they were back on the street again, REHABILITATED, right? They'd lucked into the house in Somerville because the previous tenants had found it necessary to depart for the West Coast at a great rate of speed, if you know what I mean, and then Cass and me coming along like completed the picture—well, especially with me paying the rent. And it was a big house, so we had us some room to breathe. And Cass thought Garvin and Lorraine were better than Nichols and May, like their act really cracked her up. Yeah, it wasn't too bad there for a while. A man can get used to anything, right?

WELL, YOU know what's funny? If Cass and me had never moved in with Garvin and Lorraine at all, like if we'd just hung on crashed in the camper, everything would have worked out fine. You see, weird Pam Zalman came back to town, and John moved in with her, and if anybody needed to get laid, he did, and believe me, he was one happy man. And that left his rat-hole apartment standing empty, so we could have gone back there, right? One of those famous missed opportunities, right? Well, it depends on how you look at it. Like my mom says, there's always the silver lining. After my good buddy Ethan came back to town, things got a little hairy for me and Terry, but guess what? I still had a key to John's apartment.

There's this thing about fucking your brains out. After you do it enough times, you get to the point where you can TALK TO EACH OTHER. So I'm laying there one night with Terry on that foamie at John's, and we're in that sweet blown-away state you get into when you're totally satisfied, and I look down at those big dark eyes, and it finally dawns on me I don't know zip about her. "Hey, babyshake," I say, "just who the hell are you?"

She makes like she don't know what I'm talking about, so I say, "Look, it's real simple. My name's Thomas Samuel Parker and I spring from a long line of crazy Scotsmen who settled out in the Dakota Territories back in the days when the Sioux Indians would drop in for breakfast. So the good book says go forth and multiply, and that's one thing they had covered. I got aunts and uncles and cousins scattered all over the place, and North Dakota may be the asshole of the universe, but it's MY asshole, so if things ever get too harsh, I can always go back there. And guess what? I can roll a smoke with one hand while riding a horse, which is something I bet you can't do. OK, you getting the picture? Now let me ask you again—JUST WHO THE HELL ARE YOU?"

I didn't think she was going to answer me, but eventually she gives me this funny little smile and says, "What it says on my birth certificate is Margaret Teresa Flaherty."

That one really cracked me up. I just couldn't stop laughing about it. "Sweet Jesus, a little mackerel snapper."

"Oh, shut the fuck up, man. It's not that funny."

"Oh, yeah it is. An honest-to-God Irish Mick."

Well, OK, she had to admit to it, she says, but Maggie Flaherty died in the summer of sixty-seven. You know, with the help of good old Ethan and a few hits of pure Sandoz acid. Yes, Maggie Flaherty had been a nice Catholic girl who had her life all planned out for her, and she was just walking straight down the middle of the road the way she should, like going to BU and dating nice Catholic boys and all that, but then she died, kind of suddenly and horribly, and the person that got born in her place was what I was seeing before me—TERRY THE WITCH. Maggie Flaherty was no dumbbell, she said, like she had the straight scoop on a lot of things but just twisted—like the way THE CHURCH twisted everything.

Terry was real down on THE CHURCH. She couldn't say anything bad enough about THE CHURCH, what with them burning witches and doing their Spanish Inquisition and I don't know what all. "Whenever those dudes saw something REAL, man, they always tried to kill it." She figured what was wrong with THE CHURCH was they were hung up on sex. It wasn't Jesus' fault, it was all those assholes who came after him. Like when he had a human body, he was probably getting it on with Mary Magdalene, and now whenever he looked down on the world, he probably wept because of how wrong we'd got it and how bad we'd fucked it up. And what we were living through now was what the Hindus called THE KALIYUGA, and that meant the worst possible age in the entire history of the universe that went back quadrillions of uncountable years.

It's funny, but she believed exactly the same thing that Ethan did: SEX IS THE KEY TO THE UNIVERSE. "That's all well and good, sweet stuff," I say, "but what do you think he'd think about YOU fucking ME?"

"Oh, he wouldn't be delighted . . . But, shit, man, that's HIS hang-up."

Where we were headed, she said, was THE AGE OF AQUARIUS, and when we got there, everybody would fuck everybody whenever they felt like it, but it was going to take a hell of a lot of pain and suffering to get there because we all had some heavy-duty hang-ups to work through. She had a few real ugly ones herself, she said.

So anyhow, Terry and me got to know each other a little. It was nice. I never felt, you know, COMFORTABLE with her—the way I did with Cassandra when we first got together—but I enjoyed her company. Her show was highly entertaining. She was checked out on the Hindus and the Buddhists and the Native American Indians and the Tarot cards and the witchcraft and all that other hippy-dippy shit, and she could rap about it for hours. And I remember . . . This is funny. One night she said to me, "We all got our hang-ups . . . except for YOU, Thomas Samuel Parker." Yeah, I had to laugh at that one. "Oh, yeah, that's me all right," I said, "one hundred percent sane."

FOR A while there, we were all looking good. Back in the old days before she'd accepted Sweet Doogie as her personal Lord and Savior, Lorraine had done an incarnation as a housewife, so she was thoroughly checked out in the culinary department, and she was also one of the world's most accomplished rip-off artists. Like she'd come home with incredible things stuffed under her clothes—six game hens or a whole leg of lamb or a bohunking big fish—and there was always plenty of smoke, and we'd lay around having these far-out dinners and wrecking ourselves for the rest of the night. So Garvin and Lorraine were doing REHABILITATED, and Cass was doing DOMESTIC, and Terry and me were getting our rocks off on a fairly regular basis and not bugging anybody in the process. Even Ethan was happy as a clam. He kept talking about how the *Weasel* had been a millstone around his neck, and what a relief it was for it to be gone, and most nights he had his nose buried in a seed catalogue, planning HIS NEXT CROP. We didn't see much of John because him and Pamela the Great were heavy into each other, but I'd fall by their place sometimes to drop off a little smoke, and . . . well, I don't know if SEX IS THE KEY TO THE UNIVERSE for the rest of us poor fools, but it sure was for them. Like they were in bed even when they weren't, and sometimes I couldn't get out of there quick enough.

I laid it on John that I might have some USE for his apartment, although I did not specify exactly what that use might be. He didn't give a shit. He'd left a lot of his stuff there because he and Pamela weren't really LIVING TOGETHER. This rap was man-to-man, you know—like one night when Pamela was off with the chicks doing her women's lib thing, so him and me could give each other the straight scoop. "Oh," I said, "is that right?" Because they were about as LIVING TOGETHER as two people could get.

"Yeah," he says, "we're maintaining our AUTONOMY."

"Well, shit, old buddy," I say, "I'm sure glad to hear that. Yeah, is that ever a relief. I'd sure hate to see a man lose his AUTONOMY."

So the long and the short of it was that I kept on paying his rent—which was nothing, which was like pocket change—so he could maintain his AUTONOMY. And so I could maintain mine.

———

A PAUSE like a dip out of time, and then they were gone—out from behind the Japanese screen and cut loose into the slanting sunlight of the late afternoon, driven by a fury of manic energy. More than speed-rapping—a torrent of words, an explosion of words—words blazing up and out and away. "Dig it. That defining moment. What did you . . . ?"

"A gathering point . . ."

"Yeah, and so there you are, and . . ."

"When it all comes together . . ."

"Yeah, man, right on."

Tingle at his fingertips, deepening in his breath, amber filaments tickling his stomach, zing of current up his spine, prickle at the base of his neck, the light in the room leaping up to meet him—"So there you are in your Alice costume," she was saying, "and you've got it right . . . all the way to the patent leather shoes. The mandatory fetish. Not like in Freud, like in *primitive*. Ritual object. Imbued with power. And you're what . . . ? Scared to death? Like embarrassed?"

"You better believe it."

"And that little girl . . . ?"

"Nancy Clark."

"Yeah, and she says, 'Come on, Alice, sit by me,' and it's like, 'Sure you can be on my side. Sure you can *be like me.*' What a great little girl. What a fantastic little girl."

"Wait, wait," he said, "let me get it right." He couldn't get the words out fast enough. Pacing up and down, waving his arms, practically bouncing off the walls. He wanted to throw away the last vestiges of safety and swing away into a high wild dance, ride it straight through to the blue and golden edge of nothing. "I'd love to show you her picture, and that picture of me, but they're in Toronto. Along with every other damn thing I own that matters."

The glass of the windows, the dazzling whiteness, the pinks and greys, the lovely blend of emptiness and object—he loved everything. Yes, he was moving, it was true, and there was absolutely nothing left to protect, absolutely nothing he could possibly lose. He was more than euphoric; he was ringing higher than the highest tone in the upper partials—he'd made it out to where the air was clear and thin. There was no way they could ever misunderstand each other now, not when they'd just spent hours in her huge white bed—where he'd come twice and she'd come God knows how many times. It was incredible how many times she could come.

"Sometimes it feels more like me than me," he said. "I don't remember what I thought when I was seven . . . you know, the words in my head . . . but I remember the mind-feeling. I was a girl. Anybody who didn't think so could go straight to hell. But having to pretend to be a boy seemed . . . phony. Oh my God, so much work."

"Do you still think you're a girl?"

"No, but . . . OK, this is weird. When I was on acid, I found this thing that lurked and had time. And it was . . . OK, like there's a track . . . This is hard to talk about . . . I mean, I want to talk about it, but words are no damned good. And at the end of the track is . . . like exactly what I've just told you. That gathering point. When I was seven. Halloween. And back there along the track, at that point, there's a divide and a whole other life continues from there. And that's me as a girl, and she's been alive that whole time, kind of living parallel to me . . ."

"Wow."

He could see the dancer Pam had once been—her luminous eyes that she still painted as though she were going on stage every day, her flushed face that didn't need any makeup now with the heat of blood in her cheeks. Her radiance—that brilliant living flare. "Jesus, I can't believe this," she said. "It's perfect." She lit the joint she'd been rolling, dragged, added the scents of grass and licorice to the mix—to the unmistakable animal pungency of her sex, and of his, and her own subtle signature that he'd learned by now was two drops of vanilla oil rubbed into the veins of her throat.

"I knew we had to do something together," she said. "I thought it was anarchism, but wow. Just the tip of the iceberg. OK, let me ask you something. If you could cross that divide and *be* that girl, would you do it?"

"I don't know." He let the possibility of it move through him. "I don't think so. Not unless I could go back and forth."

"Yeah, man, diversity. Fluidity. Yeah, right on. You don't know how much *sense* this makes to me. Like it's all the stuff I've been thinking about. But . . . OK, suppose somebody waved a magic wand and ZAP, you're on the other side. How would you feel about that?"

"With no choice in the matter? Like Tiresias? This is weird, but I wouldn't mind all that much. I'd be losing some things but gaining others. I've got used to being a boy, but . . . I'd probably adjust. I mean without much trouble. And that makes me feel kind of freaky. Like I'm a traitor to the male sex, or like. . . . Most guys wouldn't adjust, would they? That easily?"

"OK, and here's the sixty-four-million-dollar question . . . *should* you have been a girl?"

He didn't know how to answer that one.

"I never wanted to *be* a boy," she said, helping him, "but I used to think I'd be *better off* as a boy. You dig?"

"OK. Sure. Sure, I would have been better off as a girl."

"You ever make it with a boy?"

"No."

"Did you ever want to?"

"I don't *think* so . . . but like subconsciously . . . ?"

"Fuck subconsciously. I mean do you ever think about boys and get a hard-on?"

"No," he said, laughing, "but this girl I was dating at WVU . . . She was absolutely convinced I was gay."

"Yeah, sure she was. Of course she was. They always want to make it simple. Binary. On-off, stop-go, up-down, black-white, gay-straight, *male-female*. But it's not simple . . ."

"Oh, hell, no. It's like what Jung calls *scintillae* . . . a million glittery fragments. Guppies in a fishbowl." He almost had it. He was chasing its tail: "Not the content, the energy . . . the carrier, the kick." What the fuck did that mean? Something from McLuhan.

"Oh, right *on*," she said. "And we've got to follow that kick." She took his hand and pulled him into her small white kitchen. "And we've got to *eat* or they're going to be carting us both off to the bin."

The late-afternoon sunlight was pouring through the west windows—the golden autumn light that catches up to you when you've spent the day in bed. They were glowing with it, and glowing with each other—*I want to tell you everything.* Pamela, whose skin had never been tanned, was still wearing nothing at all—had radiated to an angelic pallor, flushed with pink, filigreed with tracery blue. At the stove, she measured brown rice into a sauce pan; at the sink, he washed carrots in water that burned with light. The speed and focus of that mind-feeling-thing he called "the whole track inside" had delivered him to nowhere else but here. That burden he'd carried all of his life—he hadn't known how heavy it was until he put it down.

11.

PAMELA WAS on a run. She didn't need to set her alarm clock; her own ideas woke her. She liked to be up and at work while it was still dark. She brewed a lethal coffee—Mocha-Java and dark French—and drank it black. She paced up and down, organizing her thoughts, and then blasted words onto paper with her small purring Olympia. John woke to her typing, to the insistent smell of her coffee, to the indigo at her windows where the night was giving up, and found that he was, and wanted to be, nowhere else but *here*—for once perfectly situated in that time-place-thing that's usually called "life." It was a kind of happiness, surely. In the ordinary language that people used every day, he could say that he'd never been happier; he called it "luck" for short, but he knew that luck didn't have a damned thing to do with it. He lay in her bed still warm from her body, still marked with her scent, and thought about feeding her. She would eat two or three buckwheat pancakes if they were not much bigger than fifty-cent pieces, but she wouldn't use butter or syrup on them. She would eat fresh fruit. She would eat yogurt.

"Now you'll get to see how crazy I really am," she'd told him. He wouldn't have called it "crazy"—although her need for order did seem excessive to him, as compulsive as her need to fit the entire universe into a total critique, but he regarded her space as sacred and occupied it with awe. He folded her towels the way she liked them, put his clothes away in the places she'd assigned them. Then he began picking up after her, putting away *her* clothes. He'd never ironed anything in his life, but he learned to iron her shirts. He swept the floors, emptied the ashtrays. He did all the shopping, all the cooking. He didn't understand exactly why or how he'd become a vegetarian—something to do with Terry, with his acid trip—but his new diet seemed to suit her. She had no great interest in meat. She too would eat vegetables and fruit, brown rice and tofu. "There's just one basic rule, man," she told him. "I can't eat anything that resembles Jewish cooking."

She said it was a relief not to have to think about food—not to have to buy it and not to have to cook it. As soon as they'd eaten, he washed the dishes and put them away. "I can see why men want wives," she said. "Everybody ought to have one."

They made love in the afternoons, and slept. She woke to evening driven by a mad energy. Every day she had to feed her body enough exercise to keep her from going nuts; it was more important than food. They walked for hours, talking. She wouldn't let him read what she was writing. "Not yet," she said, "it's too raw." But she told him about it. At the center was what she'd discovered while she'd been gone—her breakthrough, her higher level, that flash of insight that had made her change her ways—*the theory of androgyny*. She'd been busily rewriting her own life ever since; now she was busily rewriting *his*.

"Dig it, man," she said, "there's six sexes. Maybe more . . . but at least six major categories. First you divide into male and female. And then you subdivide. Into straights. And gays. And *us*, the androgynes. Maybe at some point in the future everything will dissolve and we won't need distinctions at all, but what's required at this historical moment is to *clarify* the distinctions. Nobody's ever heard of us. They don't even know we're here. Most of us don't even know we're androgynes."

Before she'd realized she was an androgyne, she'd thought of herself as a "girl." The women in the Movement said the word was demeaning, but she'd never felt demeaned by it. The first shrink she'd ever seen had told her, "You're afraid of growing up, Pamela. You don't want to be a woman." She'd thought, "*Asshole*. He doesn't understand. I'm a dancer. I just want to be a few pounds lighter," but years later, she'd admitted to herself that he'd been right—that she'd wanted to go on being a girl forever. She'd hated her periods, her breasts. For years—until she went into the hospital for the first time—she'd shaved off her pubic hair. The thought of getting pregnant still nauseated her. "Just dig it, man. Like the full horror of it. A parasite. An *alien*. Living inside you. Sucking off your energy."

Her childhood, his childhood, she said—let's consider how sick they must have looked. Abnormal. But they hadn't been sick; it was straight society that was sick, so of course there'd been cognitive dissonance. They'd felt guilty—mad and bad. They'd been self-destructive. His "anorexic episodes" had been exactly like hers. "They were *political* acts," she said, "acts of refusal. I didn't want to be a woman, you didn't want to be a man. And that was *normal* for us . . . because we were androgynes. Refusing to eat was the only power we had."

"At those *gathering points*," she said, "when you were seven, when you were fourteen . . . when you wanted to be a girl . . . you didn't even have a way to think about it. Like we can't even *think* about something new until we've created a whole new theoretical structure, a whole new vocabulary. We repeat everything that hasn't been analyzed, that hasn't become conscious. That's why neurotics repeat the same mistakes over and over and don't even know they're doing it. They've built an elaborate set of defense mechanisms to prevent themselves from becoming *conscious*. But the proletariat is becoming *conscious* now as in no previous time in history. Don't you see how *revolutionary* this is?"

Sometimes he believed her—entirely, with no reservations. Sometimes her words sank deeply into the mind-place-thing where thoughts began—flared there, burned there, said *this is right*. He could feel the urgency of her need to find a theory that would organize everything. If she kept on going, she would write a critique as elegant as the mind diagram that organized her apartment. It would be, to use her favorite words, "coherent" and "total." Of course he wanted to believe in it; he could feel how seductive it was—so soaked in sexual energy it was a continual turn-on. But at other times he could feel her working too hard—like the unenlightened man in the Zen story, pulling on the grass to make it grow. He wanted to give himself to her—entirely, with no reservations—but he could feel himself holding back. Lying next to her as she slept, he was afraid that her theory might account for everything but the eerie shiver in his mind.

A NEW underground paper had been hitting the streets. It called itself *Zygote*, and the lead editorial in the first issue said, "A zygote is a cell created by union. We are the coming together of the Lost Tribes of the Age of Aquarius. We believe that whenever we focus on the negative—the dark, the demonic, the destructive—we give those forces energy. *Zygote* will always present creative, positive, life-affirming alternatives. We believe that even now, here in America where so much is tragically wrong, there is still room for all of us to dream, to live out our dreams, to envision and create a brave new world. Dig it, gentle children, *we are what we envision, and the war is already over."*

It made John sad, but Pam said, "I can't believe anybody's still writing that flower-power crap."

Zygote was beautifully produced. It had a slick four-color cover. The columns were perfectly justified. The layout was open, airy, and easy to read. The graphics looked like something from an art college. There were articles—some of them quite good—on ecology, meditation, organic gardening, alternative schools, and communal child-rearing. The section called "the Scene" was such a thorough listing of everything going down in Boston—movies, music, plays, "alternative" events—that *Zygote* was clearly the paper to buy if you wanted to know what was happening. "And check the ads," John said. "How did they sell all those goddamn ads?"

"Easy. They haven't got any politics. They're probably funded by the CIA."

But they were both thinking the same thing, and John said it—"Getting published is better than not getting published."

The Weatherman National Action was coming up—the Days of Rage planned for Chicago. "We've got to criticize it," Pam said. Oh, right, John thought, we're *a council*. He'd almost forgotten that.

She took the two angry, disconnected paragraphs he'd written alone in his small box, laid them out next to her Olympia, and turned them into a coherent statement. When he read what she'd done, he saw how easy it had been; she'd simply built a logical bridge from his first fragment to his second and added an anarchist coda about creating the new society in the shell of the old. It was good, he thought, and a good length—fewer than eight hundred words. They took it into the *Zygote* office where the walls were freshly painted and all of the equipment was new. The editor called himself Adam Kabir Das. He was as pale as Pamela, as thin as John, and dressed top to toe in one hundred percent cotton. He'd obviously been growing his hair and beard for years. He had eyes like the Jesus in Sunday school paintings. "We used to work on the *Weasel*," John told him.

"Groovy," Adam said. "The *Weasel* was one of my inspirations . . . the old *Weasel*, not the death-trip bullshit they're putting out now."

"Right on," Pam said. "We hate that shit too. That's why we got purged from the staff. That's why we're here. And dig it, man, you don't have any politics."

Almost anyone else, John thought, would have accepted their piece politely and showed them to the door, but Adam sat down and read it while they waited. Then he rose gracefully to his feet, pressed the palms of his hands together, and bowed to them. "We didn't have any politics," he said, "because we were waiting for you."

Zygote, Adam told them, was operating on a new and revolutionary principle, one that he hoped would help to make it the best alternative paper in Boston—they *paid* their contributors. Raymond Lee and Pamela Zalman each received a check for twenty-five dollars. Adam invited them to become part of the *Zygote* family—to write a regular column, help with the layout, become *involved*.

They had to talk about it. "Will we be instantly spectacularized?" John said.

Yes, probably, she said, but that was true of anything. Every gesture anyone made was instantly recuperated into the Spectacle. And maybe *Zygote* really was funded by the CIA, but even if it was, Adam was on his own trip. "Yeah," John said, "he's been to India."

Their title had been "You *Don't* Need a Weatherman," but Adam changed it to "BRING YOUR BALLS TO CHICAGO." What they'd written together, and published in *Zygote*, was not an exercise in theory; they had criticized real people. They kept hearing pings coming back on the Movement sonar; Weatherman did not see it as comradely criticism but as a declaration of war. "How the hell can you and Karen Vance still be in the Collective together?" John asked her.

"She's not in it anymore."

Pam's hint of a smile told him that there was more to the story. "You purged them?" he said.

"Oh, we wouldn't do that. We just had a sub-caucus meeting . . .

you know, the women in our tendency . . . and discussed the situation. And then, when we were planning the next meeting, we didn't bother to tell the Weatherwomen when or where it was."

In October, the Weatherman NATIONAL ACTION finally arrived—the DAYS OF RAGE. Thousands of angry street-fighting kids were supposed to converge on Chicago to join their Vietnamese comrades in armed struggle against the might of the AMERIKKKAN EMPIRE, but only a few hundred Weatherpeople showed up. They came dressed for WARGASM—in construction boots and helmets, the women in padded bras, the men in jock straps with cups. They were armed with pipes, hammers, chains, and blackjacks. They built a bonfire in Lincoln Park and listened to speeches from Weather heavies. They ran screaming into the Loop, smashing windows, trashing and burning parked cars, flattening any hapless pedestrians who happened to get in their way. Two days before, someone had blown up the statue of a cop in Haymarket Square, so the two thousand perfectly real cops who had been called out to deal with the Weatherman menace were not in a good mood. They beat the crap out of anybody they caught, threw them in the slammer, even shot a few. The Weatherpeople had over two million bucks worth of bail laid on them—and that was a quarter of a million cash up front. Many Weatherpeople were badly injured; both Karen and Phil Vance ended up in the hospital. The Weather heavies called the action a GREAT VICTORY.

"History has demonstrated that we were correct," Pam said, her wry tone undercutting the jargon. "Doesn't that make you feel good?"

"No," John said.

In November, the mainstream anti-war movement, under the umbrella of the Moratorium, brought three-quarters of a million people to Washington. It was the largest single protest demonstration in the history of the United States. At the Washington Monument, Pete Seeger led that crowd of mostly straight people in the singing of "Give Peace a Chance."

"Pathetic," Pam said.

Yes, he supposed it was pathetic, but back along the track, strands were winding together. John was playing that Stella of Ethan's every day, and if it wasn't for Pete Seeger, that grand old man, he might not be doing that. John saying no to the draft, going to Canada, coming back to try to change something—if it wasn't for Pete Seeger and folk songs, Kerouac and Gary Snyder and Buddhism, Carl Oglesby's speech about "making love more possible," he might not have done any of that. Those strands made a pattern, a tapestry. It was *his* tapestry, *his* subjectivity, and wasn't that where Pam said everything had to start? That huge crowd of ordinary people at the Washington Monument, Pete Seeger leading them in song—he felt a significance, a resonance. "How long has it been," he said, "since all we wanted to do was end the war?"

A splinter group had broken off from the main demonstration—Weathermen, some of the reports said—and attacked the Justice Department with a battering ram. The pigs blocked all the side streets and laid down so much tear gas that Attorney General Mitchell got a good dose of it in his office. That splinter demonstration of several hundred people got far more press coverage than the peaceful three-quarters of a million at the Washington Monument. "Of course it did," Pam said.

———

WINTER WAS setting in and things were starting to come apart on us. Like there was no one big bummer crashing down like where you could say, oh, sweet Jesus, I got to deal with that motherfucker. No, it was like my mom says—JUST ONE THING AFTER ANOTHER. It started with bread . . . Well, with Garvin and Lorraine, bread had always been a problem. Garvin never did find work. Lorraine used to have a waitressing gig there for a while, but then one night the owner threw the make on her—not just assing around but in a fairly sleazeball way—and she kneed him in the balls, and that was the end of that. And it never crossed Cassandra's mind that she should contribute to the household finances. So guess what? Here's old Tommy Parker supporting four people instead of two, and I was doing pretty good in the import and retail business, but I wasn't doing that good. I was starting to fray around the edges.

OK, the next thing I know Garvin decides he's going to score a little doogie. "I've got to get some bread happening," he says. Well, yes. "This is motherfucking ridiculous," he says. "I know we been depending on you, man, and it hurts me. Yeah, it really does, swear to God. Shit, man, I always paid my own way my whole fucking life, you know what I mean? Don't worry, man, I'm not going to USE, you dig? I'm just going to MOVE IT AROUND TOWN. So if you could maybe do me a little bread up front . . ."

I could have written that movie, but what the hell. So I slipped him some coin and he scored, and he paid me back, every damn cent—at least that first time he did—and then we entered a short sweet period of DEAD CALM. Because in the evenings there wasn't much to disturb the sounds of silence except the occasional THUD as Garvin or Lorraine's head bounced off the table top.

But it didn't stay calm for long because Garvin and Lorraine knew every junkie in the Greater Boston Area—especially all the REHABILITATED ones—and within a week the word went out that our place was WHERE IT WAS HAPPENING. And then it's people looking to score falling by, and people looking to deal falling by, and people with some smack they want to give away for some crazy reason, and pill freaks and weirdoes and rip-off artists, and teeny-boppers who think junkies are neat, and just every imaginable lame dude falling by. Some of those mind-fucked junkies were around so much they practically moved in with us, and I swear to God they had names like Joe the Mooch and Betty Delirious, and you'd never know when you got up in the morning who was going to be crashed on the floor, some mornings wall-to-wall bodies in the living room and even in the halls, for Christ's sake, and some of those dudes made Houdini look like a rank amateur the way things VANISHED whenever they came around—like you couldn't lay a thing down and expect it to be there thirty seconds later. I never caught one of them with his hand in my pants, but it came pretty close to that. And then one night Garvin came back late and found that somebody had locked him out and everybody inside was too wasted to manage to crawl the six feet to the door and let him in, so he just kicked the door in and broke the lock bigger than hell, and after that, our front door was always open and anybody could come strolling in any damn time they pleased. Well, I suppose I could have fixed it, but I was thinking, fuck the front door and fuck all you assholes. Somebody wants in here, any window will do—like they had a nice selection to choose from, all of them at ground level—so I fell by the lock store and said, "Give me the biggest meanest one you got," and guess where I screwed that motherfucker? ON OUR BEDROOM DOOR.

The camper got stripped to the bone in nothing flat, so I had to keep it locked and parked way the hell and gone so the skagheads wouldn't know where it was, and you know what? Right at the heart of this whole sick scene was our bathroom. Yeah, our bathroom was starting to look like the neighborhood community center, and one night Cassandra says, "Jesus, this place is a motherfucking SHOOTING GALLERY," so that's what we started calling it.

So one night I decide to drive somewhere, and I trot over the six blocks to where I'd parked the camper, and I detect the fact that somebody has managed to unlock my fine vehicle and there's a pair of legs with old beat-to-shit cowboy boots attached to them sticking out from under the dash. I give the boots a kick and out crawls this sorry son of a bitch that called itself Joe the Mooch. He'd been crashed on our floor for a while—the same dude I'd seen like an hour before with a spike in his arm in our bathroom—and I say, "What the fuck you doing, asshole?" but it's kind of obvious what he's doing.

"Hey, I'm sorry, man," he says, "I didn't know this was YOUR truck. I wouldn't have gone anywhere near it if I'd known it was YOUR truck."

Well, that was an interesting theory, and I did stand there a minute and consider it. And I gave myself a little lecture. Like, OK, Tommy boy, do not go off half-cocked. Even though your patience has been sorely tried, that will accomplish nothing. What is required here is what they call A CALM RATIONAL DECISION. OK? And my CALM RATIONAL DECISION was that I should get the word out to the skaghead community that Tom Parker was not somebody to fuck with. So I gave the bastard my best Roy Rogers smile, and I offered him my hand, and I said, "Well, shit, man, no harm done, right?"

He's kind of startled, but what choice has he got, right? He's got to shake on it, and that means he's got to take a step toward me.

So he does that, and I take his right hand in my right hand, and I deposit my left fist in his gut. Did I tell you I'm a southpaw? And he goes OOOF and kind of folds up, and I slap his head one way, and then I slap it the other. I'd been so pissed off for days it just did my heart good, you know what I mean?

I get him in an arm bar and choke him for awhile, and then I turn him loose and boot his ass right on down to the ground. He lays there on his face kind of sobbing and moaning, and I just stand behind him and wait. He tries to scrabble up and run, and I boot him down again. He tries to run a few more times, and every time, I boot him down again. I just want to make sure, you know, that the old knees and elbows are getting a good workout on that fine Somerville pavement. Well, I finally let him go, and he makes his break but good, and I'm left with that wonderful feeling of GRIM SATISFACTION, because I'd done exactly what I'd wanted—like no serious damage, but I was pretty sure I'd scared the flaming bejesus out of that junkie asshole, and that was the point. And, yeah, it was sad that things had got down to that, a fairly sorry day when things had got down to that, like so much for love and peace and brotherhood and flower power, right? But that stuff only takes you so far, and then you got to revert to basics.

STRANGELY, THE way everything seemed to be happening now, without his having to do much about it, John's life changed again— or that track usually called "life" continued to carry him. He had a job again, something to do, something that might mean something. He was even getting paid for it. Although money never seemed to be a problem. "Who's supporting us?" he asked Pamela.

"Mainly my father. Don't worry, he can afford us."

John never stopped being astonished that he was *living with a woman*. She was still saying they were "a council," but he thought— although he didn't say it to her—that they might be turning into "a couple." He was getting used to her, to her strange ways, but she could still surprise him every day.

She owned dozens of records but not one that anybody would describe as "cool." She was the first person he'd ever known who actually *liked* classical music. He tried, but he couldn't groove on her taste; everything ran together in his mind. Was that fat wash of melancholy strings Mahler or Bruckner? Or maybe even Brahms? He did become fond of the records she chose for the afternoons when they were making love—Shostakovich's pieces for the piano, Beethoven's stately *Eroica*. He played the guitar for her, picked through every tune his fingers remembered. She said she liked hearing him play—except in the morning when she was working. He never sang. He still didn't trust his voice, and now he knew why. To sing, you have to use *words*.

She'd brought pictures back from New York to show him—a studio glossy of herself *en pointe*, the weight of her entire body balanced on the curve of a single immaculate foot, on the tiny tip of one gleaming pointe shoe. "Oh, my God, you were beautiful," he said.

"Oh, yeah," deadpan. "Sure I was. A real doll."

"What did it feel like?"

"It's hard to . . . I'd give you the experience if I could, but . . . It satisfied something in me in a way that nothing else ever has, but I was always worried. Like anxious. Like nerve-twitchy teenage awful chalk-on-the-blackboard anxious . . . Like that's the highest level of stylization you can achieve with the female body, and I sensed it, and I wanted it, but there's no way I could have verbalized it. I never thought I was good enough . . . perfect enough. I honestly believed that perfection could be achieved. And that's the ballet death-trip, right there, man, WHAM."

She showed him an album of family snapshots, starting when she was a child and ending when she was a teenager. She kept getting older but her clothes stayed the same—hair ribbons, blazers and kilts, short skirts and Mary Janes. "I drove my mother nuts. I was in the vanguard of fashion, but we didn't know that. She kept trying to put me in heels, but I refused. Like who needed that shit? If I wanted to do high femme, I had pointe."

The last picture was a publicity shot of herself in her only solo role—Clara. She was sixteen but looked twelve—in a child's flounced white dress, a ribbon in her hair (the one she'd pinned up by her bed), clutching a gigantic nutcracker to her flat chest, a look of dewy expectancy on her face. "Talk about being perfectly cast," she said, "oh, my. You can keep that if you want. I've got a dozen of these damned things. Yeah, when you get back to Toronto, put it next to the picture of yourself as Alice. They go together."

Sleeping in the same bed with her never stopped feeling magical. "Something you should know about me," she said. "I'm not cuddly." She needed a foot of space between them; every night, from her side of that foot of space, she kept on talking until sleep sandbagged her. He loved lying in the dark next to her, listening as her mind scattered. That's when she would say things that trailed free—loose and airy things that were not yet fully nailed into her total critique.

"We androgynes get turned on by ambiguity," she said. "We have a wider range of sexual response than other people. You could make it with straight girls. You could make it with boy androgynes. Just don't ever try to make it with straight men. Wow, is that ever a bummer."

"You actually *liked* little girls," she said. "That's so groovy, man. You identified with little girls. You should be proud of it. Most little boys don't like little girls, and look how they grow up."

Some of her probes were so right-on they stopped his breath. "I understand about Zoë now," she said. "It isn't just that she was your little sister. You were *her* sister."

"You didn't fall for those girls in high school because they were *young*," she said. "You fell for them because they were *androgynous*. Like they hadn't been defined yet. Linda was just learning how to be a girl, and that fascinated you because you wanted to do it too. And Cassandra's an androgyne just like us."

Even as a child, she'd adored the pretty boys in her ballet classes. As a teenager, she'd had terrible crushes on some of them. "Like it wasn't conscious, but I kept falling for femmy boys. I didn't know what it was, but they drew me like a magnet. It was sad. They always turned out to be gay."

"*Back along the track*," she said, giving his own formulation back to him, "you were a pretty boy in my ballet class, and I let you wear my pointe shoes. When you were fourteen, I dressed you up just like me . . . so we looked like twins, girlfriends . . . Does that turn you on?" reaching a cool hand across that foot of space to see if it did—and of course it did.

Ah, sex—more potent, more all-encompassing, more compelling than any drug he could imagine. He'd always thought that if you had as much sex as you wanted, you might eventually get enough of it, but no—the more you had, the more you wanted. She told him about her first girlfriend, Melanie. They'd been in ballet school together, had lived together at Melanie's house, slept in the same bed. "I couldn't wait for bedtime. I thought about it all day. So did she. I could look at her across a room, and . . . like I could get her wet just by looking at her."

"Being with a girl still feels more natural to me," she told him, "and it probably always will. Like there's different balances to androgyny, you dig? And I'm naturally balanced toward the lesbian side. Just like you're naturally balanced toward the straight side. But we're a good match . . . for right now." He didn't like "for right now."

Sleep always came to her before it did to him. Sometimes it would take her out in the middle of a sentence. He'd lie next to her and listen to her breathing. He was different from her in this—sleep slithered over him gently, from unexpected directions, untangling him, and then, as he'd been doing ever since his acid trip, he'd go back along the track to that point before it had all divided. It was never anything that could be explained—not by any maneuver he might make and not by Pamela's total critique either. Then, as he entered into his nightly journey through interlinking mind-feeling-things, he found that behind each image was yet another image—as far back as he'd yet been able to travel—but he wanted to keep on going until he arrived at the back of everything where there was nothing left but an emptiness that would make everything simple.

IN THE cool blue mornings, John felt a sharpness returning, an edge he'd lost, the ability to *use* things, and he knew that he was finally recovering from his acid trip. He found himself thinking—day-dreaming—about being a grad student again. He could write a paper on the myth of Achilles, do a real Northrop Frye number on it. Something obvious that nobody seemed to have pointed out yet—not only had Achilles been the original draft dodger, but when he'd been hiding out with the girls, he'd looked so much like a girl, acted so much like a girl, that it had taken the cleverest man in all of Greece to ferret him out. John thought it would have been a better myth—better for the good of humanity—if Achilles had stayed right where he was, playing dolls and dressup, instead of going on to become Auden's "man-slaying Achilles who would not live long."

John hadn't written a word since he'd moved in with Pamela; now he sat down at his own typewriter and blasted out a one-paragraph summary of her theory of androgyny:

```
Reich: if the dominant ideas in any age are always
ruling-class ideas, then the dominant sexuality in any
age is always ruling-class sexuality. The State needs
to produce the kind of people who will reproduce
the State. Straight male sexuality is dominant and
oppressive, and that's exactly what is required
to continue the world as it is--to maintain the
oppression of workers, women, children, gays, blacks,
Vietnamese, everybody--including, in the end, even the
straight males themselves because their personalities
are warped and stunted by the process. The entire
project of spectacularized capitalism, of imperialism,
rests on the bedrock of straight male sexuality. If
you want to get to the root of everything, that's
where you have to start. Androgyny, then, doesn't
define merely a separate sexual category. Androgyny is
revolutionary sexuality.
```

"Well, that's like the bare bones," she said.

"Yeah, I know it's not *total*, but is it *coherent*?"

She had to think about it. "Yes."

"OK. Don't you think other people need to hear it . . . at this particular time in history?" He knew that argument would get to her.

John expanded his paragraph into a hippie-style rap. Pam corrected it four times before she allowed him to take it to *Zygote*. Adam wanted to run it under the title of "Beyond Women's Liberation."

"Oh no, you won't," Pam said.

They settled on "Androgyny in the New Age," and Adam printed it over a ten-percent screen of the compassionate image of Kuan-yin—"She who listens to the cries of the world." He explained to them that in India she had been a male deity, Avalokiteshvara, but when she'd come to China, she'd changed her sex.

———

SO ONE night me and Cass come back fairly late, like maybe four in the morning, and the minute we stroll though the front door, I detect the fact that things had achieved TOTAL QUIET. Like there's nowhere near the usual number of fuckheads, and the ones we've got are passed out like corpses, and Cass says, "Shit, what is this? Sleeping Beauty's palace?" And the only one who's even remotely near consciousness is good old Garvin. He's sitting . . . Well, sitting ain't quite right. PROPPED is more like it. He's PROPPED up at the kitchen table. And it takes him, oh, maybe a century and a half to get his eyes open, and they look like little red coals at the back of an old fire. He goes, "MMMMM . . . laid some groovy shit on us," and he nods off. So we go trotting upstairs to our room, and I get out my key to open the big mother lock, and I immediately notice that I don't need the key.

The door is splintered and cracked, looks like somebody went at it with a battering ram, and we've been CLEANED OUT. That little stereo we'd bought when we'd been crashed at John's is gone, naturally, and all the records, and Cassandra's books, and, when you get right down to it, pretty much EVERYTHING is gone except for the bed Cassandra had made me buy when we'd moved in there. But they'd tried to get the mattress out the door, for fuck's sake, like they'd got it jammed in the doorway and had to give up on it. I shoved it back in the room and we stood there for a while contemplating this fine little twist of fate, and Cassandra starts laughing. "Well, old Thoreau says to simplify. We just been motherfucking SIMPLIFIED."

So I go back downstairs, and I prop Garvin up into a somewhat more upright position, and I lean down so I can whisper in his ear, and I say, "OK, buddy, so tell me. WHO laid this groovy shit on you?"

"Ummm," he goes. "It was Joe the Mooch." Oh, I loved that. I simply ADORED it.

You think things can't get worse? Want to bet? Eventually I noted the fact that there were a couple dudes in a grey car who seemed to spend a lot of time parked directly across the street, so I laid it on Lorraine—"Hey, have you caught those guys in the Chevy?"

"Yeah. They're narks."

"Oh, yeah? Well that's NICE."

And then . . . Well, this is going to sound like I made it up, but I swear it's the truth. This strange dude started hanging around the house, and he was a tall skinny guy in BRAND-NEW cowboy boots, and BRAND-NEW blue jeans, and VERY SHORT hair, and WRAP-AROUND SUNGLASSES. He'd fall by and give everybody free drugs, prescription drugs straight from the bottle. He had a camera, one of these tiny jobs that fit in the palm of your hand, and he didn't even try to hide it. He took pictures of everybody in the house. By that time I was beginning to figure that maybe it was ME that was nuts, so I went around asking people—you know, just doing my own reality check—"Hey, could it be possible that dude just might possibly be a nark?"

The skagheads said, "That's his thing, man. He gets off on bringing everybody down by pretending he's a nark."

I say, "Now wait a minute. How do you know he's not a nark?"

They say, "Well, Christ, man, he's laying all this groovy shit on us." And so even I believed it for a while. Well, sort of believed it. I thought, shit, he looks so OBVIOUSLY like a nark, there's no way in hell he could really be a nark. But then I decided to check with Lorraine, because if anybody would know, she would, and she says, "Oh, him? He's a nark, man. Works for Lieutenant Vincenti."

"Well, for Christ's sake. WHAT THE FUCK ARE WE DOING HERE?"

She just shrugs. "They're not going to bust the house, man. They're pulling too much information out of here. Besides, they'd just send me back to the hospital again." Well, that's OK for you, Lorraine old buddy, but what about me and Cassandra who don't happen to be lucky enough to be junkies? And you know what was the craziest thing of all? We kept right on living there just like it was perfectly normal.

JOHN LOVED to see Pamela dressed for the winter—how much she looked like a boy—and sometimes when they'd come home in the evenings from the *Zygote* office, she'd deliberately pretend to be a boy. As soon as they stepped into her apartment and the door clicked shut behind them, she'd slam him into the wall and thrust her tongue into his mouth. If she was heavy into the fantasy, she'd push on his shoulders, an unmistakable command—*down*. Kneeling at her feet, he'd unzip her boots and pull them off, undo her belt, unbutton her jeans, unzip her fly, work her jeans down her hard thighs—slowly, teasing her—and peel off her underwear. She'd sink into the firmly rooted karate stance that said *boy*, and he'd press his mouth into the tender patch of dark curly hair between her legs, pretending he was taking an erect penis into his mouth—although he couldn't maintain that fantasy for very long. He loved the taste of her that was not boyish at all.

"I keep thinking about you down there with a mouthful of hair," she said. "It really bothers me. Like vile, man."

They both knew it was only an excuse. She let him begin with scissors. "Just like Zoë's eyelashes," she said, "be *careful*."

She finished the job herself—with a razor in the bathtub. Looking down at herself, she said, "Yeah, that's how I ought to look, the real me." Smooth, clean, not yet defined. Just as he'd known it would, it turned him on, but it made him uneasy too. Standing next to her, he looked too male—and she'd gone somewhere else, dispersed through a mind-feeling-place of her own and left him behind. "But maybe just a few pounds lighter," she was saying.

"Oh, for Christ's sake."

"Hey, whoa, I'm just putting you on. Well, mostly putting you on. But if I went down to . . . like maybe a hundred and five . . . I wouldn't have any breasts *at all*. But no, I'm not even going to think about that, am I, man? OK, your turn."

He was surprised, but not that surprised. Of course he would let her do it—was even prepared to like it—but the scissors snipping away so near his balls and penis terrified him. "Wow," she said, giggling, "I've never seen you so limp. Cool out, man. I'm not

Valarie Solanis. Trust me . . . How about the rest of you? Would you like that?"

Having his public hair shaved off was not a turn-on, but having the rest of him shaved obviously was. Now his erection felt like a length of steel pipe. "Bizarre," she said. "Men's bodies . . . so strange."

He stood up in the bathtub so she could shave the backs of his legs. He turned to face her so she could shave the front of his legs—and his stomach and chest. She even shaved his underarms. It took forever. She had to keep changing blades. He kept phasing in and out of the turn-on; sometimes he was hard and sometimes he wasn't. It didn't matter. Wherever she'd gone, he was catching up to her, and he allowed the words in his head to come and go and leave nothing behind but slender vapor trails. Later, he would remember saying, "Now there won't even be hair between us."

"Oy, you're such a Romantic." Someone had told him that before. It was probably true.

She rinsed him in the shower, dried him, massaged his hairless body with apricot lotion. It made him tingle all over. "Sexy, sexy, sexy," she said, "but wow, is it ever a bitch when it grows back. You'll see."

He wanted to look at himself in the mirror, but she wouldn't let him. "Not yet. Wait till I'm finished."

They blew some weed. It made her even more single-minded and intent. She rummaged around in the back of her closet, found a plastic bag filled with old makeup. She brushed his hair smooth, parted it in the middle, and tied it into two ponytails with black ribbons—cleaned his face with cream, wiped it off with Kleenex, patted it with astringent, and smoothed an ivory foundation over it. "Oh," she said, murmuring, "you're going to look . . . just so . . . absolutely . . . far out."

She kept saying, "Trust me." She told him to stare at a fixed point on the far wall. She drew lines around his eyes with a kohl pencil, shadowed his lids with smoky blue powder. He'd often seen her like this before—meticulous, determined, rapt, obsessive—but now he felt the full purity of the mind-focus-thing that took her and distanced her. If they were playing dolls and dressup, he was the doll, and he wanted to be the doll. She was doing to him what she said men did to women all the time—turning him into an object—but he wanted to be objectified. Maybe later he would be able to untangle these fabulously complex knots of mind-stuff—the lines and threads of these interwoven tapestries—but, for now, all he knew was that he wanted to be an object of her desire.

She curled his eyelashes, coated them with mascara—let them dry and coated them again. "Oh, darling," she whispered, "I'm going to make you look *just like me.*"

She walked quickly to her dresser, opened a drawer, searched for something—came back with a pair of her panties and handed them to him. He took them reluctantly. They were a shiny pale pink, made of some heavy-duty stretch fabric. They looked far too small. He stepped into them, tried to pull them up, but his hard-on made it impossible. It felt entirely independent of him. "Think about something that's *not* a turn-on," she said.

But the whole world was a turn-on. "What do you think I am?" he said. "A goddamned yogi?"

She stared into his eyes for a long moment. "What was Bakunin's central objection to Marx's idea of the people's state?" she said.

A ragged fracturing. "Bakunin?" It took him a moment even to translate her bizarre question into an intelligible sentence. "*Bakunin!* What the fuck . . . ?"

"Yeah, Bakunin. You know. His objection to . . ."

"For Christ's sake, Pam, why are you . . . ?"

"Seriously, man. Tell me. Come on. The dictatorship of the proletariat . . .?"

John looked away. Her small white world they were occupying was vibrating like an anthill. Spinning off, wobbling, he heard himself say, "If the proletariat becomes the ruling class, who's it ruling? Is that what you mean?"

"Yeah. That's it exactly. Go on. Tell me."

"OK. The proletariat then becomes a class itself, and that implies . . . Jesus, Pam. Why are you doing this? Jesus, it's motherfucking freaky . . . like . . ."

Smiling slightly, she glanced down. He followed her eyes. He had gone limp.

Not daring to think, he worked the panties up quickly, over his hips, folded himself into them and drew them up tight. As soon as he felt that damnable stretch fabric trap him and hold him down, the full heat of the turn-on came back like the door swinging open on a blast furnace. Something scary about that. He was shaking all over. Tuned in to him, she said, "Oh, baby, are you all right?"

The last thing he wanted was for her to turn into a mom. "I'm OK. I'm fine."

She took his hand and led him to the mirror. "I'm OK," he said again to convince her—and to convince himself.

He looked and saw that they had become two slender white entities with ribbons in their hair, their smooth hairless bodies gleaming with apricot lotion, every muscle clearly edged with light. Two sets of huge eyes stared back at them—eyes like images painted onto ritual masks. He was no longer a boy. He looked something like a girl but not really like a girl. It was hard to say what he looked like. And his ambiguous presence next to Pam undermined her image so that she didn't look like a girl either. The shaved triangle between her legs looked as strangely chaste as if it had been carved from marble. They were as sexless as angels. "Oh, aren't we pretty?" she said.

It was true. They *were* pretty. She kissed him, her tongue in his mouth. With her fingertips, she drew delicate lines of fire on his thighs and stomach, over his curled, compressed cock. She turned slightly so that she could see herself kissing him, touching him. "Sweetheart," she whispered, "my pretty girl," and that was exactly what he wanted her to say.

He was connecting back to countless high school make-out sessions, to Linda in the gazebo, mounting him like a horse, and to Carol, of course, who'd teased him to a fearful nausea. Pamela was not teasing him, was doing something else entirely, but he was so turned on, had been turned on for so long, it was twisting back on him, gutting him, making him sick. "Pam," he said, "you're killing me."

She led him behind the Japanese screen, but once he was there, he changed his mind. No, he wasn't ready to stop yet. If he'd become a girl—or something like a girl—he wanted to go on being one. Attached to him by a million tiny filaments, Pamela took him into her arms and kissed him slowly, in excessive detail, but the burning ache between his legs kept reminding him that he wasn't a girl. It was that old despair—that he couldn't hold either position, the boy's or the girl's. That was the mistake he'd seen so clearly on acid—that the two sides of himself still made up a demonic construction, that he was at heart unstable, irresolvable. But no, maybe there was a way out, a possible resolution. If Pam was right about him, he was an androgyne, and an androgyne is something like an angel. She had made him into something like an angel, and she had called him her angel. But angels don't have sex. Angels are pure, and that purity gave him a resting place, a stability. He had a man's body, not an angel's, so it would be painful, but if that's what she wanted, that's what he would give her.

That must not have been what she wanted. She was sliding the stretchy panties down. He was almost disappointed. But why had he been working so hard in his head? Once again, he'd missed the point—it was hers to choose and always had been.

As soon as it was freed, his cock leapt up—a sensation far more compelling than mere relief. Not able to think about anything now but physical immediacy, he sank onto the edge of the bed. She followed, swung herself onto his lap, spread her legs and straddled him. Unlike herself, she seemed to have arrived there with no plan; wide-eyed, astonished, she stared into his eyes. He grasped the cheeks of her ass. As tall and substantial as she seemed to him sometimes, it was an illusion; she really was a small girl, not heavy at all. He lifted her up. He could support all of her weight if he had to. And then it was as though his polarity had reversed in an instant—he wanted to be a boy just as badly as, only a few seconds before, he had wanted to be a girl. For the first time since they'd become lovers, he had the sensation—what he thought must be an entirely *male* sensation—of *impaling* her. She whispered: "Oh"—a released breath—"God."

After a moment, his sense of being male—and different from her—melted away and they were again what they had been so often, twins joined at the hip. But in that position, he couldn't do anything.

What needed to be done was something *she* would have to do. As she always did.

He kissed her. She opened her mouth so his tongue could enter her. He knew that she liked being kissed, could feel it in her shiver, but she didn't respond. Her tensely drawn power seemed to have left her entirely—all of her fierce boyishness—and she seemed unable to do anything but look into the eyes she'd made up to look exactly like her own. He had always thought that aggressiveness defined her sexually; without it, she'd become someone he didn't know. Maybe she didn't know him either. She kept staring at him with a focused, dazzled expression he could call "wonderment." And then he understood what must have happened, or at least something of it—her body had caught up with her unawares and blown her mind as empty as the Buddha's. Even though she was free to move, she couldn't move. She couldn't do anything. She was so turned on she was utterly helpless.

For a moment he was baffled, but then he allowed himself to understand her perfectly. He grasped her again, took all of her weight, and rolled backward onto the bed, carrying her with him. On his back, he arched under her, held her by her sharp pelvic bones and pushed her up high enough to give himself room to move. "Ah," she said, gasping. She began to move with him.

Her bed was low enough for him to press his feet into the hardwood floor; he needed to push his legs and feet *down* so he could push his pelvis *up*—but their bodies, linked at even a deeper level than their minds, had already got the idea. She didn't kiss him as she usually did but stared blindly into an emptiness a few inches above his head, her mouth hanging open, and he felt how alive they were—not images, not angels—but vulnerable animals caught up in a motion that was undeniable. Ah, yes, he thought—it *was* an animal thing, and *this* is what you did with the jangle. The sound of her voice ignited a pulse in his throat, and he cried out right along with her.

She melted, flowed out over him, her energy lines cut, her ballerina's legs splayed flat. She didn't, as she usually did, withdraw at once. She didn't, as she usually did, start talking. He could feel her heart racing. Then, strangely, after they'd finished, she broke into a sweat, her skin beneath his hands going suddenly moist. The whole world stank of apricots.

She kept her hips glued to his. He was still inside her. He saw that she could see him again. "I don't believe this," she said. "I just don't fucking believe it. Did you come?" she said.

"Jesus, Pam, what do you think? Couldn't you feel it?"

"Of course I could feel it. My God, man, we just had *a simultaneous orgasm*. And I thought it was a load of crap, a male chauvinist myth. But it's real. Jesus, man, do you know what that means? Reich wasn't just right about the mass psychology of fascism. He was right about *sex*."

He laughed. "What?" she said, wrinkling her nose. "Is that funny? What's funny?"

"The way your mind kicks in," he said, but he was laughing at himself too.

"Yeah, it's weird. I always told you I was weird, and it's . . . Wow, it's fucking amazing, man. You know, that's the first time in my life I ever understood why straight people bother to do it."

12

AND THEN there was another little thing that was bugging me. Cassandra and Lorraine were getting real tight, and I don't know why I should give a shit, but I did. Cass seemed to think that Lorraine was some kind of guru, like she had the ultimate scoop on the ways of the world. Cass would go, "Some of her stories, man, whew."

Yeah, Lorraine was just full of stories, and every one of them was more horrible than the last one, and the more horrible they got, the funnier she made them. "So there I am in the slammer AGAIN." If you know how to do it, you can deliver a line like that so you crack up everybody in the room. "And fuck your due process. 'Lorraine,' they say, 'you are going to tell us some interesting tales, and until you start telling, you are going to remain here.' And it was the worst fucking place I've ever been, man. The only way I could keep the dykes off me was to tell them I had hep . . . which was true, I DID have hep. And periodically I'd say, 'Hey, didn't I hear something once about one phone call?' And they thought that was real funny. And there I am ten fucking days and I haven't even been charged. And finally one day I'm in this big exercise room with all the other prisoners, and what do I see but a pay phone hanging on the wall. And the matron has to split for some reason, so she says, 'Now I don't want any of you trying to use that phone.' And there are all these women in there. They all want to make a phone call, but they're all TOO FUCKING SCARED, some of them even saying to me, 'Hey, she said not to USE it.' Like a bunch of fucking sheep, man. And if I hadn't got that phone call in, I'd be there still."

Cassandra says, "Yeah, I know about those fucking California cops," and she tells her story about the time they busted her, sitting in the hole for twenty-four hours buck naked with no smokes and all the other profound joys of that experience.

So Lorraine's got to top that one. "Shit, so he says to me, 'Put out, bitch, and put out quick.' I look out the window of the cruiser and there's nothing but warehouses . . . nothing, not a soul. I mean, even if there was, who's going to stick around when the MAN comes cruising down the street? And they know I've been hustling, and they know I'm into doogie, and they know I've got a record long as Interstate Ninety. Well, to make a long story short, I fucked the one of them and sucked off the other, and that wasn't so bad. What was bothering me was the mean one, the real son of a bitch . . . the way he kept saying he was going to jam his billy club up my ass if I didn't get right down to it. Amazing how friendly you can get under some circumstances."

So Cassandra gets to lay out her rap about how women are fucked over from day one, and Lorraine agrees with her totally, and Lorraine has got ten stories to every one of Cassandra's because Lorraine's had every number run on her that it's possible to run, and she's had her ass drop-kicked from San Francisco to Boston and back again, and it's NO NEWS TO HER. "You're born a woman, you're just out of luck. You know, I used to wish I'd been born UGLY."

"Yeah," Cassandra says, laughing. "I've thought of that myself." And Cassandra and Lorraine are yucking it up and just getting tighter and tighter.

OK, so there was this old-time beatnik bar called the Incision, and it was a regular hangout for junkies—of both the REHABILITATED and the NONREHABILITATED variety—and it was cool as all hell, like it had a lot of blacks going in there, and a lot of hip types going in there, and a lot of deals going down—nothing changing hands, you dig, but all the good words taken care of. And Lorraine would fall by there damned near every night to hustle drinks and bread. She knew all the regulars, and she could sit and drink for free, and before the night was out, she could always hit some man up for a LOAN, so she'd come home with five or ten bucks in her purse, and I guess that five or ten bucks was better than nothing. I used to watch her getting fitted out for her run to the Incision, and fuck, it was awe-inspiring, like watching somebody paint a battleship, it was that deliberate. She'd lay on the makeup with a hand trowel, and check it out in the mirror to make sure it was enough to DO THE JOB, and then she'd check out her ass to make sure the skirt was short enough and tight enough to DO THE JOB, and then she'd give me a little grin like, "Yeah, well, I guess I'm still worth ten bucks."

The next thing I know, Cassandra's going with her. I couldn't believe it. Here's the same chick who just a few months ago was chasing some poor secretary up the street like a mad dog, the same chick who's worn nothing but jeans ever since I met her, and here she is shaving her legs and painting her face and climbing into one of Lorraine's miniskirts and checking her ass in the mirror to make sure it will DO THE JOB, and pretty soon Cass is coming home every night with five or ten bucks in HER purse—and before that, you couldn't have got her out in public with A PURSE if you'd held a gun to her head. But what the hell, at least she was bringing home a coin or two, and besides, wasn't she just DOING HER OWN THING? I tried to keep my big mouth shut, but upon occasion, I would let slip words to the effect of how scoring drinks and coin with Lorraine at the Incision was maybe a little bit farther down the old road toward sleazedom than Cass should be traveling, and she'd snap back at me, "Fuck you, man. You deal your drugs and I'll deal mine. You're a great one to talk. What about Bobby Lyons? Jesus, that guy's a half-pint Mafioso. He's a motherfucking asshole, man."

By then I knew perfectly well that Lyons was a half-pint Mafioso and a motherfucking asshole—I mean, I knew it a hell of a lot better than Cassandra did—but he was my main source, so I was kind of touchy on the subject. I'm saying, "Well, you see, sweet stuff, there's this strange savage ritual the natives conduct here in Somerville once a month. It's called paying the rent."

It's not like I didn't have other sources, but they were not RELIABLE, you know what I mean? And Lyons was always reliable. And the weird thing about him was he never stopped asking me to come in with him—PARTNERS, right? And I got to admit, I thought about it. I mean, Lyons never burnt me. Not once. In fact, it was just the opposite, he went out of his way to help me out, and a lot of times he'd just lay shit on me for no good reason. Except that—well, Christ, maybe it really was that simple, the son of a bitch LIKED ME. And I probably WAS the only dude in town he could trust. And, you know, it would have been easy. Of course he was into some things that filled me with those famous DOUBTS AND RESERVATIONS—but I could have swallowed my pride, right? And it wouldn't have to be FOREVER, right? And I'd have bread out the ying-yang, and I could even salt away a coin or two for the old rainy day. Yeah, I knew it was a lousy idea, but I couldn't stop thinking about it either.

————

INTERRUPTION FROM another galaxy, a spaceship *bong*—the voice of a lightly struck marimba. Lying in Pam's bed, doing what they always did when the day had so beautifully concluded itself far beyond the hard edges of anybody's agenda—smoke and licorice and vanilla oil—and now what? At one in the morning. The doorbell. "Oh, Jesus," she said, "who the fuck . . . ?"

Paranoia was shredding him like a grater. "Don't," he said, "just let it . . ." but she was already up and moving, pulling on jeans and shirt.

He grabbed up his own clothes and shot straight into the bathroom. Blown-out dumb as a brick, he ran water, soaked a washcloth, smeared soap on it, and scrubbed away the eye makeup that had seemed—well, up until a few seconds ago had seemed not merely innocent but so natural he'd forgotten he was wearing it. Through the closed door, he heard footsteps, a *man's* voice, and John's shaved armpits blazed with sweat. He felt seared, end to end, hairless as a slug, and for one lunatic's moment, imagined himself simply staying in there, safely locked away in there, until it was all over. Pam was the boy; she could deal with it. But no. Pam was not the boy. She was the same as he was, and they were a council, and he prayed to Whomever to give him some useful center in this tintinnabulating real. Why did he have to be so utterly, so goddamned stoned? Then, scrubbed and dressed—that is, masked—he unlocked the door and stepped through it. A man was sitting at the kitchen table. John had never seen him before in his life.

"Time to intensify the struggle, you dig?" the man was saying to Pam. The man turned; his eyes met John's, and he smiled—a sad thin warmth. "Ray," he said, then, shrugging, "Come on, man, it's *me*."

Who? The skinny bald man, hunched forward, bending,

apologetic. A little old man, collapsed in on himself. No, he wasn't like that at all. He wasn't old at all. Wire-rimmed granny glasses and a Harvard boy's Harris Tweed jacket. Pert, pursed, lips—sharply cut, almost too pretty. And (oh, my God) the picture finally blew itself together—it was Phil Vance with his beard and mustache shaved off.

"He's dropped out," Pam said.

"Yeah," Phil said. Shrugged. "Fuck."

"What?" John said.

"Out of Weatherman," Pam said. "You want to do some smoke?" she said to Phil.

"Oh, Christ, no. My head can't deal with that shit right now. You got anything to . . . I don't know. You got anything *to drink?*"

Pam's eyes met John's. Neither of them drank anything stronger than Oolong. "Maybe Deb left something," she said, and he heard the unspoken message: Come on, man, function. He sat down at the table with Phil.

"Shit, man," Phil said, "I don't know. We got back from Flint, and like our cadre. Heavy, man. Criticism, self-criticism. Day after day. We've been dropping acid and . . . like day after day. Everybody's onto everybody. Watching everybody. Like nobody can be alone. Not for ten minutes. You've got to report . . . like, 'Hey, I'm going to crash now. Is that OK? I'm going to the can now. Got to take a dump. Is that OK?' Jesus, I'm not putting you on. *Everything*, you dig? You've got to report, and Ben . . . you know, Ben Pavalick. He's kind of emerged as the . . . He lays out this rap like, 'Nobody can leave now. Dig it, we all know that by now. It's really clear by now. We'll have to kill anybody who tries to leave.' And I just . . . snapped. Something in me . . . Like I just waited like . . . And I said, 'Hey, I'm going out for smokes. Just up to the corner, OK?' And I never went back."

Pam had found—of all wacko things—a bottle of sherry. She poured a splash of it into a teacup. Phil knocked it back. "You want anything to eat?" she said.

Phil was staring down at the table top. "I'm never going back," he said. "They can fucking kill me, I don't care. I'm going home. If they want to find me and kill me at home, they can do that." Voice planed flat. John watched him. Pam was making a cheese sandwich.

"Jesus," Phil said, "how'd we get here?"

"I'm really fucked," Phil said. He was trying to tell them how fucked he was. He was back in the *Days of Rage* now, laying out that rap—getting busted in Chicago, getting the crap kicked out of him in Chicago. A cracked rib—among other things. He'd recovered from the other things, but the goddamn rib still hurt. "Those Chicago pigs were not fucking around, man." And then they murdered Fred Hampton. The Chairman of the Illinois Black Panther Party. Slaughtered him in his bed. Came in, guns blazing, fired hundreds of bullets into that goddamned place. "Shit, you can still see the bullet holes. They didn't give a shit. The motherfuckers. They just riddled the place, man."

The Weatherbureau freaked. A crucial event. "Like now was the time to intensify the struggle, you dig?"

All of the Weather collectives met in Flint, Michigan, in an old hall in a black ghetto. A huge cardboard machine gun was hanging from the ceiling. On the wall were the enemies of the people—LBJ, Nixon, Mayor Daley, Sharon Tate . . .

"Fuck, I heard that," Pam said, "but I didn't want to believe it. Sharon Tate?"

"Yeah, sure."

"Look, was it . . . ? Sharon Tate and those other . . . the ones the Manson Family killed?"

"Yeah. Sure. Yeah, the Tate Eight."

"It was in LNS, for fuck's sake," John said.

Her eyes zapped him into silence. "The Tate Eight, Jesus," she said. "I want to hear it. I want to hear it from somebody who was there. OK, Phil, so tell me . . . just how the fuck were those . . . ? How was Sharon Tate supposed to be an enemy of the people?"

"Fuck, I don't know. That's where it was at, you dig? That was *the line*, you dig? She was rich. Decadent. A sleazy actress. White skin privilege . . . I don't know. They didn't spell it out. She was like a symbol."

"Some symbol. She was pregnant."

"Yeah, I know. Jesus, Pam, I'm just trying to tell you. Listen. Bernardine laid out this rap. She was . . . God, you should have seen her. She was way out there. She said we were going wimpy. Like after the pigs offed Hampton, we should have burned Chicago to the motherfucking ground. She was . . . Sexy? Jesus. These thigh-high black boots. Stomping around, yelling. Turning everybody on . . . men, women, everybody. Like everybody wanted to fuck Bernardine."

"But killing *Sharon Tate?* How was that . . . ?"

"Fuck if I know. It was nuts, OK? I know it was nuts. Just listen. I'm trying to *tell you*, for Christ's sake. It's what Bernardine said. 'Weatherman digs Charlie Manson.' Like Charlie wasn't wimpy. Charlie had balls, right? Like Bernardine says, 'First they killed those pigs, and then they ate dinner in the same room with them. They even shoved a fork in a victim's stomach.' Yeah, Bernardine really dug that shit. She thought it was wild. And she did this." He thrust his hand into the air in a stiff salute—three fingers spread. "That's the fork, you dig? That's what she did. So after that, we all went around giving each other the fork, you dig?"

SMASH—like something blew up from the strain. Jerking back in his chair, John saw the fragments of the plate Pam had winged into the sink. "Fuck," she said. "I didn't want to believe it. I thought that was . . . I thought it was just a bunch of fuck-ass agitprop. But it's true, isn't it? Murdering *women?* Murdering *pregnant* women? This is a revolutionary act?"

Watching this shit go down, John was a strobe misfire. Freaky echoes. Contact high from Phil's acid? Fuck, some things you shouldn't have to live through stoned.

"Jesus," Pam said. She wasn't yelling. Most definitely, John thought, she was not yelling. "They're motherfucking male-identified," she said. "Like totally. And it's not politics, it's religion. It's motherfucking demonology. Was Karen into that shit?"

Phil shrugged again. "We were all into it."

"Tell me. This is important. I've got to know."

Their cadre, Phil said. It was still going on. It was going on right at this minute. Criticism self-criticism. "You know what we call it? 'Weather Fries.'

"Everybody sits around in a circle. Ben passes out the acid. These fucking weird neon-orange capsules. You can't say no. Nobody can say no. Everybody drops. And when you're tripping, you get criticized for your counter-revolutionary actions and thoughts. There's no way out. Only one way to survive. You've got to admit your crimes against the people and criticize yourself. You ever read *Darkness at Noon*? I get it now. Makes perfect sense now . . . how all those dudes could have been kissing Stalin's ass right up to the minute he had them shot."

The cadre attacked Phil for being wimpy. He'd been hiding behind white-skin privilege, male privilege, intellectual privilege, every goddamned kind of privilege. They really went after him. The women were the worst. Karen was the worst of the women. "Like we've been married for five years. She knows me really well."

Phil's head fell forward. He was hiding his face. He was crying. "Sorry. Sorry, man, sorry. Jesus, I'm sorry."

Pam stepped to the back of his chair—not looking at him, not looking at his face—pressed her hands into the muscles of his shoulders and squeezed. "Fuck that shit," she said. "Fuck those assholes. Fuck sorry."

"When you're criticizing somebody . . . There's nothing that's off limits. You're allowed to say *anything*, you dig?"

He stopped crying. He simply turned it off—CLICK—pushed himself upright, his eyes scraped down and shiny. "There's one more thing you've got to know," he said. "We're going to start offing pigs. That's the next phase . . . for our cadre, you dig? We renamed ourselves 'the Fork.' We've got some guns . . . a couple hunting rifles and a pistol. Shit. I don't know anything about guns. Fuck, I don't want to know anything about guns."

Their cadre made up a hit list. They started with the BIG PIGS. Politicians, judges, cops. And then they made a list of PIGLETS. Small-time motherfuckers, counter-revolutionary swine, traitors, so-called revolutionaries who've sold out the revolution. "You guys are at the top of the Piglet List. That thing you wrote in *Zygote* . . . 'Bring Your Balls to Chicago.' That puts you right at the top of the list. As soon we move into action, you're going to get offed."

The BIG PIGS would just be blown away wherever they were—in their beds, taking a walk, sitting in a restaurant. But there'd been some discussion of what to do with the PIGLETS. It had been decided that

Piglets should die, squealing, on their knees. Like it was a political act, you dig? So people would get the message—here's what happens to counter-revolutionary swine. Yeah, you'd make them drop acid, and then you'd hit them with the revolutionary criticism. However long it took. By any means necessary. And when you finally got them to the point where they were admitting their counter-revolutionary bullshit, where they were squealing and crying and begging for mercy, they'd get a single bullet in the base of the skull. And then the cadre would make a circle around the corpse and eat dinner.

"There was some discussion," Phil said, "about who was going to do the people on the Piglet List, like who was going to fire the bullet. We were talking about killing people we *know*, right? So offing the piglet would be a test of revolutionary commitment." He looked at Pam. "The cadre decided that Karen was going to do you."

The color was gone from Pam's face. Not a gradual thing. It was just gone. "She agreed to do it?" she said.

"Shit, Pamela, what do you think? We've been tripping for . . . God, I don't know how long. Days. Of course she agreed to do it. She hated the . . . It made her fucking sick . . . But she knew she had to do it. We were like . . . turning ourselves into tools of the revolution. And if you could kill *a friend* . . . If you could do that . . . Fuck. You'd *be there*."

Pam and Karen had been more than friends—John had figured out that much. "Ideology is," Pam said. "Is the collec tive . . . the collective . . ." She made a pushing gesture: *Get away from me.* "The super-ego becomes . . . co lec tive, and the, and the . . ."

Disaster had struck her deep in the body. She contracted, gagging. Gulping air. Sweat beading up on her forehead. She struggled to breathe, head thrown back, brushed off John's hand, pushed him back, pushed herself back, walked away. Stood, her back to them. Directed out the nothing window, her voice came back. "I can't deal with this shit."

John, desperate. "Hey, it was a fucking acid trip. A fucking bad acid trip. An evil jerk-off fantasy. Motherfucking sick porn. They're not going to off anybody."

Dry-eyed now, Phil was grinning reflexively, slack-faced and stupid as a clown, and John saw that, yes, it was real death they were talking about. Phil might have run from it, skittering away like a rat, but the threads of it were still all over him. John's anger was immaculate. "Shit," he said, "so who was supposed to off me?"

The shopkeeper's apologetic shrug—*sorry, we're sold out of that.* "Me."

———

SO I go see Lyons. By that stage of his career—what with him being a highly successful man of business—he always kept lots of chicks at his place, and he made sure they were always whacked right out of their pretty little gourds, and they were there for exactly the same reason he kept plenty of food and booze and smoke and doogie and crystal laying around—like you were supposed to help yourself. But he always picked one of the chicks to be his GIRLFRIEND, like at his beck and call twenty-four hours a day. He'd been trading up on the girlfriends for a while, always looking for the new and improved model, and eventually he'd settled on one named Susie. When she first turned up at Lyons' place, she was like a little ray of sunshine, one of those apple-cheeked girls with real sparkly eyes, a real oh-wow kid. She just made you smile. Of course she didn't stay that way for long.

Now, paying attention to Lyons' chicks was not high on my list. No, usually what I was paying attention to was BUSINESS. But that night, I didn't have much choice in the matter. We do what we always do when we want to have some WORDS—go in his bedroom. Susie's trailing right along with us. Lyons and me are rapping away, and I haven't quite got around to telling him how wonderful things are at the Shooting Gallery, but I'm getting there. And Susie's being real annoying. Like if you decide you want a teenager for a girlfriend, that's exactly what you're going to get. She's hanging all over him, getting in his way, interrupting everything he says, and so finally, without any warning at all, he just hauls off and whaps her one. Knocks her flat. And she's down on all fours on the floor crying and he just goes on rapping away like nothing's happened. She gets up and he whaps her again. He says, "I didn't tell you to get up yet, cunt."

He rolls a joint, giggling and laughing, and she's whimpering to herself, and my stomach's tightening up like a vice. A few minutes drag by and she says, "Can I get up now, Bob?"

He says, "No, not yet."

I can't see her face because it's, you know, kind of pressed into the rug, but I can see the back of her neck, and it turns bright sunset red. I have this very strong desire to take Lyons and crack him over my knee like a stick. And he looks at me, and I look at him, and I can see by that merry little twinkle in his eye that he knows EXACTLY what I'm thinking.

OK, so there's a number of possibilities about what's going down. Maybe Lyons wanted to teach her a lesson, and he went about it in kind of a crude way. Or maybe he wanted to teach ME a lesson—because I could take him out in less than half a second and I wouldn't even work up a sweat doing it, and he KNOWS THAT, so maybe he was saying, OK, old buddy, I got the top card now. Yeah, you may think the way I'm treating this poor little girl is shitty and disgusting and worthy of your wrath, but you won't do dick about it because YOU'RE IN IT WITH ME UP TO YOUR EYEBALLS.

Or maybe it didn't have a damn thing to do with Susie or with me. Maybe he was just nuts. Like I always knew he was nuts even back at Ton Son Nhut—of course we were all nuts at Ton Son Nhut—and four million hits of crystal sure hadn't helped any.

Or maybe nuts didn't have anything to do with it either. Maybe he was just doing it because it was fun—like they say, THE EXERCISE OF POWER FOR ITS OWN SAKE. I know that one. I've been there myself a few more times than I like to admit, and I know it feels pretty good. That's probably the way Lyndon Johnson and Richard Nixon felt too. But anyhow, I'm thinking about all this shit, and to put things in a nutshell, I am not having a real good time.

So I've got to sit there listening to him giggle and squeak like a bat, and she's got to lay there on the floor—and I swear he made her lay there for damned near an hour—until he goes, "Susie, my sweet, why don't you make us some tea?"

She gets up and makes us some tea. She can't look at me, and I can't look at her either. "OK, Tommy," he says, "what can I do for you tonight?"

What I needed was a key. And I needed it up front because I was tapped right out. And I needed it pretty damn quick. But I just couldn't do it. "Nothing, man. I just fell by to check out your ugly ass."

"Well, shit, a man always needs SOMETHING."

"Not me, Robert. I'm looking good."

OK, SO I might have won that little head game with Lyons, but I was, like they say, running on empty. I checked my other sources, and lo and behold, they were dry as a bone. OK, so talk about swallowing your pride, I fell by to see Ethan. He's always glad to see me. He misses my company when I ain't falling by. He thinks I'm his good buddy. He pulls his nose out of his seed catalogues and rolls us a big fat doobie, and we lay back on the pillows on the floor in the living room and start emitting the good words. Terry's in the background the whole time, you dig, making tea and slicing up the home-made bread for us dudes. And of course she can hear everything I say when I'm asking him if, hey, maybe he's got a source I could tap into along with him. She don't even look at me, but I can feel how disgusted she is.

Ethan is loving it to pieces. Me with the friendly neighborhood source I wouldn't let him in on? Me who always has grass out the ying-yang? Coming TO HIM? Oh, you better believe he's happy. Maybe he'll help me out and maybe he won't, but he's got to make me squirm first. "Well, you know how it is, man. Boston's in kind of a dope drought at the moment. It's all a matter of the ECOLOGY." And that gives him his chance to lay it on me how we're all in it together—THE WHOLE EARTH—like it's like one big interconnected system, man, and air pollution in China ends up on the North Pole bothering Santa Claus, and the state of the grass supply in Boston is directly related to the political situation in Mexico. I go, "Oh, yeah, is that right?" and we do that one for a while until he gets around to admitting that, yeah, maybe one of his sources might have a few extra keys coming in.

Well, after that I was scrambling. Ethan always got dibsies—I mean, after all it was HIS SOURCE, right?—and so I was welcome to the seconds if there was any. And I had to keep checking back with my other half-assed sources—like I always had to be somewhere sometime checking out something, not to mention moving my little bit of grass when I could get my hands on it, and the general public was beginning to get annoyed with me because I was no longer what you could call RELIABLE, and when you start losing the good will of the general public, you've lost it all. Shit, there were times when I figured I could do better selling the *Encyclopedia Britannica* door to door in North Dakota.

JOHN WOKE in the cool blue mornings to the smell of Pam's coffee and a strange openness, a chasm in the array of sound where her fingers on the keys of her typewriter should have been. He heard, instead, her bare feet padding from one side of the room to the other. Later in the day, she would tell him about what she'd been thinking, or at least some of it. She talked about religion infecting political movements: "Like Vaneigem says, the old hippie of Nazareth worms his way into everything." She talked about the Jacobins, the Puritans, Oliver Cromwell, the Spanish Inquisition, the Albigensian Crusade. She talked about ideology becoming a collective superego, the individual members of the group forced to become masochistic in order to survive. And all of that theoretical crap, of course, was going into her total critique—which John had begun to think of as *The Critique*. Or maybe it wasn't. She didn't seem able to write anything down.

And she didn't seem able to eat. Dozens of carrots, an occasional apple or pear, a handful of nuts or a spoonful of yogurt, once an entire head of lettuce with a splash of French dressing on it, and lots of coffee, lots of water—that's all he'd seen going down her throat since Phil had been there. It was scary how quickly the weight could drop away from her. When they went to bed now, her bones hurt him. "Hey," he said, "you're getting too thin."

"Listen," she said, "don't *ever* try to make me eat, OK? It just makes things worse. When I get freaked, it's like . . . I don't know, something shuts down, and food just . . . It's my way of working through things, OK? It's just temporary. Don't worry, I've been here before. I'm keeping track of my weight."

She could still talk. Oh, yeah, she could do that all right—

compulsively. He'd seen her going nuts before—hurt, driven, and distanced—but not as bad as it was now. She didn't use the word "betrayed," but he was sure that's what she was feeling—rapping about Karen and the other Movement women who'd been sucked into Weatherman. "The minute I hit town, they're all coming on to me. What? I'm supposed to provide everybody's lesbian experience? Jesus, there's not enough of me to go around. Why don't all of you just go off and sleep with *each other?* They're going on and on about the joys of sisterhood, and they're afraid to hold hands. I had my first girlfriend when I was fifteen, for Christ's sake. What were you guys doing at fifteen, getting ready for the junior prom?"

"Did you say that to them?"

"Oh, no. Are you kidding? It's everything I *wanted* to say . . . And Karen's really persistent. Phil's over at the *Weasel*, so we hop into bed. And she turns into the most terrified little girl you ever saw in your life. Well, we get through that one eventually, and then, oh, wow, I'm the greatest thing since sliced bread. The stars and stripes fly out of my ass, man. I'm *her first*, you dig? She'll never forget me. She'll always love me . . . for ever and ever and ever. Yeah, you bet. A bullet in my fucking brain, that's how much she loves me."

He said the same thing he always said: "It was a bad trip on bad acid. A sick jerkoff fantasy. They're not going to kill anybody." But he didn't know what to believe.

When he'd first moved into Pam's clearly articulated space, he'd been able to bracket off his paranoia, but he couldn't do it any longer—and neither could she. When the doorbell sounded, she no longer ran down to see who it was; she used the intercom. She locked her father's car. She set up an elaborate arrangement with the women in the Collective to call each other at specific times; if someone wasn't where she was supposed to be when she was supposed to be there, then the group would go into action to find her. When she and John walked anywhere, they checked out everyone around them. To avoid a car snatch, they kept well back from the edges of sidewalks, sometimes walking single-file. They never went out at night if they could help it. When they were separated, they established fail-safe times. She made him memorize the phone numbers of all the women in the Collective—and her father's, doctor's, and therapist's numbers in New York. Nothing was to be written down.

It wasn't just Weatherman—their paranoia now extended to everything and everyone. There was, for instance, that long-haired, vacant-eyed young man they kept running into. Why was he always walking around the Square at the same time they were? Twice they'd caught him standing across the street from their apartment doing absolutely nothing. But if he was an agent, whose agent was he?

"It wouldn't take much effort to bug this place," John said. "They'd just have to memorize our routine and then wait till we go to the *Zygote* office."

"We better not have a routine then."

"But what if they've already done it?"

She shrugged. "Shit, there's some things you just can't . . . Well, OK, if they've got a bug in here, I hope they dig our sex life."

Their sex life? Right, he thought. How would that look to an agent? Shaving his face took ten minutes; shaving his entire body took over an hour. Within days, it was growing back, a constant annoyance. For a while, he'd gone around smelling like a gigantic apricot; then Pam had bought him mentholated skin cream—a delicious tingle, a pothead's groove—so now he smelled like mint leaves. It was addictive—sleek, shiny, smooth skin. He loved the way he looked. Staring into the mirror, feeling what? Turn-on, of course, and a complex bittersweet pleasure. It made him want to lose weight too, join Pamela in her madness—*anorexia nervosa atypical*—so they could firmly and finally bracket off their paranoia, lie on her white bed, display themselves to each other on her white eyelet lace, and admire each other's emerging bone structures as they thinned out quietly into sweet Romantic death.

But he could never do that. It was a sick fantasy, and the paranoia wouldn't stay bracketed off for long, and he could never take anorexia as far as Pam did. Acid had left him with a vivid sense of himself as a body in a world full of bodies, and bodies need to be fed. Part of him was still the Zen monk who throws down his hoe and laughs when the dinner bell rings—and there was a point, too, beyond which Pam would become too thin, would stop turning him on. He'd already seen her there once—the gaunt driven speed freak she'd become after the Chicago convention. He didn't want to see her there again, but that's where she was headed. What was driving her now? Paranoia cranked up to an unsustainable pitch? Grief?

He'd been sure that he'd already run every possible disaster through his mind. Back in his wretched little box off Central Square, the radio blatting away, or the TV, stoned to the eyeballs, he'd sweated through every brilliantly imagined detail. The agents who turn up at the office. The groovy Movement dude—or chick—who's really an agent. The bust on the street, the bust at the airport, the thunderous KGB knock at four in the morning, the too-tight handcuffs in the back of the car, the slow hours of interrogation, the days in solitary, the passage of time. The sit-ups and push-ups and all the poetry he remembered—doing anything he had to in order to survive. The writing—if they gave him anything to write with. Now he had another lovely story to add to his repertoire of bummers. His naked, shivering, hairless body would reveal him to be the most loathsome of subversives—a depraved little sissy faggot—and that's exactly how his gleefully self-righteous pig captors would treat him.

He'd even become afraid of writing. He was afraid of what he'd already written. Why in God's name had he ever laid out his and Pam's utterly mad ideas in print, in *Zygote*, for everyone in the world to see? The only response that had yet come back from the world had been from women in the Collective: "How the hell did you ever get *a man* to sign that with you?"

"What did you tell them?"

"I said you weren't a man, that you were an androgyne just like me . . . and you'd renounced male privilege. I told them that we were playing with reversed sex roles."

It was true enough, but he felt—to use Pam's word—"demeaned" by her cool summary. He didn't tell her that.

THEY DIDN'T find out about the townhouse explosion all at once. Bits of information kept dribbling out day after day. The first reports suggested that it might have been gas pipes blowing up. "I know that neighborhood," Pam said. It was in Greenwich Village—trendy, chi-

chi, the big bucks. "I've walked by that house a million times," she said. Movie stars lived around there.

The explosion must have been a real motherfucker. It had shaken the entire area, punched out a hole in the house next door, shattered windows across the street. Several people had stumbled away from the blast but couldn't be found to comment. The townhouse had burned so badly that the whole damned thing had collapsed in on itself. When the fire was out and heavy equipment had been brought in to stabilize what was left, firemen finally managed to go inside where they discovered the first body—a young man in jeans. "It wasn't gas," Pam said.

Reports the next day said that the house was owned by a James Wilkerson; he was away on vacation. One of the people who had escaped alive and gone missing was his daughter, Cathlyn. "Shit," Pam said, "Cathy Wilkerson." Weatherman.

When the first body was identified, it turned out to be someone named Ted Gold. "You know him too?" John said.

"Of course I know him. Fuck, man, I'm going to know them all."

The police found SDS leaflets. The press said that the townhouse had been a Weatherman bomb factory, and something must have gone terribly wrong. The police found two more bodies—one was that of a young woman. Her head and hands had been blown off; she had been riddled with roofing nails. The other body was a torso so badly mutilated that the sex couldn't yet be determined. They found blasting caps, alarm clocks, wires, dynamite.

"*Roofing nails*," Pam said. "That's motherfucking anti-personnel, man. That's bombs you use *against people* . . . I kept hoping, like, hey, maybe it's just another big show. Like let's see who has the biggest mouth, who can run the heaviest rap, but . . . Part of me just didn't want to believe it, but it's true. The whole scene's fucked, man. If murdering a pregnant woman is a revolutionary act, then that's exactly where you're headed . . . like it's inevitable. Fuck, I just wish I wasn't so goddamned *right* all the time. Jacobins, Cromwellites, motherfucking religious fanatics . . . *Religion*. Once you're there, anything's justified."

In New York, bombs went off in the headquarters of IBM, Socony

Mobil, and General Telephone and Electronics. Weatherman didn't take credit for them, but the press blamed them on Weatherman nonetheless. In the townhouse, the cops had found a fingertip belonging to the headless, handless body of the young woman; the identification came back and was released to the public—Diana Oughton. Pam couldn't stop crying.

John didn't know what was happening. Up until the moment she'd got the news—one of the women in the Collective had called her up and told her—Pam had seemed to be just as cold and angry as he was. Now she sat at her desk where *The Critique*, untouched for weeks, was stacked up in a neat pile. She stared in the direction of the window, tears running down her face. "She was a good person," she said.

What? he thought. She's mourning the death of a Leninist asshole who was making bombs to kill people?

"Can you imagine what they had to do to get there?" she said. "To get themselves cranked up to that fever pitch? Can you imagine the *violence* they had to do to themselves?"

He took her hand. She allowed him to lead her to their bed. Once she lay down, she gave up—drew her knees up to her chest, wrapped her arms around them, and sobbed. "Oh, baby," he said, stroking her hair. He never would have imagined Pam as inarticulate, but that's what she was now—her words forced out in small, tear-soaked bursts. "Like that thing Laing . . . the forces of violence called 'love' . . . What if you're doing it to yourself?"

He wanted to shake her out of her grief the way a terrier shakes a rat. "Jesus, Pam, you were talking about the split in the Movement the first night I met you. Well, this is it, you dig? Not PL. PL's always been totally irrelevant. It's motherfucking Weatherman. We should have seen it coming. We never should have tried to do anything with Leninists. They were always the enemy. They're just as much the enemy as the CIA."

"You don't understand."

How could she say that to him? He'd never in his life worked harder at understanding anyone.

"She was a good person," she kept saying. "She was sweet. She was kind and gentle." She hadn't known Diana very well, but they'd had a long rap once, really intense. "She was . . . I don't know how to tell you. She was why I was in SDS. She was the best we had."

"They want *to kill us*," he said. "Not metaphor. Like right smack down in the real."

"Oh, just shut up, man. You've got to let me feel what I'm feeling."

OK, he thought, I'm not going to say another fucking word. He lay down beside her. "The tip of her finger," she said. "Jesus fuck, man, her head, her hands . . . motherfucking *roofing nails.*"

Yes, he thought, roofing nails. Of course, roofing nails. But now her telegraphic fragments were no longer about Diana Oughton; they were about Karen Vance. He could sense the connection between Diana and Karen—an elusive vibration—but his head wouldn't move fast enough to bring it into focus. "It's what happens to women," Pam was saying. "Like it's a . . . Shit, in a warped mirror. What did Karen have to do to herself so she could . . . ? Like male-identified . . . No, it's more than that. Like how could she . . . ? Oh, fuck, man, *Karen did love me. She did. It was real.*"

She allowed him to take her in his arms. She felt thin—tiny, bony. Like a child, she pressed her face into his chest. She hadn't cried since Phil had dropped by to deliver his terrible news, so she must have been storing up these tears. "We've got to get clear of men," she said to the man holding her. *But no,* he had to remind himself, *she doesn't think of me as a man.*

He thought she'd cried herself out, but when she pushed him back and stood up, he saw that she was still crying—soundlessly now, but the tears streaking her cheeks. "I'm going to call Deb," she said, already across the room, already picking up the phone and dialing.

"What? In New Mexico? The motherfucking phone's tapped."

"Fuck that shit," and into the phone: "Hey, it's me. Pamela. Is Deb . . . ? Yeah, OK."

He followed her. Holding the phone to her ear, waiting, she looked into his eyes. He'd learned to read her wordless communications, but he couldn't read that one. "Deb?" she said into the phone. "It's me. Did you hear . . . ?" and then she was crying again—full tilt, flat out, doubled over with it.

He was appalled at what he was thinking: *I can't take any more of this shit.* Heading for the door, he gave her a stiff wave. "You don't have to go," she called after him, covering the mouthpiece of the phone. But, yes, he did have to go.

As angry as he was, he couldn't leave without a word. "I'll be back," he said.

HE WALKED around Harvard Yard four times, fast, before it made even the slightest dent in the jangle. What a stupid exit line, he thought. "I'll be back," implied that he'd considered not coming back. He should go back now. He didn't want to go back.

Cut loose. Out alone again in the dreadful real with the paranoia grinding him like a million rolling boulders. All the assholes involved in the townhouse explosion had been NO—or at least he thought they'd been—but what about Karen Vance's whacked-out little underground cell in Dorchester? Maybe they were still dropping acid every day and following their own sick path—revolution as violence as pornography. With their brains irradiated to a putrid day-glo orange, would they see the townhouse explosion as a SIGN? Yeah, the time is at hand, motherfuckers. Ready or not, here we come. Now we're going to off some pigs and piglets—and he and Pam would be easier to kill than some goddamned senator.

He didn't know where the hell his politics were these days, but there was one thing he did know—he must never allow himself to get drafted into anybody's murdering club. Just like Pamela, he'd thought that the murdering clubs were exclusively male—and just how goddamned naive had *that* been? OK, so if he knew better by now, where did that leave him? Nowhere. Everywhere. Fucked, God help him. *Man, woman*—the way those words were used these days, he didn't want to be either of them. He wanted to be as elusive as one of those weird subatomic particles—the moment you try to pin it down, it's gone.

After six times around the Yard, he walked back to the Square. The jangle had backed off a bit, but he could still feel it waiting to jump him. He'd been gone too long—Pam didn't know where he was—but he still couldn't go back. Having a car had spoiled him, but shit, he still knew how to ride the MTA. Even better than that, he had some money in his jeans from his last *Zygote* paycheck. He hailed a cab and told the driver Somerville.

Without a clue what he was doing, he stood a moment on the sidewalk, looking up at the crappy old house Cassandra had labeled the Shooting Gallery. The last time he'd been there, it had been death-trip winter—ice-bound, snow-clogged, locked into black stellar cold—but the sky tonight was translucent blue, and the wind felt wet, not icy. The snow had melted, spring was coming; the seasons were rotating through their old comforting cycle just as though the world wasn't about to end at any minute. He didn't bother to knock, stepped into a curious quiet like a pause in the general proceedings. A radio in the kitchen was playing bebop—the metalwork of some disassembled tune. He followed the sound and found crazy Lorraine sitting at the kitchen table, smoking. "Hey, Raymond, what's happening?" She was cooking something—pasta maybe. Her boiling water had steamed the windows. The scene looked almost normal—damned near *domestic*—but the whole house stunk of cigarettes and dope. "She's upstairs, man," she told him, gesturing *up* with her head.

He found Cassandra alone in the bedroom she shared with Tom. Nothing in there but the bed and a pile of clothes in the corner and an old crooked stand-up lamp that looked like it had been scavenged from the Cambridge dump—nothing else, not a picture on the wall, not even a chair. Cassandra was lying on the bed reading; she looked up when he stepped through the door, and he felt the force of her grey eyes—their accuracy. "Far fucking out," she said, laid her book aside, stood up, and hugged him. He was still scrabbling, and it took him a moment before he could hug her back. "Hey, Cass."

"You sorry asshole," she said, "I didn't know how much I missed you till I saw you walking through the door." Wow, that wasn't her usual hip persona that found things mind-blowing or trippy or a drag but never simply human. Could he do it too—express something that was simply human? "What the fuck's happening, man?" she said.

"I couldn't tell you." Space travel, moon landing—from Pamela's world into Cassandra's too fast, his head left lagging behind, ruminating paranoia in the cab or pursuing empty circles in Harvard Yard. He'd forgotten how short Cassandra's hair was these days. If you put a blazer on her, she'd look like a pretty British schoolboy. "You want to do some smoke?" she said. Of course he wanted to do some smoke.

They sat down on the edge of the bed, and she rolled a joint. Being here had brought his head into painful focus. He didn't want to be living anywhere else but in Pamela's little white box, but life there had begun to feel closed in, hermetically sealed, almost like a trap.

"You ever read this?" Cassandra said, tossing her book into his lap—Carlos Castaneda. "Everybody and their dog has been telling me I've got to read this damn thing, and I'm going, fuck, I don't want to read something *everybody's* reading. But they were right, man, it's a real trip."

"Oh, you bet your sweet ass."

"'Learning is never what you expect.' Shit. If there was nothing in there but that one line, it'd be worth the price of admission. So what the fuck you doing? Still working for *Zygote?*"

"Oh, yeah." She passed him the joint. He fired it up.

"Wow," she said, "that androgyny thing you guys wrote. Motherfucking blew me away, man. Like I had to go scrape my brains off the wall and stuff them back into my skull, and I'm not just bullshitting you. I started reading it, and every word, I'm going, 'Oh, far out. Wow, that's true. Why didn't I think of that years ago?'"

"Hey, thanks. It wasn't just me, like most of it's Pam . . . So what're you doing? Where's Tom?"

"Oh, he's *out*, man. Flat out, far out, running on a tight schedule, fuck if I know where he is."

"How about those evil dudes in California? You heard any more from them?"

"No action on that front, but I haven't checked it out, so what the hell do I know? Nothing is what I know. Sleeping dogs lie, I think that's how it goes."

He passed her the joint. "Zoë keeps threatening to come up," she said, "and I keep going, 'No, no, no, it's not quite . . . um . . . auspicious. Yeah, the omens and portents haven't aligned themselves up properly yet.' Maybe I should go down there again, pay her a little visit, like head her off at the pass, but fuck, man. I love her dearly, but she's straighter than a Barbie doll. So what's happening with your love life? How's Pamela the Great?"

"She's bummed out about the townhouse explosion. You heard about that?"

"Oh, yeah. Heavy. It's like that thing from Pogo . . . 'We have met the enemy, and he is us.'"

"That's good," he said, laughing. "It's too easy, but it's good."

The dope felt good too—and he realized that dope hadn't been feeling good for a while. Too much paranoia, too many weird complexities, and then, WHAM, he caught up to where he was. His obscure inner compass had told him exactly where to go; he'd just walked into that good, solid, well-built sense of coming home, and all it took to get there was Cassandra. Maybe now, eventually, in an hour or two, he could go back and deal with crazy Pamela.

"Hey, Dupre." Cass had been rapping about something. She'd just interrupted herself in mid-sentence, her voice suddenly shifting into the tone she would have used if she'd said, "Hey, look, a falling star!" She was staring at his chest. "What have you done, you asshole?"

A burst of fiery pin points, scalp to crotch. He knew exactly what she was seeing. Why the fuck hadn't he been more careful? She reached out, snagged his t-shirt, and pulled it down. He batted her hand away, sprang to his feet.

"Oh, you fucking jerk," she said, laughing. Jumped up and pursued him. Backed him against the wall. Thrust her hand down the front of his t-shirt. "Blow me away, man. Smooth as a baby's ass. What the hell are you doing?"

Not a single word was available to him. "Oh," she said, grinning, "I get it. You guys are really doing it. You're motherfucking *androgynous*. Far fucking out. How much more?"

"What do you mean, how . . . ?"

"Your *legs*? Did you shave *your legs*?"

He squirmed away from her, slid along the wall, was stopped by the corner. Still laughing, she dropped to the floor and pursued him on all fours. Intoning: "Did. You. Shave. Your. Legs. You asshole."

She grabbed his left ankle with one hand, with the other reached up under his jeans and felt his skin. "Far out. You honest-to-God motherfucking did it."

Appalled, John heard a high-pitched sound coming out of himself like a teenager's hysterical giggle. She was undoing his belt. "For Christ's sake," he said.

"Take it off, Dupre. Come on, I want to see it *all*, man." She grabbed his jeans in both hands and jerked them down. "Whew. Beautiful."

"What if Tom . . . ?

"Fuck Tom. Tom's long gone."

She sprang to her feet, yanked his shirt over his head. "Come on, come on, come on. No half measures. Let's see the full catastrophe."

Lickety-split, she stripped him down to his underwear—even his socks—and stepped back to take in the full view. He was so embarrassed all he could do was stare at his bare feet. He could have sworn that every inch of his body was blushing.

"Wow," she said, "you are *so* skinny, and *so* smooth . . ."

He looked up, met her eyes. She was smiling slightly. "I bet you know where the clitoris is *now*, don't you, old buddy?"

Of course he was laughing—what else could he do? He was laughing so hard he couldn't stand. He backed up until he felt the wall behind him and slid to the floor, laughing.

Then he was stopped and so was she. Flipped out of time, they regarded each other in one of those somber grey pauses that could have been anywhere back along the track all the way to the first night they'd met. "Oh, yeah," she said, "I bet Pamela just eats you up with a spoon."

He couldn't look away from her eyes. "But seriously," she said, "you got to ditch those Jockeys. They don't do a thing for you, sweetie. I mean, you shouldn't wear little pink bows or, you know, anything motherfucking ridiculous. But not *Jockeys* . . . You wear dresses?"

Anger—a steel defense in him closing up and locking. "No."

"Well, why not? She might like it. I know *you'd* like it. I don't mean Cinderella, for fuck's sake. But you've got to feel what it's like in a skirt."

He already knew what it was like in a skirt—although he hadn't worn one since he'd been a kid. He didn't want to tell her that. "Androgyny's like a middle ground," he said.

"Oh, yeah. I can dig it. But, skirts and . . . hey, *stockings*, man. How could you possibly resist? You got to try stockings."

Still looking into her eyes, he finally flashed on it—this was *Cassandra* and there was nothing he had to defend. "I don't know if Pam wants to go that far."

"You might be surprised, man."

Yeah, he might be. He was continually surprised these days. And a tearing—or no, more like a fracturing. Awareness. Amplified distractions. One of them was right there—Lorraine's distant skittering of bebop. It had been there all along, reminding him that they weren't alone. He kicked the door shut, retrieved his clothes. Watching him get dressed, Cassandra picked up the dope and the papers. She used plain old Zig-Zags. He was glad of that. "Let's really do it," she said. "Let's get motherfucking ridiculous."

The curtain was going up on the next act—whatever the hell it was going to be. He sat on the edge of the bed and inhaled smoke. "Remember the night you took me to the Louis Armstrong concert out at the park?" she said.

"Of course I do. You think I could ever forget that?"

"Well, that was . . . It wasn't the first time I'd ever had stockings on, but it was the first time I ever understood why anybody would bother with the damned things. I'll never forget the feeling. It's hard to describe. There's this sleek, smooth . . . but a kind of raspiness too, almost scratchy. Not quite scratchy. But your legs kind of . . . zzzz when they slide against each other. Oh, wow, man, I was like right in the center of everything, like I had it all. School was out, and in the fall I was going to be a motherfucking *sophomore*, and I had a new dress and a boyfriend in university and I had *stockings on*, man. Yeah, I was looking good, and, wow, did I ever know it."

"And I'd never seen a girl in my life as beautiful as you that night."

"Yeah? Well, you always liked me, so your taste can't be trusted. But it's like . . . Being a girl's a bummer most of the time, but there's moments when it feels just great. That's how they suck you into their whole sick trip . . . So how is it?"

"How's what?"

"You like being a girl? Or androgynous . . . or whatever you are?"

"Yeah."

"You dig the sex."

"Oh, yeah. Christ, I don't how to . . . It's wonderful. It's like a drug." And he realized that he'd come to complain about Pamela—at least that had been one of his *conscious* reasons—but now he had no intention of doing that. His loyalty to Pamela couldn't have felt any more compelling if they'd been married. "She's sexually very aggressive . . ."

"*Sexually aggressive?* Oh, gee. Oh, wow, is that ever a surprise. I'm just blown away by that. I never could have guessed that . . . I bet you're the first man she's ever been in bed with in her whole goddamn life."

Yes, he could still be surprised. Maybe it was true—or at least partially true. If Pam had been in bed with men before him, it probably hadn't counted for much. He was probably the first androgynous boy she'd ever met who hadn't been gay.

In the same way he would have watched on old film clip, he watched Cassandra drag, hold the smoke in, let it go. "Oh, I got her number right away," she said. "Takes a chick to get it. Like all this energy zapping between us. I even thought about it . . . for maybe half a second. Like, hey, wow, I've never made it with a chick, it might be kind of interesting. That's why she rubs dudes wrong. Like Ethan and Tom. They're too dumb to figure it out, but they can sense it. She walks in the room, and they go, 'Oooh, something's not right here.'"

She passed him the joint. What a strangely inhuman thing to do, he thought—inhale the smoke from a burning plant. "Pamela thinks you're an androgyne just like us," he said.

"Oh, she does, does she . . . ? Well, of course I am. Whatever that is. Like 'X people,' you don't want to pin it down too much. Then it gets like . . ."

"A box."

"Right on."

276

He understood her perfectly. "And nobody's going to put you in a box, right? You're Cassandra, the cat who walks by herself."

"And you're still the guy who'll try anything. Remember telling me, 'Ordinary experience isn't enough'?"

"Did I lay that rap on you?"

"Shit, man, you laid it on everybody."

The dope was running his pulverized brains through a flour sifter. Yes, he knew that he'd met her the spring of his senior year in high school, but it felt like he'd known her forever. "Cassandra," he said, "I am so glad to see you." And not far from there—only a few hundred miles—the great Ohio was rolling along right at the edge of everything.

"When I was tripping out on that weird fucking acid," he said, "you came and helped me out."

"Groovy. What did I do?"

"I asked you how I could get off . . . like off that crazy roller-coaster . . . and you said, 'You don't get off. You just hang on.'"

"Shit," she said, laughing, "that wasn't an acid blip. That was me."

———

SO ONE night Terry and me are doing our rendezvous number, and we'd been doing it for so long, it was getting kind of casual. Like we parked in different places and met up on this corner where there's no street light, and then we zipped real quick into the building, and it was always a relief to get off the street. Not a huge relief, just this little whew—like everything's cool, like hey, we did it again. And so we're trotting down the stairs and on back that long hallway, rapping away, not thinking much of anything, and I unlock the door to John's apartment, and the minute I step inside, I detect the fact that things are somewhat different. Like the place has been THOROUGHLY TRASHED.

I'm standing there going, what the fuck? All the bookshelves pulled down and crap flung every which way like a twister hit. And my first thought is, shit, why would John do that? He must have been really pissed off about something. But if you give me a half a chance, I'll usually get there, so eventually I catch up to my second thought—hey, it wasn't John who did it.

Terry agrees with me. Yeah, it's obvious, she says, somebody's been through there looking for SOMETHING. And she's real upset because we'd got kind of fond of John's place, like it had kind of turned into OUR PLACE. Of course Terry thinks it's A SIGN.

"Sure, it's A SIGN," I say. "It's A SIGN that somebody's one jump behind John's ass."

No, no, no, that's not what she means. She knows that down here on the EARTHLY LEVEL it was somebody after John's ass, but it's the HIGHER REGIONS she's talking about. You know, the COSMIC FORCES. And she figures it's A SIGN FOR US. "Yeah?" I say. "So what do you suppose that SIGN might be?"

She's not sure, but it's heavy, she knows that much. Maybe it means that Ethan's onto us—or if we're not careful he's going to be onto us. Or maybe it means that we can't keep on running things in our usual half-assed way, that we've got to make some kind of DECISION.

Well, I don't know about any of that shit, but one thing I do know is that I've got to give John the straight scoop, so after I get done conducting my business with Terry for the night, I give him a call, wake the poor fucker up, and lay it on him that we need to have some words. Like this is HEAVY, man, like this is JUST BETWEEN THE TWO OF US. I didn't want Pamela the Great around. I figured this one called for a sniff of that old autonomy.

———

"IT'S BEEN jimmied," John said. "See the scratch marks."

"Hey," Tom said, "you're really checked out on this secret agent shit."

"Constant paranoia's good for something," John said, and it was true. He'd rehearsed this scene a hundred million times before so if it actually happened, he'd go on automatic pilot—*this* is what you do next, and then *this*, and then *this*. OK, he told himself, don't freak. Breathe. What you're feeling doesn't matter a sweet goddamn; it's what you do that counts. Start by checking it out. Try to figure out who they were, what they wanted. "I've got to think," he said out loud.

"Yeah?" Tom said. "So think."

Something echoey here, something spacey. Was he going blooey?

Hell, no. He'd never fainted in his life, and he wasn't about to start now. "They didn't do any nasty fuck-you shit," he said, "like writing PIG on the wall or taking a dump in the middle of the floor. And it wouldn't be Weatherman anyway because everybody knows I'm living with Pamela. Like everybody in the Movement knows that. They were looking for something. But looking for what?"

Now *he* was looking—for clues, signs, tiny details, omens, anything. "All my papers are over at Pamela's," he said, "so there's nothing here that could identify me."

But how about all the pictures of Zoë on the walls? Could anybody figure out who Zoë was, connect him that way? No, that was sheer lunacy. All they'd know about the guy who lived here was that he was one horny son of a bitch.

"Arthur T. Jones," he said, "that's who the landlord knows. Yeah, that identity's blown. Well, shit, Mr. Jones didn't have much of an identity anyway."

Wait a minute, John thought, *the money*. The book was right in front of him—*Memoir of a Revolutionist*. It had been tossed onto the floor along with all the other books. He opened it, and the bread was still in there. "Shit, man," he said, "you'd think if they were going to all this trouble, they'd flip through the pages, right? Does that mean they were amateurs, or does it mean they were in a hurry?"

Could he read their minds from the chaos they'd left behind? "Were they looking for Raymond Lee? Or were they looking for *me*? Raymond Lee really *exists*, you know." John had made sure of that, had dropped lots of clues. Raymond Lee was from Akron, Ohio, had been out in the Haight for a while, but then he'd drifted into Boston, worked for the Resistance, worked on the *Weasel*. He was an anarchist. He'd written those crazy articles with Pam Zalman in *Zygote*. He lived with Pam Zalman. "Everybody in the Movement knows him. That means the agents know him too."

"Yeah, right. So who knows who you really are?"

"Ethan and Terry and you and Cassandra and Pamela."

"That's all?"

"Yeah, that's all. That damn well better be all, or . . . Shit, if the agents know who I am, that means they're just toying with me."

"Either that or they figure you're more useful out running loose. Like you're going to lead them somewhere. Just like the narks at our place."

"You know," John said, "that could be right. They honest-to-God believe the Movement's run from Peiking or Hanoi or Havana, the dumb fucks."

But what the hell did John know about *Tom?* Ping down the backbone. "Hey," he said carefully, "when you said you had some use for this place, just what were you using it for?"

He saw Tom go silent and hard. Oh, shit, John thought, I'm dead. But then Tom shook his head and laughed. "Fuck, man, it was kind of dumb, but . . . Like I'm sorry, man, but I was using this place to store grass."

John laughed too. He'd been right; all of his instincts had told him that—if he couldn't trust Tom Parker, he couldn't trust anybody. "Why didn't you tell me that before? They were looking for dope. Did they get anything?"

"No. I was in between shipments. Hey, I don't think they was looking for dope. I think they was looking for you."

Tom had been standing, too tall for this cheese box; now he sank into a squat and began rolling a joint. "Tell me, old buddy," he said, "why I shouldn't be driving you to the airport."

"You know why," John said.

"For that chick, huh?"

John sank to the floor too. He took the fat joint Tom was offering him, lit it and dragged. "I can't leave Pamela right now." It wasn't that he hadn't thought about it. But he couldn't leave her when she was as fucked up as she was.

"I thought you was going to tell me you was doing it for the revolution," Tom said.

"Oh, yeah. Right. Sure that's what I was going to say."

"Hey, old buddy, check it out." Tom made a sweeping gesture— the trashed room. "Don't that look dumb to you? Don't that look clumsy to you? Was that some sneaky bastards or just a couple assholes doing their job? Don't that say standard-issue cops to you? But the thing you got to remember . . . cops may be dumb, but they keep on coming. You got a little bit of room to maneuver, buddy, you better take it."

Why, John asked himself, was he smoking grass? Why was he doing it *now?* They weren't cops, he thought, because they'd jimmied the door. That was a good point, but he couldn't get himself to say it. He passed the joint. Tom took a wickedly long toke, held it, and then, like a magician's trick, let the smoke filter slowly out of his nose. "I respect you, old buddy, you know that?" Quiet, nearly meditative.

"Yeah?"

"Coming back here, risking your ass. Trying to do your bit. Yeah, we got to do something even if it's wrong. You like this shit, man? This is Columbian shit. Top of the line."

The dope was coming on too fast, a swirl of rotating distractions, and times like this, times when one should be able to keep one's mind simple, focused on what was right in front of one's goddamned nose and not go spidering away down some obscurely tugged strand— "Shit, man," Tom was saying in the same quiet dreamy voice, "you want to . . . Fuck me, but Mister Charlie's one evil dude, and we get over there, we get just as evil as Mister Charlie. Do you understand what I'm telling you? Yeah, like let's all climb down in the sewer together, right? Yeah, we're having ourselves such a damn fine time, all down in the sewer together, right?"

John felt the joint being pressed between his fingers. Oh, what the hell, he thought.

"You know," Tom was saying, "guys will show you the ears they collected. Proud as can be. Show you their pictures. Why the fuck anybody'd want to take pictures of that shit, I'll never know. Like, 'Hey, man, dig this one. We shoved a grenade up her ass. Pretty cool, huh?' Or like . . . Jesus, there was this one picture . . . I'm going like, 'Jesus, what the fuck happened to him?'

"'We peeled him, man.'

"'What the fuck you mean, you peeled him?'

"'Shit, man, you ever peeled a peach? Just like that.'

"Yeah, man, it's just . . . And then there's . . . Shit, like some things are like standard issue. Chucking Mister Charles out of the chopper. Standard issue. Happens every day. Zips falling out of the sky regular as raindrops. And the Bell Telephone Hour. You know that one, don't you? The field telephone wired up to the old testicles. Happens every day. Even chicks. Wires shoved up their cunt. Lots of laughs, right?"

What could John say to that? "Fuck, that's heavy," he said.

"You don't know the half of it, old buddy. Yeah, so why did they go after that poor son of a bitch, Calley? Because fucking Nixon needs him, that's why. Yeah, folks, it was just that crazy dude, Calley. Everybody else is sane. Yeah, you bet your sweet ass. Jesus Christ, man, My Lai's going down over there every fucking day, and everybody knows it."

He's right, John thought, and I don't know the half of it—and don't want to know.

"But I was field maintenance, right?" Tom was saying. "The air force's primary mission is to fly and maintain aircraft capable of flying. Yeah, that's the truth, and it's a fucking joke, man. I'm just supposed to keep the fuckers up in the air, right? I'm not supposed to be out there playing Doc Holliday at the OK Corral."

"What did you say?" John said. "What are you talking about?"

"Did I ever tell you about Tet, old buddy? Shit. You know, we should have seen it coming. I mean the night before, there was all these fireworks and shit going down, because it was, you know, the new year, but that night it was motherfucking *quiet*. Like the mama-sans didn't show up. Like they knew there was going to be some heavy shit, you know what I mean?"

"Yeah," John said. "Yeah, I do know what you mean."

"*Incoming*, that's where it starts. I mean where the hell else would it start? There's supposed to be a truce on, but do you think Mister Charles gives a fuck about any truce? And you know what? It took us forever to get any weapons because they locked them up at night. That's how swift they are in the You Sure Are Fucked United States Air Force. It was awe-inspiring, I don't know what else to call it. The choppers drawing all this fire, like these green tracers going up, and Charlie's out there all right, I mean thousands and thousands and thousands of those motherfuckers out there . . .

"You know, I heard one of those Harvard assholes in the *Weasel* office, he said it was *symbolic*. Yeah, that's what he called Tet.

Symbolic. And I just motherfucking lost it. *Symbolic* my fucking ass. Charlie wanted Ton Son Nhut, and Charlie had a pretty good idea he could take Ton Son Nhut, and Charlie came within an inch and a half of taking Ton Son Nhut, and the main thing stopping him was the SPs. Motherfucking light infantry is what they were, and there were just waves and waves coming at them, and they held. I still can't believe it. And then the choppers got into it, and a lot of them went down too, a bad sorry day when the army's got to provide air support for the goddamn air force, but that's what it was, a bad sorry day, so it was pretty much touch and go there for a while until the Three Quarter Cav showed up, and you could hear them coming in, man, like a herd of elephants, and it was the best sound you ever heard in your life, so don't tell me it was motherfucking *symbolic* . . .

"A lot of good men bought it that day. And the dudes in the choppers, and those SPs on the ground . . . I really owe those fuckers. Yeah, nothing's too good for those dudes. When we say we were brothers, that just ain't bullshit, and to my dying day I'll be grateful to those dudes, and whatever any of us did that day, we did it for each other, and it's a fucking crime the way they're wasting our fucking lives over there, man, for fucking *nothing.*"

John had been staring at something, a dark blur like a cloud of gnats, but now he saw that it was just another mental trick, not a real thing in the room with him. Tom had stopped talking. He looked over, found Tom sitting quietly, watching him. "You going to waste your life for fucking nothing, man?" Tom said.

"Shit," John said.

"You want to go to the airport?"

John couldn't say a word.

"Hey, old buddy," Tom said, "I know you been getting your rocks off, and I know how good that feels, believe me, I do. But listen up, it's me, old Mad Tom talking to you now, and I ain't going to bullshit you. I just want to ask you something. Just between us two dudes with our hammers hanging down, don't you think that skiddly chick might be leading you a little bit off course?"

13.

"ALL THE way!" Twisted tin-can voice crackling from the sound truck. Like a parody of a fifties football coach, saying the same goddamned things—this interminable pep talk. "Yeah, yeah, yeah, we're going all the way. The Red Army's on the march. All the way to Harvard Square."

Red Army? John thought. Give me a fucking break.

A lot of the people had gone home, but plenty were still left, still on the move. The asshole in the sound truck seemed to think that he was in charge of them, but this was not anybody's army, and it was certainly not *marching*—a word that implied a strategy, or at least some tactical order. The only vibe John could pick up from the kids around him was a simple need to keep on going.

He was lousy at guessing crowd sizes, but he would have said a couple thousand were still left, maybe more. On the Common, he and Pam had seen lots of people they knew, the usual faces at demonstrations, the leftover politicos who'd lost their homes—old Resistance types, SDSers who hadn't been able to go with either PL or Weatherman, RYM II people, or the just plain unaffiliated—now brought together temporarily under the flaccid umbrella of the November Action Committee. But they were only a fraction of this freaky parade; who the rest were was anybody's guess. The ones right around them—Pam had been talking to them—were from Dedham High, fifteen- and sixteen-year-olds out on a lark. Some of them, girls as well as boys, had brought laundry bags stuffed full of rocks. Then, not too far ahead in the pack, was a knot of dudes the straight papers would have called "youth." They were wearing leather jackets, construction boots, and football helmets. They were carrying baseball bats.

But John and Pam's most intimate comrade in the Red Army, their constant companion—they'd tried, but they hadn't been able to shake her—was a plump teenager in ripped black pants. When she'd told them her name, John had thought at first she'd said "Flashlight" but, waving her pale, dimpled, oddly lovely hands in the air, she'd said, "No, no, no, man . . . Flash*line*." At first glance, her waist-length hair had appeared to be braided, but when John had got a closer look, he'd seen that it was merely filthy—matted into strands like tar-soaked ropes. He hoped that Flashline had grown herself a good set of calluses; she was walking from the Boston Common to Harvard Square barefoot, and she was tripped out of her everloving skull. "Oh, wow," she said in her cheery little-kid's voice, "conglomerate Kensington, farther than fetchington, out of the fencington, out of the . . . out of the . . . Blop."

"Right on, Flashline," Pam told her.

As Pam had pointed out to him, women's lib was well represented—members of the groups she called "centrist"—but, except for herself, there were no women from the Collective. What was going on today was absolutely irrelevant to them. Why should they be interested in the struggle between the *men* in Hanoi and the *men* in Washington? "A point of view to which I am not entirely unsympathetic," Pam had said with a wry smile. What she and John were doing at the demonstration was covering it for *Zygote*.

"What the fuck's happening?" somebody yelled. They'd been walking slower and slower; now they bumped to a halt. John could see the end of the Harvard Bridge; it was just ahead of the sound truck. "Pigs," somebody else yelled. John couldn't tell if it was a warning or an explanation. Something about the parade permit.

"Get that lawyer dude up there. Where's that fucking lawyer dude?"

"What the fuck is this? We're cleared all the way to Harvard Square."

The girls right around them started up a halfhearted cheer—"Hey, hey, all the way, Dedham's going to win today!"—then collapsed into giggles.

"Oy," Pam said to him, "this is the agency of change?" but she was grinning. She seemed to be enjoying this insanity. It was the first time in a hell of a long time that she'd seemed to be enjoying much of anything.

Pam looked as freaky as Flashline; she looked as freaky as anybody there. He didn't know how many layers she was wearing at the end of this fine spring afternoon, still warm even though the sun was rapidly dropping out. Her top layer was an old duffel coat, the hood up, her hair hidden inside. In a thin jacket, unzipped and hanging open, he'd worked up a sweat walking, but she had gloves on—her navy-blue dress gloves, the ones with the tiny bows. She'd lost so much weight her nose looked damned near as sharp as a bird's beak; her cheekbones were as clearly defined as tennis balls with pale pink rubber stretched over them. She looked like a scrawny scruffy starved little boy, a twelve-year-old with his eyes elaborately made up—a scary image. When you got right down to it, he thought, you'd have to say that she looked like hell.

Deep shambling roar—motorcycle cops turning around and beating it back to Boston. And cop cars right along with them—a whole phalanx of the Imperial Legions. "Piggy, piggy, piggy better GO now," the helmeted youth chanted, banging out the time on the pavement with their ball bats, "Oink, oink . . . bang, bang . . . DEAD PIG." Who the hell's been organizing *them?* John thought. Weatherman? But no, Weatherman had gone deep underground, and these dudes didn't have quite the fully cranked Weatherman craziness. Maybe they were the kids the NAC was supposed to be organizing—if you could call it organizing.

The clotted-up mass had been given the go-ahead, was moving again, was turning onto the bridge. Some poor son of a bitch had stalled his car there, and the kids flowed around it and sat down. Cars trying to get from Cambridge to Boston kept oozing forward; the kids pounded the fenders and windshields—nothing serious, just assing off, but the folks inside, windows rolled up, looked terrified.

"What the fuck is this?" an NAC marshal was yelling. "What the fuck *is* this? Is this the motherfucking *front?* Come on, move it. We're going all the way to Harvard Square."

Moving again. Leaving Boston, crossing the bridge and entering Cambridge. It felt like a significant moment, supercharged, but maybe it was just the bridge, the water, the archetype of it—"it behooves one to cross the great water"—and the sky must have dropped acid right along with Flashline, was supplying "portentous," was supplying "ominous," going pink-tinged and smoke-green, recreating itself as a painting from the cover of an old *Galaxy* magazine. John looked for

Pam; she'd gone on ahead of him. He caught up to her now, saw only her silhouette, the stark outline of her hooded head with the sickly iridescent sky glowing behind her. The other silhouettes were the Dedham kids—and Flashline, of course: "Or if it's constant, horrific content, more of it concrete, Mortifer comet . . ."

Mass Ave was lined with cops; some were just ordinary cops, but others were in full riot gear. "They got dogs," somebody yelled.

"Dogs? What the fuck? *Dogs?*"

"Dogs. You know, woof woof."

Far behind them in the crowd, a chant started up: "Free Bobby Seale, Free Bobby Seale!"

The kids right around them answered with: "Hey, hey, what do you say? Rock and roll is here to stay!"

Pam laughed. "Too fucking much."

He didn't know what to do about her—if there was anything he could do. She was freaking him out, had been freaking him out for a while now. In some bizarre way, they'd never been closer; except when they were asleep, their two-person council was engaged in constant dialogue, and she seemed to be working through all the shit that had been dumped on her lately, doing it the way she did everything—by adjusting her theory—but she didn't seem to be grooving on it the way she used to. It seemed to have turned into a grim interminable job for her, and he didn't know where she was going half the time—quoting not only Vaneigem and Debord, Emma Goldman and the sainted Rosa, but Freud, Reich, Adler, Karen Horney, Erich Neumann, Lukacs, Marcuse, Laing, Szasz, and Rollo May. Although he couldn't quite see the big pattern yet, the things coming out of her mouth were always fascinating.

"'Polymorphous perverse' is an incorrect label," she said. "Like 'sissy' and 'dyke,' it's pejorative, just *slimy* with pre-judgments. A good label might be 'nascent androgyny.'"

"Dig it," she said, "the archetypal significance of the looking glass. Neumann says consciousness first manifests itself in girls by an attention to their own appearance. I always thought he was just another male chauvinist pig, but if you can tear the term 'girl' loose from biological sex, then he's got a point."

But everything was theoretical these days. They hadn't made love since the townhouse explosion, and it had been damn near that long since he'd seen her naked. It had taken him a while to admit to himself that she was really doing what she was obviously doing—hiding from him. Adding layer upon layer of clothes. Changing her clothes in the bathroom with the door locked. Sleeping with her clothes on. She didn't seem to be eating anything—unless you could count the gallons of black coffee.

Tech Square was packed with cops. Hundreds of the fuckers. Riot helmets, tear-gas guns, stone blank faces. Simply standing there, watching the crowd go by—"Piggy, piggy, piggy." They didn't seem to give a shit. But, no, that wasn't right. John could feel their thick male energy, pent up and hungry for release, but they still didn't move even when some of the kids started chucking rocks through windows of MIT buildings. Not impassive, not indifferent, certainly not bored—no, it was more like, "Go ahead, punks, we've got more time than you've got." The sound truck—"Don't get hung up. We're going all the way to Harvard."

"They thought we were going to do MIT," Pam said. She was a small black shape with an invisible face, the lurid sky a backdrop. "The dumb shits. Who does their intelligence work, the Smothers Brothers?"

More trashing in Central Square. The Cambridgeport Bank was getting its windows remodeled. "Good choice," Pam said. NAC marshals worked their way back through the crowd—"Hey, dig it, working people live here. Cool it, cool it. We're going to Harvard Square where the pigs are," and the crowd took up the chant: "Cool it, cool it, cool it."

"The motherfuckers just don't get it," Pam said.

"Yeah," John said, "nobody gets it. Tomorrow the straight press is going to blame it on Abbie." In his speech on the Common, Abbie Hoffman had told the crowd exactly what it had wanted to hear: "Boston was the cradle of liberty . . . How many hands going to rock the cradle? How many hands going to cradle a rock?" A nice turn, John had thought—although he doubted that Abbie would be out on the street backing up his words with his body.

Through Central Square and moving steadily, nearly there. The famous end of the road, John thought—Shangri-La, Mecca, lair of the dragon, the eternal playing field where everything would be revealed. The kids were catching each other's vibe and firing it back, the collective tension rising to whistle pitch. Shit, and it was the same damn thing that always happened to him when the action was coming down—keyed-up and frightened, he couldn't shut off his smart-ass mouth: "OK, folks, anybody got any chickens that need their heads bit off? The Geek Army is slouching toward Harvard Square to be born." He didn't know if Pam had heard him over the noise—or had heard him right—but she laughed anyway. He couldn't see any good coming out of this.

There were no cops in Harvard Square. Well, on second glance, he saw a few cops, maybe a dozen, but plain ordinary Cambridge cops. They weren't ready, and there weren't enough of them, and they looked scared shitless. A whole hell of a lot of people were walking into the Square. The sound truck made a last squawk—nobody could hear the message—then turned around and scooted into the thickening twilight. So much for the leadership. "Shit," Pam said, "I don't believe this. It's ours."

DENSE PRESS of the crowd, no way to go but forward—"Trash it, trash it, trash it!"—cheering from the high school kids, the women's libbers doing the weird ululation out of *The Battle of Algiers*, and everywhere now, from all the shops on all the streets, that brilliant sound of *windows*—John heard it in silly cartoon capitals: POW, WHAM, SMASH—the shattering of clear shiny glass. Pam was yelling, quoting some famous asshole, "We are a force," and, for once, it was true; they really did have the numbers. *Demonstrators*, the straight press might call them—no, probably *rioters*—thousands of moving bodies, more than enough to fill up the Cambridge Common, to clog the Square itself, to stop the traffic dead, to outnumber the pigs so badly they couldn't do a thing but watch. Night had closed down the sky, and hundreds of young voices defined the Square—"One, two, three, four. We don't want your fucking war"—and a single old voice, distant, was pleading on a bullhorn—some forlorn Cambridge cop doing his best—"I've got a son in Vietnam. I want to see this over as much as you do." Jeers and boos from the Red Army.

Kids swarming onto the roof of the MTA station. Trash cans set ablaze. The news stand ripped to shit, the boards chucked into the bonfire the kids had made. A constant rain of rocks through windows—razor-brilliant splinters of light, ice on the sidewalks, the rioters' rhinestones. Add the smoke and crackle of fires going up, more yelling and running, more chanting, more windows—POW SMASH. Krackerjacks, that purveyor of glitz and psychedelica—its elaborate stained-glass windows gone in an instant. Dudes in helmets made the first pass, smashing with their ball bats; the looters were right behind them, young kids, pouring through the broken windows, flinging out the commodified images of spectacular capitalism—skirts and tops, flamboyantly colored pants, gleaming dress shoes, purses and coats, even goddamned underwear. From Saks Fifth Avenue, from Bobbie Baker, from the Harvard Coop, from the Andover Shop. Window mannequins thrown into the street—stylish effigies of straight decadence. Kids running by with portable radios, TVs, stereo components, armloads of records. Somebody had thrown Flashline a looted peasant skirt; she'd pulled it on over her black pants, was whirling in circles, singing her song from another galaxy—"Confusion of stains, contusion of rains, conclusion of pains . . ."

"Tell me again," Pam said, "what the fuck we're doing here," then, smiling, gave him Proudhon's line from when he'd first seen the mob on the streets of Paris—"But they don't have any ideas."

"Yeah?" John said. "Maybe most of them don't, but Flashline's got plenty."

"Right on." They were coming up to the Northeast Federal Savings Bank. Pam stopped.

She looked at the bank, and then she looked at him. She said it in exactly the same tone she would have used for any of her flipped-around Hegelian pronouncements. She might as well have been saying, "We need a theory of incoherence to deal with the incoherence of theory," but what she said was, "Fuck ideas."

"Hey," she said to one of the Dedham kids who was toting a bag, "lend me some rocks?"

Pam didn't throw like a girl. Why was he surprised? She glanced back at him over her shoulder—self-conscious, embarrassed, excited. Christ, she was cranked to the eyeballs—and something else. Figure it out later, he told himself, and she'd already turned away from him—was throwing rocks as fast as she could haul them out of the laundry bag. Helmeted dudes joined her with bats. The bank had just become an open-air facility, and Pam was darting by him quick as a wasp.

He shambled along behind her—what, me worry?—but then saw her clawing at the burning trash in a blackened can. "Pam. Jesus!" She shot by him again before he could begin to make any sense of it, waving a burning board in her gloved hand, and sent the fire spiraling through the window of the bank. Stopped, bent over, panting, her hands on her knees.

"Pam. Pamela. What the fuck are you doing?"

"Jesus, man, that felt good." She straightened up.

Now he saw the little kid she'd once been—the sparkling eyes, the flush, the dangerous excitement—staying up too late after the birthday party, staying up long past her bedtime And he saw the ancient crone she'd one day become, if she lived long enough—the pinched skin, the sunken cheeks and sunken eyes, the stretched flesh ready to rip away with a breath. Saw both images, each showing through the other, neither dominant. *Christ,* he thought, *she's sick. She's sick as a dog.* "What do you mean, *fuck ideas?*" he said.

She didn't answer him. "That's motherfucking Weatherman," he said. "That's what we criticized them for. Action-faction horseshit. *Incoherence.*"

He was waiting. He wanted to hear the theory—if there was a theory. "What are we going to say in *Zygote*? '*And then we burned the bank?*'"

But her torch didn't seem to be catching. Maybe she hadn't burned the bank after all. "What?" she said. "We're supposed to be objective? Fuck, man, the illusion of objectivity merely objectifies the illusion."

He was furious. "Jesus, Pam, I don't even know what that *means.*"

As they stood there staring at each other, the lights went out.

It felt like he'd done it with his mind, but that wasn't possible, was it? That wasn't the way the real was supposed to work. "What the fuck?" he said. "Somebody cut the . . . ?"

"Oh, hell, no. The pigs have turned off the street lights, that's all."

"Why would they do that? Now they can't see worth a shit."

"What they're going to do, they're going to do in the dark."

"Hey, that's good," he said. "That's positively Shakespearian."

"Oh, it's going to be Shakespearian, all right," and, grabbing his hand, tugged him along to check out the action. The pigs that were showing up now weren't pathetic Cambridge cops. These were pigs from somewhere else, in full riot gear, lining up in front of the Hayes-Bick. If they kept on coming, pretty soon there might be enough of them to get the job done. "Yeah," Pam said, flat and declarative. "Don't worry, we'll have plenty to say in *Zygote*."

Keeping well back, a knot of demonstrators was chanting: "Where are your badges, where are your badges?" The pigs paid them no mind. But a last car—God help the crazy fuckers—was trying to inch through the Square. The pigs surrounded it, jerked the doors open, hauled the passengers out by their hair. Middle-aged guys in suits—protesting, pleading, waving their arms. Without a moment's hesitation, the pigs clubbed them down.

The Hayes-Bick was still lit—so were the other restaurants—but on the street only smoky fires with fat sparks going up, trash cans and one honest-to-God bonfire. Up to this point, it had felt like nothing more serious than a sports event gone out of control—the Academy versus Raysburg High—but the game had changed, and things were about to get heavy.

"WALK, WALK, walk." He slowed to a jog, looked back for Pam. He'd got a good healthy whiff of gas that time—burning eyes, churn in the belly—and it had scared the bejesus out of him. If he ever got the full dose, there'd be no choking it back, he'd barf up his guts for sure—and, Christ, what was happening now? Pam had sunk to her knees. He ran back for her, scooped her up. Jesus, she felt little. "Fuck. Are you all right?"

"Yeah. Yeah, sure." She was panting.

What was happening to his dancer, his quicksilver girl? He wanted her off the street. "Are you OK? I mean really?"

"Yes, I'm OK, for fuck's sake."

"Come on, enough's enough. For what? Let's go home."

"Fuck that shit," she said. "We've got to see how it ends."

The pigs had cleared the Square four times. They always did it the same way—formed a military line, held it a minute or two, and then advanced. They fired gas canisters. The demonstrators fired back paving stones and bricks and bottles. The pigs weren't bothering to make more than a handful of arrests; they just beat the motherfucking shit out of anybody they could catch. And they must have wanted the game to go on forever; they never blocked any of the side streets, left the demonstrators free to melt away through those open passageways, regroup, and take the Square again. It had been going on for hours. John hadn't liked capture-the-flag much when he'd been in summer camp, and he liked this warped-out grown-up version even less, but he couldn't do what he'd done at camp—simply walk away to the crafts table and join the girls.

Now they were back at Harvard, hard to know where they were, hard to keep track of anything in the dark, following the crowd—coughing, guts churning. The gas by these dorms was as thick as the London fog in a Fu Manchu book. "Water! Water!" Some helpful souls were passing out soaked towels. He took one and wrapped it around his mouth, and they were walking away from the worst of it; he could breathe again, or almost breathe.

Pam, pressing a towel to her face, gestured with her head—rows of yellow lit windows, Harvard boys, leaning out like jack o' lanterns, giving them the V sign. "Music, music," somebody yelled, as the good guys, pig-free for the moment, were streaming through the gentle lanes of Harvard University. Laughing, chanting, yucking it up, taking a break before going back to the action.

They'd asked for music, and music's what they got—sixty watts at full crank, the Stones bawling out "Street Fighting Man." The kids cheered, waved clenched fists or V signs—"Right on!" A street fair, a frat party, a freshman's conception of the revolution, a Mardi

Gras, for Christ's sake—all these loony adolescents, some of them wearing looted finery tied around their waists, on their heads. A tall boy just in front of them was wearing a pair of pink lace panties stretched over his football helmet. So damn young, and they kept on coming. More now than when they'd started. Where the hell were they coming from? Riding in on the MTA?

Everybody knows what a *mob* is, he thought. Yeah, he could write that in *Zygote*—a *mob* is something really scary. A mob is a dark, anarchic, murderous, terrifying mass with all the orderly laws of civilization stripped away—humanity reduced to its lowest level, a seething amorphous blob of pure animal evil. But whatever they were in now—this living civic body—it was not a mob. There was no name for it—or no name that he knew. It was a fluid, flexible *organism*, continually in motion, continually redefining itself, and yes, of course it was frightening, but it was also exhilarating. Polarization had made things simple, the sides as clearly defined as the "shirts" and the "skins" at camp, and you had to trust the people on your side, whoever they were, because you didn't have any choice—just as they had to trust you. There was no room now for bystanders. If you were on the street, you were in the game—as the straight reporters found out when the pigs clubbed them to the pavement.

He sensed a motion coming down the line—a diversion, something heavy. Then saw it—off to one side, three cops in full riot gear. The motherfuckers had gone freelance, were chucking bricks through the windows of a Harvard dorm. The helmeted youth were not about to let that one go by—"Hey, pigs, having fun? Piggy, piggy, piggy."

The cops swung around to confront the kids. "Come on, chicken shits. Come on, come on, come on," making clucking noises, gesturing—come *on*, come to *me*, come to *daddy*. From the broken Harvard windows, a rain of beer bottles erupted onto the pigs' heads, and the helmeted youth waded in, half a dozen of them, swinging ball bats. John saw one pig go down. From somewhere else—"Pigs, pigs, pigs." He shot Pam a look. They turned and ran.

HE DIDN'T have a clue what street they were on, but they were free and clear again, slowing to a walk. Dark shapes were clotting up, and he bumped into the back of one of the Dedham kids, a tall boy with the beginnings of a wispy beard—"Hey, man, what a fucking trip." Voices assembling all around him, laughing, yelling. They must have run far from Harvard—no more jack o' lantern faces—and it was darker than the city had any right to be, no light but stars and a hunk of moon. The shapes were congealing into individual people he was getting to know pretty damn well—yeah, their *affinity group*. Pam had stopped again to bend over and pant. "You all right?" he said, his hand on her shoulder.

"Yeah," she said. "Sure. *You* all right?"

"Yeah, I'm all right, but . . . Jesus, the gas. Come on, Pamela, let's go home. This shit's going to go on all night."

"No. Not yet."

A shaft of light from a high window—it was making a long, large shape on the street gleam like patent leather. As they came abreast of it, they saw what it was—a cop car. Parked. Not a pig anywhere around it. Big and official and deadly and black. Shiny. "Motherfuckers," Pam said and kicked the fender.

"Come *on*," he said.

"Hey," she said, "if we get separated, go straight back to the apartment, you dig? Like fail-safe. No matter what happens, you dig? I'll meet you there."

Oh, he thought, you're planning on losing me, are you, Pamela? Think again, babe. "Yeah, sure," he said.

Now they were walking into music, but what music? Weird. And there was a crackle of fire coming up. He was sure that he'd been everywhere in and around Harvard Square, but he'd never seen that particular street before—yellow lights high up in the medieval black, and a smoky bonfire in the middle of everything. A Breughel painting, an ancient wood block, a city that lived at the edge of dreams, and the music was more than merely unlikely—it was fucking *impossible*—but he couldn't deny what he was hearing. It was *Greek* music. A single man was dancing to it.

Acid flash. Jagged edge where the real had sheared off. An old man with white hair. Rapt, intent, inward face. Body drawn upward into an elegantly focused line. Arms raised. Stepping in a ritual pattern that might have been thousands of years old. A Greek man doing a Greek dance to Greek music, lit by a bonfire set somewhere near Harvard University in the Year of Our Lord Nineteen-Hundred and Seventy. "Beautiful," Pam said. "Motherfucking beautiful. You see why we're still out here?"

The kids were pouring into the scene, clapping along with the music, chanting, "Go, Zorba, go," and another bunch, farther back, responding in the same rhythm, "*One* two *three* four *we* don't want your *fuck*ing war." The old man danced on, deep into his own thing, and John thought how profoundly and naturally and eternally people were meant to be utterly harmless.

"Pigs, pigs, pigs."

"Oh, fuck," John said, "here we go again." The heavy-duty ones, the mean ones in full-riot-gear—coming from the far end of the street, from the direction where the crowd had been headed, pacing forward slowly in one of their orderly, military, street-clearing lines. John looked back to where the old Greek man had been dancing, and there was nobody. The music was still playing, but the old man was gone.

"Let's split," John said. Pam didn't answer him. "What's the fucking point?" he said, but he knew it was hopeless.

The organism called "our side" was already forming its own ragged line, gathering up bricks and rocks and paving stones, preparing to make a stand—for however long it could make one—and here was Flashline right on time, trailing a dozen teenage girls behind her. She whirled into the empty space where the old man had been, dancing to the beat of his ancient music, the girls whirling along behind her, circling the fire.

The pigs were firing gas—PWAK, PWAK, PWAK. It took John a moment to figure out what they were doing. They weren't aiming in front of the crowd, but higher, firing their canisters *behind* the crowd. Yeah, they were laying down gas on the only way out. When the crowd ran, it would have to run through it. "The bastards," he said.

Now one of the pigs—John couldn't believe it—was aiming directly into the people. PWAK. A canister hit a boy in the chest, sent him sprawling, howling. Somebody grabbed it up—hissing evil—and threw it back. The kids were throwing everything they had at the pigs. Dudes in helmets, NAC people, even some crazy teenagers—running *toward* the police line. Jesus, insanity—the air full of bricks and stones. The pigs stopped, holding their formal line, drew themselves up, waiting to absorb the charge and then roll on through the demonstrators, flatten the goddamned punks—and that same pig, that rotten sadistic prick, was aiming directly at the people again. PWAK. That time he got no one, the canister shooting back at him like a volleyed tennis ball.

The son of a bitch was aiming again. Flashline was dancing in front of the fire, facing the pigs, her arms raised, imitating the vanished old man. Oh, fuck. "Flashline!" John yelled, and the canister struck her full in the face.

John ran for her. Sprawled on her ass, her mouth a huge O, scream pouring out of it, explosion of blood—oh, God, her fucking nose. John grabbed her to haul her up. She clutched his shirt. A helmeted dude grabbed the other side of her—a bearded NAC guy. Flashline had become a siren they couldn't turn off. "Get her the fuck out of here," Pam yelled.

NAC dudes, three or four of them. Picked up Flashline, ran with her. John and Pam ran along with them. "Shit. Fucking bad, man. Bummer. Infirmary."

"She's tripping," John yelled at them.

"Holyoke?"

"No. Pigs. Won't let anybody through."

"The church?"

"Yeah. Move it."

Pam just ahead of him. Stumbling, crying—"Shit, shit, shit." She stopped, and he slammed into her, nearly knocked her down. She spiraled away, howling, clawed at herself, yanked her hood back, shaking out her hair. Unknown stretched face gleaming with tears. "Fuck," she yelled at him. The NAC dudes were running with Flashline straight into the cloud of gas. They vanished into it. For a second or two, he could still hear Flashline screaming. "Pam?" but she was already gone. She'd spun again—a fabulous pirouette. She was running straight at the police line.

He ran after her. Jesus, she was fast. The pigs were throwing shit back. A rain of shit. Bottles smashing. Rocks and bricks. Pam was grabbing up shit and throwing it—softball girl, outfielder, star of the team. Coiling with each throw, her whole body into it, and, Jesus, she wasn't going to stop—a goddamned kamikaze charge. She was going to run straight into the pigs, and they'd beat the piss out of her.

Mouth full of lead. Sprinting nightmare. Almost had her. But fuck, she was gone again—one jump ahead. Coiled back to throw, and he grabbed her waist, lifted her off the feet—howling, kicking. "Pamela! Jesus fuck, Jesus fuck, Pamela." PWAK, PWAK, PWAK— canisters falling all around them. Gas, fucking gas. Set her down. Spun at him, clawing.

"Pamela. Fuck." Pushed her back, pushed her the way he wanted her to go. *The other way.*

Jolt of something in her eyes. Then she was running. The right way, thank God. He was right behind her. But no way he could keep up. Pamela—that darting needle he'd seen before. Hey, great stuff, he thought. She could thread any crowd—and she'd got the message, was making her break. Darting through kids and NAC dudes. Those fuckers were running full tilt, but she was running faster. She ran into the gas cloud and was gone.

Fast, fast, fast, he chanted to himself, gulped air, held his breath, hit the cloud, ran into it, and the gas bit down. Nothing. Fog. Blind. Running. Kicked stone, brick, some goddamned thing. Nearly down. Caught balance. Staggering. Had to breathe. Poison. Lungs ripped, slaughtered. Just keep running. Breathing Clorox and steel shards, running free of it, but he was done—slowing to a jog, shuffling forward, bent at the waist. He jerked his head, twisted head, and barfed his guts out. Firing it away from him, BWAH. Had to stop, panting. Sweat. Swimmy misery. Impaled on a drive shaft. Wiped barf off his jeans—stinking clumps—flung it off his fingers. Stomach still jerking in on itself. Don't fall, for Christ's sake. Keep moving. Sounds of kids barfing. "Jesus, Jesus. Oh, fuck. Water. Oh, Jesus Christ," and a girl's voice going, "Mommy, mommy." Other voices—heavy, male—"Move it, move it, move it."

Not too far back, gas guns firing, and he was jogging, wobbly, dizzy. Eyes burning, saw Pamela. The first one to get there. To the shiny death machine. Of course she was the first one to get there, to that motherfucking police car. There was nothing left in her head to slow her down. She was hammering the windshield with a brick. The smash. Her voice. Lower-pitched than a scream but loud enough. Shocked him because he'd never heard a voice like that come out of her. Yeah, it was plenty loud enough. "TRASH IT."

"Pamela," he yelled, running toward the car. She hadn't broken through yet, glass spiderwebbing out from her blows. "TRASH IT."

Some kids too sick, but helmeted dudes drawn like filings to a magnet. Rocks on the windshield, the windows, the fenders. Guys using ball bats. Glass. POW, SMASH. There went the headlights, the taillights. Metal, the car a huge drum. Pam lifted her brick high over her head and brought it straight down. It penetrated. She stood there openhanded. Perplexed. Saddened kid in the playground. Lost her toy. Brick had gone straight through, was inside the car. She looked up, looked right at him, but he didn't know if she could see him. He shot a look back for pigs, but none yet. He ran toward her.

"FLIP IT," she yelled. Bent her knees, grabbed the bottom of the car like she could lift it herself. Then so many kids swarming over the car, it was blotted out. Seething boiling mass of people, and, miraculously, the goddamn thing began to rise, to levitate, and faster than he would have thought possible, the fucker was on its side. Glass shattering, metal tearing, and it was over, was upside down. The goddamned fucking police car was upside down. Kids cheering like somebody had just scored a touchdown. John smelled gasoline, pouring out, pooling. "TORCH IT," Pam yelled. She was running straight at him. "MATCHES."

"Jesus, Pam."

"Fucking matches, man. Matches, matches, matches. Give me the fucking *matches*." She was all over him, pawing in his pockets, a bird pecking, a bony flurry. Gone, her bootheels hammering, jeans flapping, right to the edge of the spreading pool. "Get back," kids were yelling, "Jesus fuck." The crowd got bent the other way, surged back, away, as Pam knelt to the gasoline, lit a match and threw it. Out. "Pam!" Nothing. "STOP IT." He was just too fucking slow.

She was bending down, inches away. Gasoline sheet, spreading—Jesus, the *smell* of it. Already lighting. The next match. Memorize fire-trickle from her gloved fingers.

Flame at the pool licked itself, curled. John grabbed at her and yanked. Flame cleared its throat and coughed—a deep throaty HUMPF. She pulled away from the flame, pulled away from him, ran ahead. Turned back, reached for him, and he risked a glance back. Saw—useless blip—a *mythic* image, tower of fire.

Looped and jerked, something at his hips. She was. Dragging him by his belt. "John, John, John." He stumbled, she caught him—stutter of bones, too fucking little—they both went down, knees and elbows on the pain. Up again, go.

Flame took a breath and inhaled itself—CAWOOMF, FWAH—blew through the real. Heat *there*, faster than they were, running motherfuckers. Solid broken, disestablished and whizzing, metal hail, black high, and another look saw the black curling. Flame, street lit, bonfire, car's ruined core to the fog hole. Open. Through. Pigs poured like shit.

Stench. Gasoline, burning rubber, fucking gas. Boots pounding. FUCK YOU, FUCK YOU, FUCK YOU. Thud, nightsticks, ball bats. Thud, thud. Screaming. MOTHERFUCKER. And heat. FUCK YOU, MOTHERFUCKER. Thud, thud, thud. No mind. Run.

NOT A clue where he was—Mt. Auburn Street, maybe, was where he was—but far from Harvard, avoiding crowds, watching for pigs, ducking into shadows at the first sign of another human being—any human being. He'd been walking. He'd been walking for a long time. Fighting to reassemble himself. Maybe he should just keep on walking, point himself away from this insanity and walk until the city lit itself up again. His head was stuttering with a million ragged thoughts, but he couldn't get them to stick together. Here was one thought: if he got through this shit, he'd never be afraid of anything again, not ever, not in his entire life—fear so big now the entire world was fear. And here was another thought: just how fucking much adrenaline could his system take before all his circuits blew? Maybe they'd already blown. He should do something serious and meaningful, but he couldn't figure out just what that might be. He'd given up searching for Pamela, his lost Maenad. Meet her at the apartment, she'd said. Yeah, right. How the fuck was he supposed to get there? Pigs everywhere.

When he'd felt the club on his head, he'd thought, hey, that's not bad. "A light glancing blow," his absurdly chatty mind had labeled it. He touched it now, winced—a lump the size of half a tennis ball just behind his left ear. It left blood on his fingers. Shit. Should he try to see somebody? Like a doctor dude? Where? At one of the beleaguered infirmaries? But he hadn't been knocked *out*. He'd just been knocked *down*—flattened, face on the pavement—and kicked. They hadn't even kicked him that hard. Not really. If they'd wanted to cream him, they could have done it—but they'd had other things on their minds. Fighting off NAC dudes, for starters. But he was OK. Well, maybe he was OK. Fuck, he didn't know if he was OK. Anybody out on the street tonight without a helmet was just fucking nuts.

A plan, that's what he needed. Something *coherent*. The coherence of our critique implies the . . . Oh, fuck, give me a break. OK, start looping back toward home. Don't go directly. Stick to the side streets, get back to the apartment by any means necessary. Shit, and he'd been wrong, his judgment badly off. He hadn't wandered very far from Harvard. The Yard was right over there, through that gate—closed and locked. The sidewalk was slippery with vomit, and a dozen kids were stumbling toward him—teenagers. The boys holding up the girls, the girls weeping. They must have been gassed. Yeah, he was getting a whiff of it again—the fumes of the barf machine—and he knew exactly where he was. The apartment was not even half a block away, thank Christ.

He could hear the same old shit going down—the pigs versus our side going into overtime. Close, maybe just a few streets over—and for what? Hey. Some pigs, wandering loose, aimed his way. He jumped back, felt for a wall, found it, found something even better, a doorway, made himself into a black paper cut-out. He counted six of them. They were actually talking to each other like normal human beings. He couldn't make out what they were saying. They walked right on by him. He couldn't stand it anymore, sprang out of his hole and ran. Knew he shouldn't be running—he was calling attention to himself by running—but he just fucking didn't give a shit. Mindless, made it to the front door of Pam's building. Worried his key into the lock, jumped through the door, slammed it behind him, pulled until he heard the lock click into place.

She was sitting huddled on the stairs. Lit by the single harsh overhead light, she looked like a small burrowing animal, all eyes. "Jesus," he said, "are you all right?"

She didn't answer but stood up. He wrapped his arms around her and squeezed, felt all the padding she'd wrapped around herself. After a moment, she hugged him back—lightly. It felt what? Perfunctory? Tentative? "Yeah, I'm all right," she said—quiet, composed, absolutely expressionless voice. "Are you all right?"

"Yeah, sure. I got hit, but fuck. I think it's . . . Yeah, I'm all right."

She allowed him to lead her up the stairs and into their apartment. "I was so worried about you," she said in the same spooky voice. "I was afraid something had happened to you."

The fear had been like a tourniquet; now that he was safe inside their familiar white box, he felt it loosening, the first trickle coming back that might eventually resemble human life. Words seemed to be coming with it—"Jesus, that was heavy . . . That's as close as I want to get to . . . Jesus Christ, Pam, you scared the absolute living shit out of me." He pulled off his boots, was halfway through stripping off his stinking jacket, and he was stopped. She'd fallen to her knees as softly as a pillow. Jesus, he should do something about that. His mind wasn't working. She'd extended one hand, the palm pressed against the wall. "Hey," he said.

He picked her up. She was so fucking light. "You stay here, baby," she said. "I'm going to go back."

"What? Are you fucking nuts?"

"It's not over yet."

"Oh, for Christ's sake."

She hung limply in his arms. She smelled as foul as he did. He should get them both into a shower. Yeah, it was that simple—he had to start somewhere. He pushed her hood back and released a pungent nasty smell. The stench of burnt hair. Horrified, he pawed at her hair, ran his fingers through it. No, it hadn't burned, but it had been close. He could smell the fire in it. "Don't," she said.

She wanted to be free. It would have taken scarcely four ounces to hold her, but he let her go. She pulled back from him and sank to the floor. Only someone that ballet-limber could have arrived in such a sadly splayed, hip-sprung collapse. "Nobody hit me," she said. "Jesus, those motherfuckers kept trying. They really wanted to. But none of them got me." She laughed. "I'm unscathed. Jesus, man, they were beating the fucking crap out of everybody, and they didn't get me once. Not once. I've got to go back."

Oh, fuck, he thought, she's in shock. Badly. "Pamela," he said as gently as if he'd been talking to a sick child, "you can't even stand up."

"Yeah, I can't, can I?"

He peeled off his vomit-soaked jeans, threw them behind him, and his shirt. Yeah, shower. That was right. He sank to his knees in front of her. "Come on, baby." He tugged at one of her boots.

She tried to crawl away from him. "Don't. Please don't."

"For Christ's sake, Pam, you're not going out there again." He pulled her boots off. She made a crying sound like "Oh, oh, oh, oh," crawled away, rolled up, hugging herself. "Come on, baby, you're filthy."

He took one of her hands, drew it toward him. She let him do it. The navy blue glove was cut in a dozen places, blood in the cuts. He peeled off her gloves. Her hands were cut and scraped. He lifted her up. He wasn't sure that she could stand on her own two feet—that is, simply stand there, erect, like a primate—but she did it. He unfastened her duffel coat, and she started to cry—not just making the sounds but for real, her head hanging down and tears pouring into her eye sockets. "It's OK, it's OK," he said and tugged at her coat.

"Please don't," she said, but she raised her arms like a child.

Her took her coat off. And then her sweater, and then a boy's shirt and a t-shirt and another t-shirt. Naked, she pushed him away, crying, and turned away from him. He stared, paralyzed. Well, what the fuck had he expected? She hadn't been able to hide *her face*. Yeah, fuck, he'd been seeing *her face*. He could have guessed what her body would look like—

No. That was wrong. There was no way he could have guessed what her body would look like. Stripped. Bone. Hideous deep pockets in her like holes. And *bone*. She'd turned away, but he'd seen the horrible shapes of her hipbones, the deep hole under her ribcage, her stomach muscles exposed under stretched white skin—a vivisection, an anatomy lesson still miraculously kept alive.

She wandered away from him, hugging herself—"Oh, oh, oh, oh, oh." Her knees and elbows were lumps of bone. Just by looking, he could count her vertebrae. For God's sake, don't exaggerate, he told himself. He was a witness, and he had to see, and remember, and tell the truth—to himself, and to her if she would ever listen to him—so he had to be exact. She didn't look as bad as a Dachau victim—not yet, she didn't. But she was close, and that was exactly where she was headed, and once she got there, she wouldn't be able to come back, and then she would die. She crawled into bed and pulled the blankets over herself.

I CAN'T deal with this shit, he thought. The whole rotten works fell on him then, an unbearable load. It was all just too fucking much, and he couldn't understand how he could have made it that far. Yeah, he was fucked good, he was nothing. Christ, he had to lie down. He got into bed with her. She was still crying. She didn't maintain her one foot of space, pressed herself into him. Weird. She was as cold as something dragged out of the river. "Oh, baby," he said and rubbed her hollowed-out back. Her breath stank. It was the smell of her body eating itself.

John fought to stay awake. He should think of something to do, something to say. He should study the situation, make concrete plans. He should tell her that she goddamn well had to start eating. He should tell her that things were going to get better. But his body was desperate for sleep. The soft blurring of her breath, the cold hard shape of her, the memories of the street—all of it kept winding itself around him like thick dark cords binding him to the bed. Every few minutes he'd wake with a start, not sure where he was. First he'd think, Christ, what do I do now? Because he knew he had to do something. Then he'd think, no, everything's ruined, totally fucked. Everything's so wrong it can never be fixed.

Later he woke from a murderous sleep and knew he'd been out for hours. His head was pounding like hell, and he was dying of thirst. He got up, drank two glasses of water, brought a glass to Pam. Her eyes were open. He was afraid she wouldn't drink the water, but she did. He crawled back into bed with her. She started to say something. Her voice was hoarse. She cleared her throat. "You know what my mother used to tell me? She'd say, 'Pamela, you should have been scraped from the side of my womb.'"

HE WOKE to thick oppressive heat. The pain in his head was beating him damn near blind. He sat up, and the movement hurt him, the blast of light. Searing. When was he going to stop drinking so much? Sweat it out, you asshole, he told himself. The *Seventeen* he'd been reading was lying next to him on the bed, and there was something seriously wrong with the cover, something peculiar and disturbing. The model was wearing white ankle socks with navy Mary Janes, a cute navy winter coat with tight little navy dress gloves—and that wasn't right. But then he thought, oh, wait a minute. They're just showing the fall clothes. That's all it is. There's nothing wrong with that.

He threw the magazine aside, jumped up, and stepped out onto his balcony. The day was huge, close, and stifling. He lit a cigarette and stared down at Front Street. It was empty and silent. The light was appalling, a hideous smeary dazzle, and he heard—from far away, maybe from all the way out in the middle of the river—a sound like a car horn. Well, not like that but something like that. It didn't make any sense, but the message was clear enough. He had to get out of there.

He walked quickly down the hall and found his father in the living room reading the paper. "Hey, Dad," he said, "can I have the car?"

His father looked up—freshly shaven jaws, sparkling chocolate-brown eyes, big con-man's grin. He smelled like Vitalis and Chesterfields and whiskey. He fished the car keys out of his trouser pocket, spun them around his finger once—a twirl of light—and tossed them. John felt the hard metal land in the palm of his hand. "You're only young once," his father said with a wink, and John woke to the stink of the bed. He was too hot under the blankets, sweating, and Pam was clinging to him. He didn't know what time it was, but it was full daylight—maybe afternoon. The knot on his head was damned near killing him, and he thought, I've got to get out of here.

He disentangled her bony arms, slid out of bed, pressed his bare feet into the hardwood floor—feeling for the real. Shit, the dream had been just as real as *this* real. Why should he be stuck with *this* real when almost any other real would do?

Out from behind the Japanese screen, confronting the what? He paced back and forth, swinging his arms, hauling the air down to the bottoms of his lungs, trying to get himself back into himself—whoever the hell that was. Sore in a dozen places. Jesus, his head. He drank a glass of milk, took two aspirin. His body was telling him he needed salt. He stripped a banana, salted it and ate it. Back behind the screen to check on her. Eyes open. Huge shining eyes surrounded by black smears. Not sad or frightened. Not anything that he could see. "Are you awake?" Nothing.

He paced to the front window and back again. "Hey. This is motherfucking ridiculous. You've got to eat something." Nothing.

She was looking right at him. "What the fuck are you thinking?" Nothing.

I can't deal with this shit, he thought.

He walked to the front window and stood, looking out. The sun was shining merrily away just as though everything in the universe was just Jim dandy, just peachy keen. Jesus, his father in the dream had been as real as anybody. When his mother had called to tell him that his father was dying, he hadn't flown into Pittsburgh but into Detroit—a logical destination for a Canadian. Every card in his wallet had identified him as Don McCann from Mississauga,

Ontario. That's how he'd got to Raysburg, and that's how he'd got back to Toronto. Christ, he had to get back to Toronto now. It was too late to do it today, but maybe tomorrow.

He went to look at her again. "How do you feel? Are you all right? Do you feel like hell?" Nothing.

When John's father had been dying, he hadn't been conscious most of the time. He'd been fighting emphysema. During those brief periods when he'd seemed to be awake—his eyes open, searching, obviously aware of *something*—he'd done nothing but try to breathe. If he'd known that John was there, it hadn't seemed to matter to him one way or the other. He'd said a few things, things like, "Gotta shit," and, "Hurts."

"Pamela," John said. "You've got to talk to me." Nothing.

Oh, fuck this, he thought, I'm gone.

Back at the window, staring at the damnably cheery sunshine. He wasn't a Christian, so he didn't believe in sin, but as a Buddhist— even a half-assed Buddhist—he'd always tried to find Right Action. He knew that if he left her now, it might be the worst thing he'd ever done in his life. "Pam," he called to her. "Where the fuck are you? Come on, give me a sign." Nothing.

No, he really could not deal with this shit. He grabbed up Ethan's old Stella, sat down on a kitchen chair, and kicked into "Spike Driver's Blues" hard and fast, stamping out the time with his bare left foot. That tune slid right on into "Reuben" and, after that, he didn't bother to think of the names of the tunes. He didn't give a shit about making a mistake because there were no mistakes. Everything he was playing was right—even these strange twisty variations with their unexpected pull-offs and loopy slides and bass runs, even the tunes that were like nothing he'd ever heard before. The music rolled on, nameless and wordless; he could never get to the end of it. He played for over an hour. He set the guitar aside, jumped up, and ran directly to her. "Pamela," he said, "you're not a mistake."

She closed her eyes. Then opened them. Back of the real, something changed. The light. She made a gesture—pushing. It took him a moment to get it. She didn't want him to see her naked.

He walked to the window, heard her get up, heard her cry,

making that terrible "oh, oh, oh, oh" sound again.

He had to see. Her sad stripped body was standing directly in the center of the bathroom scale by her bed. Her eyes were searching for him. She pointed down. The scale read 89 pounds. She seized his hands with her cold hands. "Help me."

14

IT WAS getting kind of obvious by then that Cassandra and me were rapidly approaching that famous end of the road. We were still sleeping in the same bed, but I wasn't seeing too much of her otherwise. She was spending more time with Lorraine than she was with me, and one night I detected the fact that Lorraine had just fixed herself in the bathroom and Cass was leaning against the sink and having herself a little SNIFF, just to get a glow on, right? But I didn't say a thing because Cassandra's favorite line lately was, "Don't play daddy with me, Tom," and I didn't want to hear it again. She saw that I was watching her and she said, "You ought to give it a try. It's rather pleasant." And I thought, PLEASANT. So it's PLEASANT, is it, you overeducated little fucked-up hillbilly bitch? It kind of shocked me that I'd be thinking about Cassandra like that, but there it was in my head.

All right? And a lot of other dandy things were going down. We'd got together in the first place because it was easy, but it wasn't easy anymore. We weren't just wearing away at each other like two pieces of sandpaper, we were having the kind of knock-down drag-out fights where you go for blood. When you're living with somebody, you can have lots of fights like when the sun comes up in the morning, you clean your teeth and life goes on, but there's some you never get over.

The way it started out was like this. I'm rapping about Terry and her Tarot cards, and Cassandra says, "You'll fall for anything, won't you?"

My first thought is, whoops, she must have FOUND OUT. But then we get into it, and I can see she hasn't found out, it's just Terry IN GENERAL that pisses her off. But I start out real careful. "What? What do you mean?"

"That witch business. Christ, Tom, what a crock of shit."

"I thought you liked Terry. I mean the way she took care of you when you were sick and all."

"I do like Terry. I'm not saying she doesn't have a good heart, man. I know she has a good heart. All I'm saying is she's full of shit."

"Well, I don't know."

"What do you mean, you DON'T KNOW? Don't give me that. That shit she's laying down . . . you just lap it up like a fucking dog." And then she runs this imitation of Terry. Cass is great at imitating people, like she's got a real talent for it. She grabs her left tit and stares off into space and says in this slow heavy voice that sounds EXACTLY like Terry, "I'm a WOMAN. Double you oh-em-ay-en, say it again. And I've got a CUNT, motherfuckers, and that's all I need. You better believe it. Whole world come out of my cunt. Make the grass grow and the sun shine with my cunt. 'Cause I'm a WOOOO-MAN!"

She's got me laughing, but I'm pissed off too. "Shit, Cass, that's not fair."

"Oh, Tommy, you're incredible. You really are. You've got this naïve romantic streak in you a mile wide. Like you'd be a sitting duck for anything . . . little-old-lady astrologers, the Hari Krishna boys, whatever's going. Yeah, you're like a little kid at the carny show, 'Come on, DO IT TO ME.' And when it's a young pretty GIRL with LONG BLACK HAIR and BIG FUCKING DOE EYES telling you the whole world comes out of her CUNT, well, man, you're GONE . . . She dyes her hair, by the way."

We've pissed each other off so much by then that neither of us is going to give one little inch, so I've got to insist that Terry really is a witch and knows all kinds of heavy shit and Cass has got to insist that Terry is just a fucked-up little girl who don't know her cunt from a snowdrop. "You know what she is, man," Cass says, "she's just Ethan's house nigger. She makes a religion out of her own slavery."

Something in my head finally goes CLICK. It wasn't just Pamela the Great, although Cass and her used to be real tight there for awhile, so maybe Pam was the one who'd started the ball rolling, but where Cassandra had got herself to now, that was HER THING, like that was WHERE SHE WAS AT. "Hey, sweetheart," I say, "what are you doing . . . turning into one of these crazy women's libbers on me?"

She goes up like a rocket. "Fuck you, Tommy, you goddamned PLASTIC COWBOY."

After that any hope I had about holding back on my mouth is GONE. I'm on her about me supporting her, I'm on her about that little hero-worship number she has going on Lorraine—and, while I'm at it, I've got to mention that Lorraine is maybe the lamest, most hopeless loser ever to stumble down God's turnpike—and I'm on her about sniffing doogie and calling it motherfucking PLEASANT, and of course I'm on her about peddling her ass in the bars.

She's right back at me. "You're goddamned right I'm PEDDLING MY FUCKING ASS. I was born a girl, right, and that's what I'm supposed to peddle. And I'm going to get some fucking cash for my goddamned ass. If some limp-dicked drunken asshole in a bar wants to stare at my fucking ass, he's going to PAY for the privilege, cash on the barrelhead. If he wants me to listen to his miserable sorry stories, he's going to damned well PAY. And that's the only kind of fucking honesty there is, man. You know what, Tommy? I'm sick to fucking death of all you goddamned MEN and your goddamned messed-up fucked-over minds, and as far as I'm concerned YOU CAN ALL TAKE YOUR GODDAMNED PRICKS AND SHOVE THEM UP A DRAINPIPE."

The weirdest thing about that fight was that we managed to go on living together. We even managed to stay halfway friendly most of the time, even managed to sleep in the same bed and get a fuck in now and then, but nothing was ever the same after that, and we both knew it.

––––––––

THE RULES were Pamela's. She had dictated them, and he had written them down, and they followed them to the letter. John had to get up when she got up because he had to watch to make sure that she didn't cheat. She had to be naked. She had to pee so her urine wouldn't be counted as part of her body weight. She wasn't allowed to move the scale from its fixed position, not even by a fraction of an inch. She had to step on and off until the same number appeared three times, and then John could write her weight into a log book. If her weight had gone up, she was allowed to eat—or not eat—anything she wanted. If her weight was unchanged, she had to eat two small extra meals that John gave her during the day. If her weight had gone down, she lost her privileges and she had to eat anything John gave her.

According to the contract she'd signed with her doctor, she should have been in the hospital a month ago, but she and John were reproducing the regimen of the hospital. That made him her doctor—or her nurse, or her keeper, or her prison guard, or at any rate some heavy-duty authority figure. He hadn't volunteered for the job, and he knew damn well that he was the wrong person for it, but he seemed to be stuck with it. As long as they were playing by her rules, he was in the hospital right along with her; the only way to get himself out was to get *her* out—to feed her until her body generated the round perfect number, 100. He'd never before hated an inanimate object the way he hated her smartass, grinning, bland, white, little know-it-all bathroom scale.

He consulted with Terry the Witch. He fed Pam a tea brewed from ginger root, milk thistle, red clover, dandelion, and peppermint. (He tasted it himself, and it wasn't half bad.) He fed her tofu and eggs, yogurt and oatmeal. He fed her fruit and steamed vegetables. He fed her raw wheat germ and brewer's yeast, blackstrap molasses and fish oil, tons of vitamin C, and as much brown rice as he could stuff down her. It took her forever to eat anything. She would sit at the table, staring straight ahead; she'd take a tiny bite and chew—and then she'd take another tiny bite and chew, and then another, and then another. She wouldn't get out of bed except to eat, and she wouldn't talk. "I just can't right now, OK?"

He'd loved her for her words, had learned to read her heart by interpreting that constant flow of glittering words, and now he couldn't find any way in. She was wrapped in silence and clothes. Surely she had to be getting warm—she was eating again, for Christ's sake—but she lay in bed wearing sweatpants and a sweatshirt and thick wool socks. Sometimes she did nothing but stare into space, but most of the time she read. She pulled old books off her shelf, ones she'd obviously read before, and read them through again from beginning to end. She read her undergrad anthropology textbooks. She read Ruth Benedict and Margaret Meade and Jules Henry. He tried to imagine what she was thinking. Was she planning to work more anthropology into *The Critique*, or was she simply making the time pass?

She didn't want to go anywhere or talk to anyone. He made her call the Collective so they'd know that she hadn't been arrested or kidnapped by Weatherman. He heard her say that she had a bad case of the flu, and she might as well have had the flu—or double pneumonia, or sleeping sickness, or the plague—because she was no company at all. He was playing Ethan's stiff old Stella so much that he had to smooth out the calluses on his fingertips with an emery board. When he couldn't stand to be trapped a minute longer inside the small white box with his silent patient, he walked.

Checking out the real—constantly, obsessively—so he wouldn't be taken by surprise by pigs, agents, or foaming-at-the-mouth Weathermen, he walked along the Charles River and longed for the Ohio. Somewhere back along the track—from the acid, the constant paranoia, the collapse of the Left, the Harvard Square riot, Pam's breakdown, the general motherfucking craziness, or all of the above—he'd cracked. He didn't know how much longer he could go on holding the broken pieces of himself together, and he didn't know what it would look like if he allowed himself to fall apart. But he couldn't fall apart. She'd gone away and left him in charge. He kept trying to talk to her. "*The Boston Globe* says we fought fiercely with the police."

She looked up from her book, met his eyes. "Well, we did," she said.

She hadn't washed her face lately; she was looking at him from pale, strange, shining, distant, alarmingly beautiful eyes surrounded by thick oily black smears. It was a day when she'd "lost her privileges," whatever the hell that meant. She'd never fully defined it, but maybe it meant that he could tell her what to do. "For fuck's sake," he said, "wash off your makeup." She looked at him a moment longer, then laid her book aside, went into the bathroom—leaving the door ajar so he could watch her—and washed her face.

He couldn't believe it. Was it really that simple? "While you're in there, take a bath," he told her. She did that too, and he finally flashed on the obvious. It was worse than being in charge of a mental patient; it was like having *a child*. He didn't know if she wanted to be a child, or, if she did, how much of a child she wanted to be. But maybe she didn't have any choice. Maybe she was wandering through some chilly inhuman landscape like the one where he'd been lost after his acid trip.

Lying in bed with her made him sad, made him remember how it used to be—how she'd say wonderful things when they were going to sleep, really interesting things—in the dark, from her side of the mandatory one foot of space. "We've got an article due for *Zygote*," he said. "I don't know what to write about."

She didn't say anything, and, by now, that didn't surprise him. But he had to keep trying. "Should I write a critique of the Harvard Square riot?"

"Oh, fuck no."

"We've got to say something. We could say, yeah, it's raising the level of chaos, making it harder to conduct the war, but it's a thin line . . . like between what's going to help bring the war to an end and what's going to bring down the repression. We could say that it's only a matter of time until somebody gets killed."

"That's fucking obvious, man. Everybody knows that."

He was almost asleep when she said, "I'll tell you what to write about. Write about how we've come to the point where it's damned near impossible to believe anything. Write about how we've lost trust in damned near everybody. Write about how anybody could be lying."

PAM WAS waking up earlier and earlier, so—bound by her rules—he had to get up right along with her. One morning she set the record for sheer pointless pain-in-the-ass craziness: four fucking forty-three AM. After the weigh-in—she was 92.5 pounds—she went back to bed with Margaret Meade's *Male and Female*. Groggy, resentful—thoroughly pissed-off, as a matter of fact—John brewed coffee and drank it. He'd been carrying her words around for days, hadn't known what to do with them, but now he found that something resembling a coherent statement had congealed in his mind. It surprised him because it wasn't about the Harvard Square riot; it wasn't about the Movement at all—at least not directly. He was coming at things from a queer sideways angle, but it felt like the only way to do it. He used her Olympia to write the beginning:

Everybody knows by now that anybody could be lying. Those who are supposed to be speaking with authority-- government officials, scholars, or journalists-- could be lying, but so could anyone in the Movement. The flip side of total skepticism is a readiness to believe almost anything. Lately we've begun to collect strange underground stories we've been hearing with ominous frequency. They are based upon no verifiable evidence whatsoever, and don't have to be, because no one any longer believes that anything can be verified.

One of these stories has achieved mythic proportions. We've heard three accounts of it told with complete sincerity and conviction. Of course it really happened, man (in Wyoming, in Georgia, in New York City); it was a friend of so-and-so. He was hitchhiking, picked up by the cops who found traces of grass in his pockets. They held him for weeks without charging him or allowing his one phone call. Every day they beat him on the head with billy clubs until he was reduced to a vegetable.

For those of us who live in the east, California has become a demonic land where anything can happen. Here are a few California stories. Among the jaded Hollywood hip-drug set, favorite party games now feature ritual whipping, rape, castration, and murder. If you have enough money, you can buy snuff films and get to see girls beheaded for real, or, better yet, you can have still-warm corpses delivered to your parties. The Manson Family was only a tiny corner of a vast conspiracy involving top government officials and the CIA.

You've probably heard some of these stories too. The United States did not land on the moon; the event was staged in Hollywood. Nixon (in another version it's J. Edgar Hoover) has been dead for years; he's been replaced by an actor. One of the Beatles is dead; if you play parts of the White Album backwards, you'll find out all about it. The drug trade is now run entirely by the CIA; they're trying out weird new drugs, using hippies and street kids as experimental animals; they're perfecting a super drug designed

315

to keep everybody totally whacked out and harmless.
Blacks in Roxbury (or the paramilitary Right in the
South, or the Weathermen, or whoever you're feeling
most paranoid about at the moment) are buying vast
quantities of weapons--including tanks, machine guns,
grenades, and rockets--and are storing them in secret
warehouses. A radical women's liberation group in
New York (or San Francisco or wherever) has taken to
murdering men at random. An organized male-supremacist
group has taken to murdering women's liberationists
at random. The government has quietly sealed off the
border with Canada. All left-wing groups are now run
by CIA agents-provocateurs. Within a few months, all
of us--freaks and politicos both--will be rounded up
and put in concentration camps. The Vietnam War is
about to be extended again, with full-scale operations
in Cambodia and Laos, and this time they're going
to use tactical nuclear weapons. The Vietnam War is
really over, but the news media, controlled by the
government, won't tell us.

The most terrifying thing about these stories is
not the possibility that some of them might be true--
as indeed some of them might be--but rather that
we're living in a social climate that makes all of
them sound so goddamned plausible.

He was afraid she wouldn't read it, but she did. "You've got it,"
she said. "Right on."

"Thanks. But you'll notice I said 'we.' It's *our* piece. That's just
the beginning. Adam's looking for *positive alternatives* ... OK, so
how's it going to end? Where the fuck are *you*?"

Of course she didn't answer him. Hours later, as they were lying
side by side on the bed again—ruined by getting up in the fucking
middle of the night, cat-napping their way through the interminable
afternoon, careful, as always, not to touch each other—she said,
"You're right. It's got to have an ending. Nihilism just lets the old
world in through the back door."

He waited to hear the rest of it. He was afraid that there was no
rest of it.

"The despair of a critique has to be turned into a critique of despair," she said—and then, in something like her old hard speedy voice—"Oh, fuck, man, I hate myself sometimes. What a fucking load of crap. It always comes out sounding like pure crap."

It was a warm day, and he'd opened all the windows to try to get rid of the sick-room stink of the place. He felt the air moving, not strongly enough to call it a breeze, but a liveness, a quiver. "We've got to find something basic," Pam said, "something simple, something rock solid. Like the one simple truth that lies under everything. The one thing we're going to believe no matter what."

"Is that what you've been looking for?"

"Yes. That's exactly what I've been looking for."

"Have you found it?"

"No. Listen. I mean *basic*. As basic as basic can be. As basic as *'Sh'ma Yisrael adonai elohaynu adonai echad.'*"

———

ONE NIGHT we're doing our usual number at the Shooting Gallery, a million people falling out of nowhere and you can't possibly tell how many of them are narks, but what the hell. Some very fine weed for us potheads, and a little acid floating around in case standard-issue reality gets tedious, and, of course, the skagheads lined up for the bathroom. I'm rapping with some people—Lorraine and I don't know who all—and eventually it filters into the dim recesses of my smoked-out brain that I haven't caught Cassandra's act lately. It's not really bothering me, but I figure I better check it out, so I say to Lorraine, "Hey, you got any idea where Cass went?"

She gives me this real careful look across the table. Like a real junkie's look. "Oh, she split a couple hours ago."

"Split?" I say, kind of surprised.

"Yeah, she split with Imhoff."

"Imhoff? Who the fuck's Imhoff?"

She says, "You know, the old guy you guys were rapping with."

"You mean that FUCKING OLD MAN?"

Imhoff was another one of those junkies who didn't have a first name. Lorraine had known him forever, like he was a friend of her ex-husband Carl's, and Imhoff was a real old-time old-style junkie from way back. A fairly far-out cat, I'd been thinking there for a while—for somebody the same age as my goddamned FATHER. Bald on top, stringy grey hair, little pointed grey beard, pot gut hanging out over his pants, deep rumbly voice that sounds like it's coming up from some ten-mile hole way out in the wind-swept desert. And funny? Oh, yeah, rapping to us about THE GOLDEN AGE OF JUNK, and that's right after he got out of the service, and that's WW TWO he's talking about, and Cass was lapping it up with a spoon, like, "Hey, John should be here. He'd just love this shit," so I was thinking, oh, well, that's what's happened. She's probably gone off with that old dude somewhere because she DIGS HIS MIND.

She never did come back. Well, that's not right. She never came back that night, but she came creeping in around seven in the morning. I hadn't been sleeping that great, and I was awake in a flash. "Hey," I said, you know, kind of casual, "where you been, old buddy?"

She says, "I've been laid," just blank like a wall.

"Oh? How was it?"

"Christ," she says, "he couldn't do it with a screwdriver."

I kept telling myself I should be pissed off, but somehow I couldn't get there. The thing about Cassandra was she'd always been straight with me, and that was a fuck of a lot more than I'd been with her. And besides, we'd never said we'd be true and faithful to each other or any of that crap, but it bummed me out.

She lays down on the bed with me, and I say, "A fucking old junkie with a pot belly, for Christ's sake? Old enough to be your father, for Christ's sake?"

"Shit, man," she says, "he made me laugh, and that's kind of rare these days."

He took her to this little hole-in-the-wall run by some old-time Mafia family, and Cass is a sucker for joints like that, and she loves the grub, and the grub was good. She told me all about it. Like dish by dish.

"You know, Tommy," she says, "it just seems so pointless sometimes . . . whether you do or you don't fuck somebody. I mean, what's the big deal? It's just skin rubbing together. Well, we ended up back at his place, and it was pathetic, man. He didn't really want to fuck me, he just wanted a pretty young chick to pay some attention to him. He went through the motions, but shit. And we sat up and rapped half the night, and he laid some bread on me for a cab, and he fixed himself and passed out."

I didn't know what to say to that—or God knows, what to do about it. I figured maybe go to sleep is what we should do about it. So I say, "Take your clothes off, babyshake, and come to bed. Like it's a new day." So she got undressed and got in bed with me, and she says, "Promise me something, Tommy?"

"Yeah? What's that?"

"That you'll get the hell out of Boston."

And I thought, fuck, we're splitting up. That's about as clear as it gets. So I told her, yeah, I was going to get the hell out of Boston. Like it was fairly high on my list. "So what are you going to do?" I ask her.

"I don't know," she says. "Nothing right away. Is it OK if I stay here for a while?"

"Oh, sure. Hey, Cass, you don't even have to ASK ME shit like that. Don't worry about a thing, sweet stuff. We got no problem but the rent, and the rent's paid."

"Thanks. You're a good man, Tommy, despite your appalling idiosyncrasies. I just need to cool out for a while before I make my next jump. I'm kind of fried around the edges, you know what I mean?"

Yeah, I did know what she meant. I was getting a little crisp there myself.

Then just about the time I was drifting off asleep, she says, "Hey, man, we've had a great run. I'm glad I got to know you."

I told her it was mutual, and then, with both of us beat to shit like two old dogs, and right after she'd just been fucking somebody else, we made love. No, I did not just fuck her. Yeah, I meant it exactly how I just said it. WE MADE LOVE. And after it was over, I thought, shit, if that's the way it had been all along, I never would have looked twice at silly-ass Margaret Teresa Flaherty.

———

THE SEETHING swamp of their bed was beginning to drive John nuts. He couldn't understand how Pam could stand it. She'd always been so *clean*. "Get up," he told her.

"I don't want to." She didn't even look up from her book. Her hair—lank and stringy and unbrushed—was hanging in her face. He was damned well sick of her. "I don't care what you want," he said. "Get up anyway."

She got up and retreated to the far side of the room. He stripped the bed while she waited, standing, her book in her hand, marking her place with a finger, and watched him with no expression on her face at all. "Get dressed," he told her.

"Fuck you, man."

"We're going out. We're going to the laundromat."

"I don't want to go out."

Try reasonable, he told himself. There's got to be a reasonable person still in there somewhere. "If you were in the hospital, they wouldn't just let you lie around in bed all day, would they? They'd make you do something, wouldn't they?"

"No, they wouldn't. Not if they saw how *motherfucking depressed* I was." That flash of anger was the first sign of real feeling he'd seen from her in days.

"You've lost your privileges," he said. "Get dressed."

It was so warm that some of the Cliffies were wearing shorts, but Pam had put on jeans, a t-shirt, a shirt, a sweater, her Levi jacket, and even gloves—another prissy kid-leather pair, tight and girlish and pale beige. He knew that she wasn't ready to drive a car, so they walked, each carrying a laundry bag. He felt as though they were getting the evil eye from a million directions. He had to keep reminding himself that the pigs still had at least some legal restraints placed on them, that they hadn't got to the point yet where they were busting people for simply looking bizarre.

In the laundromat she threw herself onto a chair, sat huddled up there, hugging herself, and watched him like a hostile cat. "Put some bleach in the white load," she said.

I'll bleach *you*, he thought—but then, considering it, he took it for a good sign. On some level, she still gave a shit.

He separated the whites from the colors, used two machines, put bleach in with the white load, and sat down next to her. She must have been waiting for him to sit down—must have been drafting the statement in her head, twisting it around this way or that, polishing it until it came out short and simple: "Refusing to eat is *not* a political act. Refusing to eat is masochistic and stupid."

"Yeah?"

She was staring at the washing machine directly in front of her as though she'd never seen one before. "It's bad enough they're trying to kill us, but they've also trained us to try to kill ourselves."

"But we don't have to cooperate," he said.

She met his eyes a moment, then looked away.

"Listen," he said, "when you told me the story, about the hospital and everything . . . You told me the story like you'd been cured."

"*Cured?* Fuck, man. It's like a drug addiction. You're never cured. All you can ask is that you're not doing it."

He waited for her to tell him more about it, but she didn't. When their laundry was clean, he dumped it into a dryer. She made no move to help him. "Hey, man, I'm sorry." she said. "Like I know I'm a stone drag, but . . . Like I *am* depressed. Like textbook. It's no fucking joke. They used to bring the medical students in to look at me."

He probably should have said something encouraging, but he couldn't find a goddamned thing—and he was tired of trying to coax words out of her. He was tired of everything. They watched the laundry go round.

"I'm not sorry I burned the police car," she said.

"Oh, yeah? You scared the shit out of me."

"I scared the shit out of me too. I'm sorry that . . . The only thing I'm really sorry about is you. When I think about it, it makes me sick. I risked *your* ass. You could have been hurt . . . like badly hurt. You could have got busted. And, I'm sorry about . . . Shit. I hate putting you through this, man. I'm so ashamed. I fucking hate myself."

She hadn't taken her gloves off. He took her hand, felt the bones under the smooth expensive leather. She let him hold her hand a moment, then, with a squeeze, pushed him away. Her eyes sent him a sad message, an apology. "What have you been thinking about?" he asked her.

"I can't talk about it. It's like . . . I don't know . . . It's just too big an effort. It all seems hopeless anyway."

They carried the clean laundry back to the apartment. Without being asked, she helped him fold it and put it away, helped him make the bed. Then she went into the bathroom and shut the door firmly behind her.

After half an hour, he began to wonder what she could possibly be doing in there. He hadn't heard the toilet flush, didn't hear water running. It was none of his business—or was it? *Depressed?* He'd been nuts to leave her alone so long. Maybe she was cutting her wrists or doing some other strange weird sick thing in there. Frightened, feeling like a fool, he jerked the door open. She was standing, motionless, staring at herself in the mirror. She'd obviously heard him come bursting in, but her eyes never left the mirror. "How could you let me go out on the street looking like this?" she said in the voice of a hurt angry betrayed little girl. "I look like motherfucking *death*."

THE RAINBOW of nutrients John had been stuffing into Pam seemed to be working. Her weight gain was averaging just under half a pound a day, and she was talking again. Not the way she used to—non-stop, frantically, morning till night—but in short bursts. "Don't let me stay in bed," she told him, and he finally got it. *He* wasn't in charge of her life; *she* was still in charge of it, but in some occult way she'd been using him as an intermediary. It was a comforting thought.

"Get *up*, Pamela," he said every day, and she got up and got dressed. Sometimes she even sat at her desk and tapped out words. She wasn't *writing*, she said; she was *making notes*. He didn't understand the distinction, but it seemed important to her.

He no longer had to tell her to take a bath or wash her hair or clean her teeth or change her underwear. She put on makeup every day—not her old *Sylphide* eyes but something new, a different kind of makeup for a different purpose. She dumped everything out of her old plastic makeup bag, arranged it neatly on the bathroom counter, and did an old-fashioned *Vogue* production, beginning with foundation and ending with blush and powder and pale pink lipstick. A trace of her old sense of humor was coming back: "After this," she said, "I can always get a job doing the makeup in a mortuary."

She really did seem to be rethinking everything, revising herself. "History has demonstrated that our analysis was incorrect, *comrade*," she said.

"Incorrect how, *comrade?*" he said, playing along with her bleak joke.

"Straight male sexuality is not the root of all evil. That's not what the State needs to reproduce itself. Violent, oppressive, murderous sexuality is what the State needs to reproduce itself, and that kind of sexuality has long been associated with men in our culture, but it is *not exclusively male.*"

In her new incarnation, she was obsessed with words and definitions. "The ability to define is the ability to control," she said, quoting somebody or other, Franz Fanon maybe. She kept chewing on the word *lesbian*. "Deb and I used to have these terrible arguments. We were lovers. You knew that, didn't you?"

"I don't know," he said, keeping his voice neutral. "I didn't think about it." But of course he'd known it. He just hadn't wanted to think about it.

"We weren't together that long. We spent more time on the dialectic than we did in bed. She kept telling me that I had to declare myself . . . like it was politically important, and I'd say, 'Sure, I'll call myself a lesbian in public if you want, but just between you and me, babe, that's not everything I am,' and she'd say, 'For Christ's sake, Pamela, your first sexual experience was with a woman, all your sexual partners are women, what the hell else could you possibly be?' And I didn't have any answer to that. Usually I do what my head tells me, but I was going on my guts. I hadn't discovered androgyny yet. The main thing I knew was that I didn't want to be *defined.*"

He took her out of the apartment once a day. He guessed that she saved her most personal transmissions for when they were walking— maybe so she could talk to him without having to look at him. "Hey, John, I'm sorry about our sex life, man. But it's just . . . When I get too thin, I don't just get androgynous, I get *neutered*. Like I don't want to be touched . . . and the way I look, you probably don't feel much like touching me."

There was nothing he could say to that. She was making an effort now, but—makeup or no makeup—she was still so thin she freaked him out. He loved her, but, no, he didn't want to touch her. He was glad that he'd found that limit in himself. He was glad that she didn't turn him on when she was sick.

NOTHING WAS tying them into the real, and it scared the shit out of him. She wouldn't go to the *Zygote* office, wouldn't go to Collective meetings, wouldn't see any of their friends, wouldn't talk on the telephone. She was talking to *him* now, but he knew damned well that he was hearing only a fraction of what she was thinking, and he could sense a depth of convoluted mind-stuff lurking underneath that he couldn't begin to touch. Lying in her bed, staring into the dark, he flashed on the full intensity of his fear—just who the hell was this weird scary freaky incomprehensible alien sleeping next to him? She couldn't have been any stranger if he'd found her under a mushroom. What if she was genuinely nuts? What if *her* craziness was resonating with *his* craziness so eventually he'd end up just as nuts as she was?

He clung to routine like a lifeline—established set times for meals and stuck to them, cooked honest-to-God dinners every day and served them at exactly six o'clock. One evening, as he was chopping vegetables, she got out of bed and joined him in the kitchen—arriving barefoot with no warning, not a word at all, a quiet helpful presence suddenly materializing at his left side. He was blown away, tried not to show it. He'd laid out everything in a row—carrots and potatoes and turnips, onions and celery and garlic and peppers, chard and kale and parsley. Like the other half of the council they used to be, she saw what needed to be done and began doing it—washing the carrots. "Thanks for not giving up on me," she said.

"You're welcome," he said.

She presented him with the faintest suggestion of a smile, then curtseyed, lifting an imaginary skirt, and looked away. For an odd, misplaced moment she'd been a shy little girl, and he didn't know what to do with that image. Of course she hadn't meant it straight. It had been a gentle parody of a stereotype, but there'd been a flicker of real in it too. Had it been a glimpse of the child he'd been taking care of? And she seemed to know what he was thinking—or something of it. "Fuck, man," she said quietly, "I've got to come back. I can't just . . . Like if I run it any farther, it's pure self-indulgence."

"You are coming back." She was, in fact, flirting with the magic number, 100. Some days she was there; other days she was 99.5. She said she wanted to see her weight nailed at 100 for seven days straight before she'd believe it. She was looking better too—no longer like a patient mistakenly let out on a day pass from the terminal ward. Now she looked like a malnourished teenager improbably wearing prom makeup. Cliffies sometimes turned to stare at her on the street.

"I know it's sick and weird putting you in charge of me," she said "but it's keeping me out of the hospital. In some ways this has been the worst time . . . I don't mean physically. When I was seventeen, I damned near died. But this time . . . Shit, it's hard to talk about. Maybe I could have stopped it . . . No, I couldn't. I feel so ashamed. Although it's not my fault. I keep telling myself it's not my fault. But like my head was just fucking *destroyed*, man. I've got to make an effort now. I know it's a shlep, but I've just got to do it."

"You can do it," he said automatically. He hoped she could do it.

"Oh, God, sometimes I think that all I'm doing . . . all I've *ever* been doing . . . is trying to work through endless childhood crap, and if that's all I'm doing, then how fucking long . . . ? Oy. It's like my therapist used to tell me all the time, *'The dreadful has already happened.'* And every time she'd say it, we'd go through the same number. Like we must have done it ten times. She'd attribute it to Laing, and I'd say, 'No, it's Heidegger,' and she'd say, 'It doesn't matter a damn who it is, Pamela. *Get out of your head.'*"

He was laughing. He could see in her eyes that she'd meant him to laugh, and that gave him hope. Yeah, she really was trying to come back. "That's like what Terry told me," he said. "Remember that night she read my Tarot, did her heavy witch thing on me? She said, 'Don't try to *think* your way out . . .'"

"Well, of course she'd say that. But it's like . . . It's easier for you.

It's sick the way I'm stuck in my head all the time. Like the thing I do with *androgyny*. For me it's an organizing principle, almost an abstraction, but for you, it's straight from your guts."

"Is it?"

"Yeah, it is. Because you're girl-identified."

Was that true? Well, it felt at least partially true, but he didn't like being summed up so neatly—defined—any more than she liked it.

He watched her chop the tops off the carrots. She was doing it with single-minded concentration—as though it was the only thing in the world worth doing. Just who the hell *was* she? "Pamela? Did you ever have sex with men . . . like before me? I mean really?"

Startled. "Yes. Twice. Did you think I made it up? Hey, I've never lied to you. Never. Not about anything."

No, he thought, but from time to time you've sure left some heavy things out. "How was it?"

She didn't hesitate. "Once it was OK, and once it wasn't. The OK one was during the Columbia action. We were like . . . just keyed up on the action, and it seemed like the thing to do. It *was* the thing to do. He was this baby-faced kid, a lot younger than me, like nineteen or twenty. It was nice. Sweet. He was so grateful . . . and the other time . . .

"Oh, fuck. I got manipulated into it. This motherfucking SDS heavy. 'Come on, baby, why are you so uptight?' I was repressed, bourgeois, you know, all that crap. And I should have just told him to shove it. It was kind of . . . I felt raped. *Felt?* Hell, I *was* raped. And I kept thinking, shit, is this normal, does this schmuck think this is *normal?* The way Freud thought women are naturally masochistic . . . like, 'Come on, girls, adjust to rape. It's your biological lot in life, and you'll get to like it because it's *normal.*' The male chauvinist asshole. And that's when I decided I'd never go to bed with a straight man again. Like what the fuck did I think I was doing? Research?

"No birth control either time, oy gevalt. I was lucky. But I was so sure I was going to bed with you, I went on the pill in New York before I even came back here . . . Oh, you're *so weird.* Why is that making you cry?"

"Because you wanted me. Because you were so sure."

"Arrogant is more like it," she said. "I can be such an asshole sometimes. Come on, baby, don't *cry.*"

He felt like he'd been cracked open. He didn't know why he couldn't stop crying. "Oh, baby, baby, baby," she said, "I'm so sorry."

He hadn't cried that hard when his father had died. He hadn't cried that hard for years—not since he'd split up with Linda when he'd been eighteen. He couldn't control it; he kept gasping for breath. He was blinded by tears, choked and silenced. She led him out of the kitchen. They lay down on the bed, and she held him while he cried.

Somewhere along the track he'd misplaced himself. Not surprising when he was Raymond Lee or Joseph Alfred Minotti or Arthur T. Jones but hardly ever John Dupre. Not surprising when he was an androgyne—whatever the hell that was, however Pam defined it, some mythic creature as grotesque as a griffin, more girl than boy, but never a real girl. Back in the days before the riot, before the townhouse explosion, before the dire visit from Phil Vance, before Pam had decided to starve herself to death, he'd been happy to be *something* like a girl—but never a man, God forbid, and not even the boy who'd run track, got drunk with his buddies, and gone out with Linda Edmonds, that perfect fifties doll. Maybe he was like one of the primitive people in Pam's anthropology books; maybe his soul had been stolen in some demonic ritual. Maybe Pam was the one who'd stolen it. He didn't know how much longer he could stand to be trapped with her in this small white prison.

A part of himself detached, drifted away, and watched him cry—was even finding words to pin on it—weariness, fatigue. Hell, more than that, *exhaustion.* And *despair*—yeah, that was another good one, and he heard a voice in his head singing in that old nasal country tenor, "I'd rather be in some dark holler where the sun don't never shine"—half myth already even when he'd lived there, a bargeload of coal on the river, the sun on the water, view from the sun porch window. He could vanish, become the local fool, that crazy guitar-picker, shaggy and goofy as Han Shan. But, no, the real was real. He could feel it grinding him down, metal on metal, bone on bone. "Oh, baby, baby, baby," she said. "Things are getting better. *I'm* getting better. I promise."

PAM KEPT gaining weight, crossed the magical divide of 100. That meant, by her own rules, that she was out of the phantom hospital they'd created and John was no longer in charge of her, but she still wanted him there every morning at her weigh-in, still expected him to keep the log book. By the time she'd reached 104, she'd begun to glow with the same eerie inner light that had turned him on when he'd first met her. She was, he thought, looking positively *rosy*. He knew that she wasn't able to see herself clearly, but she must have been able to see herself enough to notice her natural color coming back—she was using less makeup. She'd bought herself a new pair of Mary Janes, smooth black leather, to replace her old beat-up navy pair, and she was wearing hair ribbons again. She was beginning to look like a version of the strange girl who'd walked into the *Weasel* office so long ago. Could she have gone through all this shit just to arrive right back where she'd started?

There was no doubt about her turning him on now, but they still hadn't made love. Unable to sleep, he lay in bed next to her, separated by the mandatory one foot of space, and thought that it was even worse than being a teenager because this time around he knew exactly what he was missing.

The newly reborn Pamela had decided, she said, to reconnect with ballet. She wasn't ready to go back to the Collective yet so she couldn't go to their karate classes, and she had to do *something*. She thought that ballet might turn out to be as important to her as the guitar was for him—or maybe not, but she wanted to see. Every afternoon she changed into ratty ripped dancewear—all of it a pale pink gone faintly grey with age—set out a kitchen chair to use as a barre, put one of her melancholy violin-mad composers on the stereo, and reacquainted herself with the Cecchetti Method. "It's all still there in my head, man, every fucking bit of it."

One afternoon, after she'd been doing her ballet thing for a week, she changed into tights and leotard, and then, instead of putting on her ancient filthy ballet slippers, put on a pair of equally ancient filthy pointe shoes. Feeling like a voyeur, he watched her tie up the ribbons. Mahler or Bruckner or some other Romantic clown was filling up the apartment with audible soapsuds. She began, as she always did, with a series of pliés. As he waited, he had to stop himself from holding his breath. Although she said "Oy!" when she did it, she rose onto pointe easily, deftly. It got to him just the way he'd known it would.

She'd gone through four or five exercises before she glanced over and saw how he was looking at her. "Oh, God," she said, "*pointe.* You're so goddamn predictable."

He'd been preparing and rehearsing a short speech. "Maybe you've been neutered, but I haven't."

"Oh, God, I'm not neutered anymore, believe me. It's just . . . Well, when you were taking care of me, you turned into some version of my father, and I love my father, but I don't sleep with him, you dig?"

Fully aware of him now, smiling at him from time to time, sending him, he was sure, exactly the same look she'd used from all the way across the room to get her high-school girlfriend wet, she moved through a series of exercises, all of them on pointe. "High femme is about balance," she said, a lilt in her voice that was a turn-on too. "In our culture, boys are supposed to be planted firmly on the ground, but we make girls fight for balance. Pointe . . . high heels . . . you dig? Hey, man, I can't figure out what's turning you on. Do you want to *fuck* me or do you want to *be* me?"

"Is that a serious question?"

The record ended. Making it something of a performance, she walked to him, took his hands, and drew him to his feet. She rose onto pointe, her legs pressed together into a tight closed position, bent down, and kissed him. He had to look up. She was taller than he was. "How's this for ambiguity?" she said and kissed him again, thrusting her tongue into his mouth. "Come on, Alice, make me feel like a boy again."

15.

"NORTH VIETNAM in the last two weeks has stripped away all pretense of respecting the sovereignty or neutrality of Cambodia," the image on the TV screen was saying. "Thousands of their soldiers are invading the country from the sanctuaries; they are encircling the Capital of Phnom Penh. Cambodia has sent out a call to the United States . . ."

The small, talking, black-and-white image was called "Richard Nixon," and it was meant to represent the President of the United States. It looked haggard and tired. It was gesturing at a map. "If this effort succeeds," the image said, "Cambodia would become a vast enemy staging area and springboard for attacks on South Vietnam . . ."

The last time John had watched an American president lying had been in the hot greasy summer of '65. As miserable as that time had been, it now looked enviably simple. "Jesus, I hated LBJ," John said, "but at least he was a human being."

"Was he?" Pam said.

". . . jeopardizing not only the lives of our own men but the people of South Vietnam as well," the image said.

Pam was too agitated to sit still any longer. She sprang to her feet to watch. "The Spectacle," she said. "Fuck."

"In cooperation with the armed forces of South Vietnam," the image said, "attacks are being launched this week to clean out major enemy sanctuaries on the Cambodian–Vietnam border."

"The Spectacle is not the images," she said. "The Spectacle is relations *mediated* by images."

Debord, that crazy Frenchman, had never made more sense, and, for once, John found that a thought of his own had fallen naturally into the weird flipped-around style of the SI: *The illusion of meaning is the meaning of the illusion.* He wouldn't write it that way though— not for *Zygote's* hippie readership. For those dudes, he had to be simple and clear. He'd say that the image that they were watching was designed to create the illusion that the people of the United States had a meaningful relationship with their government.

"We live in an age of anarchy both abroad and at home," the

image said. "We see mindless attacks on all the great institutions which have been created by free civilizations in the last five hundred years."

"Hey, that's a good one," John said. "Do you like that one?"

Pam made a shushing gesture—and she was right to want to focus so singlemindedly on that small, monstrous, flickering image. The words emanating from the image were lies, but they couldn't afford to miss a single one of them, because hidden in those lies might be omens. If they interpreted those omens correctly, they might be able to predict what their lives were going to be like, now and in the future—what was possible and what was not.

"Here in the United States, great universities are being systematically destroyed," the image said. Yep, John thought, the repression was going to be coming down heavy.

"I would rather be a one-term president than be a two-term president at the cost of seeing America become a second-rate power and see this nation accept the first defeat in its proud 190-year history," the image said.

"Oh, fuck," Pam said, "and you know what we've been talking about in the Collective? Karate and daycare centers."

"It is customary in a speech from the White House to ask support for the President of the United States," the image said. "Tonight, what I ask for is more important. I ask for support of our brave men fighting tonight halfway around the world . . ."

John turned off the TV.

"Hey, man," she said, "did you ever see *Triumph of the Will*? They're not that good yet . . . but they're going to be."

John felt too squashed to talk. No way he could rise to the occasion, make some smart-ass lefty joke, say something clever and bleakly funny about the Nuremberg Rallies. After the years of protest—peaceful demonstrations and not so peaceful ones, draft card burnings and building occupations, all that work, all that organizing—after three-quarters of a million people had marched on Washington, they'd arrived at this? He almost turned the TV back on—just to fill the room again with more images, with the illusion that they were mysteriously connected to everyone else in the whole damned country. "Shit," he said finally, "we're going to be in

Southeast Asia for the next twenty years. Maybe forever. But what's it going to cost them?"

"The State still controls the means of violence. Come on, baby, let's get out of here. It feels like a goddamn terrarium in here."

They walked around Harvard Yard. Of course that's where she would lead him. "Sanctuary?" she said, embracing the university with an outflung arm. "Oy gavalt, half of me feels like crawling into a hole and never coming out, and the other half of me wants to burn six more cop cars. I used to think I could . . ."

She didn't finish her thought and didn't need to. She'd told him often enough how she felt about universities. She'd never put it into words, but he'd known that she was keeping her options open—that if she ever needed to crawl into a hole and vanish, she would always be able to find it somewhere in the green groves of academe. But maybe now even that option was being closed off. She walked away.

She stopped, turned back to look for him, waited until he caught up. "John?" she said. "Whoever the hell it was that broke into your apartment . . . What do you think they wanted?"

He should have an answer to that. Right after it had happened, they'd talked it to death, and he'd certainly thought about it plenty. "I don't think they were looking for anything. Not for dope, not for incriminating documents, not for information, not for anything. I think it was a kind of fuck-you. Like, 'We know who you are. We can get you any time we want.'"

"Why would they do that?"

"I don't know. What are you thinking?"

She didn't answer immediately. Springtime in the Yard—the trees coming into full leaf, old John Harvard on his pedestal looking over it all from a benign distance like a minor tutelary deity. Yeah, it really was another world in there. In the Yard, you could almost feel some hope.

"Cambodia," she said. "Jesus. Not just sneaking in and denying it, but official, right out there in plain sight, and . . . OK, so what are they going to do now? They won't be able to tolerate dissent much longer. Not *any*. And like . . . If they can pick us up any time they want, when are they going to do it? We've got to get the fuck out of here. You do know that, don't you?"

They'd stopped in front of Widener. "One of the great academic libraries," she'd always called it.

"I'm going to New Mexico," she said. "Where are you going?"

He couldn't breathe for a moment.

"Oh, baby," she said, "I didn't mean it that way. Do you want to come to New Mexico with me?"

It had never crossed his mind. "Shit, Pam. Give me some warning, why don't you? Fuck, I don't know. It's a long way from Canada."

JOHN DIDN'T want to think about Pam going to New Mexico, and he didn't have to yet because history blew them away once again. US forces poured into Cambodia. Protests broke out on campuses all over the United States; Pam and John could have predicted them. At Kent State University in Ohio, National Guardsmen shot and killed four students. Pam and John could have predicted that violence too—although the location took them by surprise. They would have guessed that nothing much was going to happen at Harvard; the politicos there had sunk into a morass of ideological squabbles, and the riot in the Square seemed to have left the students stunned, exhausted, and apprehensive. But they might have predicted Yale; a lot of heavy shit was going down in New Haven; a huge meeting there had called for a national student strike. Or they might have predicted Berkeley, or Pam's alma mater, Columbia—certainly one of the big schools with a strong radical tradition. Nobody had ever heard of Kent State. It was a little university right smack in the middle of America.

"It's true," Pam said. "They really will kill their own children."

Students everywhere went out on strike. There were massive demonstrations from coast to coast. John and Pam couldn't stand to be boxed inside her apartment; driving her father's car again, Pam kept them in motion—from Brandeis to MIT to Wellesley to BU and back to Harvard—checking things out, trying to connect. They told each other that they were going to write something for *Zygote*—God knows what. Twenty thousand students gathered on the Boston Common and demanded that the flag at the Statehouse be flown at half mast—and it was flown at half mast. Was that worth writing about?

"I didn't think I had any tears left in me," Pam said, crying when she saw pictures of the kids who'd been murdered at Kent State. "They were so young. They were just babies."

A HUNDRED thousand people marched in Washington. It seemed impossible to keep track of all the actions and demonstrations— although the students at Brandeis set up a National Strike Information Center and tried to do exactly that. Many schools closed down—the BU administration simply stopped classes and told everybody to go home—but others limped along, trying to function in the whirlwind that had swept up thousands, maybe even a million kids. "Action everywhere," Pam said, "but no coherence. SDS could have provided the coherence."

John wasn't so sure of that. He'd never had much faith in SDS, but maybe she was right. "Not as a motherfucking Leninist vanguard," he said.

"No, but it could have been the beginning of the councils. Fuck PL. Fuck Bernardine. Fuck Weatherman."

Throughout the spring, things had been blowing up at an average of roughly one a day; that was their best estimate based on sources they could trust, or maybe could trust—the *Boston Globe*, the *New York Times*, the *Christian Science Monitor*, the *Guardian*, *I. F. Stone's Weekly*, and the packets from the two versions of *Liberation News Service*. Government offices and ROTC buildings were blown up, and so was the Chase Manhattan Bank and the Bank of America. In California, somebody bombed a Safeway. This was not shit coming out of Weatherman—it appeared to be the work of independent groups or individuals—but Weatherman took credit for bombing an army base in San Francisco. Except for the three Weatherpeople dead in the townhouse explosion, the bombs had killed nobody yet, but they knew that it was only a matter of time.

Adam kept asking them for *commentary*, but they had run out of commentary. Neither of them could think of any conclusion to John's "anybody could be lying" article—because, as Pam said, anybody *could* be lying. They knew that Adam wanted them to end with an uplifting positive alternative, and nothing at the moment seemed particularly uplifting or positive, so they transformed themselves into reporters, simply collecting information about who was doing what—when, where, and, insofar as they could figure it out, why. "*Zygote's* readership deserves to hear the truth," Pam told Adam, and of course he couldn't do anything but agree with that.

"Do we have anything to say?" John asked her. "Will we *ever* have anything to say?"

"If I think of anything, I'll tell you."

She let John write up their news reports. She wasn't writing anything now. She said she'd had it with *The Critique*—couldn't even bear to look at it. "That phase of my life's over, man. It was pure chutzpah . . . vanguardism. What did I think? I was going to be the next Rosa?"

She might not be writing, but she was finding plenty to do. She was on a run again, driving through the mad Boston traffic with the élan of an old-time cabbie, checking out the real—rapping with people, taking pictures, taking notes. John banged out copy in the *Zygote* office while she paced up and down and fed him words and phrases. She helped him with the layout. She was going to Collective meetings again, going to karate classes. She'd changed her appearance to match the mood she was in—skinned her hair back into a single ponytail, put on no more makeup than mascara and eyeliner, wore her boys' shirts and jeans. She looked streamlined and efficient and young. She'd stopped gaining weight, but she wasn't losing it either—holding steady day after day at 108—until the morning when she stepped on the scale and it said 107. "Fuck! Oy, misery. Jesus, man, I just can't eat any more than I'm eating. I'm eating all the fucking time."

John stuffed her knapsack with several flavors of yogurt, baggies of nuts and raisins, slices of Terry's whole-grain bread, plastic containers of brown rice. It didn't help. By the end of the week she was down to 104.

She stepped off the scale and exploded into tears. "What am I doing? What am I *doing?*" She was vibrating like a twanged wire. She paced up and down naked. "Jesus, man, you know what all this shit adds up to, don't you? *Everything?* Bupkes, that's what. It's just motherfucking action-faction shit. 'Oh no, man, we don't know what we're doing, but we're sure as hell going to keep on doing it.' Jesus, John, *look at me.* You've got to be my mirror. I'm too thin, right?"

"Yeah, you're getting there. You sure as hell don't want to lose any more."

"God, I'm sick. Part of me says, 'Shit, Pamela, you're OK. You look OK.' I don't look OK, do I?"

He knew by now that what was required on his part was infinite patience. "No, you don't look OK. You're still too thin. But not much . . . I mean, you don't look *terrible* . . ."

"I wanted a few extra pounds so I could . . . I've got to be able to go nuts and feel *safe.* And we're . . . Oh, what the fuck are we doing, John? We might as well be watching a nuclear explosion, man, for all the effect we're having on it.

"I just don't know about . . . Like the Collective. They seem so . . . I never told you the shit I get from them. I was loyal to the Collective, like some things I wouldn't discuss outside the Collective, but . . . OK, here's what I'm getting. 'You're not part boy, Pamela, you're *all woman.*' What? Like I don't know what biological sex I am? And what they're . . . 'Oh, it's tragic about the kids at Kent State. Oh, it's tragic about Cambodia. But as women, our focus has got to be on smashing the nuclear family and building a strong autonomous women's movement.' And living with you? At first they thought it was kind of cute, the role reversal, but now they're saying, 'One of these days you're going to have to face it, Pamela. It doesn't matter how much male privilege he gives up, he's still a man.' I need that shit? I mean, like really."

When she was on a particular kind of crying jag—he could identify it by its hard metallic edge—she couldn't stand to be touched, and for once he was glad of that. If he touched her, he might give himself away, and he was trying to show nothing, no reaction at all. He told himself that he'd chosen it—yeah, right here in this goddamned apartment that very first night. She'd revealed herself to him clearly enough, and he'd chosen to jump over the edge anyway, and now he was going to splatter on the rocks. Shit, there was no way he could fight the Collective.

But she must have really heard what she'd just said—or maybe he wasn't looking as blank as he'd thought he was. "Oh, baby." She wiped her face with her bare hands, flung the droplets away. He saw her stop herself from crying. "Hey, man, listen. How could I possibly be a separatist? The only two people who never gave up on me are you and my father."

"Thank you." What an absurd thing to say.

"Thank you too."

Then, as though she'd just caught up with her vulnerable, naked, exposed self, she grabbed up panties, t-shirt, and jeans, began pulling them on. "Make me something to eat, please. Some oatmeal or something. Oh, Jesus. They *are* watching us, aren't they? It's not just paranoia, is it?"

Was she intentionally changing the subject? Where was she going now? "Yeah, it's true," he said. "They really are watching us."

That empty-eyed long-haired dude they'd identified as an agent had vanished for a while, but lately he'd turned up again. They'd been seeing him in the Square, on side streets far from the Square, and—just like last time—standing across the street from Pam's apartment doing nothing whatsoever. And now there was another one—a hippie chickie who seemed a little too old, a little too hard-bitten, wearing just a few too many beads. They were seeing a lot of her too.

"What are they waiting for?" Pam said. "I keep having this absolutely absurd fantasy. The door gets kicked in, and here come these two huge motherfuckers in full riot gear, and they go, 'OK, we know who you are. You're the mad bad little girl who burned the Pigmobile. Come along with us. We're going to take you to a quiet out-of-the-way place and beat the living shit out of you . . .' Do you want to go to Santa Fe?"

No, she hadn't changed the subject at all. "Pam, you might as well be asking me to go to Mars. Boston's a short flight to Toronto, but New Mexico . . . Shit, they could bust me there as easy as here, and . . . God, I've never in my life even *thought* about New Mexico. Listen. Do you want to go to Toronto?"

He could see a reaction in her—a tightening, a focusing down. To what? She might still have crying jags, but she was a different person now.

"I'd be at York," he said. "It's all raw and new, but it *is* a university. I'd have a TA-ship, so there'd be some money . . . Your father could send your checks to Toronto as easy as he sends them to Boston."

She was looking straight at him. Her speckled eyes were radiating light, but he couldn't read them. "Yeah," she said, "and I could finish my PhD . . . if I wanted to finish my PhD."

She looked away; it was in the gesture—something in the way her head turned—that and a barely noticeable movement in her shoulders, a hint of a shrug. "I don't know," she said.

Oh, fuck, he thought, she's going to leave me.

———

WELL, SPRINGTIME was upon us once again, and guess what that meant? Ethan had to get back up to the Liberated Zone and deal with his own little slice of the ecology, and this year it was real heavy because he was figuring on moving him and Terry up there for good. Yeah, he kept telling me, THE SIGNS were coming down. Like it had started with the *Weasel* being taken over by assholes, and then we invaded Cambodia and those kids got killed at Kent State and most of the damn schools in the country were going up like firecrackers—shit, even the high schools—and the hard rain was going to fall now, old buddy, like we were just one step away from the two-headed chickens and the fiery green meteorites. Yeah, it was time, friends and neighbors, for us to get our pale white asses out of town. Why didn't I come up with him and Terry and have a look? I'd really dig it up there, and maybe Cassandra would too. Shit, there was still plenty of cheap land.

"Right," I told him, "me and Cass had us such a groovy trip the last time we were up there, what with that smooth easy-going day-glo acid and all, we're just dying to get back to New Hampshire." I did not bother to tell him that me and Cass was an act that was no longer playing. I didn't figure it was any of his business.

So Terry goes off with Ethan, and she stays up there doing Earth Mother for as long as she can stand it, and then, like always, she finds some excuse to come tooling back down to Boston. She said her little trips to the Liberated Zone were real enlightening, like they slammed her up against that famous HARSH REALITY. "It's clear as a bell, man. I don't WANT to live all alone with that crazy old billy goat in a geodesic dome on the top of a hill in the deepest darkest woods of New Hampshire."

By then, it wasn't just Ethan saying, GET OUT OF TOWN— everybody and their dog was saying it—and so Terry was beginning to inquire about the nature of life in that fine progressive state of North Dakota.

"Dig it, sweet stuff," I say, "if you think New Hampshire's nowhere, you ought to see North Dakota."

"But at least it's OPEN, isn't it? New Hampshire feels like, I don't know . . . like a Grimm fairy tale. Like all these woods packed in and around your ears, and you can't see out. And the vibe I keep getting from those woods is just something I can't groove on. But at least out where you come from . . . like isn't there some sense of space and light?"

"Oh, yeah, if it's space and light you want, you're there. Yeah, we got that covered. Nothing else, you dig? But space and light we got."

Yeah, North Dakota wasn't such a bad place. Like I knew it really well, and I could go there and VANISH if that's what I was inclined to do, and I'm not just talking *National Geographic*, I'm talking PEOPLE. But I couldn't see Terry vanishing. No, it'd be more like she'd be wearing a big fat flame-red sign around her neck saying WEIRDO FREAK FROM SOMEWHERE ELSE. And the other thing was, I just couldn't see me and Terry growing old together. Not that we didn't like each other, but she always felt to me . . . Like the main thing we had in common was in bed, but when we were out of bed, we had about as much in common as a codfish and a gopher.

But Terry didn't see it that way. "The day you fucked me in the bathroom . . . You didn't think it was AN ACCIDENT, did you? Well, nothing's ever AN ACCIDENT, man. We can't see the pattern in things because OUR VISION HAS BEEN CLOUDED." And she figured that we'd got together from SOME PURPOSE.

We're having this conversation on the living room floor in Terry and Ethan's apartment. Like we didn't have a whole hell of a lot of choice in the matter, but being there didn't make me exactly what you'd call COMFORTABLE. "Look, sweetness," I say, "you're not really thinking of leaving old Ethan and taking off with me, are you?"

"Why not?"

Well, shit. That one took some getting used to. Yeah, I was having a little problem wrapping my head around that. But I got to thinking, well, maybe. Like me and Cassandra was long over, and maybe Terry and Ethan were getting to the end of the road too. Yeah, maybe it was one of those moments when the music stops playing and you all change partners. And Terry was an amazing chick, no doubt about it. They don't come any prettier, and she was real smart, and she was heavy into PRACTICAL—like the old coin was never far from her mind—and maybe that would balance me out because when it comes down to PRACTICAL, there are times when I'm not everything a girl might wish for. And, you know what? Maybe fucking her in the bathroom really WASN'T an accident, and maybe it all DID mean something. But Hubbard, North Dakota? "Hey, I've never been to California," I say, "but they tell me it's a stone groove."

———

PAMELA QUIT the Collective. He couldn't believe it. Did she do it for him? Maybe she wasn't going to leave him after all.

"You want to know what I said?" she asked him. "I said, 'For a long time now I've constituted an overt tendency inside the Collective, but the dialectic is getting us nowhere, and to be absolutely frank, I'm goddamned tired of being a minority of one. It's not that you're not doing useful work. Like one of the tasks of women's liberation is to advance the cause of women in the internal power struggle between women and men inside the Spectacle, but I'm just not interested in that. You've never liked where I'm coming from, and the contradictions between us are real, not merely apparent, and if you want my formal resignation, this is it . . .' Oh, they tried to talk me out of it. There were even some tears. But I could see that they were relieved. We parted in the spirit of sisterhood.

"I'm relieved too . . . although I feel like somebody's died. I don't know if I believe any of the shit I said, but it felt good to say it. Oh, fuck. There's always going to be a place for me in the women's movement somewhere, but that just wasn't it."

By the middle of the summer, neither John nor Pam was writing anything. Still part of the *Zygote* "family," they helped with the layout. Then Pam decided she didn't want to do even that; with a check from her father once a month, she didn't need the money, so John went into the office by himself. He liked doing mindless mechanical work, and he liked getting paid; he'd never felt right about being supported by Pam's father. "We've dropped out of the Movement, haven't we?" he said.

"Yeah, it looks that way, doesn't it? I keep thinking I could work with Bread and Roses." A moderate women's-lib group. But she couldn't bring herself to go to any of their meetings. Several of her best friends had dropped out of the Collective too, over ideological differences she didn't have the energy, she said, to explain to him. "They're organizing around women's health issues," she said. "It's good work. I could do that." But she didn't do that either. She didn't do much of anything but run through the Cecchetti syllabus for an hour a day. Her weight was up to 110, and she looked wonderful.

Color was draining out of the real everywhere but in bed. "Have you been enough of a femme?" she asked him. "Have you got to do all the things you ever wanted?" He knew perfectly well that her question meant that they were running out of time. They'd already made love—around noon—and now she was making an exploratory probe to see if they were going to make love again. He'd felt, lately, an edge of desperation to their sex life. He wondered if she could feel it too.

"I don't know," he said. "I can't think of anything."

"Oh, I bet you can. Come on, there's lots of things we could do. Do you want to wear makeup again? Want me to set your hair in ringlets? That'd be kind of fun . . . although it'd take fucking forever. You'd look like one of those pretty Cavalier boys in the paintings . . . You want to do any of those old predictable cornball fantasies, like wear an apron and be the maid? . . . You want to learn to walk in high heels?"

"I thought you hated heels."

"I do. On *me*."

Their eyes met. He couldn't look away, but he couldn't say anything either. She clapped her hands like a little kid. "Oh, I love it. You're actually blushing."

She reached under the sheet to check him out. "Do I have your number, or what?"

PAM KEPT gaining weight. John still didn't have a clue where the reborn Pamela was going. Sometimes he thought she might be going *straight*. "I hate all this nonsense about the *counter-culture*," she said. "It's just hippy-dippy bullshit. Like the drug thing, 'better living through chemistry.' Enlightenment? Give me a fucking break. What? We're supposed to drop Soma and be happy happy happy?"

She said she didn't want to smoke dope anymore. He was blown away; she'd been one of the biggest potheads he'd ever met. "I've had it with grass," she said. "I'm paranoid enough as it is."

That was true of him too; his paranoia had gone completely out of control, and, yes, dope only made it worse, so he quit right along with her. But even straight, he couldn't shut down his mind. Now it wasn't agents or Weatherman; it was the fear that she would leave him, and then he'd be right back in the dark center of the eclipse. No matter how obsessively he searched for a way out, he couldn't find one. Shit, he should have seen it coming. For all of her talk about androgyny, her main sexual focus was on women—she'd never led him to believe anything else—and she'd dropped lots of hints, starting with, "We're a good match . . . *for right now.*" But, oh God, he did not want to turn back into that miserable, sick, self-pitying adolescent who wrote things into his diary like "alone always, no real contact ever, nothing done and nothing ever will." He vowed to himself that however bad he felt, he'd never allow her to see him like that.

Early in July, Pam finally made it to what she'd weighed when she'd come back from New York—112. "It's weird," she said, "for the first time in my life, I'm getting off on eating. And like I know everything you're cooking's good for me, but does it have to be so *bland?*"

He fed her vegetarian chili and corn bread, curries and chapattis, braised peppers and eggplant sprinkled with olive oil and feta cheese, squash soup flavored with toasted cumin, spinach cooked with onions and freshly grated ginger. She went up to 114. "Do I look all right?" she said. "You know I can't see myself. Come on, tell me the truth. Am I fat? Do I look all right?"

"Are you kidding? You look fabulous. How do you *feel?*"

"I feel great. Like I could actually pick up something heavy. Yeah, I feel *strong.*"

At 116 she had to buy new jeans. "Are you *sure* I look all right? Jesus, my ass feels the size of Boulder Dam."

"Do you still feel all right?"

"Fuck what I *feel like* . . . Yeah, I feel fine. What the fuck do I *look like?*"

She'd crossed a line. None of her extra weight seemed to have gone onto her waist; it had all gone onto her hips and breasts. Nobody could possibly have called her fat, or even plump—but nobody, no matter what she was wearing, could have, for even half a second, taken her for a boy. "Most women," he said, and meant it, "would kill for your figure." How could she look like that when she was planning to leave him?

PAM CALLED Deb in Santa Fe. "She makes it sound like paradise." There was no paranoia out there, Deb told her. People were sad— about the war, about Cambodia and Kent State—but they weren't paranoid. The sky was too big, the light too brilliant, for paranoia, and there was that Western tradition of "mind your own business, live and let live." They were four young women living together in a nice big old house in Santa Fe, and nobody seemed to think it was the least bit strange that none of them had boyfriends. There was plenty of room in the house for another woman. "She kept saying I had to change my entire consciousness, and New Mexico was just the place to do it . . . you know, Georgia O'Keeffe, the whole bit."

"What on earth would you do in New Mexico?"

"I don't know. Maybe I'd teach in some dumb little ballet studio,

343

teach the kiddies. The place I was taking classes in New York actually offered me a job, did I tell you that? Fucking blew me away. I didn't think I had any technique left after all these years . . . Yeah, sure, I could teach," and then, laughing, "I'd put the little boys on pointe just to strengthen their feet."

She wanted, she said, the same things she'd always wanted—to see an end to the war, to live in a peaceful non-repressive society. "I want to be able to walk out the door and not have to worry about getting busted, shot, snatched, or raped. I want to be able to wear a skirt in hot weather without feeling up-for-grabs or that I'm selling out the cause. I want to be able to see a good production of *Swan Lake* and enjoy it . . . without feeling guilty that I'm wasting my time on frivolous, counter-revolutionary bullshit."

All John really wanted was to stay with her forever, but he didn't want her to know that. He told her that he wanted to play his Martin again instead of that piece of shit of Ethan's. He wanted to play in his band in Toronto again—good old Hot Dirt. He wanted to read Northrop Frye and think about archetypes. He wanted to write poetry. "Are we talking about some post-revolutionary utopia or about something possible?" he asked her. "Like some places are better than others. Do you want to come to Toronto with me?"

"No, I don't think so. I think if I was going to leave the country, I'd go to France."

That was so firm, so sudden, so unequivocal, so goddamned *unilateral* that he was devasted. He wasn't sure he could say a word.

"Do you want to come to Santa Fe with me?" she asked him again.

"And do what?"

"We could stay with Deb in the commune and see what happens."

"What? Me and five radical lesbian feminists?"

"Is that what I am?"

They were lying in bed together. That was where they seemed to be spending most of their time these days. He wanted to get up and walk out, but he didn't.

"OK," she said, "let's go through it term by term. Radical? I suppose so. An anarcho-syndicalist or maybe a council communist. But not a Marxist-Leninist. I'll never again pretend that a Marxist-

Leninist is on the same side I'm on. I don't even want to *talk* to another motherfucking Marxist-Leninist. Lesbian? Well, OK, I've got some problems with men, and I might as well admit it. By and large, I don't like men very much. But some men I like a lot. I liked the boys in my ballet classes, and I liked my gay friends at Columbia, and I like my father, and I like you, sweetheart. But the chances that . . . well, after you, I might never find another man I want to go to bed with, and I like sex, so *lesbian?* I guess so, if you don't define it too narrowly. And feminist? Well, *of course.* So long as it doesn't mean separatist, so long as it doesn't turn into a superego riding my ass, trying to make me do things I don't want to do."

"That's very eloquent," he said. There was someone emerging in the new Pamela who knew her own mind and delivered her pronouncements with a dry no-nonsense crispness. He appreciated her clarity, but he was afraid of her now. "But what about me in New Mexico?"

Her eyes met his and held. She didn't say anything.

"You're going to leave me, aren't you?" he said.

She was beginning to answer him, but she'd waited too long. "Jesus," he said, his voice riding over hers, "I saved your fucking ass, and now you're going to leave me."

He saw a blaze of anger in her eyes. Whatever she'd been about to say died in her throat.

"John," and he could hear her holding herself back, "listen, OK? Don't lay that crap on me. I mean just *don't.* Yeah, you saved my ass, but I saved your ass too, bubbie. It was mutual . . . like mutual aid, you dig? We don't need the Church or the State . . . hospitals, doctors, experts, authorities. Like Goodman says, we can heal each other. And we did."

He knew that if he said a single word, all of his fear, anger, and resentment would come pouring out, so he kept his mouth shut. "OK, my *basic.* My rock-solid basic. Right now I need . . . I'm not talking about independence. That's just a load of crap. Nobody's independent. It's like . . . Like I'm still fragile. And I can't let anybody define me. Right now. Because I have to define myself first. Do you understand what I'm saying?"

"Yes."

"We came together as anarchist revolutionaries. If we're going to go our separate ways, then let's do it the same way." She was still using that crisp voice, but he could see how sad her eyes were. "We're both of us totally different people than we were before we met each other," she said. "Isn't that enough?"

———

I KEPT checking it out with Terry, and she seemed pretty goddamned determined, so it looked like I'd just acquired myself another girlfriend, and wherever we were going to go, I sure as hell needed a little scratch to get there, but lately I was having trouble catching even Abe Lincoln's face on a circular bit of metal. I'm thinking, fuck the scruples, and I go back to see Lyons. Susie's still with him, and that bums me right out. She's wearing the shortest skirt you ever saw and no panties at all and she's TOTALLY SILENT. We're in Bob's bedroom, and he's squeaking away. "Well, well, well, Tommy boy, is there any little thing I can do to assist you on this fine night?" And he reaches up between Susie's legs and starts playing with her pussy—kind of absent-minded, the way you'd pat a dog. "Ask and it shall be given, right?" he says. She bends over a little and spreads her legs wide open and stands there without moving a muscle and stares down at the carpet. It's SICK, you know what I mean?

"OK, Robert," I say, "here's what's happening. This penny-ante bullshit is beginning to grow old on me, and I was wondering if it was possible for me to enter the game at a somewhat higher level."

He gets a good laugh out of that one, and he smacks Susie on the ass and makes this little jerk with his head and she's gone.

"Well, Tommy," he says, "you're right on time." And he rolls us some smoke and starts laying it on me about his business—the WHOLE OPERATION. He's rapping away like a million miles a minute, and he can't sit still. He keeps jumping up, and sitting down, and walking around in circles, and banging on the table with his fists, and giggling away the whole time. He keeps peering over at me with these weird poppy eyes and laying it out so fast I'm having trouble following him.

You got to STAY DIVERSIFIED, he says. Got himself a

motherfucking FINANCIAL ADVISOR. Got him one heavy INCORPORATED ENTITY. Buying him the old stocks and bonds, chips of the brightest blue. Buying him the old real estate. "You got to be SWIFT, you know what I mean, Thomas? But shit, man, if you got the motherfucking beans, you can HIRE SWIFT." That one strikes him so funny he's just howling.

I'm not believing too much of this shit. By then Lyons was spending so much of his time running in fantasyland with Frodo and the boys that he probably didn't have a clue what was REALLY REAL, but I figured some of it had to be real. "Now getting around to YOU, Tommy," he says, "the main problemo is in THE MANUFACTURING END OF THINGS." Did I recall the fine gourmet chef? Well, he'd set that dude up in a brand-new shiny kitchen over in Brookline and laid on him everything necessary. And the chef started out by cooking up the acid, and that went real good, but you know what turned out to be the real money-maker? Crystal meth. Shit, who would have thought it? Crystal don't take a gourmet chef, any old short-order cook can do it, and it's motherfucking CHEAP. But you gots to move the QUANTITY, you dig?

And so what he wanted me to do was be the middle man between him and the Brookline Operation because, like always, I was the only dude in town he could trust. And I was thinking, CRYSTAL METH? I'd sure come a long way from Robin Hood.

So I'm the driver. I get to do a lot of walking too. They tell me it's good for your health. And John wasn't the only one who got to play secret agent. I park the camper like eight or ten blocks away, a different place every time, and then I have myself a nice stroll through this neighborhood where it's easy to see if you've picked up any new friends. If I'm still alone at that point, I allow myself to arrive at a garage. I've got the key to it. Inside the garage there's a vehicle. Sometimes it's an older-model car, usually just a blue Chevy. Looks like nothing, right? Other times it's a panel truck with the name of some plumbing company on the side. Whatever it is, I go for a little drive in it, checking the rearview to make sure that nobody's decided to accompany me on my journeys.

Then I slide over to Brookline, and the minute I appear in the back alley, somebody's looking out for me because the garage door pops up. I put her in the garage, and the garage door goes down, and I wait. Some people take out whatever I'm transporting, and they give me something to take back, and then I do the whole thing in reverse. The only one in the Brookline Operation who ever talks to me is the gourmet chef. His name's Peter, and he looks like a worried college kid. I don't bother to tell him my name. Shit, I ain't even got a name.

I never inquire as to what I'm transporting. Every few days I check in with Lyons. He tells me when the next run's going to be, and he lays the heavy coin on me. And why am I doing this shit? Is it really so I can take off somewhere with Terry?

Then there's this other odd little thing that goes down one day. Part of the arrangement was that I should always fall by Lyons' place in the middle of the afternoon because that's the only time the freak show ever quiets down. So there I am, and I hit the button on the door outside, and Lyons' voice comes out of the speaker, "Yeah?" And I say, like always, "What's happening, man?" so he can hear my voice and buzz me in. I slip into the front hallway, and what do I see before me but two guys in suits stepping out of the door to the stairs. And my first thought is, gee, I wonder why they didn't take the elevator.

They're wearing grey suits and striped ties, and one of them's carrying this little briefcase job, like an attaché case. They walk right by me and they don't even slow down. They both check me out, and then they both look away. They don't say a word. They're like BLANK. They keep right on walking out the front door and they're gone. And I'm thinking, hey, that's kind of weird.

Very nice suits. Nice ties too. And the thing about cops—well, unless they're heavy-duty under cover—is they always got short hair. They just can't help themselves, they get it buzzed right off, and those dudes didn't have short hair. No, it was fairly long. So shit, they couldn't have been cops. Or could they? What about their eyes?

There's different ways to look BLANK, you know what I mean? When a junkie looks at you BLANK, it's like, "ME? I don't know nothing." When a cop looks at you BLANK, it's like, "I got a million files in my brain, and one of them's YOURS, buddy, and it's got everything in it you've ever done in your life including what you thought about the last time you jerked off, so don't give me any shit." Cops can do something about their hair, but they can't do a damned thing about their EYES. Jesus, I'm thinking, what the hell were they doing HERE?

I've never thought much about Lyons' building before, but I'm thinking about it now. It's an old building but kept up real nice so they can charge the big bucks for it. And it's not like one of these mansions somebody's chopped up to make apartments—like it's always been apartments, but built back in the old days when nobody worried about parking, so Lyons rents a separate garage, right around back, where he keeps his custom-painted midnight-blue Lincoln.

I stick my head out the door and read what's on the door buzzers. There's an apartment in the basement that says SUPERINTENDENT, and if he's your standard-issue super, he's down there at that very moment dead drunk. The building's got four floors, and every floor's got two apartments except for the top, and up there Lyons has the whole floor, what he calls "the penthouse." Feeling like an asshole, I zip down the stairs to the door that says SUPERINTENDENT, and yep, I can hear the TV going on the other side. Then I zip back up the stairs and check every fucking apartment. All I hear out of them is DEAD SILENCE—it's like two in the afternoon—except for one on the second floor where I hear a mom and a kid. By this time, I've got it figured. I trot on up to Lyons' place, and he says, "Hey, Tommy. What took you?"

I waltz him into his bedroom and shut the door. "There's two fucking cops just been in here," I say. "Shit, if they weren't cops, they sure as hell looked like cops to me. And I'll give you ten to one they been having a nice little chat with the super about you."

What I expect him to say is, "No shit? When was that? Jesus, man, you sure they was cops?" and like that. But that isn't what he says. He gives me a little grin. "Well, Tommy boy, I hate to tell you this, but there's some things you just shouldn't NOTICE, if you follow me."

I'm looking into those nutty eyes of his, and I'm thinking, hey, nothing adds up right. He's too fucking blown out on crystal to be running the kind of operation he says he's running, and if he was running that kind of operation, he wouldn't be living here in this nice apartment in this nice neighborhood with all these weirdoes falling by every night and fourteen different illegal substances laid out in plain sight. No, he'd be locked up in a fortress somewhere out in the country surrounded by fences and dogs and bodyguards with motherfucking nukes. So what were those dudes doing here? Buying? Selling? Making some kind of deal, that's for sure. But then it flashed on me that I couldn't tell anymore what was REAL. Yeah, I was getting to be as damned near as fucked up as Lyons.

———

THE PLAIN manila envelope arrived the first week in August. It was addressed to Pamela Zalman and Raymond Lee. Inside the envelope was a booklet on how to make bombs. It had everything a prospective bomber would ever want to know—from making Molotov cocktails out of wine bottles, through using clock timers and dynamite, to fabricating your own explosives from ingredients you could buy easily without attracting attention to yourself. "Shit," John said. "Wonderful stuff. Who's this from? Weatherman?"

The address had been written on a typewriter. So had the return address—some place in Dorchester. There was no name above the return address, and no one had taken credit for writing the booklet. "Who knows I'm living with you?" John said.

"Everybody in the Movement."

They kept running into people who'd received the booklet in the mail. Women's libbers, old SDS types, kids in the *Zygote* office, even some of the women in the Collective. Pam called friends in New York, and they'd received the booklet too—sent from an address in Brooklyn. "Jesus, they must have sent out hundreds of the damned things."

It took them a day to make sense of it—talking about it, speculating, trying out crazy ideas, forgetting the whole damned thing, coming back to it again. They drove to the return address in Dorchester and found a vacant lot. "Very funny," John said.

They thought about what was *not* in the booklet. How to fuck up university computer centers. How to disable power lines or phone lines. How to construct barricades. How to check for agents. There was not a word of politics. All it had in it was how to make bombs.

It was a very well produced booklet. "FBI?" John said.

"Yeah, maybe. Or maybe another agency. A really secret one. But you're motherfucking right it's from the government."

"What do they want?"

Why would the agents have trashed John's apartment not really looking for anything? To keep up the pressure, the paranoia. To make him fuck up. The agents had *wanted* the Harvard Square riot. Some of those NAC guys had been agents-provocateurs. They wanted more chaos—more trashings, burnings, and lootings. They wanted bombs. They wanted people killed. The more the better. "They want the Reichstag fire," Pam said.

The image called "Richard Nixon" had sent the signal on TV, and he'd been continuing to send it—the American people were fed up with anarchy and disorder. The boys in Washington were going to pass the most repressive legislation in the history of the United States. They were going after the Left big time. What they were about to do would make the Alien Sedition Acts and the Palmer Raids look like child's play. It was all going to come down in September when the schools reopened, and most ordinary Americans wouldn't give a shit any more than they had about Kent State. Of course the agents knew who John and Pam were; they'd been watching them. They were watching them right now. They'd get picked up on the first sweep.

But there was one more step to go. "We should have believed Chomsky," Pam said. He'd laid it out clear as a bell—the only revolution possible in the United States at that particular time was a fascist revolution.

"The dreadful has already happened," Pam said. "The revolution's over . . . a revolution not from the bottom but from the top. We're already living in a fascist state."

They were walking by the Charles River in the deepening summer twilight. She took John's hand. "We've been fucking nuts," she said. "We're both gone by the end of the week."

But they weren't gone by the end of the week. They couldn't seem to be able to get out of bed. "If we never get together again," she said. "No, shut up. Just listen. I know you, and I know what you're thinking. You're going to think that you're never going to be able to love anybody but me. I'm not being . . . Like I'm not just being *stuck on myself*." She rolled her eyes at the silly high-school phrase. "We're running out of time, so I've got to tell you the truth. If you think I'm the only girl in the world for you, that's just . . . It's just *bullshit*, man. So don't drown in Romantic misery, OK? You've got a weakness for that."

She was obviously trying to think of everything. "The rent's paid till the fifteenth of September . . . although I want you out of here long before that, like as soon as you can get it together, you dig? I want you to call me *from Toronto*, you dig? Joan and Sarah are moving in on the fifteenth. That's when their lease is up. I'm leaving all my stuff for them, so you don't have to . . . Don't stick around to get your money's worth, for fuck's sake. Just make sure it's really clean . . . Oh, I know you'll do that. You're a good girl . . . I cut keys for them, so you don't have to . . . Just walk out and lock the door."

He was shocked to find out that she was leaving *The Critique* for him. "Do whatever you want with it. It was always *ours* even when I wouldn't let you read it. We'll always be a council no matter what happens. Read it or don't read it, I don't care. Maybe there's some articles you can pull out of it."

She couldn't stop making lists—most of them advice to him, things she'd already said. "Don't try to cross the border with any papers. Not with *The Critique*, you dig? Oy, they'd have your ass. Mail all that shit to somebody up there. But I don't have to tell you, right? You know all that."

THE LIGHT fell away from the windows until the room went dark—making a small space outside of time, a place to live for a while. He tried to turn off the voice in his mind that kept wailing, "Oh, please, please, please, please *stay* . . . just a little bit longer." Pam reached over and lit the light on the bed table. Her eyes were clear and alive. "I love you," she said.

He was so blown away he couldn't even make the standard reply. "See," she said, "I can say it all on my own. You don't always have to say it first."

"I love you too," he said. That was usually her line.

The look in her eyes now was unmistakable. Yes, it was going to be one of those days when they did it twice. He waited for her to make the first move. She was always the sexual aggressor. But she just kept looking at him, her eyes shining with the yellow light from the lamp shade. "There's one girl you haven't been yet," she said.

He actually thought about it. He didn't have a clue what she meant. "Who?" he said.

"Me."

Again, he thought about it. How on earth was he supposed to *be* her? But of course he knew how.

They were both still naked, so he simply pulled the sheet down and exposed her. It was the sort of bold dramatic gesture she liked to make. She slid down from her sitting position, let her head fall back onto the pillow—just as he would have done. She was smiling, he thought, just as he would have been—with the same warm, dreamy, inviting expression. He was remembering all of the times before when she'd come onto him fast and a little bit rough and that had been exactly what he'd wanted her to do. He kissed her the way she'd always kissed him—imitating her aggressiveness. She opened her mouth for him just the way he'd always opened his mouth for her.

There was nothing to do now but continue to follow the line of force that was already flowing, but he'd never been on top before. He stopped, hovering over her, feeling the first brush of panic that would ruin him, but then she did the easiest thing in the world—took his cock into her hands, opened her legs, and guided him into her. She was beautifully wet.

She let her arms fall back to either side, inviting him to pin her down—just as he'd done for her. He caught her wrists and pressed her hands into the bed. He began moving his hips in the subtle, teasing way she'd often used when she was just getting started—but then he felt a hot contradictory urgency. To hell with everything. He'd never felt more *male* in his life, and now, suddenly, he wanted to drive her all the way to China. She gasped with every stroke.

But it was too much—was forced, exaggerated, was a kind of revenge. He didn't like the feeling of it. He slowed down. He released her wrists, and she wrapped her arms around him. He drew his hips back, giving her room to move—just as she'd always given him room to move when they were getting near to the end—and she moved with him. They made a simple perfect rhythm. "Who's the boy and who's the girl *now*?" she said.

He smiled, but she must have really wanted an answer. *"Who's the boy and who's the girl now?"*

"It doesn't matter," he said.

"You're goddamn right it doesn't matter."

They rode the rhythm out to the end of the song, and he didn't have to ask her because he'd felt it—once again they'd achieved that exquisite mind-blowing epiphany; they'd come together. He let his body collapse onto hers. She whispered, "I'm sorry, baby. I get claustrophobic."

He rolled to one side. She followed him across the one foot of space he'd created, and he took her into his arms. He thought for a moment that she was going to say something, but she didn't. He didn't know how he knew it, but he did—*now* she could leave him.

16.

WHEN, LATER, John would try to reconstruct the first few days, he wouldn't be able to remember much except for a haze of pain. Just as he'd done in Morgantown years ago, he wrote himself a note and pinned it above Pam's desk: FIND THE NEXT THING TO DO AND DO IT. But there was no next thing. After Pamela, there was nothing.

He would remember walking along the Charles River for hours. He would remember watching the tube for hours. When he did find something to do, that simple thing struck him with the force of a revelation—he would *clean the stove*. Then, as that one simple thing led to the next simple thing, he scoured the sinks, the toilet, and the bathtub. He washed the windows, swept and washed the floors. On his hands and knees, he waxed the hardwood where she'd practiced the Cecchetti Method. The morning she'd left, neither of them had been able to stop crying. "Oh, baby," she'd said, "I knew it was going to be hard, but I didn't know it was going to be this hard." She'd driven away crying. As long as he could still smell her vanilla oil and her sweat and her sex in their bed, he would not wash the sheets.

He received, as they'd planned, the collect person-to-person phone call for Emma Goldman that meant, "I'm safe in New York, and everything's fine." As they'd planned, he said, "Emma's not here right now," and that meant, "I got the message."

A dozen times, he sat down at her desk and tried to read *The Critique*. It opened with references to Vaneigem and Debord; in order to follow her writing, he would have to go back and read those obscure dudes again, and he wasn't ready to do that yet. He flipped through her typewritten pages—three hundred and nineteen of them. The manuscript was divided into numbered sections—two hundred and four of them. On many of the pages she'd added handwritten notes to the margins. It was positively Talmudic. Although he wasn't able to read more than a few random pages here and there, *The Critique* gave him the first suggestion of hope. Simply by looking through it, simply by handling the paper she'd touched, he'd found a purpose. He would respond to the *The Critique*—meet her subjectivity with his subjectivity. One day he would show her that everything she'd thought and written dovetailed beautifully with everything he'd thought and written to make a perfect whole.

ON THE seventh day after she'd left, he wandered around Harvard Square for a while, trying to look like someone cheerfully, aimlessly strolling. He was checking for agents. Then he walked to the phone booth that he and Pam had chosen—near the Square but not too near. He waited. She called exactly when she'd said she would. "Oh, baby, you should see it out here. It's true . . . the light, the landscape, the *feeling*. God, I must sound like the most spaced-out little chickie, but it's . . . *transcendent*. It's mind-blowing."

"Are you all right?"

"Oh, yeah. I'm fine. I lost two pounds, but it doesn't matter. I had that . . . like, you know, that extra cushion. I'm glad it's gone . . . Hey, this is hard, isn't it?"

Hard for *you?* he thought. I'm damned near dying.

"We've just got to keep moving forward step by step and see what happens," she said in the crisp, matter-of-fact voice of the new Pamela, the one that drove him nuts. Maybe it was the crappy phone line, but he heard her New York accent as harsh, unfamiliar, almost alien. "When I get settled, I'll stabilize my weight," she was saying. "I think I'm going to keep it around 112." He could hear, behind the words, something that wasn't being said. Of course it wasn't the time or the place to have an intense, meaningful conversation.

"Deb keeps telling me that my entire consciousness is going to change," she was saying, "just from the light."

Deb, he thought. Right.

"It really is the West out here. The women all wear cowboy boots. Can you see me in cowboy boots?"

"Oh, yeah, white ones."

He heard her laugh—a sound like someone deciding to laugh. "Of course you'd like that . . . the ambiguity . . . So, are you ready to go?"

"Yeah, just about," although he hadn't even thought about leaving yet.

"Come on, baby, you've got to get your act together. You've got to . . ." He heard her hesitate. Even calling from one phone booth to another didn't feel entirely safe. " . . . get settled." Back at York, she meant. "Listen. I *told you.* Just go through the motions, OK? That's what I keep telling myself. You're drowning in Romantic misery, aren't you? I can hear it in your voice. Well, stop it."

"I'm OK," he told her. "I've been trying to read *The Critique* . . . Some of the entries are kind of . . . well, personal. It surprised me. They're almost like journal entries. But not many. Most of it's so damned theoretical . . ."

"What did you expect? I have a theoretical mind. You know that. You know me."

He didn't know what he was trying to say to her. Something important. The line, or series of lines, that connected them had a constant shush in it—a sound like distant traffic. He couldn't let her go. There was no way he could keep her.

"Baby," she said, "what are you doing? I can't . . . I can't tell where you're at. I did what I had to do. Now you've got to take care of yourself. I can't tell what you're thinking. I know we can't really *talk,* but . . . What are you thinking?"

He didn't know what he was thinking. "Are you still there?" she said.

"Yeah." There was something more he wanted to say to her.

"Come on, man, you've got to get the hell out of there. Call me when you're *settled.*"

IT WAS like recovering from acid—and it wasn't like that at all. He was trying to find *anything* he could use. Doing physical things had helped him before—sawing wood, driving nails—so he made himself go the *Zygote* office and work on the layout, and that simple mindless activity did seem to help. For months he'd been entirely focused on Pamela—his entire purpose in life to feed her, make her better, turn her back into a functioning human being. He'd succeeded, and the well-fed, thoroughly healed, and smoothly functioning human being had packed up her things and left him. She'd found her *Sh'ma Yisrael*—some kind of *clarity.* So where was his rock-solid foundation—the one simple thing he could count on no matter what?

He pinned up a note above his desk that said, DON'T DROWN IN ROMANTIC MISERY. He was probably feeling exactly what she'd been feeling after the riot—*depressed*. So what he had to do was follow her path out of it—follow it exactly, step by step. She'd gone back to her beginnings, reconstructed the entire world, had lain in bed day after day reading anthropology books. Now he would meet her subjectivity with his subjectivity. He combed through the used bookstores in Harvard Square, bought *The Dharma Bums* and *Howl*—but he knew he was really onto it when he found a collection of Rilke with both the German original and a reasonably good translation.

"Der Sommer war sehr gross," Rilke reminded him. *"Oh, Lord, it is time!"* One year ago in August he'd been up at Ethan and Terry's in New Hampshire, recovering from acid and reincarnating himself as a vegetarian. In August one year before that, he'd been in Toronto watching Chicago go down on the tube. Christ, it had been *two years* since he'd left Canada. Had he done anything to make love more possible? Well, he'd made it more possible *for himself,* and maybe that was enough—the personal is the political—but he was afraid that Pamela was the only person he could ever love truly. She'd warned him about that too.

He was stuck, not merely in Boston, but in the entire heavy, warped-out, used-up headspace that went with it. But the Movement was dead—dead for him, surely, and maybe even dead for itself—and now he belonged to a council that had only one member left in it. But no, he thought, there were still two members. He sat down at Pam's desk. *The Critique* drew him into it—the fascination of seeing her mind at work. Some of her entries were whole, powerfully argued statements, absolute models of clarity, but others were nothing more than notes to herself. Entry 203, for instance, read, in its entirety: "Check out sexual dominance patterns in primate behavior." Then, in handwriting, she'd added: "Arguments from nature dangerous. Lévi-Strauss." Was he going to have to read *all* of Lévi-Strauss to figure out what she'd meant by that?

The most tantalizing writing was on the few pages that read like journal entries—like Number 83:

Could I do it, couldn't do it, could do it, why? Not
why but how. Cut through the breast bone. Thought
fractured. The body remembers what the tiny rat
forgets. Hot crappy little studio, rat dead. Sweat,
taste sand. Black girls, Spanish girls. Standard
question: why is this coming up now? Across the
floor. Technique persists. Surplus. Fine work on hand
axes far in excess of anything required for mere
survival. Where were you trained? Good question.
Why? I need, I need, I need. Old pain. Don't forget.
Theorize personal, personalize theory.

She must have made that entry the night after her ballet class in New York—the first class she'd taken in years. She'd told him about the black girls and Spanish girls in that class—and the old pain that had cut through her breast bone. The "tiny rat" was how she sometimes described the conscious mind. Reading her entry made him feel godlike—because he knew how the story would unfold. She was on her way to the theory of androgyny, on her way back to Boston, back to *him*. He wished that he could look at himself from the same all-knowing distance. What story was he writing? Where was he going?

HE KNEW that he had to make some effort to reconnect with the human race even if he was only going through the motions. He sat with Cassandra in the kitchen in the Shooting Gallery and smoked dope. It was the first time he'd been stoned in weeks; he loved the rush of it coming on, but then it just bummed him out. He couldn't make himself talk. He sat sweating in the late-summer heat, intensely aware of the tension—the honest-to-God *pain*—in the muscles of his neck and shoulders, listening, fascinated, to the sound of boiling water on the stove. Lorraine was making tea. He'd wanted to see Cass alone, but she seemed as attached to Lorraine as a Siamese twin. What the hell were they *doing*?

"Motherfucking trip, man," Cassandra was saying, "sweet

Lorraine shows them some tit, and I show them some ass, and they salivate like Pavlov's dogs. Yeah, come on, you got to check it out. Some real freaky chicks fall by there, even freakier than us, although you might find that hard to believe. It's motherfucking boring, if you want to know the truth. What the fuck you still doing *here*, man?"

"I don't know."

"Well, shit, old buddy, if you don't know, and I don't know, then who the fuck does?"

It was the same old jive. She sat sprawled back in her chair, her feet on the kitchen table. It was a very Cassandra-like pose, and he was flashed into one of those hideously poignant mind-feeling-things, the ones with no possible resolution. She was wearing an old minidress of Lorraine's; it looked like something from '67 or '68—a white dress with a huge circle on the bodice like a target. Her bare feet were filthy. She'd shaved her legs all the way up to her white panties—a bit on the soiled side. He wanted to say, "Where have you gone, Cass?" but he didn't.

The next day Tom fell by. "Cass tells me you're kind of bummed out, old buddy. Thought you could use a pinch of smoke." He tossed a baggie into John's hands. "Magical Michoacan. Pure sunlight, trippy as all hell . . . No, no, no, don't go reaching into your jeans. Coin is no problemo. Happy days are here again, and the bread's falling out of the sky like Manna." Then, with his Sunshine Superman grin, he was gone.

The grass was clean—not a stem or twig to be seen—and just as groovy as Tom had promised. Getting stoned with people might be a bummer, but getting stoned alone felt like exactly the right thing to do. Stoned, John could read *The Critique* for hours.

"THE PROLETARIAT must become conscious as in no previous time in history," Pamela had always said, quoting somebody or other, and so of course that's exactly the way *The Critique* opened. Well, he didn't know about the proletariat, but *he* was certainly conscious, and she had made him that way.

But what was consciousness anyway? It was just a collection of words—like *The Critique* itself. Again that feeling he'd had so strongly on acid—or *after* the acid—that consciousness is nothing more than a symptom of animal jangle, but he kept sensing a greater meaning, an enticing shimmer that was only one jump ahead of him, nothing he could think about, something he would have to flash on. He wished that pure Sandoz acid was still available in the underground.

"You're not a mistake," he'd told her. It was the same thing he'd told himself when he'd been recovering from acid—it's what he'd needed to tell himself if he wanted to go on living. But it hadn't been true in either case; both he and Pam were mistakes, but when they'd been together, the mistakes had cancelled each other out and made something right. Now that they were separated, they were mistakes again— But no, she was probably doing just fine. She'd found a way to disguise herself. She could melt into the Women's Movement and lesbianism, live there, disguised and safe, but where was he supposed to melt? Without her, *he* was a mistake, and he had nowhere to go.

Then, as he drifted into his second week of living alone, he began to feel that Pamela's apartment was *his* apartment. He'd lived alone more than he'd lived with other people, so it wasn't an unfamiliar state; if he used his time right, it didn't have to be a mind-fuck, and that clean orderly space with its wonderful light was certainly the best place where he'd ever lived alone—even better than his apartment in the Annex. But he made himself get out of there at least once a day—just as he'd made Pamela get out. As he'd done all of his life, he walked. To have somewhere to go, he fell by Ethan and Terry's.

Ethan was in New Hampshire, but Terry was at home, and it could have been tense, awkward, being alone with her, but it wasn't in the least. "I wasn't going to cook for just me," she said, "but now I've got an excuse." They smoked a whiff of grass—not in the single-minded way Cassandra went at it, to get totally blasted, but just to cut the edge. He sat at the kitchen table and watched her while she made curry and chapattis.

The acid trip they'd taken together seemed like a million years ago, another lifetime. How could his head have transformed her into a demonic figure, a Kali-like embodiment of the Terrible Woman? She did have a very womanly body, it was true—one that

361

always looked better in Indian blouses and flowy Gypsy skirts than it did in jeans—but she was four or five years younger than he was, still a girl. Meandering away on a glimmering side strand, he thought how odd it was that what you looked like—something you were born with, something you couldn't help—might determine not only how you saw the world but your very place in it. She did have a very sexy body.

"Lots of bad acid in the underground now," she told him. "Not just twisted speedy shit like we dropped, but bad shit, evil shit. A lot of time, it's not even acid. The kids are getting into death-trip drugs now, heavy into them, doing smack and reds and crystal meth, drinking booze again. Bummer. Hey, and the junkies are slamming each other out over bad dope deals. Have you heard that one? Like you put Drano in somebody's shit, you dig? It's a fairly horrible way to go out. Think what it must be like when you hit your next incarnation, all the pain you're dragging behind you, whew."

Unlike Cassandra, Terry actually *listened* to him. "Yeah, sure you're bummed out about Pamela. What did you think, you wouldn't feel a thing? But don't get hung up on it. You've still got that expanded consciousness available to you. Once you've seen it, you can never have *not* seen it, you dig? It's like that thing Don Juan told Carlos. 'Go back to Los Angeles and surround yourself with familiar things.' Yeah, make yourself a space to cool out, and shiver down, and just be there."

It was good to rap with Terry; he felt almost like himself again. But afterwards, he still had to go home to an empty apartment—but that wasn't too bad either. Pam's desk was beginning to feel like *his* desk.

Sometimes he thought that *The Critique* was the only thing keeping him going; at other times he was afraid that reading it was like picking constantly at a wound so it could never heal. But this curiously detached slice of his life would have to end soon—Pamela had made sure of that. Her friends were taking over the apartment on the fifteenth of September. In the meantime, he had to find some way to connect with his own subjectivity because, right now, he quite profoundly did not give a shit.

Entry 108 made his scalp prickle. It was the only direct reference to him in the entire manuscript—in a paragraph that seemed as packed with meaning and as difficult as any of Pound's Cantos. Pamela could have explained to him what she'd been thinking—exactly, step but step—but she wasn't there to do it.

```
His words: "the whole track inside." Divide in time
as well as in space. The parallel girl. Separate
but contiguous. Patterns of point distribution,
mytheme distribution. The subjective, structuralism
personalized: Tristes Tropiques. Mead: all cultures
assign sex roles, remarkable differences from culture
to culture. A revolutionary culture would be a
metaculture. Sixteen, mad and bad, from Clara to
locked ward, let out for the paintings in the Met,
shock of recognition. Cavalier boys. Velvet and lace,
silk hosiery, delicate slippers, long soft ringlets
to the shoulders, lovelocks. I am a boy and I have a
boyfriend. Velvet and iron. Snyder's answer to Freud:
"There is nothing in human nature or the requirements
of human social organization which intrinsically
requires that a culture be contradictory,
repressive and productive of violent and frustrated
personalities."
```

———

THE MINUTE I walk in, I know something heavy's going down because the usual crew of weirdoes ain't jammed in there—just Lyons himself and Susie. He lays one of his usual raps on me, squeaking away—"Well, Tommy boy, you sure are looking good. But are you having a good time, that's what I want to know."

We plunk down at the kitchen table. Lyons gives Susie the eyeball and she's gone. He shoves the papers and bowl of dope over to me and pours me a cup of joe and goes trotting off somewhere, and when he comes back, he lays this big motherfucking gun on the table. I mean it's practically a field artillery piece. He says, "What do you think this is, Tommy?"

"Shit, Bob, it looks like a gun to me."

He's giggling away. "You got that one right, man. Them crazy radicals been saying we got to pick up the gun, right? Well, I picked it up. But not any old kind of gun, you dig? It's a SPECIAL gun, hee hee hee. It's a Ruger .44 Magnum Super Blackhawk." And he's laying it on me about how many grains in the goddamned slugs, and the muzzle velocity, and all that shit, right? I mean he sounds like the ad man for the Ruger company.

He says, "The important thing to remember about this gun, Tommy, is what it can do. This fucker will crack an engine block. This fucker punches out a hole in a man you wouldn't believe. If I was to shoot a man with this thing and I got the shot in anywhere on his body . . . dig it, anywhere at all . . . that'd be all she wrote. Because the SHOCK would stop him. Even if I was to hit him in the hand with it, right? I mean it would just fucking well tear his hand right off. And if I was to get a shot into his body, well, shit, man . . . hamburger.

"There ain't no running away from THIS gun, Tommy, no taking one in the shoulder and getting it dug out later. If you're hit, you've bought it, the motherfucking end of the road." And he's laughing away, having a good time, talking in that high silly voice, not the least bit pissed off or anything. And then he peers across the table at me and says, sort of the way he might say "pass the salt" or "nice day today" . . . he says, "Did you sell me out, Tommy?"

I sit there and I don't say a word. I just look him in the face. He looks back, and *he* don't say a word. A lot of time passes. Finally he says, "A slug from a .44 Magnum causes what they call excessive damage to tissue. Yeah, I like that. Excessive damage to tissue."

"Lyons," I say, "you fucking asshole. We were in the war effort."

"Yeah, I know that, Tommy."

"You don't have to tell me what getting shot means."

"Yeah, I didn't think I did." He says, "Did you sell me out, man?"

I fix him with a good steady gaze the way my old man always told me to do when you're having a DISCUSSION with somebody. "Lyons," I say, "if you ask me that one more time, I'm going to take that motherfucking cannon and ram it right up your hairy ass."

He rocks back in his chair and howls with laughter. Real off-the-wall shit, I mean, like INSTITUTIONAL. Then he pushes that Magnum across the table at me. "Check it out, man, it's a motherfucking monster," and goes off on another laughing jag. I'm thinking, shit, one of these days I'm going to come in here and find nothing left of him but one gigantic methamphetamine molecule. So I pick up the gun, and the first thing I do, naturally, is break it down. It ain't loaded. Not bullet one. He's grinning at me. I grin back.

I've never liked handguns. I've never liked the feel of them, never understood people who like the feel of them. I've never learned all the ways to talk about them the way a lot of guys do. I like rifles. A rifle will do anything a handgun will do, and do it better. There's something about a rifle that makes you think a minute, but a handgun . . . Well, there's something about a handgun. A kid I knew in high school shot his toes off playing cowboy with a handgun. With a handgun there's something that makes you want to whip it out and start blazing away. I look over at Lyons and think, shit.

"What's happening?" I say.

"They busted the Brookline operation. Then they tried to lay a bust on me. I'm out on what they call a motherfucking bond."

"When was that?"

"About a week ago. They got no case. They fucked it up too bad. They're going to get it in court and it's going to look like a zip's breakfast. They got no way in hell of proving there's any connection between me and that frigging house. But it makes things a little difficult, man. It makes it difficult for me to get around town. It puts a strain on the old operations, if you know what I mean. You might say it's pissing me right off. And I was set up, man. It was just too beautiful for it to be any other way."

"Hey, Robert," I say, "maybe the Maf set you up. Maybe they thought you was getting too big."

"No," he says, "I'm cool with them."

Sure that's what he'd say, but do I believe it? I don't know. "OK," I say, "like who was over there at the Brookline operation? Like what the fuck went down?"

He lays it all out, the whole picture, and I'm thinking about it. Suddenly I see where the weak link is. More than likely I should have kept my mouth shut, but it kind of fascinated me too. "Look,"

I say, "Peter. The chef. Where the fuck was he when the bust come down?"

"He was taking a break. He was back home seeing his folks."

"Well, doesn't his timing seem a little bit too good to you?"

He taps his fingers on the table. He's not laughing anymore. "I thought of that. Yeah, you better believe I thought of that. Except his old lady got busted."

"How do you know?"

And he's stopped. I mean he's stopped DEAD, like motherfucking FROZEN. Then he says, "Shit. I know what they confiscated as evidence. My sleazy lawyer found it out. And I know how much there should have been over there. There's a big fucking difference, man. Like maybe to the tune of thirty or forty thou. I'm talking street price now. So I want to know where that difference went. And you know what, Tommy boy? There's two places it could have gone. The cops could have took it. Or the person who set me up could have took it."

He jumps up and starts pacing around, swinging his hands in the air and kind of blowing off steam like a horse. His eyeballs are blazing in his head and he's yelling, "that fucking little college punk. That goddamned little motherfucking punk. You know how these fucking college kids are, Tommy? They think GIs are fucking morons, right? Thinks I ain't got brain one. Yeah, and he's been to school for twenty motherfucking years. Thinks he can pull off this shit ON ME. Jesus, man, so clumsy a three-year-old would see through it."

Yeah? Well, he hadn't seen it till I'd pointed it out to him.

One minute he's pissed and yelling, the next minute he's giggling and squeaking at me. I mean it's so quick it's like throwing a toggle switch. "Oh well, you know, Tommy, if somebody gets busted they have to appear in court, right? I mean they don't just DISAPPEAR. And goddamn it, that cunt better turn up in court or it's going to be Peter's ass. Yeah, he's going to look like Charlie after a night with the question boys. What the fuck did he think? They was going to lock me up and throw away the key?"

And he blows me a kiss. "I love your fucking ugly ass, man. I love you like a brother. Yeah, we're tight like a nut on a bolt, right? But life's a little difficult right at the moment, you know what I mean? So why don't we go straight to the source?" and he reaches in his jeans and pulls out his wallet and peels out something like a thousand bills and lays it on me. Of course I take it, what do you think?

Then he says, "Oh, by the way, Tommy, you know that loser pad where you're crashed? They're going to take it down."

"Oh, yeah? When?"

"One never knows, do one? Could be next month or could be tonight, but down she's going to go like a Tennessee whore, hee hee hee. So if I was you, I'd get your ass out of there. Like it could get a little hairy, man. They got every single one of you on CANDID CAMERA," and he's just laughing his ass off at that one. I'm thinking, thanks a whole fuck of a lot, Robert. You could have laid that on me weeks ago.

Well, of course I was planning to get out of that house, but it takes a while for a man to get his shit together even at the best of times, and a day or so later Lyons calls me up. Like late at night at three or four in the morning. He's never called me up before, day or night, and I know he's calling from a pay phone because I can hear the traffic. "Tommy!" he squeaks at me. "You remember our favorite chef. The king of the culinary arts?"

"Yeah," I say, "I remember him quite clearly."

"Well then, of course you do recollect his old lady?"

"Oh, yeah, she has managed to lodge herself firmly in my memory."

"Well, Tommy, guess what I just found out? Hee hee hee. His old lady was not visited by anybody recently. NOT EVER, MAN. She's out in California, walking around just as free as a little birdie bird bird bird. How you like them green apples, Tommy?"

That means Peter lied to him. That means Peter set him up. "That's heavy, Bob," I say.

"No, no, man. No, no, that's not heavy at all. That's just a little giggle between friends, right? And guess who calls me up? From Philadelphia? The chef himself. Clean-cut kid and been to college too. Had him a few fairy tales to tell this dumb old GI, right? Told me a few about Little Red Riding Hood and a few more about Cinderella."

I don't know what the fuck I can say and what the fuck I can't. I'm pretty sure our phone's tapped. "This is all very interesting."

"Interesting?" he says. "Oh, that's not the half of it. You know what, man? I don't have to do a fucking thing about it. That boy's going to come to me, Tommy. Yeah, HE'S GOING TO COME TO ME."

———

THE LOCK on the front door had been broken for so long it felt normal. John hadn't been planning to fall by the Shooting Gallery; he'd just been out walking, but his feet had carried him in that direction, and he'd thought, why not? It might be good to see Tom or Cassandra—either would do. He stepped inside, and the house seemed oppressively silent. He closed the door behind him and paused, listening. Maybe they were all on the nod. But no, he heard voices—distant, muffled. Feeling like an agent, he ghosted through the rooms on the first floor. Not a skaghead to be seen. He followed the voices upstairs to the closed door of the bedroom Lorraine shared with Garvin, knocked lightly. Cassandra jerked the door open, laughed at the expression on his face. She was wearing nothing but black panties and a pair of old-fashioned flesh-colored stockings held up with a black garter belt. He stepped back.

"Far out," she said. "Here's old Raymond Lee come to do some smoke with us."

"What the fuck are you doing?" he said, still backing up.

"Did you hear that shit?" she said to Lorraine. "Is that any way to start a conversation? The dude sound a little uptight to you?"

"Oh, yeah, man," Lorraine murmured. "Drawn straight out." She was wearing a pink waist-cincher, shiny black stockings, and no panties at all. Both women were whacked out of their fucking gourds.

"Hey," he said, "if you're . . . like . . ."

"No, no, no, man," Cassandra said, grabbing his hand and pulling him inside. "Dig the show. It's for free. It's just us, for fuck's sake," and then, in jive talk, "We just playing dress-up. Come on, man, join the parade. You *androgynous* now, right?"

"Oh, for Christ's sake."

"Don't mess with him," she said to Lorraine. "He flips every way there is. Yeah, he's trickier than a catfish. Come on, Raymond, do up a little smoke."

She lit a match, held it under the bowl of a tiny brass pipe. He took the pipe, inhaled. "That's not your ordinary hash," he said.

"Can't put a thing over on old Raymond Lee," Cassandra said. "He's got the taste of a connoisseur. He's *androgynous.*"

"Oh, stop it," John said, laughing in spite of himself.

"Hey, old buddy, you want to play dressup too? We got tons of groovy shit here. We could make you into the queen of the whole fucking world, man. Yeah, float around town and fuck people's heads."

"Fire him up again," Lorraine said. "The dude ain't off yet."

"I can see that," Cassandra said. "The dude ain't getting the joke."

"Yeah, I'm off." But he took the pipe and did another toke. "What the fuck?" he said, pointing the pipestem at the two large cardboard cartons with their contents spilling out. Old clothes, dresses and slips, lingerie, boots and shoes, jewelry.

"My motherfucking ex gives me a shout, right?" Lorraine said. "Carl, the asshole. He says, 'Lorraine, you come get you shit out of my motherfucking basement or it's hitting the trash.' Dig it, he's making himself a *rec room.*"

"Ain't it sleazy?" Cassandra said, pawing through a carton. "Jesus, man, sleaze don't run no farther. Motherfucking end of the line."

"You know what that mofo asshole used to say to me?" Lorraine was asking John just as though he might know the answer. "'Lorraine,' he used to say, 'there ain't nothing more boring than a naked woman.'"

"Here," Cassandra said, "let's get you really ripped."

"No, it's OK. Jesus."

He could already feel the hash, or whatever it was, scurrying up his spinal cord like a tarantula, but Cassandra was pushing him backwards until he was forced to sit down on the bed. She tapped the pipe on the edge of the wastebasket, wiped the copper screen clear with her thumb, loaded it with a new chunk, fired it up, held the pipe under John's nose, and blew into the stem. He inhaled, and an inexorable blast of blue-white smoke shot straight through his brain to arrive, baffled, at the executioner's wall at the back of his skull. He jerked his head away.

"Come on, man," Cassandra said, "more, more, more. No sense in half measures." He tipped his nose back to the pipe. She blew the smoke into him until there was nothing left in the brass bowl but grey ash.

He hauled out his handkerchief and mopped his eyes. "What the fuck is that?"

"Well, you starts with hash. And then you throws in a chunk of that good old opium. And then you finishes it all off with a hit of crystal so's you don't nod out too bad. Motherfucking trip, man."

He couldn't move. Already the world was warping around him, growing multi-faceted, shearing off into bad science fiction—spaceship doors inside spaceship doors. Cassandra was checking out the sleazy clothes again. She came up with a black bra. "Too bad I haven't got any tits."

She thrust the bra at Lorraine who compressed her large breasts into it. Cassandra fastened it up in the back. Circles the size of fifty-cent pieces were cut out at the ends of the cups; Lorraine's nipples thrust through the holes like the ends of popsicles. It wasn't sexy. It wasn't even satire. It was grotesque. He laughed.

"Hey, shit," Cassandra said, "I think the man's getting the joke."

"Well, if he ain't got it by now, he ain't never going to be getting it."

"Come here, pussycat." Cassandra painted Lorraine's nipples with a dark red lipstick. "Shit," she said, "we too motherfucking cool for the Incision. Let's fall by Daddy Imhoff's. He'd really dig the show."

"Who the fuck's Daddy Imhoff?" John heard himself saying—already fragmented into a kaleidoscope of himselves. And the voices were murmuring, overlapping, reverberating—multi-tracked:

"Old-time dude from the good old days. Seen it all."

"Yeah, man, motherfucking Imhoff, he always gets the joke."

"Always got a pinch of smoke, maybe even a sniff of doogie for his little pals."

"Digs the ladies, you dig?"

"Always slips a little something your way."

"A little coin here, a little scratch there."

"Slips it in your panties, in your bra."

"Just like them dudes watching the belly dancer, you dig?"

Cassandra had gone back to rummaging in a carton. She was drawing out a long plastic boot. It seemed to go on forever like a strand of spaghetti. "Oh, wow. What do you think of this, Raymond? Shades of my misspent youth."

"You never wore anything like that."

"You right, man. Watched it flash by me though, at the time. You and me, buddy, sitting on the outside same as always. *L'étranger*. Hey, we gots the coin for the cab?"

"Zip," Lorraine said.

"I've got some money," John said.

"All we gots to do is get there, then we looking good," and not supposed to nod out on this shit? But he'd been *somewhere*. Cassandra was clearly *there*, leering at him from behind the makeup. She'd painted huge doe eyes onto herself, a flash-pink cupid's bow for a mouth. With her boy-short hair, it made her look like a parody of a twenties flapper. And John's voice was going on and on. He didn't have the remotest notion of what he'd been saying, heard the words: "Motherfucking space and light. Space and light. Space and light. Like . . . Shit. Did you call a cab? What did you say? *What did you just say?*"

Cassandra had found a fake leather minidress to match the sleazy brown boots. It was zipped up the front, short and tight, decorated with Indian-style fringe. She did a pirouette for him. "Don't you just love me? Don't you just want to eat me up like a scoop of ice cream? Jesus, Zoë would kill me, like strangle me with her bare hands."

Then, with apparently no transition—like a jump cut from a Goddard movie—she was kneeling next to him, speaking from only a few inches away. Her voice had changed, weirdly, as though she'd grabbed up one of the accents available to her, something floating around like loose radio waves in the ether—as though she'd found a way to speak that matched, or parodied, her grotesque makeup. "We widdle ones needs a widdle mo' smoke. Yes? No?"

He took the pipe she was offering and inhaled. "Don't be so sad, honeysuckle. Come out and play wit us. Quit your moping over bad Pamewa. She's a far-out chickie, but the world's full of far-out chickies," and then, like tuning in a radio station, that disturbing voice shifted back into her own: "Even *androgynous* ones, you dig?" She winked at him. Or he thought she did, and then he was paying the cab driver, and what the hell had happened to the time in between? Well, yeah, there were memories—broken pieces, flotsam, debris, a few bricks, a bit of mortar. He remembered getting into the cab. But, Jesus, time wasn't supposed to collapse like that. He must have been on the nod.

"All time is no time," he heard himself saying idiotically to Cassandra. "Everywhere's a nowhere, you dig?" and the secret agent in him was noting the address for future reference.

Inside. A brown study in turn-of-the-century gloom. No, that couldn't be right. That wasn't what "brown study" meant. John felt himself phasing in and out. Focus, he told himself. It was funny how you could tilt words so they meant something they didn't ordinarily mean. He imagined a whole sequence of them, each one tilted slightly, leading to the next one, so you could end up really twisted. "Hey, man, what's happening?" Cassandra was saying. "This crazy dude is Raymond Lee."

"Mr. Lee, Mr. Lee," Imhoff said. Big broad hands, and Imhoff did that sneaky hermetic thumbs-up handshake and laughed—well, rumbled—a bass voice, phlegmy with a note like dirty foam. John couldn't really be hearing the big man's lungs moving like a set of bellows, could he? Especially not with the jazz playing—some kind of bebop or whatever it was that John didn't know and didn't care to know—and half a dozen men were sprawled about. No women but Cass and Lorraine; they drew the loose raspy attention to themselves like sugar water. Imhoff himself was tall and thick and old—goatee, scraggly grey hair, pot belly, broad cowboy belt, huge silver buckle with a screaming eagle on it. Oh, yeah, he was old. Everybody was old. Jesus, a beatnik's convention from the class of '49. "Ah, Mr. Lee," Imhoff was saying as though sharing a smutty joke with John. "Ah, the ladies. What brings you charming ladies to my lair in the bowels of the darkest night?"

"Your sweetest self, Daddy," Lorraine said.

To fall out, the dudes used the floor. Pillows flung around. John sank down, found the wall with his back. A cat passed him a joint damned near as big as a Havana cigar—a real honest-to-God doobie. He took it and dragged. They'd been eating Chinese takeout in the middle of the floor. Nothing was as revolting as the cold remains of Chinese takeout. Imhoff sat in one of the only chairs, and Cass sat on his lap, her tight skirt riding up, showing her stocking tops. Lorraine was curled up with another dude; she was wearing an old shawl around her bare shoulders. They'd been drinking coffee and tea; the cold cups lay on the floor. They were drinking port wine. John had the familiar sensation—all too familiar—of not knowing what the fuck he was doing there or how he was supposed to continue doing or not doing whatever it was he was supposed to be doing or not doing. The joint came around again, and he dragged. Fuck, it was strong dope. Like inhaling on a factory chimney.

Somewhat later, that Betty Boop cartoon, parody flapper, ingénue, Cassandra in disguise—her face hanging close to his, Sweeney turning into the moon at the window, Cassandra's face turning into what, what, what? " . . . asshole called my parents," she was saying. "Same asshole called Zoë. Shit, man, I deeply do not appreciate that. Said he was a California pig, right? Well, shit, the pigs don't call you up from California. They get their fellow pigs to call you up, like in whatever state you're in, you dig . . ."

"Wait a minute, wait a minute, wait a minute. What asshole?" Cassandra was the moon.

"That's the right question, man. What asshole?" She leaned closer to him. She was speaking in a small, precise, breathy voice like a twelve-year-old reciting in church. "Somebody Sweet Andrew hired, right? Not the goddamn pigs. The goddamn pigs don't call your parents up from California. They don't call your sister in New York. Maybe it was even Sweet Andrew himself. I wouldn't put it past him, the sick fuck. My old man was perfect. He said, 'Oh, if you find her, can you let me know? We've been really worried about her. Haven't heard from her in over a year.' And Zoë said, 'The last I heard she was in California. Who the hell did you say you were?' And then they both called me up. Like they did not pass 'Go.' They hung up their fucking phones and they're on the horn to me like instantly. The old man goes, 'Are you in some kind of trouble?' Zoë goes, 'Cassandra, what the hell are you *doing?*'"

"Why didn't you tell me?" John said. Jesus, he had to focus. *Golden* was the right word. No other word would do.

"I just did tell you."

Fuck, he had to do something. They shouldn't be calling Cassandra at the Shooting Gallery. Wasn't the phone tapped? No, it wasn't the moon at the window, it was the streetlight, and it wasn't golden at all. It was harsh, carbon arc, through a slit in the drapes. The ceiling—cracks and cobwebs. Not like sleeping and dreaming. Worse. But he was coming down. Jesus, that must be what it was. Yeah, it was that simple. He was *coming down.* And where was Cassandra? She'd been there just a minute ago, her face like the moon reflected in the River Plate.

When John came off the nod again, he had a headache like vile death. God, he was thirsty. His mouth was burnt and dried. And then everything was coming back more quickly than he would have thought possible; he saw the streetlight burning outside the window, and it must be already far into the night. He heard traffic going by, and everywhere in the big Edward Hopper city people must be alive and doing something. Going somewhere, driving cars, walking. Lying around their pads watching television. Straight or stoned or drunk. A lot of them must have gone to bed by now, must be snoozing peacefully or not so peacefully. And even though he wasn't there, his apartment near Harvard Square must still be existing out in the real just as inexorably as anything else; it was waiting for him, empty, with no Pamela in it. *The Critique* was in it. He could see, with perfect clarity, the veins in the back of his hand, the small hairs on his wrist. His muscles were stiff from lying sprawled against the wall. How long had he been out of it? Hours?

Then, drifting gradually sideways back into where he was, John became aware that he'd lost track of Cassandra and Lorraine. The skitchery jazz was still playing, was truly maddening, was poking little holes in his brain, and he seemed to be on his feet, walking. On his way somewhere? Maybe he was going into the kitchen for a drink of water. He looked behind him with what he hoped was a reassuring smile but saw that no one was watching. Many of the dudes had left, and the ones that were still lying around clearly did not give a shit. He opened the door in front of him, stepped through it, came upon a pre-arranged tableau—Imhoff sitting in a chair by a small table, Cassandra standing next to him, Lorraine off to one side. They all turned to look at him. John, not knowing what else to do, shrugged and grinned. It wasn't like he didn't know what was happening. Of course he knew what was happening. He'd seen Garvin fix Lorraine, had seen Garvin fix himself.

"Don't worry, man," Lorraine said, speaking quickly. "He's just going to give her a taste. Just skin popping. Nothing to get uptight about."

"Shut the frigging door," Imhoff said quietly, then added—and it sounded like an apology—"Go on back out or come on in."

John shut the door and reassembled himself inside the gradually assembling room. "Cass?" he said. Her eyes met his—grey fume—then looked away.

"She digs the point," Lorraine said as though it explained everything.

"Yeah?" John said.

"Sometimes you'll do water, you dig? Just for the point."

"It's OK," Cassandra said to John. "It's really OK."

"He's just giving her a taste," Lorraine said. "No worse than sniffing it."

"Um," John said. He'd been planning to say something after that, but he'd lost it.

Imhoff turned his attention back to Cassandra. He opened a big hand and cupped her ass, squeezed on brown vinyl. "That's where I ought to do you, babe. That's the best place for bad girls, you dig?"

"Groovy," Cassandra said.

"Oh, yeah?" Imhoff looked at Lorraine. She sent him information with her eyes. Like everything else there that night, it was in hieroglyphics and the Rosetta Stone had been lost thousands of years ago.

"I guess you must have been a bad girl," Imhoff said to Cassandra.

"Sure," she said with something like a smile—but no, not a smile, just a meaningless contortion of her face.

"Cass?" John said again.

Imhoff looked at John and said like an aside to the audience: "Nothing to get hung about. I know these chicks, you dig?"

Imhoff wrapped one of his arms around Cassandra's waist and folded her gently forward. John saw her flare with surprise, saw her begin to resist, but then, falling into a what-the-fuck flaccidity, she allowed the motion to continue. Her face vanished on the other side of the chair. Her hands, palms open, landed on the floor, pressed down and held. Maybe all she needed was the commonplace reassurance of something solid, or maybe she was seeking the bottom of the world. Now she was lying prone across Imhoff's lap, and he was regarding her with a complex gaze that looked like sorrowful amazement. Taking his sweet time, he pushed her skirt up, revealed four rows of lace on her ridiculous black panties. He slithered the panties down to just above her knees. "Yeah, I bet you been a real bad girl," he said.

"Fuck that shit," Cassandra said, "just do it, OK?"

It was twisted, John thought—to hear her voice and not be able to see her face.

Imhoff drew junk into the spike. "Easy," Lorraine said. "Cherry."

"Yeah, I know, baby. I know."

Imhoff wrote lightly on Cassandra's ass with the charged point. Then he lifted it away and waited.

"Fuck," Cassandra said. John could feel her losing it. "Jesus, man," she said.

Imhoff deliberately brought the point to rest lightly against Cassandra's bare skin. John saw her wince. Deliberately teasing her, Imhoff held the point motionless. She began to pant; John could see it in the sharp rise and fall of her shoulders. She shifted in Imhoff's lap, rolled from side to side, squirming. Her scissoring legs yanked the panties into tense stripes of shiny black bandage that bound her at the knee. John felt sick.

Imhoff pressed the point down. He was doing it so slowly John didn't think he could watch anymore. But he couldn't stop watching; it would be treasonous not to watch, not to suffer every moment of it with her. The spike penetrated Cassandra's skin. She inhaled sharply. Her legs in Lorraine's tacky plastic boots jerked upward. Imhoff continued to press down. He was still doing it so fucking *slowly*. John saw Cassandra's entire body go rigid, fists clenching, legs contracting. A quarter of the steel point disappeared into her, then half. She released a clogged-up cry like thick sludge down a drain, and Imhoff smiled.

John felt Cassandra's pain in his own groin. With half of the gleaming spike embedded in Cassandra's ass, Imhoff paused once again and waited. If he'd wanted to, John could have recited "Mary Had a Little Lamb" in the time he waited. Then, just as slowly as before, Imhoff pressed the point down. Eventually it was entirely buried, but that didn't seem to be good enough. Imhoff kept pressing until the tube that held the needle made a deep dimple in Cassandra's flesh.

She emitted a heartbreaking sound—the first hint of a kettle boiling before you're sure it's really boiling—and that must have been the signal Imhoff had been waiting for. He compressed the plunger, urging the junk through the needle deep into Cassandra's muscle. A single high-pitched infantile syllable was ripped out of her, immediately choked off. John was thankful he didn't have to see her face.

Imhoff finished. He looked directly at John and nodded—something like: well, son, you see how it's done—and, with a motion as delicate as a surgeon's, slipped the needle out.

Breathing—that is, trying to breathe—John watched the energy drain from Cassandra's body until she was lying, dribbled out, her hands spilled open, her legs gone to taffy, heels rolled out and toes pointing inward, limp as a dead cat. Imhoff slithered her panties up her thighs and stretched them into place. He tugged her tight skirt back down. He worked his arm under her waist and stood her up. For a moment she looked to John exactly like a life-sized doll someone was trying to arrange in an upright position. Imhoff obviously hadn't yet found the proper angle for her small floppy feet. Her knees began to flex, threatened to unfold her, but she magically came to life, extended a hand, placed it on Imhoff's shoulder. Her fluorescent pink mouth was hanging open, her eyes hazed into smudges of grey nothing. Tears had cut fine tracks down the makeup on her cheeks. "Aw, fuck," she murmured.

"You off, babe?" Imhoff asked her in his sad basset-hound voice.

"Yeah."

"You dig it?"

"Yeah . . . a muth . . . a muth . . ."

Imhoff levered himself to his feet, enfolded Cassandra in his arms, led her to the bed, and eased her onto it. "A mutha fuckin rush," Cassandra whispered.

"Jesus, Imhoff, you're an artist," Lorraine said.

Imhoff used the same point on Lorraine—tied off her arm with a belt and did her with no ceremony at all. "Ah," she said. Stepped across several feet of emptiness. To a chair. Sat in it.

"Want me to fix you?" Imhoff asked John.

John was too surprised to answer. He could see nothing on Imhoff's face but a distant avuncular kindness. "No thanks," he said. "Points make me . . . you know, kind of . . ."

"Have a snort," Imhoff said.

John did it the way he'd seen it done—took a pinch of the white powder between his thumb and index finger, held it to his nose, and inhaled. Laconically, almost immediately, behind the last wisps of grass, behind the last wisps of hash, he sank into a sea of fluffy gently undulating pearly grey cotton candy bliss.

17

OK, so maybe a week goes by and one afternoon I'm doing my usual scrape-your-brains-back-together routine—a coffee and a smoke and peering out the window to make sure that the US Marine Corps hasn't showed up on our front steps, and I see this little blue Mini pull up and park right behind the narks. And a chick gets out of it, and she's contemplating our house, and I say to Lorraine, "Hey, check the action."

Lorraine says, "Wow, she's sure in the wrong neighborhood." And the chick walks up the steps and knocks at our door. Lorraine and I exchange looks, like, OK, so what's coming down on us NOW?

I open the door, and I immediately detect the fact that the chick's something else. Like if you said "good looking," that don't even start. She's gorgeous—a tall skinny blond, definitely the cool and collected type. I can't get her number. She's obviously got class. It's not like she's all dressed up or anything—just jeans and a white blouse and a pair of those dead-eye silver sunglasses—and I'm still going, what the fuck? And she takes off her sunglasses, and she's got these absolutely HUGE blue eyes, and all of a sudden I know her. Of course I do. I've only spent like a million hours laying on that foamie at John's old place with her looking down at me. "Hey, Zoë," I say, "what's happening?"

And she says, "Oh. How did you . . . ?"

And I say, "Easy, honey bun, I've caught your act in the funny papers."

By that time, Cassandra's showed up. She comes bouncing down the stairs and dribbles to a stop.

Zoë lets out this big squeal and runs over and gives Cassandra a big hug and kisses her on both cheeks and launches into this speed rap, about how ugly the traffic was, and it took JUST FOREVER, and she had a little trouble finding our place, like it's not obvious how the streets run in Boston, and wow, are Boston drivers ever nuts, and, yeah, she probably should have called first but it was a spur-of-the moment thing, "I just said to Linda . . . at the agency, you know . . . 'I just can't take any more. Cancel all my bookings.'" And she absolutely HAD to be back Sunday night because she had an UTTERLY CRUSHING shoot bright and early Monday morning, some fancy-ass lingerie company, and she HAD NEVER BEEN SO FATIGUÉ IN HER ENTIRE VIE, which I thought was a riot, but all Cassandra did was stand there.

Well, I introduced myself, and I introduced Lorraine, and I did the welcome-to-Boston number, and finally Cassandra emerges from her zombie-like state and says, kind of grim, "Hey, Zo, great to see you. You bring anything with you? Tom, why don't you help her with her suitcase?"

So I bring her suitcase in for her, and I make damned sure that she locks her car, and then we go upstairs and go strolling into our bedroom. Since we'd got ourselves SIMPLIFIED, the décor in there is what Cassandra calls ZEN. Zoë does a couple blinks at that one, but she takes it all in stride, and she allows as how what she would like more than anything in the world right now is a long hot bath.

Once we've got Zoë stashed away in the bathroom, Cass about goes nuts on me. "Jesus, what the fuck is she doing here? Should have called first, my fucking ass. How did she get our address? I never gave her our address. She must have got it from the old man. Oh, great. Oh, fucking marvelous. She's up here checking me out. Jesus, she's a motherfucking SPY. She's been a little spy since she was four years old. SHOULD HAVE CALLED FIRST, YEAH FUCKING RIGHT. Jesus, Tommy, WHAT ARE WE GOING TO DO WITH HER?"

I say, "Hey, horse, what is this WE shit?" I just couldn't help it. Like we were still sleeping in the same bed—when she bothered to come home—but that was about it. I mean it was getting ridiculous.

Cassandra says, "Oh, Tommy, for Christ's sake, HELP ME. I know everything's fucked, man, but please, don't give me any grief right now. I REALLY NEED YOU."

Well, what could I say to that? So all of a sudden the world has become filled with problems, and they're MY problems. For starters—where is little sister going to sleep? There's three bedrooms in the Shooting Gallery—ours, and Garvin and Lorraine's, and the famous THIRD BEDROOM. We haven't checked it out lately, so we take a look.

There's empty pizza boxes and gnawed-on chicken bones and various other items that are difficult to identify but used to be edible once long ago, and a million cigarette butts, and four hundred million roaches, and like a dozen empty cough syrup bottles, and a weird assortment of clothes, including a shirt with lots of blood on one of the sleeves, and a whole bunch of filthy blankets. And if you've even been in a pet shop where nobody gives a shit, like where they've got puppies and kitties and birdies and monkeys and snakes all crammed into little bitty cages that nobody's bothered to clean for a while—that's what that place smells like.

We just back off and shut the door. "Tommy," Cassandra says, "we're living like pigs."

"Hey," I say, "that could be the name of a movie. You know, one of those foreign jobs. LIVE LIKE PIGS."

But she ain't up for the humor. We've got to contemplate every possible location where little sister might catch a few Zs. "How about John's?" Cass says—because he was still crashed at Pamela the Great's and he kept it real nice—but no, she says, "that would be AWKWARD," and shit, we wouldn't want that, would we? Goddamn, we can't have AWKWARD.

So we contemplate the two of us crashing in the living room with the skagheads and giving Zoë our room, and that's a fairly horrible contemplation. And we contemplate finding Zoë a good hotel, but that wouldn't be like, you know, hospitable. And the final result of all this contemplation is that Cass and Zoë will crash in the bed in our room, and I will crash in the camper. "So go get the camper," Cass says.

I hustle my ass six blocks over to get the camper, and I bring it back, and Cass zips down and rummages around in the big chest the skagheads never figured out how to crack open yet, and she gets out all these sheets and pillow cases and blankets left over from when she was doing DOMESTIC, and we make up our bed just as pretty as a picture, and we call up John because Zoë just ABSOLUTELY has to see him. He's kind of blown away, but he says, yeah, he'd be DELIGHTED to come out and have dinner with us, and Zoë says, "Should I change into something nice?"

And Cassandra says, "No, no, the way you are is just fine. DRESS DOWN."

Now we've got to figure out where we're going to catch the grub, and that leads us to another round of contemplation, and that requires a little weed. Zoë's not what you'd call a confirmed pothead, but she does take an itsy bitsy teensy weensy little toke every time the joint floats by her. "Maybe that Mafia place," Cass says, like the one Imhoff took her to, but Zoë says, "Pasta? Oh, God. I just inhale the steam, and I gain a pound. All I need's a steak and a salad. You must know HUNDREDS of places. Nothing chi-chi, just a NICE place."

Well, sure, we know HUNDREDS of places like that, you bet, especially with John being a heavy-duty no-exceptions vegetarian. Luckily Lorraine jumps in at this point. She knows the perfect NICE place. It's where they used to go and catch the grub when she was married to that asshole Carl. "Right downtown. Family-style. Real quiet."

We pick up John, and Zoë leaps out of the camper to do her squeal and kisses on the cheeks for him, and I know John could always use a pinch of weed so we do another J, and Zoë says, "Is there any time when you guys DON'T smoke?" and we get to Mama Whosiewhatsit's, and like Lorraine said, it's quiet and it's NICE.

To kick things off right, Zoë and John are having themselves big glasses of cold clear water. And Zoë orders up a filet mignon rare with a Caesar salad—the dressing on the side. And John orders up some corn bread—hold the butter—and a side of carrots and a side of broccoli and a plate of beans—no, not the BOSTON BAKED BEANS but some damn kind of beans associated with the death of no animals. But Cass and me have got the munchies, and we're already heavy into the import beer, and we decide to split the super-humungous family-sized barbequed ribs, so here's these two parakeets pecking away, and Cass and me are going at it like a couple of prime hogs.

Well, John has been just sitting there staring at Zoë with AWE AND AMAZEMENT. Like maybe he'd got so used to her up on his wall that the real thing was just too much for him. But Zoë's a nice girl—you could tell that—and she's doing her best, so she asks me what I do. God, it's been forever since anybody's asked me that. "I'm in the import and retail business," I tell her, and Cassandra gives this little snort. I put on my wow-am-I-ever-important voice, and I go, "I do mainly Mexican imports. I'm particularly favorable to products from the Michoacan region."

Zoë glances over at John's shirt. Since he turned into a skinny vegetarian, he's been impersonating a Mexican farm worker, and it fits him somehow. "Oh," she says, "they make some lovely things. And it's all IN right now. I don't know how many shoots I've done with the ethnic look. What do you import? Shirts? Skirts? Serapes?"

Cassandra just about loses it. And John says, "He's putting you on, Zo. He's a dope dealer."

And Zoë blushes. Like bright pink. And all of a sudden I can see why the photographer dudes must love her because her eyes just go FLASH, and it's the kind of thing when you see it, you think, shit, that girl ought to be in a magazine. She's going, "Oh, you guys are just so cool. You're just too cool for words," and she says to me, "They've been doing that to me ever since I was a kid. And I always fall for it. Every damn time. I never learn."

We had us a good yuck about that, and things started to loosen up, and Cass and Zoë swapped a few yarns about doing the sister act in the olden days, and then John all of a sudden emerges from his AWESTRUCK SILENCE and starts asking Zoë about the modeling biz, and one thing leads to another, and pretty soon we're having ourselves one hell of a good time. So we get the dinner stuffed down, and we decide to move the show over to John's place. Yep, that one's safe—a damned sight better bet than taking Zoë back to the Shooting Gallery.

We walk into John's, and Zoë goes bananas over THE DÉCOR. She's complimenting John on his EXQUISITE TASTE. Well, all of that EXQUISITE TASTE belongs to Pamela the Great, and I know that, and Cass knows that, and you better believe John knows that, but Zoë don't know that, and we're not about to tell her. And we do a little more smoke, and then the three of them go off on a nostalgia number straight back to West Virginia—like the Old Folks at Home, right?—and that gets us on through with zero disasters.

I don't know what Cassandra's problem was with her little sister. You'd expect a model from New York to be like . . . well, like a model from New York. But Zoë wasn't like that—anyhow, not after she mellowed out a bit—and it had been forever since I'd rapped with somebody as straight as her, and it felt good in a weird way, like stepping back into an old movie. We had us some exceedingly fine dope, and I started flashing on a whole bunch of things. Like how I hadn't really integrated myself back into civilian life—and that old movie, the one I'd just stepped back into, the one with people like Zoë in it, well, that's what you call CIVILIAN LIFE, and this weird scene where I'd been living in Boston was just more of THE WAR EFFORT.

We're sitting on the floor, and Cassandra's flopped back on me, like in the crook of my arm, and I'm thinking, hey, cupcake, ain't you laying it on a bit thick? Like the last I heard, you was telling me that all the men in the world should be shoving their pricks up drainpipes. But she was playing couple for her sister, and I was playing right along with her, and I got to thinking, hey, why the fuck AREN'T we a couple? Because I was getting that old feeling like when we first got together.

And that got me to thinking about Margaret Teresa Flaherty. You remember her? That's the chick I'm supposed to be leaving town with. Well, she was prettier than Cassandra, and she was better in bed than Cassandra—except if you count THE LAST TIME—and she was damned near as smart as Cassandra, but I never felt like I could be myself with her the way I was with Cassandra. There was, I don't know, just some kind of vibe with me and Cassandra that felt right, but with Terry . . . Like if I was really going back home with somebody, I figured Cassandra would get the joke about Hubbard, North Dakota, right away, but I didn't think Terry would ever get it. And just who the hell was Margaret Teresa Flaherty anyway? THE CATHOLIC CHURCH ON ACID, that's who she was. So, yeah, her show was highly entertaining, but it wasn't my show. And what about me and Cassandra? Well, you know, LOVE is a word you shouldn't be throwing around too easy, but I'm thinking, shit, why did THE LAST TIME have to be the last time?

SO ANYHOW, that took care of little sister, day one. And then her and Cass caught the Zs in our bed, and the next day we shoved Zoë in the camper and picked up John to ease the old social strain—like we wouldn't want things to be AWKWARD, would we?—and we drove all over hell and gone like we was motherfucking tour guides. Yep, that killed off many an hour, and we're back at the Shooting Gallery getting our act together for the evening and the phone decides to ring. Lorraine yells up at me, "Hey, Tom, it's for you."

That call was right on time, you might say. If you didn't know better, you'd think it was directed by one of those COSMIC FORCES. It's Lyons. "Guess who's dropped by to see me?" he says. "It's the chef himself."

"Oh, is that right?" I say. I'm pretty sure I'm talking over two tapped lines.

"Right as rain," he says, "and twice as lovely. Yeah, we're having us a fine time, my friend. I'd strongly suggest that you get your ass over here."

"Lyons," I say, "I can't make it. I'm with PEOPLE."

"Oh, you're with PEOPLE, are you? Jesus fuck, man, that's wonderful news. That's the best news I've heard yet, and I've heard plenty. You grab those PEOPLE and you get your ass over here, like prontissimo. The more the merrier, you dig? Yeah, we're having us a motherfucking PARTY. And Tommy? One never knows what weird shit might be going down in one's absence, do one? Yeah, man, YOU BETTER GET YOUR MOTHERFUCKING ASS OVER HERE."

My first thought was that Lyons could get bent, but my second thought was, hell, wait a minute, things over at Lyons' place could get fairly bizarre fairly fast—and I was Lyons' partner, wasn't I? And so it probably behooved me to attempt to impose my bit of sanity on the events as they were unfolding. So I lay it on Cassandra, "You and John do something with Zoë. I got to go see Lyons."

"Oh, for Christ's sake, Tommy, don't give me that shit."

"Look, babyshake, I don't want to go into the gory details, but I don't have a lot of choice in the matter."

So we bat it back and forth for a while, and she says, "Well, fuck, man, we'll ALL go over there."

"I don't think that's what's happening," I say. But I'm thinking, hey, you know that's not a bad idea. If there's a whole bunch of people at Lyons' place, they're WITNESSES, you dig? And that puts some kind of limit on the bizarre shit right off the top. But I can't figure out where Cassandra is at. "You must be putting me on," I say. "You want to take YOUR SISTER to Bobby Lyons' place?"

She gets this evil little glint in her eyes and she says, "Shit, man, she wants to see the scene in Boston? Well, ain't that the scene?"

———

"WHAT THE fuck are we doing here?" John said. He had backed himself into a far corner in this huge, brilliantly lit, baby-blue space-age kitchen—had just found himself there with his arms folded tightly across his chest, his hands pressed into his armpits. It was something you did if you were cold, but he was so stoned he couldn't tell if it was ordinary cold or only an evil head-trip cold.

"I don't know about you, old buddy," Tom was saying, still peering in the fridge, "but I'm just trying to catch the grub."

There were times, especially these days, when John shouldn't be smoking dope—certainly not this intense, no-nonsense Panamanian Red—but he'd been sucking at every passing joint like a dying man on an inhalator. He'd arrived there tonight, to this particular version of nowhere, apparently to play a bit role in some incomprehensible farce staged by Bob Lyons, and he loathed Bob Lyons. He wanted to be with Zoë, but he was still stuck in the kitchen, and it seemed he was going to remain stuck for just as long as Tom remained stuck. He walked over and stared into the fridge. Now they were both standing there like idiots, staring into the fridge. "Shit," Tom said. "The motherfucker usually treats his guests better than this."

"There's eggs."

"Fuck eggs. You got to cook the eggs."

John was unaccountably angry. "Jesus, man, you're hopeless." He grabbed the carton out of the fridge, pulled down an enormous blue bowl from the cupboard and began cracking eggs into it. "What the fuck's he doing with that gun?"

"Playing badass," Tom said.

"But he's talking like he's going to kill him."

"Fuck," Tom said.

John had lost count of the eggs, but it looked like plenty. He beat the hell out of them with a fork, found a frying pan easily enough, and even a bottle of safflower oil. "Fuck?" John said.

"OK, now listen up, old buddy, because I'm giving you the straight scoop. If he was going to kill him, would he do it with all of us watching him?"

John looked into Tom's toothy grin, saw that an answer was expected. Yup, if the straight-man didn't set you up, you couldn't do the next gag. "That wouldn't make any sense," John said.

"Well, sense is maybe just a fraction more than we should be asking for, but let's just say we got to put some limit on things, you dig?"

John had lost it again. Limit? Limit?— Oh, *cheese*, that's what he should be thinking about. John found a block of cheddar, neatly wrapped. Who did all the neat tidying up and putting away around here? No way it could be Lyons. Probably the silent girlfriend. She was in the living room, coloring in a coloring book.

Tom had been talking. What was he saying? "OK, before you get too sympathetic to innocent old Peter in there, let me tell you something about that miserable little prick. He burned Lyons good. Ripped him off and brought the fucking heat down on his ass. Ain't that one against the revolution?"

The oil was hot enough. John poured the eggs into the frying pan. He loved the sound of the hiss. He turned the heat down. "The thing you got to remember about Lyons," Tom was saying, "is he's a dealer. The main thing he wants is his bread back . . . well, as much of it as he can get anyway. And he's going to do what it takes . . . like by any means necessary, you dig?"

John grated cheese directly onto the cooking eggs. Saw a pepper grinder on a shelf, cranked that into the pan a few times. Saw the spice bottles, added some tarragon. He put the lid on. All that was required now was patience.

"You following everything I'm laying down so far?" Tom said. "Like what we're going to see is one hell of a good show. And when old Bobby Lyons gets done, it's going to be a cold fucking day in

July before Peter sells anybody out again. Yeah, most likely Lyons will scare him right out of the dope trade, which is just fine. Yeah, like afterwards Peter can go back home to mommy and daddy and be whatever it was they wanted him to be and have lots of war stories to tell his kids about his crazy days in Boston back in the bad old days. You getting the picture?"

"Yeah, I'm getting the picture." John flipped the omelet. Sometimes he was so good at dumb things like this that somebody should give him a medal.

"But another thing you might consider," Tom said. "The way things are coming down at the moment, maybe you ought to remove little sister from the premises before it gets any more hilarious."

LITTLE SISTER? Right. Every time he looked at her, he felt that the whole track inside had freed itself from its moorings, twisted back, curled around and slammed him. Her arrival into his life at this particular moment was either a grotesque karmic blunder or the last perfect crank of the kaleidoscope. Zoë was sitting as far away from the stereo speakers as she could get. The Rolling Stones couldn't have been louder if they'd been there in person. John sat down next to her. She made a gesture, cupping one ear, then shrugged, rolled her eyes: "Don't bother to say a thing. I can't possibly hear you."

He was still admiring her, not merely her clothes, but her *ensemble*—no other word would do. He was sure she'd be pleased if she knew it; she'd obviously dressed to be admired. He smiled back at her, hoping she'd read his message: "Despite all appearances to the contrary, everything here is cool. More than cool, it's just dandy."

Last night, she'd presented herself with a simplicity that was elegance itself—in sandals, jeans, and a crisp white blouse that looked as though it had been freshly ironed. Tonight, however, she'd changed into a look that he suspected was dearer to her heart—a chiffon top, pale russet, and another pair of jeans, tighter and sleeker, with butterflies embroidered on the back pockets. She was cinched at the waist by a broad belt that looked as though it had been slapped together from odds and ends of leather—black, scarlet, and a color the magazines would surely have called *mulberry*—studded with nailheads in a pattern that suggested that the craftsman who'd made it had been stoned to the eyeballs. Her purse matched her belt. It wasn't quite September yet, but she was wearing boots—not with extremely high heels by any means but higher than any self-respecting Movement woman would have worn—in a mulberry that matched the patches on her belt and purse, matched her lipstick. John had lost track of the fashion mags lately, and he hadn't been ready for mulberry lipstick. After years of white or the palest of pinks or nothing at all, it was almost mind-blowing.

Zoë herself was there too, somewhere—or at least he hoped she was—and he flashed on all the times when he and Zoë, in a previous incarnation, had sat at the back of her parents' living room, side by side, out of the way, watching the action go down and commenting on it under their breath like co-conspirators.

Tonight's show was well in progress. There were four hip types John didn't know—three chicks and a cat—taking up one wall. They seemed to be bit players or extras. Lyons' little girlfriend was lying on her stomach directly between the stereo speakers as though trying to transform herself into an extension of the sound equipment. A zillion colors of crayons were scattered all around her, and she never looked up from her drawing. She might get a line or two of dialogue later, but John doubted it. Cassandra, however, was obviously one of the principals; she'd settled against the opposite wall and looked like a cat holding itself in repose but more than ready should a mouse be so stupid as to amble by. And Lyons and Peter were still where they had been before, sitting close to each other on the couch. Tom had joined them there. He was eating the omelet John had made for him.

Zoë mimed another communication. Her spread palms said, "What are we doing here?" or "I don't get it." She aimed her fingers at him, then at herself, and finally—with a small wavy motion—at the door, asking him if he wanted to split.

He nodded, smiled. His shrug meant—or he hoped she would take it to mean—"Yeah, just as soon as there's a break in the action."

He'd taped iconic images of her to his walls for years, but he hadn't seen the real Zoë since she'd been sixteen. Her birthday was sometime in August, so she must have just turned twenty-one.

Everybody changes a whole hell of a lot between sixteen and twenty-one, and he certainly hadn't expected her to be the bubbly ingénue he remembered, but still— Well, OK, he liked this new person, and this new person seemed to like him, but he was a little in awe of her. Had she really transformed herself into the self-contained young lady she appeared to be? And God, she was lovely. He'd seen her in *Vogue*, in *Seventeen*, in the *Sunday New York Times*, so of course he'd expected her to be lovely, but he hadn't been ready for this—the living girl and not the image.

The Stones wound to an end; the tone arm lifted from the record, clearly signaling the opening of the next act. The silence was impossible. John's ears were ringing. And Peter's voice was too loud. "These *people*, man. I don't know anything about anything with all these fucking *people* here. Come on, Bob, you've got to be putting me on."

Lyons said in his silly high-pitched voice, "He thinks I'm putting him on. How do you like them green apples, Tommy? He thinks GIs are so dumb they can't get their asses over the toilet bowl."

With his mass of tangled hair, handlebar mustache, and leather vest, Bob Lyons looked more than ever like a warped incarnation of a Hollywood cowboy. John knew Peter slightly—had met him in the *Zygote* office when he'd fallen by to promote his band. He was the manager and sound man for Trackless Waste. He was sitting stiffly now, hands in his armpits, staring at Lyons, his head tilted forward—tipped, balanced. Peter had large brown eyes, something wistful about them, like a collie's.

Lyons laughed expansively, grinned around the room, and then, with no warning, slapped Peter across the face, slapped him with the hand holding the gun. Peter jerked back. Blood welled up from his lower lip. His eyes, John saw, were wet with tears.

And Zoë's eyes—intense blue flash—were checking out the entire set. Now she was looking down at her glossy fingernails. She wore clear polish—coats and coats of it.

"Peter." Lyons was talking softly, but John could hear every word. "Before this night's out, you and me are going to be tight. We're going to love each other like brothers. We're going to bare our hearts and our souls, man. We're going to let everything hang out there is to hang. We're going to get so tight, take a motherfucking crowbar to separate us. But there's a few changes you got to go through before we get there, you dig? Like one thing you've got to be clear on, man . . . I'd just as leave kill you as look at you. You know me, Peter. I was in Nam, right? I'm crazy, right? I was one of them dudes raining down death from the skies, right? I've killed more zips than a dog has fleas, right? And I wouldn't mind killing you."

"Give the man a break, Robert," Tom said quietly. "Raining down death from the skies? Jesus, you was in field maintenance the same as I was."

Lyons laughed, said in the silly cheery voice of a clown, "Susie, my sweet. I hate to interrupt your artwork, but could you please turn the record over?"

Without speaking, the girl rose and turned the record over. Sound smashed through the room. Peter's lips were moving. Zoë looked at John. He stared back at her. He couldn't move, couldn't do a damn thing. The rush of fear had swelled into such immensity that it had reversed itself. The assault on his eardrums, the fearful knots of tension between his shoulder blades, Zoë's eyes—all had more substance, more immediacy, than anything going on in that Pinter play on the other side of the room. He should do something. But what? Take Zoë by her lily-white hand and lead her out of there? But if he did that, he'd interrupt the action, call attention to Zoë and to himself. And besides, you couldn't interrupt a performance once it had started.

Lyons slapped Peter's face again—with the butt of the gun. Zoë winced, her body contracting in the chair, and then John saw Zoë trying to send a message to her sister—an SOS—but Cassandra couldn't see it. Cassandra was smoking one of Lyons' imported cigarettes and was reading, apparently with total absorption, the liner notes on one of his records.

Lyons yelled something, gestured. The girlfriend hit the button on the turntable and the tone arm lifted, allowing everyone to hear Peter's voice cracking badly. " . . . from me, Bob? Jesus Christ, what do you want? Do you want me to get down on my knees?"

"Well, that's an idea," Lyons said. He winked at Tom.

It was quiet. "You've got to believe me, man." Peter's face was wet. John couldn't tell if it was sweat or tears.

"Why don't you make us all some nice hot chocolate?" Lyons said to the girlfriend. "Now wouldn't that be nice?" He giggled. "Put a hit of almond extract in it."

Without speaking, the girl got up and walked into the kitchen.

"Bob, for Christ's sake, what do you want from me?"

"Now, Peter, all I want for us is to resume the love and affection that once made our hearts beat as one." Lyons turned to Tom. "I don't think he's getting the message. I don't think he realizes that he's teetering on that fine line."

"Maybe he needs another joint," Tom said.

"Now that's an idea." Lyons picked a joint from the pile Tom had been rolling, shoved it between Peter's lips. "Smoke, you cock-sucker," he said softly. "That's it, smoke it all up right down to the bitter end."

No sound in the room but the crackle of burning grass and paper, the sharp hissing of Peter's breath. Peter's eyes were blinking, streaming. "Good, good," Lyons said. "Now eat the roach. Waste not, want not."

"What are you trying to do to me, Bob?"

Lyons was speaking slowly in his normal voice. It was quite a deep voice. "Shit, man, we just having us a good time. Looking good and having us a good time, right? But you're not looking as good as you're going to be looking. Yeah, in a little while here, buddy, you're going to be sampling your own fine products. Start with four or five caps of that fine orange acid you cooked up. Then we're going to start hitting you every hour or so with that super-fine crystal you been cranking out. By the time the sun comes up, you're going to be looking real good, man. But dig it, maybe there's some way we can avoid that shit. For starters, why don't you tell me about the deal you did with those nasty men?"

"Bob, I didn't do any deal."

"I don't think he loves me anymore," Lyons said to Tom and lifted the muzzle of the revolver to Peter's ear. "My heart's motherfucking broken. You better move over, man. I don't want you to get splattered with the blood and bone." Tom slid off the couch, sat down next to Cassandra.

"John!" Zoë said in a small distinct whisper.

"Wait," he whispered back to her. Made a pushing gesture. *Don't move. Just sit there.*

"Lyons, for God's sake," Peter said. "What is it going to take for you to believe me? Do you want me to beg you? Is that what it is?"

"You might give it a try." He prodded Peter with the barrel of the gun. "That's it, motherfucker, down on your knees."

Peter sank to his knees. His entire body was shaking. "Bob, for Christ's sake."

"Just shut up for a minute, boy. Open your mouth."

Peter's face went slack with surprise. He opened his mouth. "That's it. Wider. Wider. Just like at the dentist's."

Lyons giggled. "That's it. Good boy. A littler wider yet." With a single explosive movement, Lyons jammed the gun into Peter's mouth. "See, Tom," he said, "now his whole fucking body will act as a silencer. There'll just be a dull thud."

"I ain't so sure of that, Robert," Tom said. "Not with a .44 Magnum."

The room filled up with the stench of human feces. Urine dribbled down from the front of Peter's pants, tears streamed from his eyes. The only sound in the room was the small scraping sound of gagging.

"Everybody sort of get back," Lyons said, grinning, "so you won't get splattered." Once again he drew back the hammer on the gun.

"I don't know, Bob," Tom said, "I think you ought to give him another chance."

"Oh, do you think so?"

"Yeah, I don't think he got the message before, but I think he's got it now."

"Oh, do you? Well shit, can't hurt to check." He extracted the gun from Peter's mouth.

Peter jumped up and ran for the door. Lyons was on his feet, crouching, swiveling, his right hand braced with his left. "Peter," he yelled.

Peter froze, his hand on the doorknob. "You think I wouldn't blow you away right here in my own apartment?" Lyons said. "You think I wouldn't blow you away in front of all these nice folks? Well, listen to me, man. You think I give a shit? I'm motherfucking nuts."

Peter released the doorknob, turned slowly, sank to his knees in front of the door, and began to cry. "I did it. I did it, I did it, I did it. I set you up. I made the fucking deal. Christ, Bob, don't kill me. I'll do anything you say, Bob. I'll give you the bread back. I spent some of it, but I'll give you all I've got. Please don't kill me, man. I don't want to die, man. Jesus, man, please. I don't want to die."

Lyons laughed, said to the room at large, "See, I told him we was going to be tight again. I can feel the love returning already." And then to Peter: "Go on in the bathroom and clean yourself up, man. You're disgusting."

Lyons scooted on his bottom down the length of the couch so he could aim his gun directly into the bathroom. "No, man. Just leave the door open so I can see you." He waved, blew a kiss. His voice had risen again into its absurd treble register. "This is the watch bird, watching you. Don't forget, man, *I can see you!*" He giggled.

"Will you please walk me to my car?" Zoë said to John. She gathered up her purse and stood up. John scrambled behind her. She strode purposefully across the room, past Tom and Cassandra, past Lyons. She didn't look at any of them.

"So pleased to meet you," Lyons squeaked. "Any sister of a friend of Tom's is a sister of a friend of mine. Goodnight, Raymond Lee, or whoever the hell you are tonight. Fall by any time, man. Always glad to catch your act. Yeah, John Dupre, there's always a little smoke here if you should care to fall by."

How did he know my name? Crashing, dope-twisted buildings of the city down around his ears—Jesus, John thought, how could Zoë walk that fast in heels? She stopped so abruptly he almost ran her down—saved herself with one hand slammed into his shoulder, then thrust her purse at him. A spattering disoriented instant before he understood what she wanted—he grabbed the purse. She pressed her hands onto the hood of a parked car, bent forward, her body contracting. Her ribcage, under the sheer blouse, heaved. Her hair swung around her face, hiding it. John heard the creaking of her leather belt. Her body was arching like a bow. She was gagging.

"Are you going to be sick?"

She walked away fast. He jogged several steps to catch up. He was still carrying her purse. "How could you all just sit there like that?" she said. "How could you just sit there and watch? How could you *do* that? Haven't you got any morals? What the hell is *wrong* with you?"

"It was . . . like a show, a performance . . . like guerilla theatre."

"Is that what you guys do for fun?"

If thoughts were things, his would have been breaking glass.

"God, I'm so stoned," she said. "I've never been so stoned in my entire life. The whole city looks ugly to me. Oh, what a grotty city! How could you just sit there like that? That was the most horrible thing I've ever seen in my entire life. It was *obscene*."

"That dude sold him out . . . Shit, Lyons got what he wanted. That was the end of the . . ."

"What is Cassandra *doing?*"

That was a question he certainly couldn't answer.

"I can't understand her. I just can't. She has more brains than . . . I just can't understand why she's living like this. I can't understand why any of you . . . You're all supposed to be smarter than me. Why don't you *act* smarter?"

There was her little blue Mini. She held out her hand for her purse. They got into the car. "Can I stay with you?" she said.

"Of course you can."

"Thanks. I'll be damned if I'll spend another night in that crappy crash pad." She pulled out like a teenage hot-rodder, burning rubber—melded into the crazy Boston traffic so quickly it stopped his breath. "Hey, Zo," he said, "are you driving too fast, or am I so stoned I can't tell?"

"I am driving too fast, but I don't care."

She pulled up in front of Pam's apartment. "Good memory," he said.

"It's not hard. It's just off Harvard Square." She didn't make any move to get out of the car.

He'd never thought that Zoë was the least bit like Cassandra. He'd seen Zoë angry before—had seen her stomp off in fine teenage snits, slamming doors behind her—but he'd never suspected that she was just as capable of fury as her sister. Her words were coming out now in short fiery bursts like the terse communications of a blast furnace.

"What are you guys doing? Why do you know somebody who even *owns* a gun? What is Cassandra doing? If it's so goddamn great to get a college degree, why didn't she do it? Why didn't she finish at Bennington? She could have done anything. A Playboy bunny, oh, my God, it's just . . . Dad was just . . . She broke his heart. Oh, I'm so unhappy. What on earth am I going to tell him? 'Oh, don't worry about her, Dad, she's living with a dope dealer. He's a perfectly nice guy.' Why is somebody calling me up, pretending he's from the Los Angeles Police Department? Was that some friend of hers playing a joke? Why was he calling *me?* I said, 'Come on, you jerk, you're not a cop,' and he hung up on me. What the hell was that all about? What the hell is she *doing?*"

ZOË HAD dutifully removed her boots at the door; now she was striding back and forth in Pam's apartment—all the way to the far wall, turn, SWISH, and then back. Maybe that's the way she walked on a runway—with that long rangy lope. Did she do runway modeling? It certainly wasn't the time to ask her.

"They're probably yucking it up right at this very minute," John was telling her. "'Oh, my God, Lyons,' Peter is saying, 'you scared the shit out of me, man. I really thought you were going to do it.' And Lyons is giggling. 'Yeah, man, I got you good.' And Lyons did get him good. He got what he wanted. The coin. That's what counts."

He couldn't tell if she was buying it or not. He certainly wouldn't have bought it. Maybe he could do better with the phone call. "A boyfriend," he said, laying it out just as fast as he could make it up. Yeah, one of these insecure possessive jealous types. Cassandra had broken his heart. He'd wanted to marry her. He was some kind of a weirdo—harmless, though. He'd been calling everybody she'd ever mentioned—friends, family, he didn't care. He'd even called John. "Yeah, he said he'd gone to school with Cassandra . . . if you could believe that. Like I wouldn't know everybody Cassandra had gone to school with?" Hey, he thought, that's not too bad. That one's totally plausible.

Zoë stopped pacing, fell into a chair. She was much taller than he remembered. "I should never smoke marijuana," she said. "Never, never, never. It gives me the weirdest thoughts and . . . Do you have anything *sweet?* . . . Oh, forget I said that. I didn't really say that . . . Do you think she'd come back to New York with me?"

Not on a bet, he thought, but he said, "I don't know. It's worth a try."

"I could get her work. She'd have to lose a few pounds, but that wouldn't be hard for her. Oh, I'm so worried about her."

He washed and cut up a peach, put it in a bowl, added several spoonfuls of yogurt and a fine drizzle of maple syrup. "Oh my God, a million calories," she said, but she took it.

Cranked and vibrating, still shorting out on the dope, he knew perfectly well that a dark immensity was sniffing at him, but he didn't want to deal with it yet. Later, he would deal with it—yeah, he'd deal with *all of it*. With Pamela and *The Critique*—Pamela who was almost certainly sleeping with Deb again. With the possibility of agents, whoever they were, poised and ready, one jump behind his ass. With the tapped phones, if they really were tapped, with his trashed apartment, and, yeah, it really had been trashed, and with every other wretched twist and turn of the real. With the image of that poor kid on his knees with a gun shoved down his throat. With the nasty puzzle of Bob Lyons, because if Lyons knew John's real name—well then, by Jesus, it was *long* past time to split, and, yeah, he would deal with it all *later*, damn it, because right now a girl from his hometown was sitting in a basket chair in his apartment, a girl he might even be able to say was a friend of his, so whatever was sniffing around out there could just go fuck itself. He would tune it out, shut it out. Zoë, he thought, please, for an hour at least, be the whole world for me.

"IF ALL I had to do was work in front of a camera, I'd think I'd died and gone to heaven." She was telling him because he'd asked her. "But there's all this other stuff in the industry . . . the money stuff, and . . . Oh, and everybody comes on to you constantly. That's the biggest pain. You can't just . . . 'Hey, baby, don't be so uptight.' Oh, God. You're surrounded by sleazeballs. You're just *drowning* in sleazeballs. Your agency's supposed to protect you from sleazeballs, but of course they never do. And even just . . . You have to be *dressed up* to go to look-sees. Oh, I'm so sick of 'Hey, blondie.' I never want to hear 'Hey, blondie' again in my life."

"I bet. But it looks good on you. I really dig you blond."

"Oh, do you? Thanks. I just went a shade lighter."

"Yeah, I remember. You were talking about it the last time I saw you. The summer just before I left."

"Really? That long ago? Yeah, I guess I was. The minute I went blond, I got a lot more work. You know what? I'm still doing teenage stuff . . . although not so much any more. It's getting harder. I'm competing with real teenagers, and some of those girls are . . . Whew. I can't get any thinner. I just can't do Twiggy. If I tried to get any thinner, I'd just make myself sick, and . . . Oh, I can't stop thinking about that poor boy. If I close my eyes, I can still see him. God, that was sickening. That was just horrible. Are you sure he's all right?"

"Yeah, he's all right. Believe me, Zo, it was just a big show, a performance . . . Yeah, that Lyons is a fucking asshole."

"What a horrible man. I wish I could believe you. Oh, my God, it sure looked real to me."

Her eyes clouded over. She turned away, stared at the wall. "So, I don't know . . . Yeah, it's . . . I was about to say, 'It's a job,' but that's just me being . . . It's more than a job. Of course it is. I'm really glad I did it. The industry's been good to me, but . . . Oh, but they want you brainless." She drew a circle in front of her forehead. "Nothing. That's what everybody expects. I've learned to keep my little mouth shut.

"And then there's all these irritating dumb stupid little things. Like I really had no business driving up here this weekend. It was crazy. If I hadn't been so worried . . . I have a shoot on Monday at the crack of dawn. Why do they do that? If I break a nail before then, I'm one dead pussycat. It's a crazy way to live, but that's what I'm paid for, and . . . You know, sometimes I make tons of money. Like just tons of it. But it's never dependable. Weeks go by when I don't make a cent . . . How about you? What are you doing?"

"I keep trying to figure that one out."

"Cassandra said you really miss your girlfriend."

"Oh, yeah, I do."

"What's she like?"

What? he thought. In twenty words or less? He picked up the picture of Pamela from his desk and handed it to her. "She still sort of looks like this . . . if you can just imagine her, you know, grown up."

"Oh, wow, she's a real doll. Cassandra said she was a dancer."

"Yeah, years ago."

"Cassandra said you were androgynous together."

"Oh, she did, did she?"

"Yeah. She gave me your article. She said it was far out, like it blew her mind. I started it, but . . . I couldn't really concentrate. I'll read it carefully when I get home."

"You don't have to read it." That didn't sound right. He didn't want to come off as just another asshole who expected her to have zero between her ears—but he was embarrassed, prickly with it. "Like you can read it if you want. It's not a big deal."

"Oh, I want to read everything you write . . . Androgyny's big this season."

He wasn't sure he'd heard her right. "What? You're putting me on."

"Oh, no. It's really big. Especially in teenwear. *I've* even done a shoot . . . like they put me in these big yellow lace-up hunting boots . . . boys' size 6. And a huge watch with a thick strap, and baggy jeans and a boy's shirt, and I did all these tomboy poses. Not at all what I usually do, but it was fun."

"Wait a minute. Like they actually called it *androgyny*? Like they used *the word*? Like they really knew what they were doing?"

"Oh, yeah. I've heard it called *androgyny* . . . although usually what you hear is *unisex*," and in a bright now-I-am-quoting voice,

"'This season boys will be dressing like girls who dress like boys, and girls will be dressing like boys who dress like girls . . . ' That was in some magazine . . . *Ingenue* maybe. I know what they're getting at, but they didn't quite get it right. I wouldn't want to be a girl who dressed like a boy dressed like a girl. Most of the boys *I* know who dress like girls wear five-inch heels and rhinestones."

He was having trouble getting his mind wrapped around this one. Well, if the purpose of theory is to present a correct analysis of the present historical moment, maybe he and Pam had genuinely been in touch with the Zeitgeist. "Come on, Zo," he said. "You're telling me that this is actually a movement in fashion right now?"

"Oh, yeah. I go to all these receptions and openings and like . . . It's part of my job. I have to show up . . . be *seen,* you know. And it's fun too. You get to see what everybody's wearing, and . . . You should see some of the boys. From across the room you'd think they were girls. I saw a boy in lace harem pants. That was kind of like the . . . But you can go too far with it. I saw a spread somewhere. I think it was in a British magazine. Little boys in kilts dressed like their big sisters. I mean exactly, even the patent leather shoes. It was cute, I suppose, but I thought it was . . . un petit fey. Those poor little boys probably wanted to shoot themselves."

How could he have been so out of it that he hadn't noticed something going down in *fashion?* He and Pam must have been living in a sealed bubble. But *androgyny?* Somewhere out there on the cutting edge of fashion, maybe, but aimed at the mainstream? Jesus, that was fast. The Spectacle worked just the way Pam had always said it did. The bastards would pick up *anything* and sell it back. Nothing was private. Nothing was allowed to exist outside the Spectacle; it absorbed everything into itself. As Snyder said, it created "hungry ghosts"—people with gargantuan appetites and throats the size of needles. The images of Zoë he'd taped to his walls for years—as lovely as they'd been—were empty reflections glittering back from the Spectacle. He'd allowed the human relationship he'd once had with her to be mediated by those images, but he'd be damned if he'd allow those images to get in the way any longer. New York model? Hell, she was a nice girl from Raysburg. She had a West Virginia accent the same as he did—exactly the same, stamped by the upper Ohio valley. He'd kissed her under the mistletoe, taken her picture, listened to her chatter about her hopes and dreams and boyfriends and clothes. Sometimes he'd even told her what was in his heart.

IT WAS after four, and they were still talking. He wasn't even close to stopping, and she didn't seem to be either. The amorphous horror sniffing around the apartment was still out there—a repulsive hum in the background—and he was sure that Zoë could sense it as well as he could, but, just as he'd done, she seemed to have bracketed it off. She hadn't mentioned the really big show at Lyons' place for hours.

"Oh wow," she was saying, "hemlines. Everybody *knows* you've got to cover your knees, the question is, how far?"

It wasn't the grass now—that had worn off a long time ago, and she hadn't wanted to smoke any more—it was his own warped head, but he was following out a side strand through the millions of twists and complications. It had started with remembering what Cassandra had always said about her little sister, "There's not an ounce of X in her"—that indefinable quality that marked both him and Cassandra, set them apart, made them different. Cassandra had meant it as a put-down, but now he saw it as a singleness, a wholeness—not a bad thing at all. Zoë was not double, or multiple, as he and Cassandra were—as Pam was. And then there was something else.

"The best place for me is just below the knee. But when I go midcalf, it changes the line and I've got to wear heels. Some of the fall shoes are really high again . . ."

If he was girl-identified as Pam said he was, then Zoë was the girl he was identified with. She was a grown-up incarnation of those little girls who'd been his playmates when he'd been a child—Cindy and Nancy. When he was with Zoë, he felt exactly the way he'd felt playing dolls and dressup with the girls at seven—that he was, for once and wonderfully, the right person in the right place. There had to be some wholeness in that—some way out.

"I'm not sorry to see the end of the mini, but all the stuff I love, like anything constructed, anything tailored . . . it's just *out* right now. Everything's flowy and soft."

"Everything goes in cycles," he said. "Tailored and constructed will come back. Those classic looks always come back . . . Hey, thanks for sending me that issue of *Vogue*. And the tear-sheets and your head shot. I really appreciated that. I should have called you or something. I'm sorry."

"Oh. Did you like them? I thought you might be interested in my career."

"I am. I'll always be interested in your career. I loved seeing you in *Vogue* . . . Do you realize we haven't talked to each other in five years?"

The personal is the way out, he thought. Just as Pam had always said—the subjective. All the things he and Zoë had shared. "Remember your go-go boots?" he said—and the vinyl skirt she'd made, knocking it off from the cover of *Seventeen*, and the photo shoots, and the nights they'd sat on the glider on her parents' front porch.

"I thought Cassandra was really mean to you," she said, "and you were . . ."

"Yeah, really fat."

"I wasn't going to say that. I knew you'd be all right once you sorted yourself out. But you went around like . . . I don't know. With your sad thoughts and your German poetry."

Amazing. "Did I talk about German poetry?"

"Yeah, you did. With Cassandra. Not with me. You thought I was a pinhead."

"No, I didn't. I just didn't think you'd want to hear a big lecture about it . . . Yeah, Rilke, my God. After all these years, I still remember a lot of . . . Nothing useful, you know? Like I couldn't go to Germany and say, 'Where's the can?' or 'Please pass the schnitzel,' but I could say, 'Whoever's alone now is going to stay alone . . . for a long time to come.'" What a great example to come up with, he thought. Yeah, that was one hell of a fine example.

"So how do you say it?"

"What? You want it in German? . . . *Wer jetzt allein ist wird es lange bleiben.*"

"Wow. You really do remember."

"Of course I remember. I even remember the one I always

associated with you." Woops, he thought. Mistake.

"With *me?* What one?" She looked as excited as a little kid.

"No, I'm not really sure . . ."

"Yes, you are. I know you are. Come on. Tell me."

"*Du im Voraus vorlorne Geliebte, Nimmergekommene . . .*"

"Come on, John. Don't tease me. What's it *mean?*"

It was a poem he knew so well he never bothered to translate it into English in his mind. He couldn't see any reason why he shouldn't tell her what it meant. It was a perfect poem—written in words that didn't lie. "You're lost already . . ." he began, saw the next inevitable word as "beloved," knew he shouldn't say that one, censored it. But the rest of it was going to be all right.

Looking away from her, concentrating, he spooled through the German, turning it into his own personal English: "You're lost already. You're never going to get here. I don't even know what songs you like. I don't look for you anymore, don't think I'm going to find you somewhere in the future. All the huge images in me . . . distant landscapes, cities and towers and bridges and all those weird twists in the road . . . and that place where the gods are still living . . . It all rises up to mean I'm *never* going to find you. Ah, you were the garden. I saw you with such hope . . ."

More than surprised—he was struck, stopped. He was choked with tears. How embarrassing. He hoped she hadn't noticed. He turned to look at her. He couldn't read anything from her expression, but, oh, Lord, she had beautiful eyes.

"Oh, I should *read* more," she said. "It's just that I'm so damned busy."

She stood up, walked into the kitchen. "I've never been much of a reader, I'm afraid. Could you put on some water for tea?"

"Sure."

"Did you really see me with hope?"

"Yeah, I did."

"I'm glad. I wanted to give you hope, and . . . You gave me hope too. You were the only one who believed in me."

He felt as though they were balanced on something fragile, something infinitely delicate. "I can *tell you* what songs I like," she said.

"OK, tell me."

"I like 'Angel of the Morning.' I adore it. And I like 'Sunshine Superman' and 'Crimson and Clover.' And I like one by the Mamas and the Papas. Can you guess which one?"

He knew immediately. "'Coming to the Canyon.'"

"Right," she said, laughing. "I was one of those young girls coming to the canyon. I thought of that whenever I was schlepping my book around town."

"And I'll bet you like Melanie."

"See, you know what songs I like after all. I adore Melanie. 'Candles in the Rain.'"

The doorbell rang, and it took him a moment to identify it—that bell note, that spaceship *bong*. He checked his watch. It was just after six. "Yeah?" he said into the speaker.

"Hey, hero."

"It's your sister," he said to Zoë.

"Oh, piss."

He ran down the stairs, jerked the door open. "Jesus, Cass, your timing is . . ."

"Fuck that shit, man, this is the only time I've got." Instead of coming in, Cassandra grabbed him, hauled him through the door and out onto the front steps. The door swung shut, and the lock clicked. He felt an icy blast coming off her.

He took both of her hands. They were wet and cold. He could feel her shaking. "He blew him away," she said.

"*What?* Lyons?"

"Yeah, Lyons. Yeah, sure, motherfucking Lyons. He blew that kid away."

"Jesus, Cass, don't fuck with my head."

"Fuck with your head? Oh, Jesus. It's true, man. He really did it. I'm fucking scared, man. I'm just scared all the time now. It's like this knot in my chest that won't go away."

They both glanced toward the closed door. They had instantly become co-conspirators. They were working against time. "She's my sister and I want her out of here. I mean like now. Like out of Boston. I want her motherfucking *gone*."

"Yeah," he said.

"Shit," she said, "we got into Lyons' car, that fucking Lincoln . . . Tommy and me and that dippy little chick in the back. The kid up front with Lyons. And you know that shit he'd been saying? 'I should take you down to Roxbury and blow you away in an alley so the pigs will think the niggers did it.' Well, that's exactly what he did. He pulled up at the end of this motherfucking alley, tight, with the car in tight, so Peter would just have one way to go. Like it was down the alley or nowhere, and he said, 'OK, motherfucker, make your break.'

"I didn't think he was going to do it. Tommy didn't either. I mean, honest to God, neither one of us thought he was going to do it. And the kid just sat there. Lyons reached across him, and opened the door, and he said it again, 'Make your break, motherfucker,' and Peter just sat there like he was frozen. He was crying, man. It was fucking pathetic. Lyons says, 'Hey, man, you know what's on the other side of death? Nothing. Nothing at all. It's the big fat zip.' And Peter's just crying. Lyons says, 'Come on, asshole, I want to see you stepping right along. You got a fighting chance here. Fair's fair, right? I'll give you to the count of ten, and then I'm going to snuff you.' He starts counting. He gets to . . . I don't know, two or three, and all of a sudden Peter jumps up like a rabbit takes off down that alley just running like a son of a bitch.

"And Lyons blew him away. Four shots. I counted them. I think he hit him with all four, but I don't know for sure. Shit, he didn't even give the poor bastard his count of ten."

18

SO WHAT happened is that Cassandra and I sat in the back of the car like bumps on a log and watched Bob Lyons kill a man. I always knew he was nuts, right? And I knew he was cranked on crystal, right? But I thought all he was only going to do was the exact same thing I would have done under the circumstances—scare the bejesus out of Peter and try to get some of his bread back. And RIGHT UP TO THE VERY MOMENT when Peter was running up that alley, I'd been thinking, well shit, Lyons, you're really doing it up right this time, yeah, you've really put that kid through some changes. But then Lyons is pointing that gun out the open door of the car, and holding down his right hand with his left so the recoil won't haul him off target, and blazing away, and from that little glimpse I got of it, those goddamned Magnum slugs tore Peter to shit. The sound of that fucking cannon going off is incredible. Lyons looks at me and giggles. I swear to God, he giggles. And he says in that high squeaky voice, "Oh, WOW, Tommy, WHAT A RUSH!" and he throws the gun down on the floor of the car, reaches over and slams the door, puts it in gear, and away we go.

Cassandra and I don't say a word. And Susie—yeah, she was there to see it too—well, she ain't said a word recently and she's not about to start now. And what the hell was there to say? He's just brought us along to SEE IT, right? He whips us back over to his place where I'd parked the camper, and we get out, and he says, "Well, Tommy, you dumb fuck, catch you in a day or two," and he slaps Susie on the ass to get her moving forward and walks away leaving Cassandra and me standing there on the sidewalk looking at each other.

Cass says, "We're accessories, aren't we?"

"Homicide law is not something I'm checked out on. But, yeah, I guess we are."

"I didn't think he was going to do it."

"Yeah, me neither."

"He's really crazy, isn't he?"

"Hasn't had a sane moment recently."

And we both just stand there. "Now what?" she says.

"Fuck if I know."

So we go back to the Shooting Gallery. Well, there's one thing to be said for the war effort—you learn to grab your Zs when you can. So after staring at the ceiling for awhile, I finally drift off. When I achieve consciousness again, Cassandra's gone, and that gives me that old iron-in-the-guts feeling. I go downstairs and make a pot of coffee, and I look out the window and detect the fact that the van's gone. Oh, Jesus, I'm thinking, where's she headed? Back to West Virginia? I just hope to God she can drive.

She turns up about an hour later. She walks in and hands me the keys. "Sorry," she says. "I didn't think you'd mind. I just wanted to make sure Zoë got her ass out of town." And she goes up to our room and starts stuffing her shit in her suitcase. "You going someplace?" I say.

"I think I got the message, Tommy. Took me a while, but it's finally sunk in. I'm going to go crash with Imhoff." That just blows my mind. Imhoff? That's motherfucking ridiculous. I tell her it's HER ass she should be getting out of town. I'm heading back to Hubbard, does she want to come with me? She says, "Thanks, man. That's nice of you, but that's not what's happening."

I say, "You are fucking nuts."

She says, "Yeah, that's probably true, but it's my life, isn't it?"

"But Imhoff? Jesus. What the fuck are you thinking?"

"In a crazy kind of way, he feels safe to me," she says.

Well, that just sounded totally bananas to me, and we kicked it around for a while, but we were both of us still kind of in shock, you know what I mean? Finally she says, "Are you going to take me to Imhoff's or am I going to have to take a cab?"

I say, "Fuck you, bitch. Take a cab," but eventually I gave in and drove her over there.

I wasn't thinking straight. All I knew is I had to keep in motion, so I kept on going straight to Terry's. Like I'd made a deal with her—well, sort of made a deal. Anyhow, I thought MAYBE I'd made a deal. I walk in the door, and the first thing she says to me is, "Ethan's back."

Yeah, I could see his shit laying around. "Where's he now?"

She shrugs. "I'd be the last to know."

So I lay it on her—"OK, sweet stuff, this is the HOUR OF DECISION. A few hairy things have been coming down lately, and I'm moving on. Like the song says, the sun ain't going to set on me. You coming with me?"

"Oh, fuck." She falls onto a chair. I fall onto a chair. "Shit," she says, "what about Cassandra?"

"That's been over a long time. You know that. I told you that."

We sit there awhile. Eventually I say, "Look, honey, I'm kind of running on a tight schedule."

She says, "Give me a couple hours. I'll meet you at your place."

Well, it was more than a couple hours. She calls me up that night and tells me things have got kind of complicated on her and she'll be over THE NEXT DAY.

Maybe junkies have a sixth sense for heat, I don't know, or maybe it was THE COSMIC FORCES. I was getting just as paranoid as John—like, you know, anything could mean anything. But remember before how the word went out that our place was where IT WAS HAPPENING? Well, now the word went out that our place was DEFINITELY NOT COOL, and then they were all gone, just that quick—Garvin and Lorraine and every other lame weirdo who'd been crashing there. Fuck, it was OMINOUS. The narks weren't parked across the street anymore, and—this is crazy—I wished they were. I kept looking out the window, waiting for them to turn up, but they never did.

So eventually Terry arrives. She hasn't got her shit with her. Like she ain't about to leave yet, she's got to TALK ABOUT IT. We get a quick fuck in, and then we TALK ABOUT IT. Can she get a job out there? What kind of job am I going to get? You can't really deal dope in rural North Dakota, can you? Do we have a place to stay? What the fuck did I mean, WITH MY PARENTS? What kind of set-up was that, man? Didn't that seem kind of off-the-wall? What were they going to think, me turning up with this weird girl from Boston? And on and on and on we go. Eventually I say, "Hey, Terry, just remain with Ethan, OK? He may be an asshole, but at least he's your asshole."

"It was an illusion," she says, "the whole thing with Ethan."

I'm trying to be patient with this shit. "Look, babyshake, I don't give a shit if it was illusion or not illusion. YOU'VE JUST GOT TO DECIDE ONE WAY OR THE OTHER."

Ethan's gone back to New Hampshire. She's supposed to join him in a day or two. They've given notice on their apartment. Yeah, they're moving out for good, and she just can't do it. No fucking way. She told Ethan OVER AND OVER AGAIN that she wants to keep the apartment, like maintain a base in the city, but he ain't hearing it. "Great," I say. "It's a SIGN from the COSMIC FORCES. Get in the fucking camper, and let's make our break."

No, we can't do that. We ain't done TALKING ABOUT IT. Things have got to be CLEAR IN HER HEAD. So more time goes by while we're TALKING ABOUT IT. Then one night it's like, I don't know, maybe four in the morning, and Terry and me are asleep at the Shooting Gallery. Like I wasn't about to crash at Ethan's place. But anyhow, it's the dead of night, and I wake up the minute I hear the car door slam out front, and I'm laying there in the dark listening to the footsteps come banging up our front steps. Shit, I'm thinking, it's Ethan. The bitch has been lying to me, and he's not in New Hampshire after all. Now why the fuck didn't I fix the lock on the front door? But one thing for sure, he's not going to catch me like a sitting duck in bed with Terry. So I jump straight out of bed in one leap and land on all fours in the middle of the floor, and that wakes Terry up and she says, "Tom? What's happening? What's happening?" And I go, "Shhhh!" because it's obvious what's happening if you listen.

The footsteps are banging right up the stairs bigger than hell, and I swear my whole body is tingling and all the hairs on the back of my neck are standing straight up. I grab a chair so if he's got some kind of weapon, I can bash his brains out. Then I hear this idiotic voice talking away, "Hey, Tommy? You up here, man? Ready or not, here I come." And WHAM, right through the door, and right into the middle of the room, walking full tilt like he's planning on making New York by morning, it's Lyons.

Then, FLASH, the ceiling light is on and I'm so cranked I gobble up the scene with my eyeballs in about two seconds flat. There's Terry, naked as a jaybird, and she's just flicked the light on, and she's grabbed a dress off the floor and she's holding it in one hand, and she's aimed out the door. Like before you could say boo she'd be gone, right behind Lyons' back, and down the stairs. But she sees who it is, and she's frozen. I guess she was expecting Ethan too. And there I am on the other side of the room, just as naked as she is, and I'm holding the chair all set to catch him on the side of the head. And Lyons is dressed up in a suit and tie, and he's carrying an attaché case in one hand, and he drops it on the floor, like immediately. Across his other hand he's got a raincoat draped, and he whips around so that his hand is pointed at my stomach. He's just laughing and talking away—"Shit, Tommy, hope I didn't interrupt you or anything like that, hee, hee, hee! I would have called first, but I didn't really have time. Funniest goddamn little things just keep happening to me these days. What the hell you doing swinging chairs in the middle of the night, Tommy?"

"Lyons," I say, "you don't know how close you came to getting your head staved in." And I put the chair down.

Lyons makes a shrugging motion so the raincoat falls on the floor, and there's that .44 Magnum pointed at my stomach. "Good thing you got good reflexes, Tommy," he says, "because I got good reflexes, if you know what I mean."

I hear a gasp from Terry. He turns to her, still giggling, and she's nailed to the spot, the dress in her hand kind of useless trailing on the floor, and she's staring at him. She's never laid eyes on Lyons before, and God knows who she thinks he is. He uncocks that fucking cannon and lays it down on the raincoat and spreads his hands, saying to her, "You can get back in bed, honeybun. Me and Tom's asshole buddies from way back."

"Who the fuck you think you are, man?" I say to him. "Wyatt Earp?"

"Didn't know who was going to be in here," he says. "Shit, ANYBODY could have been in here. Well, Tommy boy, where should I put this? In the back of the closet all right?"

"Put what?"

He jerks his head at the attaché case. It's exactly like the one those two dudes were carrying—you know, the cops or whoever the fuck they were coming out of his apartment.

"What's happening, Bob?" I say.

"Oh well, man, you know how it is, what with the this and the that, if you follow me. More than likely I'll call you in a day or two and tell you where to take it. But if I don't, then I guess you'd better go stick it in a bus-terminal locker or some damn thing. Maybe you could give it to your BANKER to keep for you," and he laughs like he's just said the funniest thing in the world.

"Jesus fucking Christ," I say.

"Yeah, man, anywhere, man. It'll be cool for a while. Don't sweat the small stuff, right? Funniest damn things keep happening to me. That little bitch sold me out. Shit, who can you trust these days?" He goes off laughing again.

"What little bitch?" I say.

"Susie. Yeah, man, she's singing grand opera. Yeah, she's sung her an aria or two by now and she's working her way up to the grand finale. So the long and the short of it, my friend, is we ain't looking too good at the moment."

He pats me on the cheek and says, "I love you like a brother." He picks up his gun and drapes his raincoat over it. Terry's still standing by the door, frozen. As he goes by her, he pats her on the pussy. "Nice," he says, "very nice." He winks at me and goes trotting off down the stairs. We hear his car door slam and we hear him drive away.

"Who the fuck was that?" Terry says.

"Oh Jesus. His name's Bob Lyons."

"What's in that goddamned thing?"

"You think I know?"

"What did you take it for?"

"What the shit is this, twenty questions?"

So we go ring-around-the-rosy with that one for a while, and then she says, "Fuck, Tom, this is just too weird. I can't deal with this shit. You never told me you were into THIS KIND OF WEIRD SHIT. What else you been LYING TO ME ABOUT? Fuck you, man, take me home."

So right in the middle of the night I drive her back to her place. I don't know if Ethan's there or not, and I don't care.

What's going down now? I'd figured Susie for a doormat, but maybe I'd figured her wrong. I couldn't help thinking, hey, Susie, good for you. But if she's singing some interesting songs, just what would those songs be about? "Yeah, there were four of us in the car when he shot that dude. There was Bob and me and that tall guy named Tom . . . No, I don't know his last name, but he's got a big mop of fuzzy hair. I think he and Bob did a lot of deals together. They used to go in the bedroom and shut the door and rap for hours, man. Bob fronted him a lot of grass. And there was Tom's girlfriend in the car. She's got a weird name . . . Oh, yeah, it's CASSANDRA."

Was I just being paranoid? Like just how much could a terrified fucked-up little teenage speed freak remember? But maybe Lyons would catch up to her, who knows? And that might mean another body in Roxbury. But he wouldn't do THAT, would he? Oh, yeah, I'm thinking, sure he would.

So eventually the sun comes up the way it tends to do once a day, and I call up Terry. God knows why, but I figured I owed her that much. The phone rings a few times and Ethan answers. I put on this voice like nothing could possibly be wrong with anything anywhere ever, and I say, "Hey, old buddy, what's happening?"

There's this long pause. Then he goes, "Tom. Yeah. Shit. But it's OK, man. Yeah, it's OK. I'm glad you called. Yeah. Real glad. That's good. Like you and me got some heavy rapping to do, man."

I'm thinking, oh, fuck, she's told him. I say, "Oh, yeah? Sounds good to me. Why don't I fall by tonight?"

Sounds good to him too, he says, and I hang up and I'm thinking, yeah, Ethan, right. I'm going to rap with you about Terry? What do you think I am, fucking nuts?

I'M STILL trying to figure out WHAT IT ALL MEANS. For starters, how did Lyons KNOW that Susie was singing grand opera? Unless he was just fucking with my head or it was all fantasyland shit. Well, let's just say she really did make her break—how did she do it? Chances are pretty good she didn't say, "Hey, Bob, it's been groovy, but I'm splitting now. Oh, and by the way, I'm headed for the nearest police station." Nope, the way you leave a guy like Lyons is you go out for a can of beans and you don't bother to come back. So who told him she went to the cops? Most likely a cop told him. Why? Well, here's one way it could have gone down. He gets picked up for something, but they don't hold him, and when he's walking out the door, they say, "We're going to be seeing you again real soon, Bob. Your chickie is singing like a canary." And then they watch him to see where he goes. That one did not fill me with joy.

OK, here's another one. He's got some arrangement with some cops somewhere, and they help him to maintain his ASININE business and he feeds them information and maybe even some coin—which would explain a lot of things. And that one filled me with even less joy than the first one.

Well, I got to thinking about Cassandra. Like maybe Terry had been messing up my mind, but now she was out of the picture, so maybe I could think straight again. And maybe Cassandra could think straight again too. And, yeah, I wanted her to decide to stick with me, but that's not what mattered. What mattered was, I had to get her ass out of there one way or another. I loaded all my shit into the camper and I drove over to Imhoff's. Guess what? Nobody's home.

I kill time—driving around, catching a meal, having a smoke— and I keep checking back at Imhoff's. It looks like a lost cause, but once I've got an idea in my head, it's hard for me to shake it. It's after midnight by then, and I'm parked right across the street when Imhoff pulls up in his old junk Chevy. He and Cass get out, and she's wearing Lorraine's clothes.

I'm out of the camper lickety-split, cutting them off at the pass, and they freak right out. Like why is this weird sinister asshole suddenly springing out of the darkness and WHAT DOES HE WANT? "I just want to rap with you a minute," I say to her.

"So rap," Imhoff says, and he makes this disgusted little motion at me, like come on in. I don't want to go into his place. It's the last thing I want to do. "Suit yourself," he says, and he goes inside and leaves me and Cass out there on the street.

"Oh, Tommy, what the fuck you doing?" Cass says. "You scared the shit out of us. This is pathetic."

"Hey, babe," I say, "I'm not trying to run your life, but there's some things you ought to know about." So I lay it on her about Susie and the cops.

"Look," she says, "do you think the cops are going to bust their asses over some freaked-out little chick? Come on, man, the world is drowning in freaked-out little chicks, and the thing about cops . . . It's not that they're stupid. Well, some of them are. But the main thing about cops is they don't have the time. Like time is money, you heard that one? And life may be long, but the coin is short. So beyond a certain point, they just don't give a shit."

"About homicide they give a shit."

"About another drug deal gone rank, they don't give a shit. And anyhow, I'm . . . Look, man, Imhoff's been around forever and he's still here. He's a survivor. And safety's relative, right? But some places are safer than others, and I'm not doing too bad right now. I'm just part of Imhoff's scene. I'm like invisible, man."

Invisible? Yeah, right. Standing there under a street light in Lorraine's plastic miniskirt and Lorraine's plastic boots. Yeah, and anybody who deals as much smack as Imhoff is bound to get busted eventually. "I'll take you anywhere you want to go," I say. "You name it, and we're gone."

"Hey, old buddy," she says, "I love you too, but you're making this messy when it should be clean."

"How about West Virginia?"

"Oh, yeah, that's a good one. Hi, Mom, hi, Dad, SURPRISE. It's me, your fucked-up daughter. You know, the SMART one."

"Fuck that shit, Cassandra. We're talking serious now. Why the hell not West Virginia? We could be there tomorrow."

All of a sudden she's yelling at me. "My parents? I'm going home AND FUCK UP MY PARENTS? You just don't get it, do you? I couldn't do that to my parents. I'm bad news, man. I'm FUCKED. I'm HEAT. I'm goddamned RADIOACTIVE."

"Look, babyshake." I'm trying to stay, you know, real calm and collected. "We ain't got time left for YOUR FUCKING BULLSHIT.

Very shortly I'm going to be driving away in that camper, and you're going to be sitting in that camper with me. You got that?"

BANG, real quick she goes DEAD QUIET. She just looks at me with those steel-grey eyes of hers. Like I know something's going on in her head, but I haven't got a clue what it is. I'm starting to feel kind of desperate, so I just keep hammering away at her. Like how it's one big motherfucking country out there. Like how I'll take her ANYWHERE. Like how she can stick a pin in a map and that's just fine with me. But there's one thing for sure, she's going with me. And she ain't saying a word.

By then, I'll try anything. "Come on, break my heart, why don't you?"

"Aw, Tommy," she says, "your heart was broken long before you met me."

IT WAS too late to be driving anywhere, so I crashed at the Shooting Gallery. I mean, why the hell not? And when I woke up, I'd never felt more alone in my life.

Now to tell you the truth, I hadn't been thinking much about John Dupre or Raymond Lee or Mister Jones or whoever the hell he was. And on the few occasions when he'd flickered through my head, I'd thought, well, he's a smart guy, and the writing's up there on the wall, and he can read it as well as anybody. But now I was having second thoughts, so I fell by, and even out on the street I could hear the goddamned typewriter going. Yeah, he was making them old keys smoke. He's real surprised to see me. "Jesus, Tom, I thought you were LONG GONE."

Well, I could have said the same thing to him. And guess what he's doing? He's sitting there in Pamela the Great's place WRITING SOMETHING. No, it's not an article—not something for *Zygote* or anything remotely sane like that. He's not sure what it is, but by God, is it ever heavy.

Why did I still give a shit? Well, I got to admit I'd always had a soft spot for the crazy fucker going all the way back to the days when I first got to Boston and him and me used to drift around town together, sailing under the black flag. And I can see right away that he's TOTALLY NUTS. Like his eyes are big as saucers, and he hasn't caught a shave lately, and he's talking a mile a minute, and . . . Well, you remember how he kept Pamela the Great's place real nice? Now it was a pigsty. Clothes thrown in the corners, and dirty dishes piled up, and paper everywhere. Like all this fucking paper with writing on it. You see, he's got this GREAT NEW INSIGHT, and he starts to lay it on me. "No, no, no," I say. "I really can't be catching your GREAT NEW INSIGHT right at the moment. Like it'd be pretty much lost on me right at the moment. But have you considered holding off on this shit until you get your ass back to Canada?"

"I don't want to take it across the border," he says. It's not the Canadian side he's worried about. He doesn't want to be in the Boston airport carrying anything that might identify him—especially any revolutionary shit. He's just a day or two away from getting it done, he says, and then he's going mail it all off to Pamela the Great, and then he's gone. You see? I always knew that skiddly chick would mess up his mind.

Well, he's going on about how he'd figured THE RAIDS wouldn't come down before October, and I'm going, "WHAT RAIDS?" and he tells me all about it. Like they're going to sweep up the whole damn Left. Like it's common knowledge. Like he honest-to-God believes that armed Federal agents are going to come kicking through the door and hauling everybody off in the middle of the night. But he's a smart guy, right? He's got it figured. They can't have THE RAIDS until they've got themselves one hell of a good excuse, and, yeah, some of them crazy radicals are going to give them one—like the bombs are going to be going off like popcorn—but not before September when the kids are back in school. So that means THE RAIDS will be in October, and he'll be long gone by then. So he's safe at the moment. Yeah, they're watching him, but so what? Paranoia's got to stop somewhere.

I swear to God, it really was like talking to somebody in the asylum. "Well, I'll tell you what, old buddy," I say. "I've had me a GREAT NEW INSIGHT of my own." And I laid it on him about everybody in the Shooting Gallery being on CANDID CAMERA, and I reminded him that he'd been known to hang out there on occasion himself. And I told him about Susie singing to the cops, and all the shit I'd been thinking about Lyons, and about me and Cassandra splitting up and her crashing with Imhoff, and about how I was ready to take her anywhere in the whole goddamned universe, but she won't budge, the goddamn stubborn little bitch.

"What the fuck you mean, with Imhoff?"

"Like Imhoff. That old World War Two junkie."

"Oh, I know who he is. But shit, she told me she was leaving with you."

Now it's my turn to go, "What the fuck?" You see, that morning after the heavy shit went down, that morning when she borrowed the camper and went over to make sure her little sister got her ass out of town—well, she told John she was splitting with me. Yeah, she told him that her and me was headed for North Dakota that afternoon. I'm going, "Where the fuck's her head?" That's what John wants to know too. So I've got to tell him everything that went down with me and Cassandra—like blow by blow, word for word.

We was spending way too much time on that shit, but eventually the whole sick scene comes down on him like full force, and he goes, "Oh fuck."

You know, when that dumbass hillbilly got cranked up to full flame, he could step right along. We were out of there in forty-two minutes by my watch, and that's from a standing start. We lost some of his shit in a dumpster across town so it wouldn't be hanging around to incriminate him, and of course he had to pack up all his revolutionary papers and mail them to somebody up in Canada, and we stopped by the post office to do that, and then we were on our way to the airport. I was kind of worried about him. He was a mess. Like he'd turned kind of grey, and he was panting like a dog. I asked him if he was going to hold it together.

"Oh, yeah," he says. "I've done this in my head a million times. I'll buy my ticket. I'll sit there and look bored. I'll buy a magazine. Yeah, I'll just go through it step by step. Yeah, once I kick into THE PLAN, I'll be all right."

So I get him to the airport, and we're standing by the camper in the you-can-not-park-here zone saying goodbye, and I ask him if he needs any bread, and he says he's still got a few bills left from Cassandra's hash deal all the way back a million years ago, and thank God, he remembered to grab that up. Jesus, I can't believe it. And he's still got some coin from his last *Zygote* paycheck, he says, and he hauls out his wallet and starts counting. He says he's pretty sure he's got enough for his airfare. Like he hadn't even thought about it, and that kind of gets to me, you know what I mean? So I roll up some bills into a little tube and shove it in his shirt pocket. And I won't let him take it back out. Like I don't want him to see how much it is. Like it's the rest of the Judas money I got for fingering Peter, but I'm not about to tell him that. He starts to thank me PROFUSELY, and I tell him to can that shit. I tell him to slip me the good word via General Delivery, Hubbard, North Dakota. "Listen, asshole," I say, "send me a postcard from the Weird Land of Mooses."

OK, SO there was my good deed for the day, and what I should have done was start driving west, but that's not what I did. I'd been telling myself a dozen different stories about Bobby Lyons, and with every single one of them, I always hit a point where it didn't make the least bit of sense. I kept having the feeling that he was fucking with my head—like somehow or other it was all going to turn out to be just one more big sick joke. Like what with everything coming down on him, where he had to be was deep underground—like the big NOWHERE—but I kept seeing him right back at his place, cranked on crystal, Susie laying on the floor coloring away, the stereo going full tilt, the usual assorted freaks in there, and me walking in and him saying, "Well, Jesus, Tommy, it sure took you long enough."

I'd had a lot of practice lately checking for tails, so I drove around for maybe an hour, and if there was anybody on me, they was a motherfucking genius. I slipped over to Lyons' place and parked a couple blocks away, and then I went for a nice stroll. The best I could tell, nobody decided to join me. I peered up at the other buildings, looking for anywhere they could be doing surveillance, and, yeah, there was a few likely spots, but they just looked like ordinary windows—blinds up, even people walking around in some of them. No strange dudes parked on the street or wandering by.

Hell, it was the most peaceful ordinary-looking neighborhood you could possibly imagine.

I zipped quick across the street and ran up and rang his bell. I waited. I didn't hear his voice coming out of the speaker. I thought, come on, Parker, you asshole, of course he's not going to be there and this is not exactly a safe place for you either.

But something told me to stay put. I sat down on the top step and lit a cigarette. And then this pretty little housewife towing a kid walked right by me and stood there fumbling with her key, and just about the time she got the door open, I jumped up with a big smile and held it for her. I waited until the elevator door shut behind her, and then I walked right in.

I didn't take the elevator. I ran up all those four flights of stairs. Like I didn't know why I was going so fast, but when I got to Lyons' door, I was out of breath. I gave a little tap. And no answer. I gave a good solid knock. And no answer. I still didn't know why I was doing any of this, but I tried the door, and it was open. I stepped in and said, "Hey, Bob?" but I knew he wasn't there. A strong harsh smell in the apartment, kind of a metal smell.

It's in the kitchen. One of the burners on the stove. Electric stove, right? It's on, bright cherry red. Nothing sitting on it, just the burner glowing away, and the porcelain around the edge starting to turn brown, and the harsh smell coming from that. And there's six cups sitting there, empty and clean, and a teapot with its lid off, and I look in and it's full of dry tea, and then there's the tea kettle, right where somebody's lifted it off the burner and set it to one side. It's full of water. Then I think, hey, and I get some toilet paper, and everything I've touched, I wipe off. I'm feeling like a damned fool, like I've just joined old John in the secret service.

I look in the fridge. Hamburger and milk and beer and some leftover pizza. The milk's still fresh. And I've got to wipe all THAT shit off. And then I recall a little conversation I had with Garvin one night. He was telling me the tricks of the trade, and he said, "No, man, you don't need to carry nothing with you. Everybody's got SOCKS." So I walk into Bob's bedroom and pick up a pair of socks and pull them over my hands. Then I go back to checking out his apartment. There's nothing much very strange. Except that six people were about to have tea, and they didn't. And they'd decided not to pretty damned fast. Then I see that his big mother stereo is gone. It's so obvious I don't know why I didn't see it when I first walked in there.

I sit in the living room, not really thinking, just, I don't know, trying to pick up the vibe of the place. The fish tanks are bubbling away, the fish are swimming around, and it's motherfucking QUIET. It's beginning to get next to me. So I check all the bedrooms. They're a mess the way they always are, lots of girls' clothes thrown around, and makeup and shit like that. I check Bob's bedroom again. The bed's a mess the way it always is. Bob's clothes are all over the place the way they always are. So I try the bathroom and something really strange starts to happen to me. I don't know what to compare it to except maybe hunting when you're tracking something and you get this funny feeling that tells you to stop and wait. I'm tingling all over. I don't know how I know it, but I know I'm onto something.

A hell of a long time goes by, and then I realize I've been looking out the window down at the garage in the back alley where Lyons keeps his goddamn big pig Lincoln. If you'd climb through the window, you'd be out on the fire escape, and you could take the fire escape right down to the ground. You'd have to hang drop to the bottom, and then you'd be right across from the garage.

I push the bathroom window open. It don't stick a bit. And I slide out onto the fire escape. No problem at all for somebody who's fairly agile and not afraid of heights. Then I see the thread. A rough edge on one of the bolts and it's got a little blue thread stuck on it. Blue-jean material.

I go out the way I came in, and wipe off the doorknob, and around to the back of the building where I can look UP at the fire escape. I'm fucking well CONVINCED that somebody has been down that fire escape. I walk over to the bottom where they'd have to drop down, and it's dirt, and I see there's footprints and somebody's tried to scuff them over.

So it's all leading to the garage, right? The garage door's unlocked, and I swing it up, and there's Lyons. He's laying on the floor of the garage by the trunk of his car, and the tire iron they'd used on him is laying right there with him. They must have laid him out with the first couple bashes and then kept right on going. To make sure. Or maybe they went nuts. Or maybe just for fun. But they've mashed his skull good. He's laying on his side, and I can see one eye, and it's open, peering up, and he's got a little smile on his face, almost like a grin, almost like he's about to jump up and say, "Well, Tommy, what the fuck's happening, you simple shit?" His .44 Magnum is laying in front of him.

I don't know why I did it, because I just wanted to get the fuck out of there, but I bent down and looked close. There was a lot of blood. Like you don't imagine somebody has that much blood in their HEAD. And I could see his brains mashed up. Yeah, there was some muscle behind that tire iron all right. Somebody waiting for him in the garage. Somebody who knew him well enough to know just when to wait, just where to wait. It was kind of sad, you know what I mean? And I said to Lyons, "Yeah, well, who CAN you trust, old buddy?" And the answer to that one was real simple. NOBODY is who you can trust. Some days you can't even trust yourself.

I stood there in that garage listening to the traffic. I didn't really give two shits about Bob Lyons, if you want to know the truth. It felt like a huge load had just dropped off my back. But, dumb fuck that I was, I was still trying to see the PURPOSE in all this, like figure out what it all MEANT.

Then it flashed on me again, something I already knew—how one minute you can be alive, trying to figure out your next move, and the next minute you can cease to exist. That one's so horrible you can only stay with it in your mind for like maybe a few seconds at a time, but when you try to pull back from it, that's just chickenshit, because you know what? It's the only thing that's real. And that's when I finally got the big picture. Yeah, standing there in Lyons' garage, I finally got THE KEY TO THE WHOLE UNIVERSE. What does it all mean? I'll tell you, buddy, it don't mean shit. You see, I didn't have to go to Boston to learn that. I'd already learned that at Ton Son Nhut.

I got the fuck out of there. And you know that attaché case Lyons left at my place? Well, I had it in the camper, and I found myself some nice quiet place to park, and I bashed it open. It was full of plastic bags of white powder. Like it could have been anything. It could have been flour or sugar or talcum powder for all I knew, but I was pretty sure that's not what it was. And I knew a few places I could go to find out what it was, but I didn't do that. I drove straight through from Boston to Hubbard, and it's kind of funny. I don't know what that shit would have brought on the street. Chances are, I could have been a rich man. But on my way out of town, I threw that shit in the Charles River.

———

THE END of the line. *Oh, my God,* John thought, *what have I done?* He couldn't see straight. The whole goddamn airport was burning wasp-yellow—light sizzling with images that wouldn't make sense, a million droplets of liquid fire breaking out on his back. The real had been transformed into a frying pan. Like acid. Mind-warp. Help. He was fucked, he was losing it, he was as conspicuous as a burning cop car. Shit, anybody could be an agent, those harmless-looking kind of goofy, like on the next bench pretending to be businessmen—they could be agents, that stern middle-aged lady holding her purse firmly on her lap could be an agent. What had he thought he was going to do—sit on his ass a million years and watch the really big show go down, the best show in town? If Tom hadn't turned up to hit him with the real, he'd be sitting there still, trying to find the perfect words to describe the fragments as they blew by his window.

Function, man, he told himself. You can do it. You've only rehearsed this scene like four hundred million times. You know what to do. It doesn't matter what you're feeling, all that matters is what you do. Don't think, just rely on the plan. Take the next step and the next step after.

What had Tom been thinking to give him all that money? Nearly eight hundred bucks, Jesus. OK, so bread was no problem. That was a good start. And he was wearing his I-go-to-Harvard outfit—Harris tweed jacket—but his hair was too long, horribly too long, and it was too late, nothing to do about that. They wouldn't embrace him with open arms at the border, but they wouldn't stop him either. He was a

Landed Immigrant, and he'd only been out of the country for a short time—right, two weeks at the most. In a minute—or two minutes, or ten minutes—when he could function again, he'd walk over to the Air Canada counter and buy his ticket. He had an hour and a half till the next flight. He would smoke a cigarette. He would find some center, something to hold onto, some way to go on living—to make it through this wasp-yellow moment, and then on to the next, and then on to the one after that, but, oh Jesus, the motherfucking buzz.

Outstripped and late. All the brilliant, glittering, fascinating words blown to shit. Not a goddamned thing to hold onto. Once there'd been a council with millions in it, but he couldn't hold onto the Movement any longer; it had disintegrated into chaos and violence. Then there'd been a council of two, but he couldn't hold onto Pamela; she was long gone. He couldn't even hold onto any hope for change; everything was hopeless. He still had a sullen dedication to waiting the motherfuckers out—being ready for them the next time—but that one was pretty goddamn remote, fairly fucking austere; in fact, that one was absolutely useless. None of his identities were any help either. He was back down to a council of one, and that one was fucked and weird the same as always—split into a million glittering fragments like guppies in a fishbowl. Why bother with anything? But that couldn't be right. What? He'd learned *nothing* in two years? Pam had found her *Sh'ma Yisrael*. Why couldn't he find his?

Something that basic had to be simple—something so simple he'd known it down in his bones forever, something he'd known for so long he'd almost forgotten it. An hour and a half till flight time. Breathe, he told himself. Count your breaths if you have to—like sitting Zazen. Count to ten and start over. That's what the plan said to do, and that's what he was going to do. Just sit there. And find it. He closed his eyes. He breathed. He counted his breaths.

Oh, fuck, what if it didn't work? Mind rattling away, the tiny rat: "You can never trade in any moment in the real for any other moment—never, never, never." Fuck that shit. He could see the sad old Ohio River rolling in front of his closed eyes. Watching his father die—no words for it. His father's last words—"I can't breathe." You

423

couldn't get any more simple than that. So breathe now while you can, animal that will die, and the dim pulse in his ears—deeper than any random flurry or distracting hum or nasty buzz of the airport—was his own heartbeat.

So fucking scared he could hear it back of his ears, a rhythm like running, first one foot and then the other—that pulse, deep thrust out, kick back of the veins, the twin beat that was music before there was music. The sun, reflected on the river, burned behind his eyelids, heating the retinae—the world a red haze, dizzying. No way he could miss it—the vivid irritability of living tissue. He would never be here again, exactly as he was, exactly at this moment—sitting in the Boston airport with his eyes shut, breathing, with this particular set of images in his mind, remembering the light.

So fucking scared. "Come on, Alice, sit by me." Washing carrots in water burning with light—Pamela, naked, and the glass of the windows, the pinks and greys, the lovely blend of emptiness and object, her pale skin filigreed with tracery blue. Glowing with light, and that ancient, monotonous drone of locusts in the trees that says, "Almost school time, almost school time." Grease and mayonnaise on the plates, small pools giving back sun; the plates are glowing, light on the bubbles in the sink full of dishes, light on their faces. Sweating, the kitchen vivid with heat, the sun everywhere—on the oak table, the silver candelabra, the marble top of the antique sideboard, the crystal in its display case, the threadbare Oriental rug on the floor, the massive wing-back chair. This light would be as brief as a suspended teardrop, and he didn't want to miss any of it—the golden light pouring through the open window, and the blue-black edge where the light had to start all over again.

Beginning in darkness, emerging in a metallic grisaille, a swelling of cool light along the edges of buildings. A slow but steady crescendo of smoky blue—dove-grey here, steel-grey there. Like a scrim was being drawn away, and the firm shapes of things were emerging, objects pushing back into reality, the wires tightening, the world reassembling itself. He'd got what he'd wanted, and he felt the impact of it shiver through him. Soon he would have everything he needed to make a world.

John opened his eyes. Now he could see the airport—clearly, usefully—and everything was different. He was in that ticklish crossover when everything is suspended, but soon the wires that defined the real would be yanked back into place, so he didn't have much time—certainly no time for bullshit. Yeah, what was basic was simple—something he'd never lost and never would lose, something he kept with him all the time. It was everything he knew without knowing how he knew it—an emptiness—and what he knew then was more real than any of their theories. Yeah, it was better than any of their theories. When you're at the end of the line, you've got to start over again. What matters is what happens between people, and love is simply love. He bought two tickets for Mr. and Mrs. Joe Minotti on the last flight out for Toronto.

IT WAS one of those brilliant wine-sap New England afternoons in early September when the clarity of the light is almost too much to bear. John used the cab ride from the airport back into downtown Boston to work out his new plan, to go over it, to make it into the new instruction manual that he would follow mindlessly, one idiotically simple step at a time. Dodging the Washington Street shoppers, he walked into the first large glitzy barber shop he saw. "Make me look like a Harvard boy."

The barber had that raw belligerent Boston accent—maybe Dorchester—that John had come to loathe. "Look, buddy, I'm a barber not a sociologist. Just tell me how short you want it."

"There," John said, pointing at a picture on the wall—a trendy young man who could have been an advertising executive or an aspiring Hollywood bit player. It was the first time scissors had touched John's hair since 1966. He didn't come out looking exactly like a Harvard boy, but, as Tom would have said, it was close enough for government work. Amazing, he thought, hair actually has weight.

He didn't have a lot of time to fuck around. He went into Filene's, strode quickly through the women's wear department, looking at the mannequins. Saw an image that was exactly what he wanted. Checked out the salesgirls until he found one who looked right. "My sister's about your size," he told her. "I want to buy that whole outfit. Yeah, everything . . . even the purse."

OK, buddy, he told himself, just keep moving it along here. No time to wallow in commodity fetishism, just buy all the goddamn accessories to match the image—pantyhose, underwear, a couple bras. He asked the girl at the cosmetics counter, "What's in at the moment?" Bought lipstick, mascara, and blush. He couldn't think of anything more, and time was chewing his ass.

On the street again, loaded down with his shopping bags and his own knapsack, he scanned the passing cabs, looking for a young driver with lots of hair. Gave that one up pretty quick and flagged down the first one that looked even remotely likely. Threw his shit into the back seat. The man turned to look at him. Mid-forties, maybe, his face marked with acne, old eyes that had seen it all—a stereotype out of a Raymond Chandler novel. So what would Phillip Marlowe do? John took out his wallet, peeled off a twenty and offered it. "I'll double your fare if you don't remember this trip."

The cabbie didn't look the least bit surprised. "Sure," he said. "Let me book off."

At Imhoff's, John said to the cabbie, "Wait for me. Like *wait*, OK? It may take a while."

John hammered the door. Nothing. He checked his watch. Fuck, what if they weren't home? Footsteps, the door swung open. Imhoff: "Mr. Lee, Mr. Lee." Inside, everything had ground to a halt; it was any time at all—no time—the blinds drawn, the yellowed shade of a brass floor lamp casting a piss-yellow circle in the corner. John was assaulted by the standard-issue stench of cigarettes and grass. It took his eyes a moment to adjust. Five or six heaps that turned out to be people, all of them heavy on the nod. Imhoff galumphed back to an overstuffed chair by the stereo. John wasn't ready for this shit. Felt the sting of adrenaline, the need to move. There was no sign of Cassandra.

Imhoff speaking—low rumble—gave it up. But in a moment had another shot at it, "Reefer?" Codfish hand flopping, pointing toward the table and a baggie of dope.

"Thanks," John said. "Later." He watched Imhoff subside into his overstuffed chair, nod off.

John found Cassandra right where he'd thought she'd be—in Imhoff's bedroom. She was sprawled diagonally across the bed, face up. She could have been asleep or dead or a waxworks figure. His heart hit a double thud; he knelt to listen for *her* heart—his ear on her chest. Found the beat, slow and steady, solid as a rock. "Cass," he said. No reaction. He put his fingers to her lips to feel her breath.

She was wearing one of Lorraine's sleazy minidresses, floral on black, and tight black boots, old-fashioned ones with thin heels. Her eye makeup was smudged into gooey black circles. The dress was hiked up to her hips, her black pantyhose ripped at the crotch and full of runs. "Cass," he said. Again, nothing. He turned her arms over and found tracks on the left one. Not much. But at least twice. Like the small discreet dots left after the doctor does a blood test. "Oh, baby," he said, "you're looking good."

What he didn't need at the moment was any interference. He poked his nose into the living room, saw that the huge dumped sacks weren't stirring. He ghosted on into the kitchen, went though the cupboards until he found a bowl, filled it with warm water, and carried it back to the bedroom. Got a washcloth, a cake of soap, and a towel. Knelt by the bed and washed Cassandra's face. If she felt anything, she sure as hell wasn't showing it. Cleaning around her eyes was a bitch. He twisted the corner of the washcloth into a point, used that to clean her lashes. It was taking forever. Slow, slow, slow, he told himself, do it right.

"What?" he said to her. He was sure that she'd just said something. A word or only a sighing murmur? But nothing now, only her steady breathing.

He'd got her face clean. She could have used a shower, but no way in hell. He stripped her naked, prayed that she'd wake up. Nothing. The inevitable metaphor—a life-sized doll. She was warm, alive, breathing, but *gone*—the ultimate logic of junk. If anybody did anything to her now, she wouldn't know it, might never know it, might only stumble upon it later—as something not right, something that hurt. "You're not lost, Cassandra," he told her. "It's the world that's lost."

Christ, who would have thought putting a bra on someone would be so fucking difficult? He hauled her up into a sitting position, folded her into his arms. He'd always hated bras, the fiddliness of their hooks. He tore open the package of pantyhose. Now what? Well, start with her toes. Wait a minute. Shouldn't her panties go on first? Yeah, of course they should. OK, and *now* the pantyhose—did they have a front and a back? Yup, they came in leg shapes with the feet outlined. He slithered the damn things over her toes and began working up her legs, going back and forth from one leg to the other. Problem at the hips. A goddamn dead weight. He tried rolling her to one side, but that didn't seem to work. He pulled them as high up as he could in the front, then turned her completely over onto her stomach. Jesus, the things were truly demonic. He tugged and jerked them over her ass, got the waistband into place, and his finger shot straight through the sheer fabric. "Shit." As he rolled Cassandra back over, he could see the run sailing merrily down her thigh. But he was finally getting some reaction out of her—in a small, thick, fogged-out voice, clearly, "Fuck off."

"Come on, Sleeping Beauty. Get your act together." But she was a traveler in a galactic spaceship, an experiment in time suspension.

He'd had it with doll dressing for the moment. Her old blue carry-on bag was in the closet. Her clothes—mainly Lorraine's clothes—were strewn on the floor. He picked the best of them and started packing. Talk about getting down to basics, she didn't own much more than Mahatma Gandhi. He put her old worn-out Frye boots at the bottom, then her navy blue sweater. She only had two books, battered paperbacks—Carlos Castaneda and Simone de Beauvoir. He found the ratty purse she'd been carrying—some stupid thing of Lorraine's—dumped everything out. Checked out her wallet. A five-dollar bill and some change, her Social Security card, her West Virginia driver's license, her student card from Bennington—expired, of course, but it would still help. He put her wallet into the immaculate brand-new black leather purse from Filene's, threw in the makeup he'd bought her.

OK, back to the doll. He wrestled the white button-down blouse onto her, did up the buttons, yanked the pleated herringbone skirt up over hips, zipped it and fastened the waistband. Her eyes fluttered open for a moment. "Fuck, man. Fuck you."

"Hey, great stuff. Consciousness. Just goddamned marvelous. Stand up, OK?" But she wasn't about to stand up. How the hell was he going to move her?

Well, first things first. He grabbed her carry-on bag, her new purse, and the jacket that went with her new suit, ran with them back down to the cab. Flung them into the back seat. "We're almost ready," he heard himself singing out cheerfully. The cabbie didn't say a word.

John ran back to the bedroom. Cassandra had rolled over onto her side and put a pillow under her head. "Terrific," John said. "Signs of life. Come on, twinkletoes."

He rolled her back over, pulled her downward until her legs stuck off the bed, worried her brand-new black pumps onto her feet. He took her hands and pulled. Her body hung back. "Cassandra, for Christ's sake," he said. He let go, and she collapsed. He checked his watch. Holy Jesus. How could he have ever thought that this ridiculous hare-brained scheme would work?

He could only imagine carrying her one way—the way the hubby carries his new bride across the threshold in countless old movies. He wrapped his left arm around her back, shoved his right arm under her knees, and picked her up. Fuck, she was heavy. He lurched through the door, pressed his shoulders against the wall to brace himself, and started down the steps—one thick, murderous, deep, impossible step at a time. Sweating, heart slamming, he heard Imhoff's phlegmy rumble. "Hey, man. What the fuck you doing, man?"

"Just walking her." Ridiculous. She was a hell of a long way from walking anywhere. The goddamned front door was closed. Panting, he set her down, hoped she might find a spark—just a small hit of juice, survival instinct—hoped that she might stay propped there a few seconds. She slid down the wall, arrived on the floor with her legs splayed. "Fuck," she said, but her eyes stayed shut.

John jerked the front door open, looked behind him, saw shapes shifting back there in the beatniks' twilight. "Hey, she'll be all right," Imhoff rumbled at him. "Nothing to get hung about. Just on the nod, you dig?"

Dutiful hubby, John picked up his bride again and staggered

through the door. The cabbie sat behind his wheel staring up at them as impassively as a toad. John started down the front steps. One of Cassandra's new pumps fell off and went skittering away—bing, a bing, a bing—down to the sidewalk. John sat down, Cassandra's body heavy as grief in his arms. This is too fucking hard, he thought. I can't do it. This is worse than Kafka. This is Groucho Marx in hell.

"Cassandra," he said directly into her ear. Her eyes opened, regarded him a moment. Not a goddamned thing in them. Closed again.

He stood up with her. His back muscles were burning. He made it down to the cab. The fucking asshole cab driver continued to sit there, motionless. John leaned her against the cab, held her up with one hand, opened the door with the other, wrapped both arms around her waist and inched her inside, fit her in with the luggage. She flopped, lying awkwardly, partially on the seat and partially on her bag. John sprinted back to get her lost pump, saw Imhoff standing in the doorway at the top of the stairs, the light behind him—the wreck of an old sea captain, watching as his ship sinks beneath him. "Mr. Lee," Imhoff yelled. "Hey, Mr. Lee. Fuck, man. What the hell do you think you're doing?"

John jumped into the back seat of the cab, slammed the door and locked it. "Move."

The cabbie turned slowly around in his seat. "She smacked out or what?"

"Yeah," John said. Gripping the handrail, Imhoff was stepping ponderously down the stairs.

"What the fuck do you take me for?" the cabbie said.

"For Christ's sake," John said, "I'm taking her home,"

"How do I know *that* ain't her home?" pointing up at the house.

Imhoff had arrived to bang on the window of the car with a thick pink fist.

"Come on, man," John said. "I got to get her the fuck out of here, man."

The cabbie had all the time in the world. "Holy Mother of God," he said. He leaned into the back seat to yell directly into Cassandra's face. "Hey, lady. Hey, lady."

This is the motherfucking end of the road, John thought.

He put his arm around Cassandra's chest and pulled her upright. "Cassandra?" She opened her eyes.

"Hey, lady, do you want to go with this guy?"

She tilted toward John, gave him a look that was fixed, glassy, and owlish. Then she smiled. "Hey, hero," she said and let her head fall onto his shoulder.

"OK," the cabbie said and pulled away.

"DRINK," JOHN said and pressed the Styrofoam cup to her lips.

She swallowed. "Too sweet," she said.

"Sweet's what you need. Come on, drink."

"Jesus fuck, man, I'm coming down."

"Yeah, I know. Drink."

He fed her coffee and watched the clock. He'd left it as long as he could. "Don't move," he said to her. "I'll be right back."

Would she simply sit there? Was that possible? He hurried into the men's room. All those million times when he'd gone over the plan in his head, this was the moment he'd always dreaded, but, yes, he had to do it now and not on the plane. There were many excellent, well-thought-out reasons why he had to do it now and not on the plane. He closed himself into a stall, took out his wallet, tore up the bits of paper that said he was Joseph Alfred Minotti, and flushed them down the toilet. Now he couldn't change his mind. He'd passed the point of no return. He was an amorphous blob of nothing, a snail without its shell. He had no identity, and he would continue to have no identity until he was on the plane and the plane was in the air. If anything happened before that, he was fucked.

When he got back, Cassandra was still sitting up. Miraculous.

"This is heavy," he told her. "This is motherfucking serious."

"Dupre, you're so full of shit."

"Can you walk?" he said.

"Fuck, yes, I can walk. Just back off me, man, OK? Jesus, man, I'm coming down."

A girl's voice, cheery as all hell, called for boarding. Wait. Don't get caught up in a crowd of people who might be curious, or friendly, or simply not inclined to mind their own goddamn business—but don't be the last ones either. He had to steady her, his arm around her waist, but she walked.

"Rough weekend," he told the stewardess—tried for a conspiratorial grin. He gave Cassandra the window seat, stowed his knapsack and her bag, fastened her seat belt, then his own. The inside of his mouth tasted like shit. *Take off,* he prayed to the invisible pilot. Cassandra lay back in her seat with her eyes shut, but at least she hadn't slumped into some conspicuously whacked-out position like a rag doll. A voice came over the PA. When it switched from English to French, Cassandra opened her eyes and stared at him. "You asshole," she said. The plane taxied down the runway. It sat there for a while—for a hell of a long time, for only a minute or two. It took off.

The no-smoking sign went off. John lit two cigarettes, gave her one. "Where the fuck are we going?" she said.

"Toronto," he said.

"Great. Motherfucking fabulous. Thanks for giving me some choice in the matter."

They were high above the clouds, and the last rays of the setting sun struck her full in the face. She turned away from him and stared into that brilliant light.

With the nail file he'd kept in his shirt for precisely that purpose, he cut the thread around the secret pocket on the inside of his knapsack, took out the Landed Immigrant card, his Ontario driver's license, Social Insurance card, York University student card—all the little rectangles of paper that attested to the fact that he was an utterly credible person named John Dupre. He filled out the customs forms for both himself and Cassandra. They had nothing to declare.

"What the fuck am I *wearing?*" she said.

"Dig it. You came to Boston in disguise, you're leaving in disguise."

"Yeah, right. Fuck me, man. What am I disguised *as?* Jesus, Dupre, you've made me into a goddamn lady."

She picked up the Filene's purse, checked out the contents. "I don't fucking believe this," she said. "Let me out."

He got out of his seat. She moved slowly down the aisle,

steadying herself on the seat backs. He watched her make it all the way to the can. When she came back, she'd combed her hair, put on a touch of lipstick and mascara and blush—just enough to complete the image created by the stockings, the pumps, and the herringbone suit. "When this is over, Dupre," she said, "I'm fucking going to murder you."

"HAVE YOU been out of the country long, Mr. Dupre?"

"No. A couple weeks."

The dude at Customs and Immigration was not smiling. He was all business. "How long will you be staying in Toronto?" he asked Cassandra.

"A few days." Her voice was right, her eyes were right. Everything about her was right—the purse, the shoes, even the way she was standing.

John watched that balding, middle-aged official check her out. No, she wasn't one of those goddamned pain-in-the-ass American radicals; she was exactly what she looked like—a girl in a herringbone suit, a nice girl, a very pretty girl. "Welcome to Canada, Miss Markapolous."

Customs didn't bother to open their bags. They walked through the basement of the airport, up the stairs and outside. The sun had set, leaving behind a clear stripe of indigo.

Cassandra let her bag fall to the sidewalk and turned on him. "OK, Dupre, just what the fuck do you think you're doing with me?"

"I'm not doing *anything* with you."

"You motherfucking kidnapped me, man."

"Listen, Cass. Dig it. Nobody knows where you are. Like the California pigs . . ."

"Fuck you, man. What the fuck are you going to *do* with me?"

They had made it. The whole bizarre plan had worked, and it was all too fucking much. He was mad enough to kill her. "I'm not going to do *a goddamned thing* with you," he yelled back at her. "Go find another man to live off. Go find another sick fuck to stick needles in your ass. Jesus, Cassandra, you can do anything you damn well please."

That stopped her.

"Listen." He wasn't yelling now. "Nobody knows where you are. Not the California pigs. Not Sweet Charles. Not Zoë. Not your parents. *Nobody*. And nobody's going to know unless you tell them. Paranoia's got to stop somewhere, right? Well, it stops here. You're out of that sick crazy fucked-up American karma. You're free and clear, Cassandra. You're vanished. You're *gone*."

He didn't know whether she'd got it or not.

"Cassandra," he said, "you're in Canada."

After a moment, she said, "Why?"

"Why what?" But he knew what she was asking. "Don't you remember what we said to each other? We're linked. We're closer than a brother and a sister."

"But, Jesus, man," she said, "I was only sixteen."

"Yeah? So? You were sixteen. Come on, Cassie, did you think I'd forget?"

She inhaled—a sound like an interrupted "Ah." Her eyes filled, spilled over. She walked away a few steps, pressed one hand over her face, and stood there crying. It didn't last longer than a few seconds.

"Is this a groovy city?" she asked him.

"It's a great city."

"We got any coin?"

"A few bills."

"Shit, man, then we got no problem. Where we going?"

"My old place in the Annex."

She shook her head—not in the least saying "no" but, oddly, like shaking off something, a scarf or a hood—a gesture that must have been left over from when she'd had long hair. She wiped the tears off her face.

"Oh, fuck, Dupre," she said, laughing, "you're such an asshole. I bet you've wanted to see me dressed like this ever since you met me."

She caught his hand and pulled him forward. Walking quickly, she led him toward the cab that would take them into downtown Toronto.

Author's Afterword

This, the fourth volume of the *Difficulty at the Beginning* quartet, bears only a tenuous relationship to the version of John Dupre's story previously published as the second half of *Cutting Through* (General Publishing, Toronto, 1982). It has the same cast of characters, but they have grown and changed enormously since their first appearance in the world, and their stories have changed just as much. I regard the *Cutting Through* version as little more than an uneven collection of rough preliminary sketches and notes, mostly now abandoned; what little I did retain, I have developed and elaborated far beyond anything implied in the original writing. Although I also read even earlier drafts now housed in the archives at the University of British Columbia library, I used hardly anything from that stratum of unpublished writing. So easily ninety percent of the writing in *Looking Good* is entirely new, and it must be considered as a new work.

Looking Good is fiction, and the content is not autobiographical. The main players in this story are entirely fictitious and are not based upon real people. I have, however, tried to be true to the times, and many of the political events and some of the off-stage people mentioned in the book are real. I feel that any curiosity some readers might have about what I made up and what I didn't is perfectly legitimate, and I will try to satisfy that curiosity.

Although *Zygote* and the *Biweekly Weasel* resemble types of "underground" newspapers current at the time, they are fictitious, as is the organization called the *Boston Radical Women's Collective*. Members of Harvard SDS did not, of course, work for a fictitious newspaper or take it over. Pam's recollections of the Columbia "action" are based upon those I found in various sources, the most useful of which were Richard Rosenkranz's *Across the Barricades* (Lippincott, Philadelphia and New York, 1971) and the excellent report compiled by Jerry L. Avorn and the staff of the *Columbia Daily Spectator*, published as *Up Against the Ivy Wall: A History of the Columbia Crisis* (Atheneum, New York, 1969).

Although my accounts of the Harvard bust and the Harvard Square riot are fictionalized (sometimes highly so), they were based upon real events. When I was constructing my story of the Harvard bust, I found it very useful to read two accounts from highly divergent viewpoints:

Roger Rosenblatt's *Coming Apart: A Memoir of the Harvard Wars of 1969* (Little Brown, Boston, 1997) and Lawrence E. Eichel, Kenneth W. Jost, Robert D. Luskin, and Richard M. Neustadt's *The Harvard Strike* (Houghton Mifflin, Boston, 1970). For the Harvard Square riot I found many fascinating and useful details in accounts published in the *Boston Globe*, the MIT *Tech*, and the *Harvard Crimson*.

For all matters pertaining to the Students for a Democratic Society, I consulted Kirpatrick Sale's meticulously researched *SDS: Ten Years Towards a Revolution* (Random House, New York, 1973). An account of Bernardine Dohrn's praise of the Manson family at the SDS National Convention in Flint, Michigan, in December, 1969, appears in Sale's book (pp. 626–629) and has also been widely documented elsewhere.

It was rumored in Boston leftist circles in 1970 that Weatherman had prepared a hit list of enemies who were to be "offed" when the revolution began, but I have found no evidence that enabled me to either confirm or deny those rumors. The particular Boston Weatherman cell I have described—with its lurid acid-driven fantasies of political murder—is entirely fictitious. "The Fork" is the name adopted by a Weatherman cell in New York; I have borrowed it for my fiction. The imposition of "revolutionary consciousness" on the members of Weatherman by the use of "criticism, self-criticism" sessions, however, has been widely reported; an excellent account appears in Mark D. Naison's *White Boy: A Memoir* (Temple University Press, 2002).

While writing this book, I read or consulted a large number of sources, both primary and secondary, and it would be pretentious of me to list them all. I do, however, want to mention Todd Gitlin's excellent, detailed, and magisterial work: *The Sixties: Years of Hope, Days of Rage* (Bantam, New York, 1987).

I feel compelled to comment on my use of the word "motherfucker." I considered not using it at all, but it was a characteristic of the speech of black nationalists, white radicals, and "underground" types at the time, and was, in fact, used so commonly and so often that it eventually lost nearly all of its shock value—as I hope it will for anyone who persists in reading this book all the way to the end.

Many of my characters hold opinions that were typical of the late 1960s; I have tried to express their ideas in language that they themselves would have used. I have also tried not to give any of them opinions that would have been impossible or unlikely for anyone to hold at the time. The extent to which sixties radicals felt alienated from mainstream American society cannot be overemphasized; many of them believed that everything they had ever been taught was, at best, a web of pitiful delusions, and, at worst, a cleverly assembled system of malevolent lies designed to maintain an intolerable and utterly mad social order. That conviction led to an assault, not only on social institutions, but on the very structure of "reality," forcing radicals to attempt to reinvent all human knowledge from the ground up—no mean task for kids in their twenties—and no idea, on the face of it, was too nutty to be considered, at least for a while.

Readers attempting to orient themselves should remember that, with the exception of Simone de Beauvoir's *The Second Sex* (first published in an English translation by Jonathan Cape in 1953) and Betty Friedan's *The Feminine Mystique* (1963), none of the books that would now be considered to be classics of mid-twentieth-century feminism had yet been published; even the use of the term "feminism" (as applied to a contemporary position) was quite new, and one heard "women's liberation" far more often. It was very much a do-it-yourself period in the Women's Movement, and young women were making up feminist theory on their own, coming up with new ideas every day. The huge energy and excitement of that intensely creative period was readily apparent even to men who were watching from the sidelines.

The writings of the Situationist International were not widely known in the United States at the time, but Guy Debord's *La société du spectacle* (1967) and the opening of Raoul Vaneigem's *Traité du savoir-vivre à l'usage des jeunes générations* (1967) were available in English translation and were taken quite seriously by a very small number of American radicals. Of Carlos Castaneda's many books, only the first, *The Teachings of Don Juan, a Yaqui Way of Knowledge* (1968), had been published, and it was still possible for a reasonable person to believe that Castaneda was an anthropologist and not, as he later proved to be, a novelist.

Pam's attempts to put anorexia nervosa into a political context is not as far ahead of the times as it might appear to today's readers; after the publication of R. D. Laing's *The Politics of Experience* (1967), all forms of mental illness were easily seen in a political context, and, of course, some New Left radicals attempted to put *everything* into a political context.

Although its recent notoriety might make crystal meth appear to be a twenty-first-century drug, it was available in the underground in the late 1960s and popular enough that one saw impassioned editorials against it appearing in the alternate press.

"Androgyny," or, as it was more commonly called, "unisex," did have a large impact on the world of fashion in the early 1970s. Zoë does not remember the exact wording of the quotation she cites; the original is: "This spring girls will be looking like boys who dress like girls. And boys will be dressing like girls who dress like boys." It appeared, not in *Ingenue*, as Zoë mistakenly remembers, but in *Eye* (February, 1969).

Just as I have described in this book, American leftists were, by 1970, suffering from that constant and corrosive anxiety commonly called "paranoia," and it eventually became difficult or impossible to make even a good guess as to what was real and what was not. Since then, we have learned that phones were indeed tapped, files on radical activity were indeed kept by various government agencies, and radical organizations were indeed infiltrated both by agents and by agents-provocateurs. When the Nixon Administration finally came tumbling down, we learned that even the wildest fantasies of the New Left hadn't been quite wild enough.

It should be obvious that I am sympathetic to my characters, but I have also tried my best to absent myself from the debate. Whether I have succeeded or not is another matter, but it was my intention that readers should confront my characters as directly as possible without the author getting in the way.

The earliest writing that I incorporated into *Running*, the first book of *Difficulty at the Beginning*, dates back to my high-school days; the most recent writing is what I was doing yesterday. I am astonished when I consider it, but I have been at work on this project, off and on, for nearly fifty years. Writing is a social act, and I could not have done it without the help I received along the way from many friends who did everything from commenting upon my manuscripts to paying the rent. A complete list would go on for pages, but I cannot bring this work to an end without mentioning at least some of the people who have been essential to my writing life.

When I really was having difficulty at the beginning, I could always count upon Mark and Maxann Kasdan, Steve Savitt and Mary Lynn

Baum, Ginger Eckert, and Jon Supak. My old pal and mentor David Omar White taught me what it means to work at one's craft. In my early Vancouver years, I relied upon Bob Harlow, Tony Simmonds, Annie Simmonds, Bonnelle Strickling, Michael Williamson, Rhoda Williamson, and Judi Saltman. Much of my writing career I owe to Ed Carson who published five books of mine, edited them superbly, put up with me when I was nuts, helped me out in countless ways, and is still my friend after all these years.

More recently, my students at UBC have been a constant inspiration. My daughters, Jane and Elizabeth, have helped me out, daily, by simply being around, being themselves, and sharing their lives with me. I could not have completed this project without my wife, Mary, who, at various times, has played the roles of editor, business manager, publicist, agent, gadfly, and coach. ("Don't worry, just *write it*.") Thanks, kid.

Finally, I must mention two people whose impact upon me was absolutely central to this writing. The impulse to revisit the John Dupre material first struck me with undeniable force one night in Charleston, West Virginia; at the center of that powerful psychic event, the catalyst for it, was my host and my friend, Gordon Simmons. *Difficulty at the Beginning* could not have appeared in the world without the enormous energy, enthusiasm, and incomparable editorial skill of Lee Shedden at Brindle and Glass.

If I got it right this time, I must offer my thanks to all of you and to everyone else I haven't been able to mention, but the responsibility for anything wrong with this writing rests entirely on me.

Denk, es erhält sich der Held, selbst der Untergang war ihm
nur ein Vorwand, zu sein: seine letzte Geburt.
—Rilke

Keith Maillard
Vancouver
May 14, 2006